Barnes reached for his desk. "Sam! Kill him!" the Old Man rapped.

I burned his legs off and his trunk fell to the floor. I stepped quickly to him and kicked his gun away from his still-groping fingers. The Old Man snapped, "Don't touch him! Mary, stand back!"

We did so. The Old Man sidled toward the body, like a cat cautiously investigating the unknown. He poked Barnes gently with his cane.

"Boss," I said, "about time to git, isn't it?"

Without looking around he answered, "We're as safe here as anywhere. Safer, probably. This building may be swarming with them."

"Swarming with what?"

"How would I know? Swarming with whatever he was."

Mary gave a choked sob and gasped. "He's still breathing. Look!"

The body lay facedown; the back of the jacket heaved as if the chest were rising. Without a word Mary handed me a fancy pair of scissors from Barnes's desk. I cut the jacket away and we all looked.

From the neck, halfway down the back, was something which was not flesh. It pulsed like a jellyfish. Grayish, faintly translucent, and shot through with darker structure, shapeless—it reminded me of a giant clot of frogs' eggs. It was clearly alive, for it pulsed and quivered and moved by flowing.

I drew back and continued to stare at it, my gun ready. I did not know what it could do and I was not taking chances.

👉 BAEN BOOKS 👈
by ROBERT A. HEINLEIN

THE PUPPET MASTERS

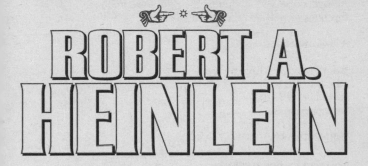

ROBERT A. HEINLEIN

BAEN

HE PUPPET MASTERS

Copyright © 1951 by Robert A. Heinlein, 1979 by
Robert A. Heinlein, 2003 by The Robert A. &
Virginia Heinlein Prize Trust

A Baen Book

Baen Publishing Enterprises
P.O. Box 1403
Riverdale, NY 10471
www.baen.com

ISBN: 978-1-4391-3376-7

Cover art by Bob Eggleton

First Baen paperback printing, August 2010

Distributed by Simon & Schuster
1230 Avenue of the Americas
New York, NY 10020

Library of Congress Cataloging-in-Publication Data:
2009016983

Printed in the United States of America

10 9 8 7 6 5 4 3 2 1

Dedication:
To
Lurton Blassingame

# Contents

☙ Introduction ☙
to
The Puppet Masters
(Robert A. Heinlein, 1951)
by
William H. Patterson, Jr.

The Puppet Masters was supremely timely, supremely in tune with the *zeitgeist* when it first appeared late in 1951. It was the first major fictional workup of the flying saucer craze, then in its fourth year (and the Air Force was still trying to put the toothpaste back in the tube, after its first official report explicitly would not rule out an extraterrestrial origin for the 1947 sightings). The sensational trials of Josef Stalin's atomic spies in the U.S., Julius and Ethel Rosenberg, that spring—and high State Department official Alger Hiss the previous autumn—convinced Mr. and Mrs. John Q. American Public that there were, indeed, aliens living undetected among us.

Heinlein was the first to work this vein of aliens-among-us cultural fear, but books and films followed like clockwork as the decade wore on and the Junior Senator from Wisconsin spun American fears of aliens-among-us into brief political capital. Jack Finney's *The Body Snatchers* went from a serial in *Collier's* to a book, to a shuddery film (*Invasion of the Body Snatchers*, 1956), following the cheesy *Invaders from Mars* (1953). Roger Corman's even more cheesy *The Brain Eaters* blatantly pirated *The Puppet Masters* in 1959 and derailed a prestige film production that was in negotiation. A quality production of *The Puppet Masters* would have capped the duck-and-cover decade's paranoia very appropriately.

When that prestige film production finally was made in 1994, Robert Heinlein's *The Puppet Masters* was back in tune with the *zeitgeist*. The complete version of the book, suppressed as too sexy and too shuddery when it was written in 1950, had been restored and published in 1990—when the aliens-among-us were no longer carriers of a deadly, insidious political meme: now they were carriers of a deadly, insidious virus.

But this coincidence of timeliness (*Invasion of the Body Snatchers* also got a remake in the 1990's) was just a cultural blip: *The Puppet Masters* had a lively publishing history between those blips, and *The Puppet Masters* continues into the Naughty-Oughties with fresh editions — two this year: the book you hold in your hands plus the publication in the Virginia Edition Collected Works of Robert A. Heinlein.

The Puppet Masters is not just a book for appropriate cultural blips, it is a perennial because it has something important to say to anyone who thinks about the self-responsible human being in relation his/her society—and how his/her society can shove him/her casually into the dirt. *The Puppet Masters*, at a level far more profound than pod people, is "about" the *real* aliens among us, the scattering of free men trying to live reasonably and responsibly among people who are cracked on the subject of the collective, of the mass man and what mass man can do politically to stamp out that disease of the human spirit, individualism. For Americans, that is a true perennial theme.

Heinlein almost never talked about his own work, but he made an exception in 1957 when he was asked to give a lecture at the University of Chicago, published as "Science Fiction: Its Nature, Faults, and Virtues." His thesis was that speculative fiction could potentially be broader, more meaningful, more relevant than so-called "mainstream" literature (which he saw at that moment as being stuck in a particularly unpleasant and tiresome rut of ironic novel conventions). In his drafts of the lecture, Heinlein selected *The Puppet Masters* as his example of that kind of broad and searching relevance, in a "discussion" section which was omitted from the published text:

> What do I think is good, or bad, about *The Puppet Masters*? It has a tired plot and was hastily written; its literary merit is negligible. I strove hard to make characterization, scene, and incident have a feeling of reality and to entertain while doing so; the mail I have received seems to indicate that I succeeded.
>
> These virtues and defects are those of the professional juggler and clown, the entertainer— which is what I think a fictioneer should be first of all. If the book has any permanent merit it

must lie in its theme, which is a thinly-disguised allegory, a diatribe against totalitarianism in all its forms. Each writer has his personal philosophy; included in mine is an intense love of personal freedom and an almost religious respect for the dignity of the individual—I despise anything which reduces these two and have, in many stories, explored the attendant problems. The trick in sermonizing through fiction is not to let your sermon get in the way of the story, to cause the story to make your point for you. Apparently I succeeded well enough in *The Puppet Masters* not to annoy most readers, so, despite the novel's obvious literary faults, I am reasonably content with it.

So when the paperback editors suggested in 1949 to Heinlein's agent they'd like to see a workup of Donald Keyhoe's *True Magazine* notion that flying saucers were aliens from outer space, they probably expected to get something like Michael Rennie's stern-but-kindly Mr. Klaatu (*The Day the Earth Stood Still*—the original one—appeared in 1951, about the same time *The Puppet Masters* was running as a serial in *Galaxy* magazine). They probably didn't expect a rewrite of *The War of the Worlds*—or "Death and Destruction!" They certainly could never have anticipated an extended meditation on the dignity of the individual.

But *The Puppet Masters* is all of these things—as well as a genuine and deeply-felt statement of the moral crisis just starting to be visible in 1951 and still gathering strength fifty-plus years later in the Neocon hagridden early years of the twenty-first century (internationalism is no substitute for individualism).

The truth of the matter is that superficial timeliness is a distraction. It is the book's perennial and enduring ideas that make *The Puppet Masters* perennially timely. *The Puppet Masters* could be remade as a film again today, and no doubt the aliens-among-us would be sleeper cells of radical fundamentalists of one kind or another. That kind of superficial timeliness only lets us not to have to think about those enduring American issues of individualism, in an era when the values of the Enlightenment are being rolled back and cast off in the name of an illusory collective "security."

Heinlein spent his entire career telling us: "focus, people—pay attention to what is important." *The Puppet Masters* talks about the dignity of the individual—and that is a message for all seasons.

☞ **Chapter 1** ☜

Were they truly intelligent? By themselves, that is? I don't
know and I don't know how we can ever find out. I'm not
a lab man; I'm an operator.

With the Soviets it seems certain that they did not
invent anything. They simply took the communist power-
for-power's-sake and extended it without any "rotten liberal
sentimentality" as the commissars put it. On the other
hand, with animals they were a good deal more than animal.

(It seems strange no longer to see dogs around. When
we finally come to grips with them, there will be a few
million dogs to avenge. And cats. For me, one particular
cat.)

If they were not truly intelligent, I hope I never live to
see us tangle with anything at all like them, which is intelligent. I know who will lose. Me. You. The so-called
human race.

For me it started much too early on July 12, '07, with
my phone shrilling in a frequency guaranteed to peel off

the skull. I felt around my person, trying to find the thing to shut it off, then recalled that I had left it in my jacket across the room. "All right," I growled. "I hear you. Shut off that damned noise."

"Emergency," a voice said in my ear. "Report in person."

I told him what to do with his emergency. "I'm on a seventy-two hour pass."

"Report to the Old Man," the voice persisted, "at once."

That was different. "Moving," I acknowledged and sat up with a jerk that hurt my eyeballs. I found myself facing a blonde. She was sitting up, too, and staring at me round-eyed.

"Who are you talking to?" she demanded.

I stared back, recalling with difficulty that I had seen her before. "Me? Talking?" I stalled while trying to think up a good lie, then, as I came wider-awake, realized that it did not have to be a very good lie as she could not possibly have heard the other half of the conversation. The sort of phone my section uses is not standard; the audio relay was buried surgically under the skin back of my left ear-bone conduction. "Sorry, babe," I went on. "Had a nightmare. I often talk in my sleep."

"Sure you're all right?"

"I'm fine, now that I'm awake," I assured her, staggering a bit as I stood up. "You go back to sleep."

"Well, uh—" She was breathing regularly almost at once. I went into the bath, injected a quarter grain of "Gyro" in my arm, then let the vibro shake me apart for three minutes while the drug put me back together. I stepped out a new man, or at least a good mock-up of one, and got my jacket. The blonde was snoring gently.

I let my subconscious race back along its track and realized with regret that I did not owe her a damned thing, so I left her. There was nothing in the apartment to give me away, nor even to tell her who I was.

I entered our section offices through a washroom booth in MacArthur Station. You won't find our offices in the phone lists. In fact, it does not exist. Probably I don't exist either. All is illusion. Another route is through a little hole-in-the-wall shop with a sign reading RARE STAMPS & COINS. Don't try that route either—they'll try to sell you a Tu'penny Black.

Don't try any route. I told you we didn't exist, didn't I?

There is one thing no head of a country can know and that is: how good is his intelligence system? He finds out only by having it fail him. Hence our section. Suspenders and belt. United Nations had never heard of us, nor had Central Intelligence—I think. I heard once that we were blanketed into an appropriation for the Department of Food Resources, but I would not know; I was paid in cash.

All I really knew about was the training I had received and the jobs the Old Man sent me on. Interesting jobs, some of them—if you don't care where you sleep, what you eat, nor how long you live. I've totaled three years behind the Curtain; I can drink vodka without blinking and spit Russian like a cat—as well as Cantonese, Kurdish, and some other bad-tasting tongues. I'm prepared to say that they've got nothing behind the Curtain that Paducah, Kentucky doesn't have bigger and better. Still, it's a living.

If I had had any sense, I'd have quit and taken a working job.

The only trouble with that would be that I wouldn't have been working for the Old Man any longer. That made the difference.

Not that he was a soft boss. He was quite capable of saying, "Boys, we need to fertilize this oak tree. Just jump in that hole at its base and I'll cover you up."

We'd have done it. Any of us would.

And the Old Man would bury us alive, too, if he thought that there was as much as a 53 percent probability that it was the Tree of Liberty he was nourishing.

He got up and limped toward me as I came in. I wondered again why he did not have that leg done over. Pride in how he had gotten the limp was my guess, not that I would ever know. A person in the Old Man's position must enjoy his pride in secret; his profession does not allow for public approbation.

His face split in a wicked smile. With his big hairless skull and his strong Roman nose he looked like a cross between Satan and Punch of Punch-and-Judy. "Welcome, Sam," he said. "Sorry to get you out of bed."

The deuce he was sorry! "I was on leave," I answered shortly. He was the Old Man, but leave is leave—and damned seldom!

"Ah, but you still are. We're going on a vacation."

I didn't trust his "vacations" so I did not rise to the bait. "So my name is 'Sam'," I answered. "What's my last name?"

"Cavanaugh. And I'm your Uncle Charlie—Charles M. Cavanaugh, retired. Meet your sister Mary."

I had noticed that there was another person in the room, but had filed my one glance for future reference. When the Old Man is present he gets full attention as long as he wants it. Now I looked over my "sister" more carefully and then looked her over again. It was worth it.

I could see why he had set us up as brother and sister if we were to do a job together; it would give him a trouble-free pattern. An indoctrinated agent can't break his assumed character any more than a professional actor can intentionally muff his lines. So this one I must treat as my sister—a dirty trick if I ever met one!

A long, lean body, but unquestionably and pleasingly mammalian. Good legs. Broad shoulders for a woman. Flaming, wavy red hair and the real redheaded saurian bony structure to her skull. Her face was handsome rather than beautiful; her teeth were sharp and clean. She looked me over as if I were a side of beef.

I was not yet in character; I wanted to drop one wing and run in circles. It must have showed, for the Old Man said gently, "Tut tut, Sammy—there's no incest in the Cavanaugh family. You were both carefully brought up, by my favorite sister-in-law. Your sister dotes on you and you are extremely fond of your sister, but in a healthy, clean-cut, sickeningly chivalrous, All-American-Boy sort of way."

"As bad as that?" I asked, still looking at my "sister".

"Worse."

"Oh, well—howdy, Sis. Glad to know you."

She stuck out a hand. It was firm and seemed as strong as mine. "Hi, Bud." Her voice was deep contralto, which was all I needed. Damn the Old Man!

"I might add," the Old Man went on in the same

gentle tones, "that you are so devoted to your sister that you would gladly die to protect her. I dislike to tell you so, Sammy, but your sister is a little more valuable, for the present at least, to the organization than you are."

"Got it," I acknowledged. "Thanks for the polite qualification."

"Now, Sammy—"

"She's my favorite sister; I protect her from dogs and strange men. I don't have to be slapped with an ax. Okay, when do we start?"

"Better stop over in Cosmetics; I think they have a new face for you."

"Make it a whole new head. See you. 'By, Sis."

They did not quite do that, but they did fit my personal phone under the overhang of my skull in back and then cemented hair over it. They dyed my hair to the same shade as that of my newly acquired sister, bleached my skin, and did things to my cheekbones and chin. The mirror showed me to be as good an authentic redhead as Sis. I looked at my hair and tried to recall what its natural shade had been, way back when. Then I wondered if Sis were what she seemed to be along those lines. I rather hoped so. Those teeth, now—Stow it, Sammy! She's your sister.

I put on the kit they gave me and somebody handed me a jump bag, already packed. The Old Man had evidently been in Cosmetics, too; his skull was now covered by crisp curls of a shade just between pink and white. They had done something to his face, for the life of me I could not tell just what—but we were all three clearly related by blood and were all of that curious sub-race, the redheads.

"Come, Sammy," he said. "Time is short. I'll brief you

in the car." We went up by a route I had not known about and ended up on the Northside launching platform, high above New Brooklyn and overlooking Manhattan Crater.

I drove while the Old Man talked. Once we were out of local control he told me to set it automatic on Des Moines, Iowa. I then joined Mary and "Uncle Charlie" in the lounge. He gave us our personal histories briefly and filled in details to bring us up to date. "So here we are," he concluded, "a merry little family party—tourists. And if we should happen to run into unusual events, that is how we will behave, as nosy and irresponsible tourists might."

"But what is the problem?" I asked. "Or do we play this one entirely by ear?"

"Mmmm . . . possibly."

"Okay. But when you're dead, it's nice to know why you're dead, I always say. Eh, Mary?"

"Mary" did not answer. She had that quality, rare in babes and commendable, of not talking when she had nothing to say. The Old Man looked me over, his manner not that of a man who can't make up his mind, but rather as if he were judging me as I was at that moment and feeding the newly acquired data into the machine between his ears.

Presently he said, "Sam, you've heard of 'flying saucers'."

"Huh? Can't say that I have."

"You've studied history. Come, now!"

"You mean those? The flying-saucer craze, 'way back before the Disorders? I thought you meant something recent and real; those were mass hallucinations."

"Were they?"

"Well, weren't they? I haven't studied much statistical abnormal psychology, but I seem to remember an equation. That whole period was psychopathic; a man with all his gaskets tight would have been locked up."

"But this present day is sane, eh?"

"Oh, I wouldn't go so far as to say that." I pawed back through the unused drawers of my mind and found the answer I wanted. "I remember that equation now—Digby's evaluating integral for second and higher order data. It gave a 93.7 percent certainty that the flying-saucer myth, after elimination of explained cases, was hallucination. I remember it because it was the first case of its type in the history of science in which the instances had been systematically collected and evaluated. Some sort of a government project, God knows why."

The Old Man looked benignly avuncular. "Brace yourself, Sammy. We are going to inspect a flying saucer today. Maybe we'll even saw off a piece for a souvenir, like true tourists."

Chapter 2

"Seen a newscast lately?" the Old Man went on.

I shook my head. Silly question—I'd been on leave.

"Try it sometime," he suggested. "Lots of interesting things on the 'casts. Never mind. Seventeen hours—" he glanced at his finger watch and added, "—and twenty-three minutes ago an unidentified spaceship landed near Grinnell, Iowa. Type, unknown. Approximately disc-shaped and about one hundred fifty feet across. Origin, unknown, but—"

"Didn't they track a trajectory on it?" I interrupted.

"They did not," he answered, spacing his words. "Here is a photo of it taken after landing by Space Station Beta."

I looked it over and passed it to Mary. It was as unsatisfactory as a telephoto taken from five thousand miles out usually is. Trees looking like moss . . . a cloud shadow that loused up the best part of the pie . . . and a gray circle that might have been a disc-shaped space ship and could just as well have been an oil tank or a water reservoir. I wondered how many times we had bombed hydroponics plants in Siberia, mistaking them for atomic installations.

Mary handed the pic back. I said, "Looks like a tent for a camp meeting to me. What else do we know?"

"Nothing."

"Nothing! After seventeen hours! We ought to have agents pouring out of their ears!"

"Ah, yes. We did have. Two within reach and four that were sent in. They failed to report back. I dislike losing agents, Sammy, especially with no results."

Up to then I had not stopped to wonder about the Old Man himself being risked on a job—it had not looked like risk. But I had a sudden cold realization that the situation must be so serious that the Old Man had chosen to bet his own brain against the loss of the organization—for he was the Section. Nobody who knew him doubted his guts, but they did not doubt his horse sense, either. He knew his own value; he would not risk himself unless he believed coldly that it would take his own skill to swing it and that the job had to be done.

I felt suddenly chilly. Ordinarily an agent has a duty to save his own neck, in order to complete his mission and report back. On this job it was the Old Man who must come back—and after him, Mary. I stood number three and was as expendable as a paper clip. I didn't like it.

"One agent made a partial report," the Old Man went on. "He went in as a casual bystander and reported by phone that it must be a space ship although he could not determine its motive power. We got the same thing from the newscasts. He then reported that the ship was opening and that he was going to try to get closer, past the police lines. The last thing he said was, 'Here they come. They are little creatures, about—' Then he shut off."

"Little men?"

"He said, 'creatures'."

"Peripheral reports?"

"Plenty of them. The Des Moines stereocasting station reported the landing and sent mobile units in for spot cast. The pictures they sent out were all fairly long shots, taken from the air. They showed nothing but a disc-shaped object. Then, for about two hours, no pictures and no news, followed later by close ups and a new news slant."

The Old Man shut up. I said, "Well?"

"The whole thing was a hoax. The 'space ship' was a sheet metal and plastic fraud, built by two farm boys in some woods near their home. The fake reports originated with an announcer with more sense of humor than good judgment and who had put the boys up to it to make a story. He has been fired and the latest 'invasion from outer space' turns out to be a joke."

I squirmed. "So it's a hoax—but we lose six men. We're going to look for them?"

"No, for we would not find them. We are going to try to find out why triangulation of this photograph—" He held up the teleshot taken from the space station. "—doesn't quite jibe with the news reports—and why Des Moines stereo station shut up for a while."

Mary spoke up for the first time. "I'd like to talk with those farm boys."

I roaded the car about five miles this side of Grinnell and we started looking for the McLain farm—the news reports had named Vincent and George McLain as the culprits. It wasn't hard to find. At a fork in the road was a big sign, professional in appearance: THIS WAY TO THE SPACESHIP. Shortly the road was parked both sides with duos and groundcars and triphibs. A couple of hastily built stands dispensed cold drinks and souvenirs at the turn-off into the McLain place. A state cop was directing traffic.

"Pull up," directed the Old Man. "Might as well see the fun, eh?"

"Right, Uncle Charlie," I agreed.

The Old Man bounced out with only a trace of limp, swinging his cane. I handed Mary out and she snuggled up to me, grasping my arm. She looked up at me, managing to look both stupid and demure. "My, but you're strong, Buddy."

I wanted to slap her, but gave a self-conscious smirk instead. That poor-little-me routine from an agent, from one of the Old Man's agents. A smile from a tiger.

"Uncle Charlie" buzzed around, bothering state police, buttonholing people to give them unasked-for opinions, stopping to buy cigars at one of the stands, and in general giving a picture of a well-to-do, senile old fool, out for a holiday. He turned back to us and waved his cigar at a state sergeant. "The inspector says the whole thing is a fraud, my dears—a prank thought up by some boys. Shall we go?"

Mary looked disappointed. "No space ship?"

"There's a space ship, if you want to call it that," the cop answered. "Just follow the suckers, and you'll find it. It's 'sergeant', not 'inspector'."

"Uncle Charlie" pressed a cigar on him and we set

out, across a pasture and into some woods. It cost a dollar to get through the gate and many of the potential suckers turned back. The path through the woods was rather deserted. I moved carefully, wishing for eyes in the back of my head instead of a phone. According to the book six agents had gone down this path and—none had come back. I didn't want it to be nine.

Uncle Charlie and Sis walked ahead, Mary chattering like a fool and somehow managing to be both shorter and younger than she had been on the trip out. We came to a clearing and there was the "space ship".

It was the proper size, more than a hundred feet across, but it was whipped together out of light-gauge metal and sheet plastic, sprayed with aluminum. It was roughly the shape of two giant pie plates, face to face. Aside from that, it looked like nothing in particular. Nevertheless Mary squealed. "Oh, how exciting!"

A youngster, eighteen or nineteen, with a permanent sunburn and a pimply face, stuck his head out of a sort of hatch in the top of the monstrosity. "Care to see inside?" he called out. He added that it would be fifty cents a piece more and Uncle Charlie shelled out.

Mary hesitated at the hatch. Pimple face was joined by what appeared to be his twin and they started to hand her down in. She drew back and I moved in fast, intending to do any handling myself. My reasons were 99 percent professional; I could feel danger all through the place. "It's dark in there," she quavered.

"It's perfectly safe," the second young man said. "We've been taking sightseers through all day. I'm Vine McLain, one of the owners. Come on, lady."

Uncle Charlie peered down the hatch, like a cautious mother hen. "Might be snakes in there," he decided. "Mary, I don't think you had better go in."

"Nothing to fear," the first McLain said insistently. "It's safe as houses."

"Just keep the money, gentlemen." Uncle Charlie glanced at his finger. "We're late as it is. Let's go, my dears."

I followed them back up the path, my hackles up the whole way.

We got back to the car and I pulled out into the road. Once we were rolling, the Old Man said sharply, "Well? What did you see?"

I countered with, "Any doubt about that first report? The one that broke off?"

"None."

"That thing over in the woods wouldn't have fooled an agent, even in the dark. This wasn't the ship he saw."

"Of course not. What else?"

"How much would you say that fake cost? That was new sheet metal, fresh paint, and from what I saw of the inside through the hatch, probably a thousand feet, more or less, of lumber to brace it."

"Go on."

"Well, the McLain house hadn't been painted in years, not even the barn. The place had 'mortgage' spelled out all over it. If the boys were in on the gag, they didn't foot the bill."

"Obviously. You, Mary?"

"Uncle Charlie, did you notice the way they treated me?"

"Who?" I said sharply.

"Both the state sergeant and the two boys. When I use the sweet-little-bundle-of-sex routine, something should happen. Nothing did."

"They were all attentive," I objected.

"You don't understand. You can't understand—but I know. I always know. Something was wrong with them. They were dead inside. Harem guards, if you know what I mean."

"Hypnosis?" asked the Old Man.

"Possibly. Or drugs perhaps." She frowned and looked puzzled.

"Hmm—" he answered. "Sammy, take the next turn to the left. We're investigating a point about two miles south of here."

"The triangulated location by the pic?"

"What else?"

But we didn't get there. First it was a bridge out and I didn't have room enough to make the car hop it, quite aside from the small matter of traffic regulations for a duo on the ground. We circled to the south and came in again, the only remaining route. We were stopped by a highway cop and a detour sign. A brush fire, he told us; go any farther and we would probably be impressed into firefighting. He didn't know but what he ought to send me up to the firelines anyhow.

Mary waved her lashes and other things at him and he relented. She pointed out that neither she nor Uncle Charlie could drive, a double lie.

After we pulled away I asked her, "How about that one?"

"What about him?"

"Harem guard?"

"Oh, my, no! A most attractive man."

Her answer annoyed me.

The Old Man vetoed taking to the air and making a pass over the triangulated spot. He said it was useless. We headed for Des Moines. Instead of parking at the toll gates we paid to take the car into the city proper, and ended up at the main studios of Des Moines stereo. "Uncle Charlie" blustered his way into the office of the general manager, us in tow. He told several lies—or perhaps Charles M. Cavanaugh was actually a big wheel with the Federal Communications Authority. How was I to know?

Once inside and the door shut he continued the Big Brass act. "Now, sir, what is all this nonsense about a spaceship hoax? Speak plainly, sir; I warn you your license may depend on it."

The manager was a little round-shouldered man, but he did not seem cowed, merely annoyed. "We've made a full explanation over the channels," he said. "We were victimized by one of our own people. The man has been discharged."

"Hardly adequate, sir."

The little man—Barnes, his name was—shrugged. "What do you expect? Shall we string him up by his thumbs?"

Uncle Charlie pointed his cigar at him. "I warn you, sir, that I am not to be trifled with. I have been making an investigation of my own and I am not convinced that two farm louts and a junior announcer could have pulled off this preposterous business. There was money in it, sir. Yes, sir money. And where would I expect to find money? Here at the top. Now tell me, sir, just what did you—"

Mary had seated herself close by Barnes's desk. She had done something to her costume, which exposed more skin, and her pose put me in mind of Goya's Disrobed Lady. She made a thumbs-down signal to the Old Man.

Barnes should not have caught it; his attention appeared to be turned to the Old Man. But he did. He turned toward Mary and his face went dead. He reached for his desk.

"Sam! Kill him!" the Old Man rapped.

I burned his legs off and his trunk fell to the floor. It was a poor shot; I had intended to burn his belly.

I stepped quickly to him and kicked his gun away from his still-groping fingers. I was about to give him the coup de grace—a man burned that way is dead, but it takes him a while to die—when the Old Man snapped, "Don't touch him! Mary, stand back!"

We did so. The Old Man sidled toward the body, like a cat cautiously investigating the unknown. Barnes gave a long bubbling sigh and was quiet—shock death; a gun burn doesn't bleed much, not that much. The Old Man looked him over and poked him gently with his cane.

"Boss," I said, "about time to git, isn't it?"

Without looking around he answered, "We're as safe here as anywhere. Safer, probably. This building may be swarming with them."

"Swarming with what?"

"How would I know? Swarming with whatever he

was." He pointed to Barnes's body. "That's what I've got to find out."

Mary gave a choked sob, the first honest feminine thing I had known her to do, and gasped, "He's still breathing. Look!"

The body lay facedown; the back of the jacket heaved as if the chest were rising. The Old Man looked at it and poked at it with his cane. "Sam. Come here."

I came. "Strip it," he went on. "Use your gloves. And be careful."

"Booby trap?"

"Shut up. Use care."

I don't know what he expected me to find, but he must have had a hunch that was close to truth. I think the bottom part of the Old Man's brain has a built-in integrator which arrives at a logical necessity from minimum facts the way a museum johnny reconstructs an extinct animal from a single bone.

I took him at his word. First pulling on gloves— agent's gloves; I could have stirred boiling acid with my gloved hand, yet I could feel a coin in the dark and call heads or tails—once gloved, I started to turn him over to undress him.

The back was still heaving; I did not like the look of it—unnatural. I placed a palm between the shoulder blades.

A man's back is bone and muscle. This was jelly soft and undulating. I snatched my hand away.

Without a word Mary handed me a fancy pair of scissors from Barnes's desk. I took them and cut the jacket away. Presently I folded it back and we all looked.

Underneath the jacket the body was dressed in a light singlet, almost transparent. Between this shirt and the skin, from the neck halfway down the back, was something which was not flesh. A couple of inches thick, it gave the corpse a round-shouldered, or slightly humped, appearance.

It pulsed like a jellyfish.

As we watched, it slid slowly off the back, away from us. I reached out to peel up the singlet, to let us at it; my hand was knocked away by the Old Man's cane. "Make up your mind," I said and rubbed my knuckles.

He did not answer but tucked the end of his cane under the bottom of the shirt and worried it up the trunk. The thing was uncovered.

Grayish, faintly translucent, and shot through with darker structure, shapeless—it reminded me of a giant clot of frogs' eggs. It was clearly alive, for it pulsed and quivered and moved by flowing. As we watched it flowed down into the space between Barnes's arm and chest, filled it and stayed there, unable to go farther.

"The poor devil," the Old Man said softly.

"Huh? That?"

"No. Barnes. Remind me to see to it that he gets the Purple Heart, when this is over. If it ever is over." The Old Man straightened up and slumped around the room, as if he had forgotten completely the gray horror nestling in the crook of Barnes's arm.

I drew back a bit and continued to stare at it, my gun ready. It could not move fast; it obviously could not fly; but I did not know what it could do and I was not taking chances. Mary moved closer to me and pressed her shoulder against mine, as if for human comfort. I put my free arm around her.

On a side table there was an untidy stack of cans, the sort used for stereo tapes. The Old Man took a double program can, spilled the reels on the floor, and came back with it. "This will do, I think." He placed the can on the floor, near the thing, and began chivvying it with his cane, trying to irritate it into crawling into the can.

Instead it oozed back until it was almost entirely under the body. I grabbed the free arm and heaved what was left of Barnes away from the spot; the thing clung momentarily, then flopped to the floor. After that, under dear old Uncle Charlie's directions, Mary and I used our guns set at lowest power to force it, by burning the floor close to it, into the can. We got it in, a close fit, and I slapped the cover on.

The Old Man tucked the can under his arm. "On our way, my dears."

On the way out he paused in the partly open door to call out a parting to Barnes, then, after closing the door, stopped at the desk of Barnes's secretary. "I'll be seeing Mr. Barnes again tomorrow," he told her. "No, no appointment. I'll phone first."

Out we went, slow march, the Old Man with the can full of thing under his arm and me with my ears cocked for alarums. Mary played the silly little moron, with a running monologue. The Old Man even paused in the lobby, bought a cigar, and inquired directions, with bumbling, self-important good nature.

Once in the car he gave me directions, then cautioned me against driving fast. The directions led us into a garage. The Old Man sent for the manager and said to him, "Mr. Malone wants this car—immediately." It was a signal I had had occasion to use myself, only then it had been "Mr. Sheffield" who was in a hurry. I knew that the duo would cease to exist in about twenty minutes, save as anonymous spare parts in the service bins.

The manager looked us over, then answered quietly, "Through that door over there." He sent the two mechanics in the room away on errands and we ducked through the door.

We ended up presently in the apartment of an elderly couple; there we became brunets and the Old Man got his bald head back. I acquired a moustache which did nothing for my looks, but I was surprised to find that Mary looked as well dark as she had as a redhead. The "Cavanaugh" combination was dropped; Mary got a chic nurse's costume and I was togged out as a chauffeur while the Old Man became our elderly, invalid employer, complete with shawl and temper tantrums.

A car was waiting for us when we were ready. The trip back was no trouble; we could have remained the carrot-topped Cavanaughs. I kept the screen turned on to Des Moines, but, if the cops had turned up the late Mr. Barnes, the newsboys hadn't heard about it.

We went straight down to the Old Man's office—straight as one can go, that is—and there we opened the can. The Old Man sent for Dr. Graves, the head of the Section's bio lab, and the job was done with handling equipment.

We need not have bothered. What we needed were gas masks, not handling equipment. A stink of decaying organic matter, like the stench from a gangrenous wound, filled the room and forced us to slap the cover back on and speed up the blowers. Graves wrinkled his nose. "What in the world was that?" he demanded. "Puts me in mind of a dead baby."

The Old Man was swearing softly. "You are to find out," he said. "Use handling equipment. Work it in suits, in a germ-free compartment, and don't assume that it is dead."

"If that is alive, I'm Queen Anne."

"Maybe you are, but don't take chances. Here is all the help I can give. It's a parasite; it's capable of attaching itself to a host, such as a man, and controlling the host. It is almost certainly extra-terrestrial in origin and metabolism."

The lab boss sniffed. "Extra-terrestrial parasite on a terrestrial host? Ridiculous! The body chemistries would be incompatible."

The Old Man grunted. "Damn your theories. When we captured it, it was living on a man. If that means it has to be a terrestrial organism, show me where it fits into the scheme of things and where to look for its mates. And quit jumping to conclusions; I want facts."

The biologist stiffened. "You'll get them!"

"Get going. Wait—don't use more of it than necessary for your investigations; I need the major portion as evidence. And don't persist in the silly assumption that the thing is dead; that perfume may be a protective weapon. That thing, if alive, is fantastically dangerous. If it gets on one of your laboratory men, I'll almost certainly have to kill him."

The lab director said nothing more, but he left without some of his cockiness.

The Old Man settled back in his chair, sighed, and closed his eyes. He seemed to have gone to sleep; Mary and I kept quiet. After five minutes or so he opened his eyes, looked at me, and said, "How many mustard plasters the size of that thing Doc just carted out of here can arrive in a space ship as big as that fraud we looked at?"

"Was there a space ship?" I asked. "The evidence seems slim."

"Slim but utterly incontrovertible. There was a ship. There still is a ship."

"We should have examined the site."

"That site would have been our last sight. The other six boys weren't fools. Answer my question."

"I can't. How big the ship was doesn't tell me anything about its payload, when I don't know its propulsion method, the jump it made, or what supply load the passengers require. It's a case of how long is a piece of rope? If you want a horseback guess, I'd say several hundred, maybe several thousand."

"Mmm . . . yes. So there are several hundred, maybe several thousand zombies in the State of Iowa tonight. Or harem guards, as Mary puts it." He thought for a moment. "But how am I to get past them to the harem? We can't go around shooting every round-shouldered man in Iowa; it would cause talk." He smiled feebly.

"I'll put you another question with no answer," I said. "If one space ship lands in Iowa yesterday, how many will land in North Dakota tomorrow? Or in Brazil?"

"Yes, there's that." He looked still more troubled. "I'll answer it by telling you how long is your piece of rope."

"Huh?"

"Long enough to choke you to death. You kids go wash up and enjoy yourselves; you may not have another chance. Don't leave the offices."

I went back to Cosmetics, got my own skin color back and in general resumed my normal appearance, had a soak and a massage, and then went to the staff lounge in search of a drink and some company. I looked around, not knowing whether I was looking for a blonde, brunette, or redhead, but feeling fairly sure that I could spot the right chassis.

It was a redhead. Mary was in a booth, sucking on a drink and looking much as she had looked when she was introduced to me as my sister. "Hi, Sis," I said, sliding in beside her.

She smiled and answered, "Hello, Bud. Drag up a rock," while moving to make room for me.

I dialed for bourbon and water which I needed for medicinal purposes and then said, "Is this your real appearance?"

She shook her head. "Not at all. Zebra stripes and two heads. What's yours?"

"My mother smothered me with a pillow the first time she saw me, so I never got a chance to find out."

She again looked me over with that side-of-beef scrutiny, then said, "I can understand her actions, but I am probably more hardened than she was. You'll do, Bud."

"Thanks." I went on, "Let's drop this 'Bud-and-Sis' routine; I find it gives me inhibitions."

"Hmm . . . I think you need inhibitions."

"Me? Not at all. Never any violence with me; I'm more the 'Barkis-is-willing' type." I might have added that, if I laid a hand on her and she happened not to like it, I'd bet that I would draw back a bloody stump. The Old Man's kids are never sissies.

She smiled. "So? Well, note it down that Miss Barkis is not willing, at least not this evening." She put down her glass. "Drink up and let's reorder."

We did so and continued to sit there, feeling warm and good, and, for the moment, not worried. There aren't many hours like that, especially in our profession; it makes one savor them.

One of the nicest things about Mary was that she did not turn on the sex, except for professional purposes. I think she knew—I'm sure she knew—what a load of it she possessed. But she was too much of a gentleman to use it socially. She kept it turned down low, just enough to keep us both warm and comfortable.

While we sat there, not saying much, I got to thinking how well she would look on the other side of a fireplace. My job being what it was, I had never thought seriously about getting married—and after all, a babe is just a babe; why get excited? But Mary was an agent herself; talking to her would not be like shouting off Echo Mountain. I realized that I had been lonely for one hell of a long time.

"Mary—"

"Yes?"

"Are you married?"

"Eh? Why do you ask? As a matter of fact I'm not—now. But what business—I mean, why does it matter?"

"Well, it might," I persisted.

She shook her head.

"I'm serious," I went on. "Look me over. I've got both hands and both feet. I'm fairly young, and I don't track mud in the house. You could do worse."

She laughed, but her laugh was kindly. "And you could work up better lines than that. I am sure they must have been extemporaneous."

"They were."

"And I won't hold them against you. In fact, I'll forget them. Listen, wolf, your technique is down; just because a woman tells you that she is not going to sleep with you tonight is no reason to lose your head and offer her a contract. Some women would be just mean enough to hold you to it."

"I meant it," I said peevishly.

"So? What salary do you offer?"

"Damn your pretty eyes. If you want that type of contract, I'll go along; you can keep your pay and I'll allot half of mine to you . . . unless you want to retire."

She shook her head. "I didn't mean it; I'd never insist on a settlement contract, not with a man I was willing to marry in the first place—"

"I didn't think you would."

"I was just trying to make you see that you yourself were not serious." She looked me over soberly. "But perhaps you are," she added in a warm, soft voice.

"I am."

She shook her head again. "Agents should not marry. You know that."

"Agents shouldn't marry anyone but agents."

She started to answer, but stopped suddenly. My own phone was talking in my ear, the Old Man's voice, and I knew she was hearing the same thing. "Come into my office," he said.

We both got up without saying anything. Mary stopped me at the door, put a hand on my arm, and looked up into my eyes. "That is why it is silly to talk about marriage. We've got this job to finish. All the time we've been talking, you've been thinking about the job and so have I."

"I have not."

"Don't play with me! Consider this, Sam—suppose you were married and you woke up to find one of those things on your wife's shoulders, possessing her." There was horror in her eyes as she went on, "Suppose I woke up and found one of them on your shoulders."

"I'll chance it. And I won't let one get to you."

She touched my cheek. "I don't believe you would."

We went on into the Old Man's office.

He looked up just long enough to say, "Come along. We're leaving."

"Where to?" I answered. "Or shouldn't I ask?"

"White House. See the President. Shut up."

I shut.

⚞ Chapter 3 ⚟

At the beginning of a forest fire or an epidemic there is a short time when a minimum of correct action will contain and destroy. The B. W. boys express it in exponential equations, but you don't need math to understand it; it depends on early diagnosis and prompt action before the thing gets out of hand. What the President needed to do the Old Man had already figured out—declare a national emergency, fence off the Des Moines area, and shoot anybody who tried to slip out, be it a cocker spaniel or grandma with her cookie jar. Then let them out one at a time, stripping them and searching them for parasites. Meantime, use the radar screen, the rocket boys, and the space stations to spot and smash any new landings.

Warn all the other nations including those behind the Curtain, ask for their help—but don't be fussy about international law, for this was a fight for racial survival against an outside invader. For the moment it did not matter where they came from—Mars, Venus, the Jovian satellites, or outside the system entirely. Repel the invasion.

The Old Man had cracked the case, analyzed it, and come up with the right answer in a little more than twenty-four hours. His unique gift was the ability to reason logically with unfamiliar, hard-to-believe facts as easily as with the commonplace. Not much, eh? I have never met anyone else who could do it wholeheartedly. Most minds stall dead when faced with facts which conflict with basic beliefs; "I-just-can't-believe-it" is all one word to highbrows and dimwits alike.

But not to the Old Man—and he had the ear of the President.

The Secret Service guards gave us the works, politely. An X-ray went beep! and I surrendered my heater. Mary turned out to be a walking arsenal; the machine gave four beeps and a hiccough, although you would have sworn she couldn't hide a tax receipt under what she was wearing. The Old Man surrendered his cane without waiting to be asked; I got the notion he did not want it to be X-rayed.

Our audio capsules gave them trouble. They showed up both by X-ray and by metal detector, but the guards weren't equipped for surgical operations. There was a hurried conference with a presidential secretary and the head guard ruled that anything embedded in the flesh need not be classed as a potential weapon.

They printed us, photographed our retinas, and ushered us into a waiting room. The Old Man was whisked out and in to see the President alone.

"I wonder why we were brought along?" I asked Mary. "The Old Man knows everything we know."

She did not answer, so I spent the time reviewing in my mind the loopholes in the security methods used to guard the President. They do such things much better behind the Curtain; an assassin with any talent could have beaten our safeguards with ease. I got to feeling indignant about it.

After a while we were ushered in. I found I had stage fright so badly I was stumbling over my feet. The Old Man introduced us and I stammered. Mary just bowed.

The President said he was glad to see us and turned on that smile, the way you see it in the stereocasts—and he made us feel that he was glad to see us. I felt all warm inside and no longer embarrassed.

And no longer worried. The President, with the Old Man's help, would take action and the dirty horror we had seen would be cleaned up.

The Old Man directed me to report all that I had done and seen and heard on this assignment. I made it brief but complete. I tried to catch his eye when it came to the part about killing Barnes, but he wasn't having any—so I left out the Old Man's order to shoot and made it clear that I had shot to protect another agent—Mary—when I saw Barnes reach for his gun. The Old Man interrupted me. "Make your report complete."

So I filled in the Old Man's order to shoot. The President threw the Old Man a glance at the correction, the only expression he showed. I went on about the parasite thing, went on, in fact, up to that present moment, as nobody told me to stop.

Then it was Mary's turn. She fumbled in trying to explain to the President why she expected to get some sort

of response out of normal men—and had not gotten it out
of the McLain boys, the state sergeant, and Barnes. The
President helped her . . . by smiling warmly, managing to
bow without getting up, and saying, "My dear young lady,
I quite believe it."

Mary blushed, then went on. The President listened
gravely while she finished. He asked a couple of questions,
then sat still for several minutes.

Presently he looked up and spoke to the Old Man.
"Andrew," he said, "your section has been invaluable. On
at least two occasions your reports have tipped the balance in crucial occasions in history."

The Old Man snorted. "So it's 'no', is it?"

"I did not say so."

"You were about to."

The President shrugged. "I was going to suggest
that your young people withdraw, but now it does not
matter. Andrew, you are a genius, but even geniuses
make mistakes. They overwork themselves and lose
their judgment. I'm not a genius but I learned to relax
about forty years ago. How long has it been since you had
a vacation?"

"Damn your vacations! See here, Tom, I anticipated
this; that's why I brought witnesses. They are neither
drugged nor instructed. Call in your psych crew; try to
shake their stories."

The President shook his head. "You wouldn't have
brought witnesses who could be cracked. I'm sure you are
cleverer about such things than anyone whom I could
bring in to test them. Take this young man—he was
willing to risk a murder charge to protect you. You inspire

loyalty, Andrew. As for the young lady, really, Andrew, I can't start what amounts to war on a woman's intuition."

Mary took a step forward. "Mr. President," she said very earnestly, "I do know. I know every time. I can't tell you how I know—but those were not normal male men."

He hesitated, then answered, "I do not dispute you. But you have not considered an obvious explanation—that they actually were, ah, 'harem guards'. Pardon me, Miss. There are always such unfortunates in the population. By the laws of chance you ran across four in one day."

Mary shut up. The Old Man did not. "God damn it, Tom—" I shuddered; you don't talk to the President that way. "—I knew you when you were an investigating senator and I was a key man in your investigations. You know I wouldn't bring you this fairy tale if there were any way to explain it away. Facts can't be ignored; they've got to be destroyed, or faced up to. How about that space ship? What was in it? Why couldn't I even reach the spot where it landed?" He hauled out the photograph taken by Space Station Beta and shoved it under the President's nose.

The President seemed unperturbed. "Ah, yes, facts. Andrew, both you and I have a passion for facts. But I have several sources of information other than your section. Take this photo—you made quite a point of it when you phoned. I've checked the matter. The metes and bounds of the McLain farm as recorded in the local county court-house check precisely with the triangulated latitude and longitude of this object on this photograph." The President looked up. "Once I absent-mindedly turned off a block too soon and got lost in my own neighborhood. You weren't even in your own neighborhood, Andrew."

"Tom—"

"Yes, Andrew?"

"You did not trot out there and check those court-house maps yourself?"

"Of course not."

"Thank God for that—or you would be carrying three pounds of pulsing tapioca between your shoulder blades this minute—and God save the United States! You can be sure of this: the courthouse clerk and whatever agent was sent to see him, both are hag-ridden by filthy parasites this very moment." The Old Man stared at the ceiling. "Yes, and the Des Moines chief of police, newspaper editors around there, dispatchers, cops, all sorts of key people. Tom, I don't know what we are up against, but they know what we are, and they are pinching off the nerve cells of our social organism before true messages can get back— or they cover up the true reports with false ones, just as they did with Barnes. Mr. President, you must order an immediate, drastic quarantine of the whole area. There is no other hope!"

"Barnes," the President repeated softly, as if he had heard nothing else. "Andrew, I had hoped to spare you this, but—" He broke off and flipped a key at his desk. "Get me stereo station WDES, Des Moines, the manager's office."

Shortly a screen lighted on his desk; he touched another switch and a solid display in the wall lighted up. We were looking into the room we had been in only a few hours before.

Looking into it past the shoulders of a man who filled most of the screen—Barnes.

Or his twin. When I kill a man, I expect him to stay

dead. I was shaken but I still believed in myself—and my heater.

The man in the display said, "You asked for me, Mr. President?" He sounded as if he were dazzled by the honor.

"Yes, thank you. Mr. Barnes, do you recognize any of these people?"

He looked surprised. "I'm afraid not. Should I?"

The Old Man interrupted. "Tell him to call in his office force."

The President looked quizzical but did just that. "Barnes" looked puzzled but complied. They trooped in, girls mostly, and I recognized the secretary who sat outside the manager's door. One of them squealed, "Ooh—it's the President," and they all fell to buzzing.

None of them identified us—not surprising with the Old Man and me, but Mary's appearance was just as it had been in that same office, and I will bet that Mary's looks would be burned into the mind of any woman who had ever seen her.

But I noticed one thing about them—every single one of them was round-shouldered.

The President eased us out. He put a hand on the Old Man's shoulder. "Seriously, Andrew, take that vacation." He flashed the famous smile. "The Republic won't fall—I'll worry it through till you get back."

Ten minutes later we were standing in the wind on the Rock Creek platform. The Old Man seemed shrunken and, for the first time, old. "What now, boss?"

"Eh? For you two, nothing. You are both on leave until recalled."

"I'd like to take another look at Barnes's office."

"Don't go near the place. Stay out of Iowa. That's an order."

"Mmm—what are you going to do, if I may ask?"

"You heard the President, didn't you? I am going down to Florida and lie in the sun and wait for the world to go to hell. If you have any sense, you'll do the same. There's damned little time."

He squared his shoulders and stumped away. I turned to speak to Mary, but she was gone. His advice seemed awfully good, and it had suddenly occurred to me that waiting for the end of the world might not be too bad, with her help.

I looked around quickly but could not spot her. I trotted off and overtook the Old Man. "Excuse me, Boss. Where did Mary go?"

"Huh? On leave no doubt. Don't bother me."

I considered trying to relay to her through the Section circuit, when I remembered that I did not know her right name, nor her code, nor her I.D. number. I thought of trying to bull it through by describing her, but that was foolishness. Only Cosmetics Records knows the original appearance of an agent—and they won't talk. All I knew about her was that she had twice appeared as a redhead, at least once by choice—and that, for my taste, she was "why men fight". Try punching that into a phone!

Instead I found a room for the night. After I found it I wondered why I had not left the Capital and gone back to my own apartment. Then I wondered if the blonde were still in it. Then I wondered who the blonde was, anyway? Then I went to sleep.

Chapter 4

I woke up at dusk. The room I was in had a real window—the Section pays well and I could afford little luxuries. I looked out over the Capital as it came to life for the night. The river swept away in a wide bend past the Memorial; it was summer and they were adding fluorescine to the water above the District so the river stood out in curving sweeps of glowing rose and amber and emerald and shining fire. Little pleasure boats cut through the colors, each filled, I had no doubt, with couples up to no good and enjoying it.

On the land, here and there among the older buildings, the bubble domes were lighting up, giving the city a glowing fairyland look. Off to the east, where the Bomb had landed, there were no old buildings at all and the area was an Easter basket of color giant Easter eggs, lighted from within.

I've seen the Capital at night oftener than most, because of my business, and, while I like the place, I had not thought much about it. But tonight I had that "Last Ride Together" feeling. It was so beautiful it hurt but it was not its beauty that choked me up; it was knowing that down under those warm lights were people, alive and individual people, going about their lawful occasions, making love or having spats, whichever suited them . . . doing whatever they damn well pleased, each under his own vine and his own fig tree with nobody to make him afraid, as it says.

I thought about all those gentle, kindly people (with only an occasional heel) and I thought about them each with a gray slug clinging to the back of his neck, twitching his legs and arms, making his voice say what the slug wished, going where the slug wanted to go.

Hell's bells—life under the commissars couldn't be that bad. I know—I've been behind the Curtain.

I made myself a solemn promise: if the parasites won, I'd arrange to be dead before I would let one of those things ride me the way one had ridden Barnes. For an agent it would be simple; just bite my nails—or, if your hands happen to be off, there are a couple of other ways. The Old Man planned for all professional necessities.

But the Old Man had not planned such arrangements for such a purpose and I knew it. It was the Old Man's business—and mine—to keep those people down there safe, not to run out on them when the going got rough.

I turned away from the window. There was not a confounded thing I could do about it now; I decided that what I needed was company. The room contained the usual catalog of "escort bureaus" and "model agencies" that you'll find in almost any big hotel except maybe the

Martha Washington. I thumbed through it, looking the girls over, then slammed it shut. I didn't want a whoopee girl; I wanted one particular girl—one who would as soon shoot as shake hands and would bite in the clinches. And I did not know where she had gone.

I always carry a tube of "tempus fugit" pills; most agents do, as one never knows when giving your reflexes a jolt will get you through a tight spot. Despite the scare propaganda, tempus pills are not habit-forming, not the way the original hashish is.

Nevertheless a purist would say I was addicted to them, for I had the habit of taking them occasionally to make a twenty-four hour leave seem like a week. I admit that I enjoyed the mild euphoria which the pills induced as a side effect. Primarily, though, they just stretch out your subjective time by a factor of ten or more, chop time into finer bits so that you live longer for the same amount of clock and calendar.

What's wrong with that? Sure, I know the horrible example story of the man who died of old age in a calendar month through taking the pills steadily, but I took them only once in a while.

Maybe he had the right idea. He lived a long and happy life—you can be sure it was happy—and died happy at the end. What matter that the sun rose only thirty times? Who is keeping score and what are the rules anyhow?

I sat there, staring at my tube of pills and thinking that I had enough to keep me hopped up and contented for what would be, to me, at least two "years". If I wanted to, I could crawl in my hole and pull it in after me.

I took out two pills and got a glass of water. Then I put them carefully back in the tube, put on my gun and phone, left the hotel and headed for the Library of Congress.

On the way I stopped in a bar for a quick one and looked at a newscast. There was no news from Iowa, but when is there any news from Iowa?

At the Library I went to the general catalog, put on blinkers, and started scanning for references. "Flying Saucers" led to "Flying Discs", then to "Project Saucer", then "Lights in the Sky", "Fireballs", "Cosmic Diffusion Theory of Life Origins", and two dozen blind alleys and screwball branches of literature. I needed some sort of a Geiger counter to tell me what was pay dirt and what was not, especially as what I wanted was almost certain to carry a semantic-content code key classing it somewhere between Aesop's fables and the Lost Continent myths.

Nevertheless, in an hour I had a double handful of selector cards. I handed them to the vestal virgin at the desk and waited while she fed them into the hopper. Presently she said, "Most of the films you want are in use. The rest will be delivered to study room 9-A. Take the south escalator, puhlease."

Room 9-A had one occupant—who looked up as I came in and said, "Well! The wolf in person, how did you manage to pick me up again? I could swear I gave you a clean miss."

I said, "Hello, Mary."

"Hello," she answered, "and now, good-by. Miss Barkis still ain't willin' and I've got work to do."

I got annoyed. "Listen, you conceited little twerp, odd

as it may seem to you, I did not come here looking for your no-doubt beautiful white body. I occasionally do some work myself and that is why I'm here. If you will put up with my unwelcome presence until my spools arrive, I'll get the hell out and find another study room, a stag one."

Instead of flaring back, she immediately softened, thereby proving that she was more of a gentleman than I was. "I'm sorry, Sam. A woman hears the same thing so many thousand times that she gets to thinking that no other topic is possible. Sit down."

"No," I answered, "thanks, but I'll take my spools to an unoccupied room. I really do want to work."

"Stay here," she insisted. "Read that notice on the wall. If you remove spools from the room to which they are delivered, you will not only cause the sorter to blow a dozen tubes, but you'll give the chief reference librarian a nervous breakdown."

"I'll bring them back when I'm through with them."

She took my arm and warm tingles went up it. "Please, Sam. I'm sorry."

I sat down and grinned at her. "Nothing could persuade me to leave. I did not expect to find you here, but now that I have, I don't intend to let you out of sight until I know your phone code, your home address, and the true color of your hair."

"Wolf," she said softly, wrinkling her nose. "You'll never know any of them." She made a great business of fitting her head back into her study machine while ignoring me. But I could see that she was not displeased.

The delivery tube went *thunk*! and my spools spilled into the basket. I gathered them up and stacked them on the table by the other machine. One of them rolled over against the ones Mary had stacked up and knocked them down. Mary looked up.

I picked up what I thought was my spool and glanced at the end—the wrong end, as all it held was the serial number and that little pattern of dots which the selector reads. I turned it over, read the label, and placed it in my pile.

"Hey!" said Mary. "That's mine."

"In a pig's eye," I said politely.

"But it is—I read the label when it was faced toward me. It's the one I want next."

Sooner or later, I can see the obvious. Mary wouldn't be there to study the history of footgear through the Middle Ages. I picked up three or four more of hers and read the labels. "So that's why nothing I wanted was in," I said. "But you didn't do a thorough job; I found some that you missed." I handed her my selection.

Mary looked them over, then pushed all the spools into a single pile. "Shall we split them fifty-fifty, or both of us see them all?"

"Fifty-fifty to weed out the junk, then we'll both go over the remainder," I decided. "Let's get busy."

Even after having seen the parasite on poor Barnes's back, even after being solemnly assured by the Old Man that a "flying saucer" had in fact landed, I was not prepared for the monumental pile of evidence to be found buried in a public library. A pest on Digby and his evaluating formula! Digby was a floccinaucinihilipilificator at heart—which is an eight-dollar word meaning a joker who does not believe in anything he can't bite.

The evidence was unmistakable; Earth had been visited by ships from outer space not once but many times.

The reports long antedated our own achievement of space travel; some of them ran back into the seventeenth century—earlier than that, but it was impossible to judge the quality of reports dating back to a time when "science" meant an appeal to Aristotle. The first systematic data came from the United States itself in the 1940's and '50's. The next flurry was in the 1980's, mostly from Russo-Siberia. These reports were difficult to judge as there was no direct evidence from our own intelligence agents and anything that came from behind the Curtain was usually phony, ipso facto.

I noticed something and started taking down dates. Strange objects in the sky appeared to hit a cycle with crests at thirty-year intervals, about. I made a note about it; a statistical analyst might make something of it—or more likely, if I fed it to the Old Man, he would see something in that crystal ball he uses for a brain.

"Flying saucers" were tied in with "mysterious disappearances" not only through being in the same category as sea serpents, bloody rain, and such like wild data, but also because in at least three well-documented instances pilots had chased "saucers" and never come back, or down, anywhere, i.e., officially classed as crashed in wild country and not recovered— an "easy out" or "happy hurdle" type of explanation.

I got another wild hunch and tried to see whether or not there was a thirty-year cycle in mysterious disappearances, and, if so, did it phase—match the objects in-the-sky cycle? There seemed to be but I could not be sure—too much data and not enough fluctuation; there are too many people disappearing every year for other reasons, from amnesia to mothers-in-law.

But vital records have been kept for a long time and not all were lost in the bombings. I noted it down to farm out for professional analysis.

The fact that groups of reports seemed to be geographically and even politically concentrated I did not try very hard to understand. I tabled it, after trying one hunch hypothesis on for size; put yourself in the invaders' place; if you were scouting a strange planet, would you study all of it equally, or would you pick out areas that looked interesting by whatever standards you had and then concentrate?

It was just a guess and I was ready to chuck it before breakfast, if necessary.

Mary and I did not exchange three words all night. Eventually we got up and stretched, then I lent Mary change to pay the machine for the spools of notes she had taken (why don't women carry change?) and got my wires out of hock, too. "Well, what's the verdict?" I asked.

"I feel like a sparrow who has built a nice nest and discovers that it is in a rain spout."

I recited the old jingle. "And we'll do the same thing—refuse to learn and build again in the spout."

"Oh, no! Sam, we've got to do something, fast. The President has to be convinced. It makes a full pattern; this time they are moving in to stay."

"Could be. In fact I think they are."

"Well, what do we do?"

"Honey chile, you are about to learn that in the

Country of the Blind the one-eyed man is in for a hell of
a rough ride."

"Don't be cynical. There isn't time."

"No. There isn't. Gather up your gear and let's get out
of here."

Dawn was on us as we left and the big library was
almost deserted. I said, "Tell you what—let's find a barrel
of beer, take it to my hotel room, bust in the head, and talk
this thing over."

She shook her head. "Not to your hotel room."

"Damn it, this is business."

"Let's go to my apartment. It's only a couple of hundred
miles away; I'll fix you breakfast when we get there."

I recalled my basic purpose in life in time to remember
to leer. "That's the best offer I've had all night. But
seriously—why not the hotel? We'd get breakfast there
and save a half hour's travel."

"You don't want to come to my apartment? I won't
bite you."

"I was hoping you would—so I could bite back. No, I
was just wondering why the sudden switch?"

"Well—perhaps I wanted to show you the bear traps I
have arranged tastefully around my bed. Or perhaps I just
wanted to prove to you I could cook." She dimpled for a
moment.

I flagged a taxi and we went to her apartment.

When we got inside she left me standing, while she
made a careful search of the place, then she came back
and said, "Turn around. I want to feel your back."

"Why do—"

"Turn around!"

I shut up and did so. She gave it a good knuckling, all over, then said, "Now you can feel mine."

"With pleasure!" Nevertheless I did a proper job, for I saw what she was driving at. There was nothing under her clothes but girl—girl and assorted items of lethal hardware.

She turned around and let a deep sigh. "That's why I didn't want to go to your hotel room. Now we're safe. Now I know we are safe for the first time since I saw that thing on the station manager's back. This apartment is tight; I turn off the air and leave it sealed like a vault every time I leave it."

"Say—how about the air conditioning? Could one get in through the ducts?"

"Possibly—but I didn't turn on the conditioner system; I cracked one of the air-raid reserve bottles instead. Never mind; what would you like to eat?"

I wanted to suggest Mary herself, served up on lettuce and toast, but I thought better of it. "Any chance of about two pounds of steak, just warmed through?"

We split a five-pound steak between us and I swear I ate the short half. While we chomped, we watched the newscast. Still no news from Iowa.

✒ Chapter 5 ✒

I did not get to see the bear traps; she locked her bedroom door. I know; I tried it. Three hours later she woke me and we had a second breakfast. Presently we struck cigarettes and I reached over and switched off the newscast. It was devoted principally to a display of the states' entries for "Miss America." Ordinarily I would have watched with interest but since none of the babes was round-shouldered and their contest costumes could not possibly have concealed humps bigger than mosquito bites, it seemed to lack importance that day.

I said, "Well?"

Mary said, "We've got to arrange the facts we have dug up and rub the President's nose in them. Action has to be on a national scale—global, really."

"How?"

"We've got to see him again."

I repeated, "How?"

She had no answer for that one.

I said, "We've got only one route—via official channels. Through the Old Man."

I put in the call, using both our codes so that Mary could hear, too. Presently I heard, "Chief Deputy Oldfield, speaking for the Old Man. He's not available. Shoot."

"It's got to be the Old Man."

There was a pause, then, "I don't have either one of you down as on assignment. Is this official or unofficial?"

"Uh, I guess you'd call it unofficial."

"Well, I won't put you through to the Old Man for anything unofficial. And anything official I am handling. Make up your mind."

I thanked him and switched off before I used any bad language. Then I coded again. The Old Man has a special code, in addition to regular channels, which is guaranteed to cause him to rise up out of his coffin—but God help the agent who uses it unnecessarily. I hadn't used it in five years.

He answered with a burst of profanity.

"Boss," I said, "on the Iowa matter—"

He broke off short. "Yes?"

"Mary and I spent all night digging former data out of the files. We want to talk it over with you."

The profanity resumed. Presently he told me to brief it and turn it in for analysis and added that he intended to have my ears fried for a sandwich.

"Boss!" I said sharply.

"Eh?"

"If you can run out on the job, so can we. Both Mary and I are resigning from the Section right now—and that's official!"

Mary's eyebrows went up but she said nothing. There was a silence so long that I thought he had cut me off, then he said, in a tired, whipped voice, "Palmglade Hotel, North Miami Beach. I'll be the third sunburn from the end."

"Right away." I sent for a taxi and we went up on the roof. I had the hackie swing out over the ocean to avoid the Carolina speed trap; we made good time.

The Old Man was sunburned all right. He lay there, looking sullen and letting sand dribble through his fingers, while we reported. I had brought along a little buzz box so that he could get it directly off the wire.

He looked up sharply when we came to the point about thirty-year cycles, but he allowed it to ride until he came to my later query about possible similar cycles in disappearances, whereupon he stopped me and called the Section. "Get me Analysis. Hello, Peter? This is the boss. I want a curve on unexplained disappearances, quantitative, starting with 1800. Huh? People, of course—did you think I meant latch keys? Smooth out known factors and discount steady load—what I want to see is humps and valleys. When? I want it two hours ago; what are you waiting for?"

After he switched off he struggled to his feet, let me hand him his cane and said, "Well, back to the jute mill. We've no facilities here."

"To the White House?" Mary asked eagerly.

"Eh? Be your age. You two have picked up nothing that would change the President's mind."

"Oh. Then what?"

"I don't know. Keep quiet, unless you have a bright idea."

The Old Man had a car at hand, of course, and I drove us back. After I turned it over to block control I said, "Boss, I've got a caper that might convince the President, if you can get him to hold still."

He grunted. "Like this," I went on, "send two agents in, me and one other. The other agent carries a portable scanning rig and keeps it trained on me the whole time. You get the President to watch what happens."

"Suppose nothing happens?"

"I plan to make it happen. First, I am going where the space ship landed, bull my way on through. We'll get close-up pix of the real ship, piped right into the White House. After that I plan to go back to Barnes's office and investigate those round shoulders. I'll tear shirts off right in front of the camera. There won't be any finesse to the job; I'll just bust things wide open with a sledge hammer."

"You realize you would have the same chance as a mouse at a cat convention."

"I'm not so sure. As I see it, these things haven't any superhuman powers. I'll bet they are strictly limited to whatever the human being they are riding can do—maybe less. I don't plan on being a martyr. In any case I'll get you pix, good ones."

"Hmm—"

"It might work," Mary put in. "I'll be the other agent, I can—"

The Old Man and I said, "No," together—and then I flushed; it was not my prerogative to say so. Mary went on, "I was going to say that I am the logical one because of the, uh, talent I have for spotting a man with a parasite on him."

"No," the Old Man repeated, "It won't be necessary. Where he's going they'll all have riders—assumed so until proved otherwise. Besides, I am saving you for something."

She should have shut up, but for once did not. "For what? This is important."

Instead of snapping at her the Old Man said quietly, "So is the other job. I'm planning to make you a presidential bodyguard, as soon as I can get it through his head that this is serious."

"Oh." She thought about it and answered, "uh, boss—"

"Eh?"

"I'm not certain I could spot a woman who was possessed. I'm not, uh, equipped for it."

"So we take his women secretaries away from him. Ask me a hard one. And Mary—you'll be watching him, too. He's a man, you know."

She turned that over in her mind. "And suppose I find that one has gotten to him, in spite of everything?"

"You take necessary action, the Vice President succeeds to the chair, and you get shot for treason. Simple. Now about this mission. We'll send Jarvis with the scanner and I think I'll include Davidson as an extra hatchet man. While Jarvis keeps the pick-up on you, Davidson can keep his eyes on Jarvis—and you can try to keep one eye on him. Ring-around-the-rosy."

"You think it will work, then?"

"No—but any plan of action is better than no plan. Maybe it will stir up something."

While we headed for Iowa—Jarvis, Davidson, and I— the Old Man went back to Washington. He took Mary along. She cornered me as we were about to leave, grabbed me by the ears, kissed me firmly and said, "Sam—try to come back."

I got all tingly and felt like a fifteen-year-old. Second childhood, I guess.

Davidson roaded the car beyond the place where I had found a bridge out. I was navigating, using a large-scale ordnance map on which had been pinpointed the exact landing site of the real space ship. The bridge, which was still out, gave a close-by and precise reference point. We turned off the road two tenths of a mile due east of the site and jeeped through the scrub to the spot. Nobody tried to stop us.

Almost to the spot, I should say. We ran into freshly burned-over ground and decided to walk. The site as shown by the space station photograph was included in the brush fire area—and there was no "flying saucer". It would have taken a better detective than I will ever be to show that one had ever landed there. The fire had destroyed the traces, if any.

Jarvis scanned everything, anyhow, but I knew that the slugs had won another round. As we came out we ran into an elderly farmer; following doctrine we kept a wary distance, although he looked harmless.

"Quite a fire," I remarked, sidling away.

"Sure was," he said dolefully. "Killed two of my best milk cows, the poor dumb brutes. You fellows reporters?"

"Yes," I agreed, "but we've been sent out on a wild-goose chase." I wished Mary were along. Probably this character was naturally round-shouldered. On the other hand, assuming that the Old Man was right about the space ship—and he had to be right—then this all-too-innocent bumpkin must know about it and was covering it up. Ergo, he was hag-ridden.

I decided that I had to do it. The chances of capturing a live parasite and getting its picture on the channels back to the White House were better here than they would be in a crowd. I threw a glance at my teammates; they were both alert and Jarvis was scanning.

As the farmer turned to go I tripped him. He went face down and I was on his back like a monkey, clawing at his shirt. Jarvis moved in and got a close up; Davidson moved over to cover point. I had his back bare before he got his wind.

And it was bare. It was as clean as mine, no parasite, no sign of one. Nor any place on his body, which I made sure of before I let him up.

I helped him up and brushed him off; his clothes were filthy with ashes and so were mine. "I'm terribly sorry," I said. "I've made a bad mistake."

He was trembling with anger. "You young—" He couldn't seem to find a word bad enough for me. He looked at all of us and his mouth quivered. "I'll have the law on you. If I were twenty years younger I'd lick all three of you."

"Believe me, old timer, it was a mistake."

"Mistake!" His face broke and I thought he was going to cry. "I come back from Omaha and find my place burned, half my stock gone, and my son-in-law no place around. I come out to find out why strangers are snooping around my land and I like to get torn to pieces. Mistake! What's the world coming to?"

I thought I could answer that last one, but I did not try

to. I did try to pay him for the indignity but he slapped my money to the ground. We tucked in our tails and got out.

When we were back in the car and rolling again, Davidson said to me, "Are you and the Old Man sure you know what you are up to?"

"I can make a mistake," I said savagely, "but have you ever known the Old Man to?"

"Mmm . . . no. Can't say as I have. Where next?"

"Straight in to WDES main station. This one won't be a mistake."

"Anyhow," Jarvis commented. "I got good pick-up throughout."

I did not answer.

At the toll gates into Des Moines the gatekeeper hesitated when I offered the fee. He glanced at a notebook and then at our plates. "Sheriff has a call out for this car," he said. "Pull over to the right." He left the barrier down.

"Right it is," I agreed, backed up about thirty feet and gunned her for all she was worth. The Section's cars are beefed up and hopped up, too—a good thing, for the barrier was stout. I did not slow down on the far side.

"This," said Davidson dreamily, "is interesting. Do you still know what you are doing?"

"Cut the chatter," I snapped. "I may be crazy but I am still agent-in-charge. Get this, both of you: we aren't likely to get out of this. But we are going to get those pix."

"As you say, chief."

I was running ahead of any pursuit. I slammed to a stop in front of the station and we poured out. None of "Uncle Charlie's" indirect methods—we swarmed into the first elevator that was open and punched for the top floor—Barnes's floor. When we got there I left the door of the car open, hoping to use it later.

As we came into the outer office the receptionist tried to stop us but we pushed on by. The girls looked up, startled. I went straight to Barnes's inner door and tried to open it; it was locked. I turned to his secretary. "Where's Barnes?"

"Who is calling, please?" She said, polite as a fish.

I looked down at the fit of the sweater across her shoulders. Humped. By God, I said to myself, this one has to be. She was here when I killed Barnes. I bent over and pulled up her sweater.

I was right. I had to be right. For the second time I stared at the raw flesh of one of the parasites.

I wanted to throw up, but I was too busy. She struggled and clawed and tried to bite. I judo-cut the side of her neck, almost getting my hand in the filthy mess, and she went limp. I gave her three fingers in the pit of her stomach for good measure, then swung her around. "Jarvis," I yelled, "get a close up."

The idiot was fiddling with his gear, bending over it, his big hind end between me and the pickup. He straightened up. "School's out," he said. "Blew a tube."

"Replace it—hurry!"

A stenographer stood up on the other side of the room and fired, not at me, not at Jarvis, but at the scanner. Hit it, too—and both Davidson and I burned her down. As if it had been a signal about six of them jumped Davidson. They did not seem to have guns; they just swarmed over him.

I still hung onto the secretary and shot from where I was. I caught a movement out of the corner of my eye and turned to find Barnes—"Barnes" number two—standing in his doorway. I shot him through the chest to be sure to get the slug I knew was on his back. I turned back to the slaughter.

Davidson was up again. A girl crawled toward him; she seemed wounded. He shot her full in the face and she stopped. His next bolt was just past my ear. I looked around and said, "Thanks! Now let's get out of here. Jarvis—come on!"

The elevator was still open and we rushed in, me still burdened with Barnes's secretary. I slammed the door closed and started it. Davidson was trembling and Jarvis was dead white. "Buck up," I said, "you weren't shooting people, you were shooting things. Like this." I held the girl's body up and looked down at her back myself.

Then I almost collapsed. My specimen, the one I had grabbed with its host to take back alive, was gone. Slipped to the floor, probably, and oozed away during the ruckus. "Jarvis," I said, "did you get anything up there?" He shook his head and said nothing. Neither did I. Neither did Davidson.

The girl's back was covered with a red rash, like a million pinpricks, in the area where the thing had ridden her. I pulled her sweater down and settled her on the floor against the wall of the car. She was still unconscious and likely to stay that way. When we reached street level we left her in the car. Apparently nobody noticed, for there was no hue-and-cry as we went through the lobby to the street.

Our car was still standing there and a policeman had his foot on it while making out a ticket. He handed it to me as we got in. "You know you can't park in this area, Mac," he said reprovingly.

I said, "Sorry," and signed his copy as it seemed the safest and quickest thing to do. Then I gunned the car away from the curb, got as clear as I could of traffic—and blasted her off, right from a city street. I wondered whether or not he added that to the ticket. When I had her up to altitude I remembered to switch the license plates and identification code. The Old Man thinks of everything.

But he did not think much of me when we got back. I tried to report on the way in but he cut me short and ordered us into the Section offices. Mary was there with him. That was all I needed to know; if despite my flop the Old Man had convinced the President she would have stayed.

He let me tell what had happened with only an occasional grunt. "How much did you see?" I asked when I had finished.

"Transmission cut off when you hit the toll barrier," he informed me. "I can't say that the President was impressed by what he saw."

"I suppose not."

"In fact he told me to fire you."

I stiffened. I had been ready to offer my resignation, but this took me by surprise. "I am perfectly will—" I started out.

"Pipe down!" the Old Man snapped. "I told him that he could fire me, but that he could not fire my subordinates. You are a thumb-fingered dolt," he went on more quietly, "but you can't be spared, not now."

"Thanks."

Mary had been wandering restlessly around the room. I had tried to catch her eye, but she was not having any. Now she stopped back of Jarvis's chair—and gave the Old Man the same sign she had given about Barnes.

I hit Jarvis in the side of the head with my heater and he sagged out of his chair.

"Stand back, Davidson!" the Old Man rapped. His own gun was out and pointed at Davidson's chest. "Mary, how about him?"

"He's all right."

"And him."

"Sam's clean."

The Old Man's eyes moved from one of us to the other and I have never felt closer to death. "Both of you peel off your shirts," he said sourly.

We did—and Mary was right on both counts. I had begun to wonder whether or not I would know it if I did have a parasite on me. "Now him," the Old Man ordered. "Gloves, both of you."

We stretched Jarvis out on his face and very carefully cut his clothing away. We had our live specimen.

☞ Chapter 6 ☜

I felt myself ready to retch. The thought of that thing travelling right behind me in a closed car all the way from Iowa was almost more than my stomach could stand. I'm not squeamish—I hid once for four days in the sewers of Moscow—but you don't know what the sight of one can do to you unless you yourself have seen one while knowing what it was.

I swallowed hard and said, "Let's see what we can do to work it off. Maybe we can still save Jarvis." I did not really think so; I had a deep-down hunch that anyone who had been ridden by one of those things was spoiled, permanently. I guess I had a superstitious notion that they "ate souls" whatever that means.

The Old Man waved us back. "Forget about Jarvis!"

"But—"

"Stow it! If he can be saved, a bit longer won't matter. In any case—" He shut up and so did I. I knew what he meant; the principle which declared that the individual was all important now called for canceling Jarvis out as a factor, i.e., we were expendable; the people of the United States were not.

Pardon the speech. I liked Jarvis.

The Old Man, gun drawn and wary, continued to watch the unconscious agent and the thing on his back. He said to Mary, "Get the President on the screen. Special code zero zero zero seven."

Mary went to his desk and did so. I heard her talking into the muffler, but my own attention was on the parasite. It made no move to leave its host, but pulsed slowly while iridescent ripples spread across it.

Presently Mary reported, "I can't get him, sir. One of his assistants is on the screen."

"Which one?"

"Mr. McDonough."

The Old Man winced and so did I. McDonough was an intelligent, likeable man who hadn't changed his mind on anything since he was housebroken. The President used him as a buffer.

The Old Man bellowed, not bothering with the muffler.

No, the President was not available. No, he could not be reached with a message. No, Mr. McDonough was not exceeding his authority; the President had been explicit and the Old Man was not on the list of exceptions—if there was such a list, which Mr. McDonough did not concede. Yes, he would be happy to make an appointment; he would squeeze the Old Man in somehow and that was a promise. How would next Friday do? Today? Quite out of the question. Tomorrow? Equally impossible.

The Old Man switched off and I thought he was going

to have a stroke. But after a moment he took two deep breaths, his features relaxed, and he slumped back to us, saying, "Dave, slip down the hall and ask Doc Graves to step in. The rest of you keep your distance and your eyes peeled."

The head of the biological lab came in shortly, wiping his hands as he came. "Doc," said the Old Man, "there is one that isn't dead."

Graves looked at Jarvis, then more closely at Jarvis's back. "Interesting," he said. "Unique, possibly." He dropped to one knee.

"Stand back!"

Graves looked up. "But I must have an opportunity—" he said reasonably.

"You and my half-wit aunt! Listen—I want you to study it, yes, but that purpose has low priority. First, you've got to keep it alive. Second, you've got to keep it from escaping. Third, you've got to protect yourself."

Graves smiled. "I'm not afraid of it. I—"

"Be afraid of it! That's an order."

"I was about to say that I think I must rig up an incubator to care for it after we remove it from the host. The dead specimen you gave me did not afford much opportunity for studying its chemistry, but it is evident that these things need oxygen. You smothered the other one. Don't misunderstand me, not free oxygen, but oxygen from its host. Perhaps a large dog would suffice."

"No," snapped the Old Man. "Leave it right where it is."

"Eh?" Graves looked surprised. "Is this man a volunteer?"

The Old Man did not answer. Graves went on, "Human laboratory subjects must be volunteers. Professional ethics, you know."

These scientific laddies never do get broken to harness; I think they keep their bags packed. The Old Man calmed himself and said quietly, "Doctor Graves, every agent in this Section is a volunteer for whatever I find necessary. That is what they sign up for. Please carry out my orders. Get a stretcher in here and take Jarvis out. Use care."

The Old Man dismissed us after they had carted Jarvis away, and Davidson and Mary and I went to the lounge for a drink or four. We needed them. Davidson had the shakes. When the first drink failed to fix him I said, "Look, Dave, I feel as bad about those girls as you do—but it could not be helped. Get that through your head; it could not be helped."

"How bad was it?" asked Mary.

"Pretty bad. I don't know how many we killed, maybe six, maybe a dozen. There was no time to be careful. We weren't shooting people, not intentionally; we were shooting parasites." I turned to Davidson. "Don't you see that?"

He seemed to take a brace. "That's just it. They weren't human." He went on, "I think I could shoot my own brother, if the job required it. But these things aren't human. You shoot and they keep coming toward you. They don't—" He broke off.

All I felt was pity. After a bit he got up to go to the dispensary to get a shot for what ailed him. Mary and I talked a while longer, trying to figure out answers and getting nowhere. Then she announced that she was sleepy and headed for the women's dormitory. The Old Man had ordered all hands to sleep in that night, so, after a nightcap, I went to the boys' wing and crawled in a sack.

I did not get to sleep at once. I could hear the rumble of the city above us and I kept imagining it in the state Des Moines was already in.

The air-raid alarm woke me. I stumbled into my clothes as the blowers sighed off, then the intercom bawled in the Old Man's voice, "Anti-gas and anti-radiation procedures! Seal everything—all hands gather in the conference hall. Move!"

Being a field agent I was a supernumerary with no local duties. I shuffled down the tunnel from the living quarters to the Offices. The Old Man was in the big hall, looking grim. I wanted to ask him what was up, but there was a mixed dozen of clerks, agents, stenos, and such there before me and I decided not to. After a bit the Old Man sent me out to get the door tally from the guard on watch. The Old Man called the roll himself and presently it was clear that every living person listed on the door tally was now inside the hall, from old Miss Haines, the Old Man's private secretary, down to the steward of the staff lounge—except the door guard on watch and Jarvis. The tally had to be right; we keep track of who goes in and out a good bit more carefully than a bank keeps track of money.

I was sent out again for the door guard. It took a call back to the Old Man to persuade him it was all right for him to leave his post; he then threw the bolt switch and followed me. When we got back Jarvis was there, being attended by Graves and one of his lab men. He was on his feet and wrapped in a hospital robe, conscious apparently, but he seemed dopey.

When I saw him I began to have some notion of what it was all about. The Old Man did not leave us in doubt. He was facing the assembled staff and keeping his distance; now he drew his gun. "One of the invading parasites is loose among us," he said. "To some of you that means something—too much. To the rest of you I will have to explain, as the safety of all of us—and of our whole race— depends this moment on complete cooperation and utter obedience." He went on to explain briefly but with ugly exactness what a parasite was, what the situation was. "In other words," he concluded, "the parasite is almost certainly here in this room. One of us looks human but is actually an automaton, moving at the will of our deadliest and most dangerous enemy."

There was a murmur from the staff. People stole glances at each other. Some tried to draw away. A moment before we had been a team, picked for temperament compatibility; we were now a mob, each suspicious of the other. I felt it myself and found myself edging away from the man closest to me—Ronald the lounge steward, it was; I had known him for years.

Graves cleared his throat. "Chief," he started in, "I want you to understand that I took every reasonable—"

"Stow it. I don't want excuses. Bring Jarvis out in front. Take his robe off."

Graves shut up and he and his assistant complied. Jarvis did not seem to mind; he seemed only partly aware of his surroundings. There was a nasty blue welt across his left cheekbone and temple, but that was not the cause; I did not hit him that hard. Graves must have drugged him.

"Turn him around," the Old Man ordered. Jarvis let himself be turned; there was the mark of the slug, a red rash on the shoulders and neck. "You can all see," the Old Man went on, "where the thing rode him." There had been some whispers and one embarrassed giggle when Jarvis had been stripped; now there was a dead hush.

"Now," said the Old Man, "we are going to get that slug! Furthermore, we are going to capture it alive. That warning is for you eager boys with itchy trigger fingers. You have all seen where a parasite rides on a man. I'm warning you; if the parasite gets burned, I'll burn the man who did it. If you have to shoot the host to catch it, shoot low. Come here!" He pointed his gun at me.

I started toward him; he halted me halfway between the crowd and himself. "Graves! Take Jarvis out of the way. Sit him down behind me. No, leave his robe off." Jarvis was led across the room, still docile, and Graves and his helper rejoined the group. The Old Man turned his attention back to me. "Take out your gun. Drop it on the floor."

The Old Man's gun was pointed at my belly button; I was very careful how I drew mine. I slid it some six feet away from me. "Take off your clothes—all of them."

I am no shrinking violet, but that is an awkward order to carry out. The Old Man's gun overcame my inhibitions.

It did not help any to have some of the younger girls giggling at me as I got down to the buff. One of them said, not too sotto voce, "Not bad!" and another replied, "Knobby, I'd say."

I blushed like a bride.

After he looked me over the Old Man told me to pick up my gun and stand beside him. "Back me up," he ordered, "and keep an eye on the door. You! Dotty Something-or-other—you're next."

Dotty was a girl from the clerical pool. She had no gun, of course, and she had evidently been in bed when the alarm sounded; she was dressed in a floor length negligee. She stepped forward, stopped, but did nothing more.

The Old Man waved his gun at her. "Come on—get 'em off! Don't take all night."

"You really mean it?" she said incredulously.

"Move!"

She started—almost jumped. "Well!" she said, "no need to take a person's head off." She bit her lower lip and then slowly unfastened the clasp at her waist. "I ought to get a bonus for this," she said defiantly, then threw the robe from her all in one motion.

Whereupon she ruined her buildup by posing for an instant—not long, but you couldn't miss it. I concede that she had something to display, although I was in no mood to appreciate it.

"Over against the wall," the Old Man said savagely. "Renfrew!"

I don't know whether the Old Man alternated men and women on purpose or not, but it was a good idea, as it kept resistance to a minimum. Oh, shucks, I do know— the Old Man never did anything by accident. After my ordeal the men were businesslike though some were obviously embarrassed. As to the women, some giggled and some blushed, but none of them objected too much.

I would have found it interesting if the circumstances had been different. As it was, we were all bound to learn things about each other that we had not known. For instance there was a girl whom we used to call "Chesty"—never mind. In twenty minutes or so there were more square yards of gooseflesh exposed than I had ever seen before and the pile of guns on the floor looked like an arsenal.

When Mary's turn came, she set a good example by taking off her clothes quickly and in a completely unprovocative manner—the Old Man should have called her first, instead of that Dotty baggage. Bare, Mary made nothing of it, and wore her skin with quiet dignity. But what I saw did nothing to cool down my feelings about her.

Mary had added considerably to the pile of hardware. I decided she just plain liked guns. Me, I've never found use for more than one.

Finally we were all mother naked and quite evidently free of parasites, except the Old Man himself and his secretary, Miss Haines. I think he was a bit in awe of Miss Haines; she was older than he and inclined to boss him. It dawned on me whom it had to be—if the Old Man were right. He could have been wrong; for all we knew the parasite might be on a ceiling girder, waiting to drop on someone's neck.

The Old Man looked distressed and poked about in the pile of clothing with his cane. He knew that there was nothing in it—or perhaps he was really making sure. Finally he looked up at his secretary. "Miss Haines—if you please. You are next."

I thought to myself. Brother, this time you are going to have to use force.

She did not move. She stood there, facing him down, a statue of offended virginity. I could see that he was about to take action, so I moved closer to him and said, out of the corner of my mouth, "Boss—how about yourself? Take 'em off."

He jerked his head around and looked startled. "I mean it," I said. "It's you or she. It might be either. Get out of those duds."

The Old Man can relax to the inevitable. He said, "Have her stripped. And I'm next." He began fumbling at his zippers, looking grim.

I told Mary to take a couple of the women and peel Miss Haines. When I turned back the Old Man had his trousers at half mast—and Miss Haines chose to make a break for it.

The Old Man was between me and her and I couldn't get in a clean shot—and every other agent in the place was disarmed! Again, I don't think it was accident; the Old Man did not trust them not to shoot when the parasite was discovered. He wanted that slug, alive.

She was out the door and running down the passage by the time I could get organized. I could have winged her in the passageway but I was inhibited by two things—first, I could not shift gears emotionally that fast. I mean to say she was to me still old Lady Haines, the spinster secretary to the boss, the one who bawled me out for poor grammar in my reports. In the second place, if she was carrying a parasite I did not want to risk burning it, not after what we had been told. I am not the world's best shot, anyhow.

She ducked into a room; I came up to it and again I hesitated—sheer habit; it was the ladies' room.

But only a moment. I slammed the door open and looked around, gun ready.

Something hit me back of my right ear. It seemed to me that I took a long leisurely time in getting to the floor.

I can give no clear account of the next few moments. In the first place I was out cold, for a time at least. I remember a struggle and some shouts: "Look out!" "Damn her—she's bitten me!" "Watch your hands! Watch your hands!" Then somebody said more quietly, "Bind her hands and feet, now—careful." Somebody said, "How about him?" and someone else answered, "Later. He's not really hurt."

I was still practically out as they left, but I began to feel a flood of life stirring back into me. I sat up, feeling extreme urgency about something. I got up, staggering a little, and went to the door. I hesitated there, looked out cautiously; nobody was in sight. I stepped out and trotted down the corridor, away from the direction of the conference hall.

I slowed down momentarily at the outer door, then realized with a shock that I was naked and tore on down the hallway toward the men's wing. There I grabbed the first clothes I could find and pulled them on. I found a pair of shoes much too small for me, but it did not seem to matter.

I ran back toward the exit, fumbled, and found the switch; the door opened.

I thought I had made a clean escape, but somebody shouted, "Sam!" just as I was going out. I did not wait, but plunged on out. At once I had my choice of six doors and then three more beyond the one I picked. The warren we called the "Offices", being arranged to permit any number of people to come and go without being noticed, was served by a spaghetti-like mess of tunnels. I came up finally inside a subway fruit and bookstall, nodded to the proprietor—who seemed unsurprised—and swung the counter gate up and mingled with the crowd. It was not a route I had used before.

I caught the up-river jet express and got off at the first station. I crossed over to the down-river side, waited around the change window until a man came up who displayed quite a bit of money as he bought his counter. I got on the same train he did and got off when he did. At the first dark spot I rabbit-punched him. Now I had money and was ready to operate. I did not know quite why I had to have money, but I knew that I needed it for what I was about to do.

Chapter 7

Language grows, so they say, to describe experience of the race using it. Experience first—language second. How can I tell how I felt?

I saw things around me with a curious double vision, as if I stared at them through rippling water—yet I felt no surprise and no curiosity about this. I moved like a sleepwalker, unaware of what I was about to do—but I was wide-awake, fully aware of who I was, where I was, what my job at the Section had been. There was no amnesia; my full memories were available to me at any moment. And, although I did not know what I was about to do, I was always aware of what I was doing and sure that each act was the necessary, purposeful act at that moment.

They say that post-hypnotic commands work something like that. I don't know; I am a poor hypnotic subject.

I felt no particular emotion most of the time, except the mild contentment that comes from being at work which needs to be done. That was up on the conscious level—and, I repeat, I was fully awake. Someplace, more levels down than I understand about, I was excruciatingly unhappy, terrified, and filled with guilt—but that was down, 'way down, locked, suppressed; I was hardly aware of it and in no practical way affected by it.

I knew that I had been seen to leave. That shout of "Sam!" had been intended for me; only two persons knew me by that name and the Old Man would have used my right name. So Mary had seen me leave—it was a good thing, I thought, that she had let me find out where her private apartment was. It would be necessary presently to booby-trap it against her next use of it. In the meantime I must get on with work and keep from being picked up.

I was in a warehouse district, moving through it cautiously, all my agent's training at work to avoid being conspicuous. Shortly I found what seemed to be a satisfactory building; there was a sign: LOFT FOR LEASE—SEE RENTAL AGENT ON GROUND FLOOR. I scouted it thoroughly, noted the address, then doubled back to the nearest Western Union booth two squares behind me. There I sat down at a vacant machine and sent the following message: EXPEDITE TWO CASES TINY TOTS TALKY TALES SAME DISCOUNT CONSIGNED TO JOEL FREEMAN and added the address of the empty loft. I sent it to Roscoe and Dillard, Jobbers and Manufacturers Agents, Des Moines, Iowa.

As I left the booth the sight of one of the Kwikfeed chain of all-night restaurants reminded me that I was very hungry, but the reflex cut off at once and I thought no more about it. I returned to the warehouse building, found a dark corner in the rear, and settled quietly back to wait for dawn and business hours.

I must have slept; I have a dim recollection of ever repeating, claustrophobic nightmares.

From daylight until nine o'clock I hung around a hiring hall, studying the notices; it was the one place in the neighborhood where a man of no occupation would not attract attention. At nine o'clock I met the rental agent as he unlocked his office, and leased the loft, paying him a fat squeeze on the side for immediate possession while the paperwork went through on the deal. I went up to the loft, unlocked it, and waited.

About ten-thirty my crates were delivered. I let the teamsters leave; three were too many for me and I was not yet ready in any case. After they were gone, I opened one crate, took out one cell, warmed it, and got it ready. Then I went downstairs, found the rental agent again, and said, "Mr. Greenberg, could you come up for a moment? I want to see about making some changes in the lighting."

He fussed, but agreed to do so. When we entered the loft I closed the door behind us and led him over to the open crate. "Here," I said, "if you will just lean over there, you will see what I mean. If I could just—"

I got him around the neck with a grip that cut off his wind, ripped his jacket and shirt up, and, with my free hand, transferred a master from the cell to his bare back, then held him tight for a moment until his struggles stopped. Then I let him up, tucked his shirt back in and dusted him off. When he had recovered his breath, I said, "What news from Des Moines?"

"What do you want to know?" he asked. "How long have you been out?"

I started to explain, but he interrupted me with, "Let's have a direct conference and not waste time." I skinned up my shirt; he did the same; and we sat down on the edge of the unopened case, back to back, so that our masters could be in contact. My own mind was merely blank and I have no idea how long the conference went on. I watched a fly droning around a dusty cobweb, seeing it but not thinking about it.

The building superintendent was our next recruit. He was a large Swede and it took both of us to hold him. After that Mr. Greenberg called up the owner of the building and insisted that he simply had to come down and see some horrendous mishap that had occurred to the structure—just what, I don't know; I was busy with the super, opening and warming several more cells.

The owner of the building was a real prize and we all felt quiet satisfaction, including, of course, he himself. He belonged to the Constitution Club, the membership list of which read like the index of Who's Who in Finance, Government, and Industry. Better still, the club boasted the most famous chef in town; it was an even chance that any given member would be lunching there if he were in the city.

It was pushing noon; we had no time to lose. The super went out to buy suitable clothes and a satchel for me and sent the owner's chauffeur up to be recruited as he did so. At twelve-thirty we left, the owner and I, in his own car; the satchel contained twelve masters, still in their cells but ready.

The owner signed: J. Hardwick Potter & Guest. One

of the flunkies tried to take my bag but I insisted that I needed it to change my shirt before lunch. We fiddled around in the washroom until we had it to ourselves, save for the attendant—whereupon we recruited him and sent him out with a message to the resident manager that a guest had taken ill in the washroom.

After we took care of the manager he obtained a white coat for me and I became another washroom attendant. I had only ten masters left but I knew that the cases would be picked up from the warehouse loft and delivered to the club shortly. The regular attendant and I used up the rest of those I had been able to bring before the lunch hour rush was over. One guest surprised us while we were busy and I had to kill him, as there was no time to save him for recruiting. We stuffed him into the mop closet.

There was a lull after that, as the cases had not yet arrived. Hunger reflex nearly doubled me over, then it dropped off sharply but still persisted; I told the manager, who had me served one of the best lunches I have ever eaten, in his office. The cases arrived just as I was finishing.

During the drowsy period that every gentlemen's club has in the mid-afternoon we secured the place. By four o'clock everyone present in the building—members, staff, and guests—were with us; from then on we simply processed them in the lobby as the doorman passed them in. Later in the day the manager phoned Des Moines for four more cases.

Our big prize came that evening—a guest, the Assistant Secretary of the Treasury. We saw a real victory in that; the Treasury Department is charged with the safety of the President.

✌ Chapter 8 ✌

The jubilation caused by the capture of a high key official was felt by me only as absent-minded satisfaction, then I thought no more about it. We—the human recruits, I mean—hardly thought at all; we knew what we were to do each instant, but we knew it only at the moment of action, as a "high school" horse gets his orders, responds to them instantly, and is ready for the next signal from his rider.

High school horse and rider is a good comparison, as far as it goes—but it goes not nearly far enough. The horseman has partly at his disposal the intelligence of the horse; the masters had at their disposal not only our full intelligences, but also tapped directly our memory and experiences. We communicated for them between masters, too; sometimes we knew what we were talking about; sometimes we did not—such spoken words went through the servant, but the servant had no part in more important, direct, master-to-master conferences. During these we sat quietly and waited until our riders were through conferring, then rearranged our clothing to cover them up and did whatever was necessary. There was such a conference on a grand scale after the Assistant Secretary of the Treasury was recruited; I know no more of it than you do, although I sat in on it.

I had no more to do with words spoken by me for my master than had the audio relay buried behind my ear to do with words it sounded—the relay was silent all this time, incidentally; my phone proper I had left behind me. I, like it, was a communication instrument, nothing more. Some days after I was recruited I gave the club manager new instructions about how to order shipments of masters' carrying cells. I was fleetingly aware, as I did so, that three more ships had landed, but I was not aware of their locations; my overt knowledge was limited to a single address in New Orleans.

I thought nothing about it; I went on with my work. After the day spent at the club, I was a new "special assistant to Mr. Potter" and spent the days in his office— and the nights, too. Actually, the relationship may have reversed; I frequently gave oral instructions to Potter. Or perhaps I understand the social organization of the parasites as little now as I did then; the relationship may have been more flexible, more anarchistic, and vastly more subtle than I have the experience to imagine.

I knew—and my master certainly knew—that it was well for me to stay out of sight. Through me, my master knew as much of the organization we called the "Section" as I did; it knew that I was one human known to the Old Man to have been recruited—and my master knew, I am sure, that the Old Man would not cease to search for me, to recapture me or kill me.

It seems odd that it did not choose to change bodies and to kill mine; we had vastly more potential recruits available than we had masters. I do not think it could have felt anything parallel to human squeamishness; masters newly delivered from their transit cells frequently damaged their initial hosts; we always destroyed the damaged host and found a new one for the master.

Contrariwise, my master, by the time he chose me, had controlled not less than three human hosts—Jarvis, Miss Haines, and one of the girls in Barnes's office, probably the secretary—and in the course of it had no doubt acquired both sophistication and skill in the control of human hosts. It could have "changed horses" with ease.

On the other hand, would a skilled cowhand have destroyed a well-trained workhorse in favor of an untried, strange mount? That may have been why I was hidden and saved—or perhaps I don't know what I am talking about; what does a bee know about Beethoven?

After a time the city was "secured" and my master started taking me out on the streets. I do not mean to say that every inhabitant of the city wore a hump—no, not by more than 99 percent; the humans were very numerous and the masters still very few—but the key positions in the city were all held by our own recruits, from the cop on the corner to the mayor and the chief of police, not forgetting ward bosses, church ministers, board members, and any and all who were concerned with public communications and news. The vast majority continued with their usual affairs, not only undisturbed by the masquerade but unaware that anything had happened.

Unless, of course, one of them happened to be in the

way of some purpose of a master—in which case he was disposed of to shut his mouth. This used up potential hosts but there was no need to be economical.

One of the disadvantages we worked under in serving our masters—or perhaps I should say one of the disadvantages our masters worked under—was the difficulty of long-distance communication. It was limited to what human hosts could say in human speech over ordinary communication channels, and was further limited, unless the channel was secured throughout, to conventionalized code messages such as the one I had sent ordering the first two shipments of masters. Oh, no doubt the masters could communicate ship-to-ship and probably ship-to-home-base, but there was no ship nearby; this city had been stormed as a prize-of-opportunity, as a direct result of my raid on Des Moines in my previous life.

Such communication through servants was almost certainly not adequate to the purposes of the masters; they seemed to need frequent direct body-to-body conference to coordinate their actions. I am no expert in exotic psychologies; some of those who are maintain that the parasites are not discrete individuals, but cells of a larger organism, in which case—but why go on? They seemed to need direct-contact conferences.

I was sent to New Orleans for such a conference.

I did not know I was going. I went out on the street as usual one morning, then went to the uptown launching platform and ordered a cab. Cabs were scarce; I thought about moving over to the other side and catching the public shuttle but the thought was immediately suppressed. After a considerable wait my cab was lifted to the loading ramp and I started to get in—I say "started to" as an old gentleman hustled up and climbed into it ahead of me.

I received an order to dispose of him, which order was immediately countermanded by one telling me to go slow and be careful, as if even the masters were not always sure of themselves. I said, "Excuse me, sir, but this cab is taken."

"Quite," the elderly man replied. "I've taken it." He was a picture of self-importance, from briefcase to dictatorial manner. He could easily have been a member of the Constitution Club, but he was not one of our own, as my master knew and told me.

"You will have to find another," I said reasonably. "Let's see your queue ticket." I had taken my ticket from the rack as soon as I reached the platform; the cab carried the launching number shown by my ticket.

I had him, but he did not stir. "Where are you going?" he demanded.

"New Orleans," I answered and learned for the first time my destination.

"Then you can drop me off in Memphis."

I shook my head. "It's out of my way."

"All of fifteen minutes!" He seemed to have difficulty controlling his temper, as if he were not often crossed. "You, sir, must know the rules about sharing cabs in these days of shortages. You cannot preempt a public vehicle unreasonably." He turned from me. "Driver! Explain to this person the rules."

The driver stopped picking his teeth just long enough to say, "It's nothing to me. I pick 'em up, I take 'em, I drop 'em. Settle it between yourselves or I'll ask the dispatcher for another fare."

I hesitated, not yet having been instructed. Then I found myself chucking my bag in and climbing inside. "New Orleans," I said, "with stop at Memphis." The driver shrugged and signaled the control tower. The other passenger snorted and paid me no further attention.

Once in the air he opened his briefcase and spread papers across his knees. I watched him with disinterest. Presently I found myself shifting my position to let me get at my gun easily. The elderly man shot out a hand and grabbed my wrist. "Not so fast, son," he said, and his features broke into the Satanic grin of the Old Man himself.

My reflexes are fast, but I was at the disadvantage of having everything routed from me to my master, passed on by it, and action routed back to me. How much delay is that? A millisecond? I don't know. As I was drawing, I felt the bell of a gun against my ribs. "Take it easy."

With his other hand he thrust something against my side; I felt a prick, and then through me spread the warm tingle of a jolt of "morpheus" taking hold. I've been knocked out by that drug twice before and I've given it more times than that; I knew what it was.

I made one more attempt to pull my gun free and sank forward.

I was vaguely aware of voices—voices which had been going on for some time before I got around to sorting them out as meaning. Someone was handling me roughly and someone was saying, "Watch out for that ape!" Another voice replied, "It's all right; his tendons are cut," to which the first voice retorted, "He's still got teeth, hasn't he?"

Yes, I thought fretfully, and if you get close enough I'll bite you with them, too. The remark about cut tendons seemed to be true; none of my limbs would move, but that did not worry me as much as being called an ape and not being able to resent it. It was a shame, I thought, to call a man names when he can't protect himself.

I wept a little and then fell into a stupor.

"Feeling better, son?"

The Old Man was leaning over the end of my bed, staring at me thoughtfully. His chest was bare and covered with grizzled hair; he showed a slight paunch.

"Unh," I said, "pretty good, I guess." I started to sit up and found I could not move.

The Old Man came around to the side of the bed. "We can take those restraints off now," he said, fiddling with clasps. "Didn't want you hurting yourself. There!"

I sat up, rubbing myself. I was quite stiff. "Now," said the Old Man, "how much do you remember? Report."

"Remember?"

"You were with them—remember? They caught you. Do you remember anything after the parasite got to you?"

I felt a sudden wild fear and clutched at the sides of the bed. "Boss! Boss—they know where this place is! I told them."

"No, they don't," he answered quietly, "because these aren't the Section offices you remember. Once I was convinced that you had made a clean getaway, I had the old offices evacuated. They don't know about this hang-out—I think. So you remember?"

"Of course I remember. I got out of here—I mean out

of the old offices and went up—" My thoughts raced ahead of my words; I had a sudden full image of holding a live, moist master in my bare hand, ready to place it on the back of the rental agent.

I threw up on the sheet. The Old Man took a corner of it, wiped my mouth, and said gently, "Go ahead."

I swallowed and said, "Boss—they're all over the place! They've got the city."

"I know. Same as Des Moines. And Minneapolis, and St. Paul, and New Orleans, and Kansas City. Maybe more. I don't know—I can't be every place." He looked sour and added, "It's like fighting with your feet in a sack. We're losing, fast." He scowled and added, "We can't even clamp down on the cities we know about. It's very—"

"Good grief! Why not?"

"You should know. Because 'older and wiser heads' than mine are still to be convinced that there is a war on. Because when they take over a city, everything goes on as before."

I stared at him. "Never mind," he said gently. "You are the first break we've had. You're the first victim to be recaptured alive—and now we find you remember what happened to you. That's important. And your parasite is the first live one we've managed to capture and keep alive. We'll have a chance to—"

He broke off. My face must have been a mask of terror; the notion that my master was still alive—and might get to me again—was more than I could stand.

The Old Man took my arm and shook it. "Take it easy, son," he said mildly. "You are still pretty sick and pretty weak."

"Where is it?"

"Eh? The parasite? Don't worry about it. You can see it, if you wish; it's living off your opposite number, a red orangutan, name of Napoleon. It's safe."

"Kill it!"

"Hardly—we need it alive, for study."

I must have gone to pieces, for he slapped me a couple of times. "Take a brace," he said. "I hate to bother you when you are sick, but it's got to be done. We've got to get everything you remember down on wire. So level off and fly right."

I pulled myself together and started making a careful, detailed report of all that I could remember. I described renting the loft and recruiting my first victim, then how we moved on from there to the Constitution Club. The Old Man nodded. "Logical. You were a good agent, even for them. "

"You don't understand," I objected. "I didn't do any thinking. I knew what was going on, but that was all. It was as if, uh, as if—" I paused, stuck for words.

"Never mind. Get on with it."

"After we recruited the club manager the rest was easy. We took them as they came in and—"

"Names?"

"Oh, certainly. Myself, Greenberg—M. C. Greenberg, Thor Hansen, J. Hardwick Potter, his chauffeur Jim Wakeley, a little guy called 'Jake' who was washroom attendant at the club but I believe he had to be disposed of later—his master would not let him take time out for necessities. Then there was the manager; I never did get his name." I paused, letting my mind run back over that busy afternoon and evening in the club, trying to make sure of each recruit. "Oh my God!"

"What is it?"

"The Secretary—The Assistant Secretary of the Treasury."

"You mean you got him!"

"Yes. The first day. What day was that? How long has it been? God, chief, the Treasury Department protect the President—"

But I was not talking to anyone; there was just a hole in the air where the Old Man had been.

I lay back exhausted. I started sobbing softly into my pillow. After a while I went to sleep.

✌ Chapter 9 ☙

I woke up with my mouth foul, my head buzzing, and a vague sense of impending disaster. Nevertheless I felt fine, by comparison. A cheerful voice said, "Feeling better?"

A small brunet creature was bending over me. She was as cute a little bug as I have ever seen and I was well enough to appreciate the fact, however faintly. She was dressed in a very odd costume, what there was of it—skintight white shorts, a wisp of practically transparent stuff that restrained her breasts, but not much, and a sort of metal carapace that covered the back of her neck, her shoulders, and went on down her spine.

"Better," I admitted, then made a wry face.

"Mouth taste unpleasant?"

"Like a Balkan cabinet meeting."

"Here." She gave me some stuff in a glass; it was spicy and burned a little, and it washed away the bad taste at once. "No," she went on, "don't swallow it. 'Pit it out like a little man and I'll get you some water." I obeyed.

"I'm Doris Marsden," she went on, "your day nurse."

"Glad to know you, Doris," I answered and stared at her with increasing appreciation. "Say—why the get up? Not that I don't like it, but you look like a refugee from a comic book."

She looked down at herself and giggled. "I feel like a chorus girl. But you'll get used to it—I did."

"I'm already used to it. I like it fine. But why?"

"The Old Man's orders."

I started to ask why again, then I knew why, and I started feeling worse again. I shut up. Doris went on, "Now for some supper." She got a tray and sat down on my bed.

"I don't believe I want anything to eat."

"Open up," she said firmly, "or I'll rub it in your hair. There! That's a good boy."

Between gulps, taken in self-defense, I managed to get out, "I feel pretty good. Give me one jolt of 'gyro' and I'll be back on my feet."

"No stimulants for you," she said flatly, still shoveling it in. "Special diet and lots of rest, with maybe a sleepy pill later. That's what the man says."

"What's wrong with me?"

"Extreme exhaustion, starvation, and the first case of scurvy I ever saw in all my born days. As well as scabies and lice—but we got those whipped. There, now you know—and if you tell the doctor I told you, I'll call you a liar to your face. Turn over on your tummy."

I did so and she started changing dressings. I appeared to be spotted with sores; the stuff she used stung a bit, then felt cool. I thought about what she had told me and tried to remember just how I had lived under my master.

"Stop trembling," she said. "Are you having a bad one?"

"I'm all right," I told her. I did manage to stop shaking and to think it over calmly. As near as I could remember I had not eaten during that period oftener than every second or third day. Bathing? Let me see—why, I hadn't bathed at all! I had shaved every day and put on a clean shirt; that was a necessary part of the masquerade and the master knew it.

On the other hand, so far as I could remember, I had never taken off my shoes from the time I had stolen them until the Old Man had recaptured me—and they had been too tight to start with. "What sort of shape are my feet in?" I asked.

"Don't be nosy," Doris advised me. "Now turn over on your back."

I like nurses; they are calm and earthy and very tolerant. Miss Briggs, my night nurse, was not the mouth-watering job that Doris was; she had a face like a jaundiced horse—but she had a fine figure for a woman her age, hard and well cared for. She wore the same sort of musical-comedy rig that Doris sported, but she wore it with a no-nonsense air and walked like a grenadier guard. Doris, bless her heart, jiggled pleasantly as she walked.

Miss Briggs refused to give me a second sleeping pill when I woke up in the night and had the horrors, but she did play poker with me and skinned me out of half a month's pay. I tried to find out from her about the President matter, for I figured the Old Man had either won or lost by that time. But she wasn't talking. She would not admit that she knew anything about parasites, flying saucers, or what not—and she herself sitting there dressed in a costume that could have only one purpose!

I asked her what the public news was, then? She maintained that she had been too busy lately to look at a 'cast. So I asked to have a stereo box moved into my room, so I could catch a newscast. She said I would have to ask the doctor about that; I was on the 'quiet' list. I asked when in the deuce I was going to see this so-called doctor? She said she didn't know; the doctor had been very busy lately. I asked how many other patients there were in the infirmary anyway? She said she really didn't remember. About then her call bell sounded and she left, presumably to see another patient.

I fixed her. While she was gone, I cold-decked the next deal, so that she got a pat hand—then I wouldn't bet against her.

I got to sleep later on and was awakened by Miss Briggs slapping me in the face with a cold, wet washcloth. She got me ready for breakfast, then Doris relieved her and brought it to me. This time I fed myself and while I was chomping I tackled her for news, with the same perfect score I had made with Miss Briggs. Nurses run a hospital as if it were a nursery for backward children.

Davidson came around to see me after breakfast. "Heard you were here," he said. He was wearing shorts and nothing else, except that his left arm was covered by a dressing.

"More than I've heard," I complained. "What happened to you?"

"Bee stung me."

I dropped that subject; if he didn't want to tell how he had gotten burned, that was his business. I went on, "The Old Man was in here yesterday, getting my report, when he left very suddenly. Seen him since?"

"Yep."

"Well?" I answered.

"Well, how about you. Are you straightened out? Have the psych boys cleared you for classified matters, or not?"

"Is there any doubt about it?"

"You're darn tootin' there's doubt. Poor old Jarvis never did pull out of it."

"Huh?" I hadn't thought about Jarvis. "How is he now?"

"He isn't. Never did get right in his head. Dropped into a coma and died the next day—the day after you left. I mean the day after you were captured. No apparent reason—just died." Davidson looked me over. "You must be tough."

I did not feel tough. I felt tears of weakness welling up again and I blinked them back. Davidson pretended not to see and went on conversationally, "You should have seen the ruckus after you gave us the slip. The Old Man took out after you wearing nothing but a gun and a look of grim determination. He would have caught you, too, my money says—but the civil police picked him up and we had to get him out of hock." Davidson grinned.

I grinned feebly myself. There was something both gallant and silly about the Old Man charging out to save the world single-handed dressed in his birthday suit. "Sorry I missed it. But what else has happened—lately?"

Davidson looked me over carefully, then said, "Wait a minute." He stepped out of the room and was gone a short time. When he came back, he said, "The Old Man says it's all right. What do you want to know?"

"Everything! What happened yesterday?"

"I was in on that one," he answered, "That's how I got this." He waved his damaged wing at me, "I was lucky," he added, "three agents were killed. Quite a fracas."

"But how did it come out? How about the President? Was he—"

Doris hustled into the room. "Oh, there you are!" she said to Davidson. "I told you to stay in bed. You're due in prosthetics at Mercy Hospital right now. The ambulance has been waiting for ten minutes."

He stood up, grinned at her, and pinched her cheek with his good hand. "The party can't start until I get there."

"Well, hurry!"

"Coming." He started out the door with her.

I called out, "Hey! How about the President?"

Davidson paused and looked back over his shoulder. "Oh, him? He's all right—not a scratch on him." He went on.

Doris came back a few minutes later, fuming. "Patients!" she said, like a swear word. "Do you know why they call them 'patients'? Because it's patience you have to have to put up with them. I should have had at least twenty minutes for his injection to take hold; as it was I gave it to him when he got into the ambulance."

"Injection for what?"

"Didn't he tell you?"

"No."

"Well . . . no reason not to tell you. Amputation and graft, lower left arm."

"Oh." Well, I thought, I won't hear the end of the story from Davidson; grafting on a new limb is a shock. They usually keep the patient hopped up for at least ten days. I wondered about the Old Man: had he come out of it alive? Of course he had, I reminded myself; Davidson checked with him before he talked.

But that didn't mean he hadn't been wounded. I tackled Doris again. "How about the Old Man? Is he on the sick list? Or would it be a violation of your sacred run-around rules to tell me?"

"You talk too much," she answered. "It's time for your morning nourishment and your nap." She produced a glass of milky slop, magician fashion.

"Speak up, wench, or I'll spit it back in your face."

"The Old Man? You mean the Chief of Section?"

"Who else?"

"He's not on the sick list, at least not here." She shivered and made a face. "I wouldn't want him as a patient."

I was inclined to agree with her.

Chapter 10

For two or three more days I was kept wrapped in swaddling clothing and treated like a child. I did not care; it was the first real rest I had had in years. Probably they were slipping me sedatives; I noticed that I was always ready to sleep each time after they fed me. The sores got much better and presently I was encouraged—"required" I should say—by Doris to take light exercise around the room.

The Old Man called on me. "Well," he said, "still malingering, I see."

I flushed. "Damn your black, flabby heart," I told him. "Get me a pair of pants and I'll show you who is malingering."

"Slow down, slow down." He took my chart from the foot of my bed and looked it over. "Nurse," he said, "get this man a pair of shorts. I'm restoring him to duty."

Doris faced up to him like a banty hen. "Now see here," she said, "you may be the big boss, but you can't give orders here. The doctor will—"

"Stow it!" he said, "and get those drawers. When the doctor comes in, send him to me."

"But—"

He picked her up, swung her around, paddled her behind, and said, "Git!"

She went out, squawking and sputtering, and came back shortly, not with clothes for me, but with the doctor. The Old Man looked around and said mildly, "Doc, I sent for pants, not for you."

The medico said stiffly, "I'll thank you not to interfere with my patients."

"He's not your patient. I need him, so I am restoring him to duty."

"Yes? Sir, if you do not like the way I run my department, you may have my resignation at once."

The Old Man is stubborn but not bull-headed. He answered, "I beg your pardon, sir. Sometimes I become too preoccupied with other problems to remember to follow correct procedure. Will you do me the favor of examining this patient? I need him; if he can possibly be restored to duty, it would help me to have his services at once."

The doctor's jaw muscles were jumping, but all he said was, "Certainly, sir!" He went through a show of studying my chart, then had me sit on the bed while he tested my reflexes. Personally, I thought they were mushy. He peeled back my eyelids, flashed a light in my eye, and said, "He needs more recuperation time—but you may have him. Nurse—fetch clothing for this man."

Clothing consisted of shorts and shoes; I had been better dressed in a hospital gown. But everybody else was dressed the same way, and it was downright comforting to see all those bare shoulders with no masters clinging to them. I told the Old Man so. "Best defense we've got," he growled, "even if it does make the joint look like a ruddy summer colony. If we don't win this set-to before winter weather, we're licked."

The Old Man stopped at a door with a freshly lettered sign: BIOLOGICAL LABORATORY—STAY OUT! He dilated the door.

I hung back. "Where are we going?"

"Going to take a look at your twin brother, the ape with your parasite."

"That's what I thought. Not for me—no point in it. No, thanks!" I could feel myself begin to tremble.

The Old Man paused. "Now, look, son," he said patiently, "you've got to get over your panic. The best way is to face up to it. I know it's hard—I've spent a good many hours in here myself, just staring at the thing, getting used to it."

"You don't know—you can't know!" I had the shakes so badly now that I had to steady myself by the doorframe.

He looked at me. "I suppose it's different," he said slowly, "when you've actually had it. Jarvis—" He broke off.

"You're darn right it's different! You're not going to get me in there"

"No, I guess not. Well, the doctor was right. Go on back, son, and turn yourself in at the infirmary." His tones were regretful rather than angry. He turned and started into the laboratory.

He had gotten three or four steps away before I called out, "Boss!"

He stopped and turned, his face expressionless. "Wait," I added, "I'm coming."

"You don't have to."

"I know. I'll do it. It—It just takes . . . a while—to get your nerve back."

He did not answer but, as I came alongside him, he grasped my upper arm, warmly and affectionately, and continued to hold it as we walked, as if I were a girl. We went on in, through another locked door and into a room that was conditioned warm and moist. The ape was there, caged.

He sat facing us, his torso supported and restrained by a strap-metal framework. His arms and legs hung limply, as if he had no control over them—which he did not have, as I learned.

As we came in he looked up and at us. For an instant his eyes were malevolent and intelligent; then the fire died out and they were merely the eyes of a dumb brute, a brute in pain.

"Around to the side," the Old Man said softly. I would have hung back but he still had me by the arm. We moved around; the ape followed us with his eyes, but his body was held by the frame. From the new position I could see—it.

My master. The thing that had ridden my back for an endless time, spoken with my mouth—thought with my brain. My master.

"Steady," the Old Man said softly. "Steady. You'll get used to it." He shook my arm. "Look away for a bit. It helps."

I did so and it did help. Not much, but some. I took a

couple of deep breaths, then held it and managed to slow my heart down a little. I made myself stare at it.

It is not the appearance of a parasite which arouses horror. True, they are disgustingly ugly, but not more so than slime in a pond—not as much so as maggots in garbage.

Nor was the horror entirely from knowing what they could do—for I felt the horror the first time I saw one, before I really knew what one was. I tried to tell the Old Man about it, letting the talk steady me. He nodded, his eyes still on the parasite. "It's the same with everybody," he said. "Unreasoned fear, like a bird with a snake. Probably its prime weapon." He let his own eyes drift away, as if too long a sight of it were too much even for his rawhide nerves.

I stuck with him, trying to get used to it and gulping at my breakfast but not losing it. I kept telling myself that I was safe from it, that it couldn't harm me.

I looked away again and found the Old Man's eyes on me. "How about it?" he said. "Getting hardened to it?"

I looked back at it. "A little." I went on savagely, "All I want to do is to kill it! I want to kill all of them—I could spend my whole life killing them and killing them." I began to shake again.

The Old Man continued to study me. "Here," he said, and handed me his gun.

It startled me. I was unarmed myself, having come straight from bed. I took it but looked back at him questioningly. "Huh? What for?"

"You want to kill it, don't you? If you feel that you have to, go ahead. Kill it. Right now."

"Huh? But—Look here, boss, you told me you needed this one for study."

"I do. But if you need to kill it, if you feel that you have to kill it, do so. I figure this particular one is your baby; you're entitled to it. If you need to kill it, to make you a whole man again, go ahead."

"'To make me a whole man again—'" The thought rang through my head. The Old Man knew, better than I knew, what was wrong with me, what medicine it would take to cure me. I was no longer trembling; I stood there, the gun cradled in my hand, ready to spit and kill. My master . . .

If I killed this one I would be a free man again—but I would never be free as long as it lived. Surely, I wanted to kill them, every one of them, search them out, burn them, kill them—but this one above all.

My master . . . still my master unless I killed it. I had a dark and certain thought that if I were alone with it, I would be able to do nothing, that I would freeze and wait while it crawled up me and settled again between my shoulder blades, searched out my spinal column, took possession of my brain and my very inner self.

But now I could kill it!

No longer frightened but fiercely exultant I raised the gun, ready to squeeze the trigger.

The Old Man watched me.

I lowered the gun a little and said uncertainly, "Boss, suppose I do kill it. You've got others?"

"No."

"But you need it."

"Yes."

"Well, but—For the love o' God, why did you give me the gun?"

"You know why. This one is yours; you've got first claim. If you have to kill it, go ahead. If you can pass it up, then the Section will use it."

I had to kill it. Even if we killed all the others, while this one was still alive I would still crouch and tremble in the dark. As for the others, for study—why, we could capture a dozen any time at the Constitution Club. With this one dead I'd lead the raid myself. Breathing rapidly, I raised the gun again.

Then I turned and chucked the gun to the Old Man; he plucked it out of the air and put it away. "What happened?" he asked. "You were all set."

"Uh? I don't know. When it got right down to it, it was enough to know that I could."

"I figured that it would be."

I felt warm and relaxed, as if I had just killed a man or had a woman—as if I had just killed it. I was able to turn my back on it and face the Old Man. I was not even angry with him for what he had done; instead I felt warm toward him, even affectionate. "I know you did, damn you. How does it feel to be a puppet master?"

He did not take the jibe as a joke. Instead he answered soberly, "Not me. The most I ever do is to lead a man on the path he wants to follow. There is the puppet master." He hooked a thumb at the parasite.

I looked around at it. "Yes," I agreed softly, " 'the puppet master'. You think you know what you mean by that—but you don't. And boss . . . I hope you never do."

"I hope so, too," he answered seriously.

I could look now without trembling. I even started to put my hands in my pockets, but the shorts had no pockets. Still staring at it, I went on, "Boss, when you are through with it, if there is anything left, then I'll kill it."

"That's a promise."

We were interrupted by a man bustling into the cage room. He was dressed in shorts and a lab coat; it made him look silly. I did not recognize him—it was not Graves; I never saw Graves again; I imagine the Old Man ate him for lunch.

"Chief," he said, trotting up, "I did not know you were in here. I—"

"Well, I am," the Old Man cut in. "What are you doing wearing a coat?" The Old Man's gun was out and pointed at the man's chest.

The man stared at the gun as if it were a bad joke. "Why, I was working, of course. There is always a chance of splattering one's self. Some of our solutions are rather—"

"Take it off!"

"Eh?"

The Old Man waggled his gun at him. To me he said, "Get ready to take him."

The man took his coat off. He stood there holding it and biting his lip. His back and shoulders were bare, nor was there the telltale rash. "Take that damned coat and burn it," the Old Man told him. "Then get back to your work."

The man hurried away, his face red, then hesitated, glanced at me, and said to the Old Man, "Chief, are you ready for that, uh, procedure?"

"Shortly. I'll let you know."

The man opened his mouth, closed it, and left. The Old Man wearily put his gun away. "Post an order," he muttered. "Read it aloud. Make everybody sign for it—tattoo it on their narrow little chests—and some smart aleck thinks it doesn't apply to him. Scientists!" He said the last word in the way in which Doris had said, "Patients!"

I turned back to looking at my former master. It still revolted me, but there was a gusty feeling of danger, too, that was not totally unpleasant—like standing on a very high place. "Boss," I asked, "what are you going to do with this thing?"

He looked at me, rather than at the slug. "I plan to interview it."

"To what? But how can you—What I want to say is: the ape, I mean—"

"No, the ape can't talk. That's the hitch. We'll have to have a volunteer—a human volunteer."

When his words sank in and I began to visualize what he meant by them the horror struck me again almost full force. "You can't mean that. You wouldn't do that—not to anybody."

"I could and I'm going to. What needs to be done will be done."

"You won't get any volunteers!"

"I've already got one."

"You have? Who?"

"But I don't want to use the volunteer I've got. I'm still looking for the right man."

I was disgusted and showed it. "You ought not to be

looking for anyone, volunteer or not. And if you've got one, I'll bet you won't find another; there can't be two people that far out of their minds."

"Possibly," he agreed. "But I still don't want the one I've got. The interview is a necessity, son; we are fighting a war with a total lack of military intelligence. We don't know anything, really, about our enemy. We can't negotiate with him, we don't know where he comes from, nor what makes him tick. We've got to find out; our racial existence depends on it. The only, the only way to talk to these critters is through a human volunteer. So it will be done. But I'm still looking for a volunteer."

"Well, don't look at me!"

"I am looking at you."

My answer had been half wisecrack; his answer turned it dead serious and startled me speechless. I finally managed to splutter, "You're crazy! I should have killed it when I had your gun—and I would have if I had known what you wanted it for. But as for me volunteering to let you put that thing—No! I've had it."

He ploughed on through as if he had not heard me. "It can't be just any volunteer; it has to be a man who can take it. Jarvis wasn't stable enough, nor tough enough in some fashion to stand up under it. We know you are."

"Me? You don't know anything of the sort. All you know is that I lived through it once. I . . . I couldn't stand it again."

"Well, maybe it will kill you," he answered calmly, "but it is less likely to kill you than someone else. You are proved and salted; you ought to be able to do it standing on your head. With anyone else I run more risk of losing an agent."

"Since when did you worry about risking an agent?" I said bitterly.

"Since always, believe me. I am giving you one more chance, son: are you going to do this, knowing that it has to be done and that you stand the best chance of anybody—and can be of most use to us, because you are used to it—or are you going to let some other agent risk his reason and probably his life in your place?"

I started to try to explain how I felt, that I was not afraid to die, no more than is normal, but that I could not stand the thought of dying while possessed by a parasite. Somehow I felt that to die so would be to die already consigned to an endless and unbearable hell. Even worse was the prospect of not dying once the slug touched me. But I could not say it; there were still no words to describe what the race had not experienced.

I shrugged. "You can have my appointment back. There is a limit to what one man can be expected to go through and I've reached it. I won't do it."

He turned to the intercom phone on the wall. "Laboratory," he called out, "we'll start the experiment right now. Hurry it up!"

The answering voice I recognized as that of the man who had walked in on us. "Which subject?" he asked. "It affects the measurements."

"The original volunteer."

"That's the smaller rig?" the voice asked doubtfully.

"Right. Get it in here."

I started for the door. The Old Man snapped, "Where do you think you are going?"

"Out," I snapped back. "I'm having no part of this."

He grabbed me and spun me around as if he had been the bigger and younger. "No, you don't. You know more about these things than the rest of us; your advice could be of help."

"Let go of me."

"You'll stay and watch!" he said savagely, "strapped down or free to move, as you choose. I've made allowance for your illness but I've had enough of your nonsense."

I was too weary to buck him; I felt nervously exhausted, tired in my bones. "You're the boss."

The lab people wheeled in a metal framework, a sort of chair, more like a Sing Sing special than anything else. There were metal clamps for ankles and knees, more of the same on the chair arms for the wrists and elbows. There was a corselet effect to restrain the waist and the lower part of the chest, but the back was cut away so that the shoulders of the person unfortunate enough to sit in it would be free.

They brought it over and placed it beside the ape's cage, then removed the back panel of the cage and the panel on the side nearest the "chair" rig.

The ape watched the procedure with intent, aware eyes, but his limbs still dangled helplessly. Nevertheless, I became still more disturbed at the cage being thus opened. Only the Old Man's threat of placing me under restraint kept me from leaving.

The technicians stood back and waited, apparently ready for the job. The outer door opened and several people came in; among them was Mary.

I was caught off balance by her sudden appearance; I had been wanting to see her and had tried several times to get word to her through the nurses—but they either honestly could not identify her or had received instructions. Now I saw her first under these circumstances. I cursed the Old Man to myself, knowing it was useless to object. It was no sort of a show to bring a woman to, even if the woman was an agent. There ought to be some sort of decent limits somewhere.

Mary saw me, looked surprised, and nodded. I let it go with a nod myself; it was no time for small talk. She was looking good, as always, though very sober. She was dressed in the same sort of costume as the nurses had worn, shorts and a skimpy halter, but she did not have on the ludicrous metal helmet and back plate.

The others in the party were men. They wore shorts, like the Old Man and myself. They were loaded with recording and stereo equipment as well as other apparatus.

"Ready?" inquired the lab chief.

"Get going," answered the Old Man.

Mary walked straight to the metal chair and sat down in it. Two of the technicians knelt at her foot and started busying themselves with the clamps. Mary reached behind her, unfastened her halter and let it fall, leaving her back bare.

I looked at this in a frozen daze, as if caught in a nightmare. Then I had grabbed the Old Man by the shoulders and had literally thrown him aside and I was standing by the chair, kicking the technicians out of the way. "Mary!" I screamed, "get up out of there!"

Now the Old Man had his gun on me and was motioning me back with it. "Away from her," he ordered. "You three—grab him and tie him up."

I looked at the gun, then I looked down at Mary. She said nothing and did not move; in fact her feet were already bound. She simply looked at me with compassionate eyes. "Get up from there, Mary," I said dully, "I want to sit down."

They removed the chair Mary had sat in and brought in another, larger one. I could not have used hers; both of them were tailored to size. When they finished clamping me in place I might as well have been cast into concrete. Once secured, my back began to itch unbearably, although nothing, as yet, had touched it.

Mary was no longer in the room; whether she had left or had been ordered out by the Old Man I do not know and it did not seem to matter. The Old Man stepped up to me after I had been prepared, laid a hand on my arm, and said quietly, "Thanks, son."

I did not bother to answer.

I did not see them handle the parasite as it took place behind my back. There was a rig which I had seen them bring in which appeared to be modified from the remote-handling gear used on radioactives; no doubt they used that. I was not interested enough to look, even if I had been able to turn my head far enough, which I couldn't.

Once the ape barked and screamed and someone shouted, "Watch it!"

There was a dead silence as if everyone was holding his breath—then something moist touched the back of my neck and I fainted.

I came out of it with the same tingling energy I had experienced once before. I knew I was in a tight spot, but I was warily determined to think my way out of it. I was not afraid; I was contemptuous of those around me and sure that in the long run I could outwit them.

The Old Man said sharply, "Can you hear me?"

I answered, "Of course I can. Quit shouting."

"Do you remember what we are here for?"

I said, "Naturally I remember. You want to ask some questions. What are you waiting for?"

"What are you?"

"Now that's a silly question. Take a look at me. I'm six feet one, more muscle than brain, and I weigh—"

"Not you. You know to whom I am talking—you."

"Guessing games?"

The Old Man waited a bit before replying, "It will do you no good to pretend that I don't know what you are—"

"Ah, but you don't."

"Or, rather, that I don't know that you are a parasite talking through the body of a man. You know that I have been studying you all the time you have been living on the body of that ape. I know things about you which give me an advantage over you. One—" He started ticking them off.

"You can be killed.

"Two, you can be hurt. You don't like electric shock and you can't stand the amount of heat even a man can stand.

"Three, you are helpless without your host. I could have you removed from this man and you would die.

"Four, you have no powers except those you borrow from your host—and your host is helpless. Try your bonds; then be sensible. You must cooperate—or die."

I listened with half an ear; I had already been trying

my bonds, neither hoping nor fearing, but finding them, as I expected, impossible to escape. This did not worry me; I had neither worries nor fears. I was oddly contented to be back with my master, to be free of troubles and tensions. My business was to serve and the future would take care of itself.

In the meantime I must be alert, ready to serve him.

One ankle strap seemed less tight than the other; possibly I might drag my foot through it. I checked on the arm clamps; perhaps if I relaxed my muscles completely—

But I made no effort to escape. An instruction came at once—or, I made a decision, for the words mean the same; I tell you there was no conflict between my master and me; we were one—instruction or decision, I knew it was not time to risk an escape. I ran my eyes around the room, trying to figure who was armed and who was not. It was my guess that only the Old Man was armed; that bettered the chances.

Somewhere, deep down, was that dull ache of guilt and despair never experienced by any but the servants of the masters—but I was much too busy with the problem at hand to be troubled by it.

"Well?" the Old Man went on. "Do you answer my questions, or do I punish you?"

"What questions?" I asked. "Up to now, you've been talking nonsense."

The Old Man turned to one of the technicians. "Give me the tickler."

I felt no apprehension although I did not understand what it was he had asked for. I was still busy checking my bonds. If I could tempt him into placing his gun within my reach—assuming that I could get one arm free—then I might be able to—

He reached past my shoulders with a rod. I felt a shocking, unbearable pain. The room blacked out as if a switch had been thrown and for an undying instant I was jolted and twisted by hurt. I was split apart by it; for the moment I was masterless.

The pain left, leaving only its searing memory behind. Before I could speak, or even think coherently for myself, the splitting away had ended and I was again safe in the arms of my master. But for the first and only time in my service to him I was not myself free of worry; some of his own wild fear and pain was passed on to me, the servant.

I looked down and saw a line of red welling out of my left wrist; in my struggles I had cut myself on the clamp. It did not matter; I would tear off hands and feet and escape from there on bloody stumps, if escape for my master were possible that way.

"Well," asked the Old Man, "how did you like the taste of that?"

The panic that possessed me washed away; I was again filled with an unworried sense of well being, albeit wary and watchful. My wrists and ankles, which had begun to pain me, stopped hurting. "Why did you do that?" I asked. "Certainly, you can hurt me—but why?"

"Answer my questions."

"Ask them."

"What are you?"

The answer did not come at once. The Old Man reached for the rod; I heard myself saying, "We are the people."

"The people? What people?"

"The only people. We have studied you and we know your ways. We—" I stopped suddenly.

"Keep talking," the Old Man said grimly, and gestured with the rod.

"We come," I went on, "to bring you—"

"To bring us what?"

I wanted to talk; the rod was terrifyingly close. But there was some difficulty with words. "To bring you peace," I blurted out.

The Old Man snorted.

"'Peace'," I went on, "and contentment—and the joy of—of surrender." I hesitated again; "surrender" was not the right word. I struggled with it the way one struggles with a poorly grasped foreign language. "The joy," I repeated, "—the joy of . . . nirvana." That was it; the word fitted. I felt like a dog being patted for fetching a stick; I wriggled with pleasure.

"Let me get this," the Old Man said thoughtfully. "You are promising the human race that, if we will just surrender to your kind, you will take care of us and make us happy. Right?"

"Exactly!"

The Old Man studied me for a long moment, looking, not at my face, but past my shoulders. He spat upon the floor. "You know," he said slowly, "me and my kind, we have often been offered that bargain, though maybe not on such a grand scale. It never worked out worth a damn."

I leaned forward as much as the rig would allow. "Try it yourself," I suggested. "It can be done quickly—and then you will know."

He stared at me, this time in my face. "Maybe I should," he said thoughtfully. "Maybe I owe it to—somebody, to try it. And maybe I will, someday. But right now," he went on briskly, "you have more questions to answer. Answer them quick and proper and stay healthy. Be slow about it and I'll step up the current." He brandished the rod.

I shrank back, feeling dismay and defeat. For a moment I had thought he was going to accept the offer and I had been planning the possibilities of escape that could develop. "Now," he went on, "where do you come from?"

No answer . . . I felt no urge to answer.

The rod came closer. "Far away!" I burst out.

"That's no news. Tell me where? Where's your home base, your own planet?"

I had no answer. The Old Man waited a moment, then said, "I see I'll have to touch up your memory." I watched dully, thinking nothing at all. He was interrupted by one of the bystanders. "Eh?" said the Old Man.

"There may be a semantic difficulty," the other repeated. "Different astronomical concepts."

"Why should there be?" asked the Old Man. "That slug is using borrowed language throughout. He knows what his host knows; we've proved that." Nevertheless he turned back and started a different tack. "See here—you savvy the solar system; is your planet inside it or outside it?"

I hesitated, then answered, "All planets are ours."

The Old Man pulled at his lip. "I wonder," he mused, "just what you mean by that?" He went on, "Never mind; you can claim the whole damned universe; I want to know where your nest is? Where is your home base? Where do your ships come from?"

I could not have told him and did not; I sat silent.

Before I could anticipate it he reached behind me with the rod; I felt one smashing blow of pain, then it was gone. "Now, talk, damn you! What planet? Mars? Venus? Jupiter? Saturn? Uranus? Neptune? Pluto? Kalki?" As he ticked them off, I saw them—and I have never been as far off Earth as the space stations. When he came to the right one, I knew—and the thought was instantly snatched from me.

"Speak up," he went on, "or feel the whip."

I heard myself saying, "None of them. Our home is much farther away. You could never find it."

He looked past my shoulders and then into my eyes. "I think you are lying. I think you need some juice to keep you honest."

"No, no!"

"No harm to try." Slowly he thrust the rod past me, behind me. I knew the answer again and was about to give it, when something grabbed my throat. Then the pain started.

It did not stop. I was being torn apart; I tried to talk, to tell, anything to stop the pain—but the hand still clutched my throat and I could not.

Through a clearing blur of pain I saw the Old Man's face, shimmering and floating. "Had enough?" he asked. "Ready to talk?" I started to answer, but I choked and gagged. I saw him reach out again with the rod.

I burst into pieces and died.

They were leaning over me. Someone said, "He's coming around. Watch him; he might be violent."

The Old Man's face was over mine, his expression

worried. "Are you all right, son?" he asked anxiously. I turned my face away.

"One side, please," another voice said. "Let me give him the injection."

"Will his heart stand it?"

"Certainly—or I wouldn't give it to him." The speaker knelt by me, took my arm, and gave me a shot. He stood up, looked at his hands, then wiped them on his shorts; they left bloody streaks.

I felt strength flowing back into me. "Gyro", I thought absently, or something like it. Whatever it was, it was pulling me back together. Shortly I sat up, unassisted.

I was still in the cage room, directly in front of that damnable chair. The cage, I noticed without interest, was closed again. I started to get to my feet; the Old Man stepped forward and gave me a hand. I shook him off. "Don't touch me!"

"Sorry," he answered, then snapped, "Jones! You and Ito—get the litter. Take him back to the infirmary. Doc, you go along."

"Certainly." The man who had given me the shot stepped forward and started to take my arm. I drew away from him.

"Keep your hands off me!"

He stopped. "Get away from me—all of you. Just leave me alone." The doctor looked at the Old Man, who shrugged, then motioned them all back. Alone, I went to the door, through it, and on out through the outer door into the passageway.

I paused there, looked at my wrists and ankles and decided that I might as well go back to the infirmary.

Doris would take care of me, I was sure, and then maybe I could sleep. I felt as if I had gone fifteen rounds and lost every one of them.

"Sam, Sam!"

I looked up; I knew that voice. Mary hurried up and was standing before me, looking at me with great sorrowful eyes. "I've been waiting," she said. "Oh, Sam! What have they done to you?" Her voice was so choked that I could hardly understand her.

"You should know," I answered, and found I had strength enough left to slap her.

"Bitch," I added.

The room I had had was still empty, but I did not find Doris. I was aware that I had been followed, probably by the doctor, but I wanted no part of him nor any of them just then; I closed the door. Then I lay face down on the bed and tried to stop thinking or feeling anything.

Presently I heard a gasp, and opened one eye; there was Doris. "What in the world?" she exclaimed and came over to me. I felt her gentle hands on me. "Why, you poor, poor baby!" Then she added, "Just stay there, don't try to move. I'll get the doctor."

"No!"

"But you've got to have the doctor."

"No. I won't see him. You help me."

She did not answer. Presently I heard her go out. She came back shortly—I think it was shortly—and started to bathe my wounds. The doctor was not with her.

She was not more than half my size but she lifted me and turned me when she needed to as if I had been the baby she had called me. I was not surprised by it; I knew she could take care of me.

I wanted to scream when she touched my back. But she dressed it quickly and said, "Over easy, now."

"I'll stay face down."

"No," she denied, "I want you to drink something, that's a good boy."

I turned over, with her doing most of the work, and drank what she gave me. After a bit I went to sleep.

I seem to remember being awakened later, seeing the Old Man and cursing him out. The doctor was there too—or it could just as well have been a dream.

Miss Briggs woke me up and Doris brought me breakfast; it was as if I had never been off the sick list. Doris wanted to feed me but I was well able to do it myself. Actually I was not in too bad shape. I was stiff and sore and felt as if I had gone over Niagara Falls in a barrel; there were dressings on both arms and both legs where I had cut myself on the clamps, but no bones were broken. Where I was sick was in my soul.

Don't misunderstand me. The Old Man could send me into a dangerous spot—and had done so, more than once—and I would not hold it against him. That I had signed up for. But I had not signed up for what he had done to me. He knew what made me tick and he had deliberately used it to force me into something I would never have agreed to, had I not been jockeyed into it. Then after he had gotten me where he wanted me, he had used me unmercifully.

Oh, I've slapped men around to make them talk. Sometimes you have to. But this was different. Believe me.

It was the Old Man that really hurt. Mary? After all, what was she? Just another babe. True, I was disgusted with her to the bottom of my soul for letting the Old Man talk her into being used as bait. It was all right for her to use her femaleness as an agent; the Section had to have female operatives; they could do things men could not do. There have always been female spies and the young and pretty ones had always used the same tools.

But she should not have agreed to use them against another agent, inside her own Section—at least, she should not have used them against me.

Not very logical, is it? It was logical to me. Mary shouldn't have done it.

I was through, I was finished. They could go ahead with Operation Parasite without me; I'd had it. I owned a cabin up in the Adirondacks; I had enough stuff there in deep freeze to carry me for years—well, a year, anyhow. I had plenty of tempus pills and could get more; I would go up there and use them—and the world could save itself, or go to hell, without me.

If anyone came within a hundred yards of me, he would either show a bare back or be burned down.

☞ Chapter 11 ☜

I had to tell somebody about it and Doris was the goat. It may have been classified information but I did not give a hoot. It turned out that Doris knew all about Operation Parasite; there was no reason to try to keep any part of it secret. The trouble was to make it not a secret—but I am ahead of myself.

Doris was indignant—shucks, she was sore as a boiled owl. She had dressed what they had done to me. Of course, as a nurse, she had dressed a lot worse, but this had been done by our own people. I blurted out how I felt about Mary's part in it. "You know that old slaughterhouse trick," I asked her, "where they train one animal to lead the others in? That's what they got Mary to do to me."

She had not heard of it, but she understood me. "Do I understand you that you had wanted to marry this girl?"

"Correct. Stupid, ain't I?"

"All men are, about women—but that's not the point. It does not make any difference whether she wanted to

125

marry you or not; her knowing that you wanted to marry her makes what she did about eight thousand times worse. She knew what she could do to you. It wasn't fair." She stopped massaging me, her eyes snapping. "I've never met your redhead, not yet—but if I ever do, I'll scratch her face!"

I smiled at her. "You're a good kid, Doris. I believe you would play fair with a man."

"Oh, I'm no angel, and I've pulled some fast ones in my time. But if I did anything halfway like that. I'd have to break every mirror I own. Turn a bit, and I'll get the other leg."

Mary showed up. The first I knew about it was hearing Doris say angrily, "You can't come in."

Mary's voice answered, "I'm going in. Try to stop me."

Doris squealed, "Stay where you are—or I'll pull that hennaed hair out by the roots!"

There was a short silence, sounds of a scuffle—and the *smack*! of someone getting slapped, hard. I yelled out, "Hey! What goes on?"

They appeared in the doorway together. Doris was breathing hard and her hair was mussed. Mary managed to look dignified and composed, but there was a bright red patch on her left cheek the size and shape of Doris's hand. She looked at me and ignored the nurse.

Doris caught her breath and said, "You get out of here. He doesn't want to see you."

Mary said, "I'll hear that from him."

I looked at them both, then said, "Oh, what the hell—Doris, she's here; I'll talk to her. I've got some things to tell her, in any case. Thanks for trying."

Doris waited a moment, then said, "You're a fool!" and flounced out.

Mary came over to the bed. "Sam," she said. "Sam."

"My name isn't 'Sam'."

"I've never known your right name."

I hesitated. It was no time to explain to her that my parents had been silly enough to burden me with 'Elihu'. I answered, "What of it? 'Sam' will do."

"Sam," she repeated. "Oh Sam, my dear."

"I am not your 'dear'."

She inclined her head. "Yes, I know that. I don't know why. Sam, I came here to find out why you hate me. Perhaps I can't change it, but I must know why."

I made some sound of disgust. "After what you did, you don't know why? Mary, you may be a cold fish, but you aren't stupid. I know; I've worked with you."

She shook her head. "Just backwards, Sam. I'm not cold, but I'm frequently stupid. Look at me, please—I know what they did to you. I know that you let it be done to save me from the same thing. I know that and I'm deeply grateful. But I don't know why you hate me. You did not have to do it, I did not ask you to do it, and I did not want you to do it."

I didn't answer; presently she said, "You don't believe me?"

I reared up on one elbow. "I believe you. I believe you have yourself convinced that that is how it was. Now I'll tell you how it was."

"Do, please."

"You sat down in that trick chair knowing that I would never let you go through with it. You knew that, whether that devious female mind of yours admitted it to itself or not. The Old Man could not have forced me into that chair, not with a gun, not even with drugs. But you could. You did. You were the one who forced me to go through with something which I would rather have been dead than touched . . . a thing that now leaves me dirty and spoiled. You did it."

She had grown steadily whiter as I talked, until her face was almost green against her hair. She caught her breath and said, "You believe that, Sam?"

"What else?"

"Sam, that is not the way it was. I did not know you were going to be in there. I was terribly startled. But there was nothing to do but go through with it; I had promised."

"'Promised'," I repeated. "That covers everything, a schoolgirl promise."

"Hardly a schoolgirl promise."

"No matter. And it doesn't matter whether you are telling the truth or not about knowing that I would be in there—you aren't, of course, but it doesn't matter. The point is: you were there and I was there—and you could figure what would happen if you did what you did do."

"Oh." She waited a bit, then went on, "That's the way it looks to you and I can't dispute the facts."

"Hardly."

She stood very still for a long time. I let her. Finally she said, "Sam—once you said something to me about wanting to marry me."

"I remember something of the sort. That was another day."

"I didn't expect you to renew the offer. But there was

something else, a sort of corollary. Sam, no matter what you think of me, I want to tell you that I am deeply grateful for what you did for me. Uh, Miss Barkis is willing, Sam—you understand me?"

This time I grinned at her. "A female to the very end! Honest so help me, the workings of the female mind continue to delight and astound me. You always think you can cancel out the score and start over with that one trump play." I continued to grin at her while she turned red. "It won't work. Not this time. I won't inconvenience you by taking up your no-doubt generous offer."

She continued to blush but she came back at me in a steady, level voice, "I let myself in for that. Nevertheless, it's true. That—or anything else I can ever do for you."

My elbow was going to sleep; I sank back and lay down. "Sure, you can do something for me."

Her face lit up. "What?"

"Go away and quit bothering me. I'm tired." I turned my face away. I did not hear her leave, but I heard Doris come back in. She was bristling like a fox terrier; they must have passed in the hall. She faced me, fists on her hips, looking cute and adorable and very indignant. "She got around you, didn't she?"

"I don't think so."

"Don't lie to me. You went soft on her. I know—men always do. The idiots! A woman like that, all she has to do is shake her fanny at a man and he rolls over and plays dead."

"Well, I didn't. I gave her what for."

"You're sure you did?"

"I did—and sent her packing."

Doris looked doubtful. "I hope you did. Maybe you did—she wasn't looking too pert as she came out." She dismissed the matter. "How do you feel?"

"Pretty good"—it was a lie, not.

"Want some massage?"

"No, just come here and sit on the bed and talk to me. Want a cigarette?"

"Well—as long as the doctor doesn't catch me." She perched up on the bed; I struck cigarettes for both of us and stuck hers in her mouth. She took a deep drag, swelling out her chest and pushing her arrogant breasts against her halter almost to the breaking point. I thought again what a sweet dish she was; she was just what I needed to take my mind off Mary.

We talked for a while. Doris gave her views on women—it appeared she disapproved of them on principle, although she was not in the least apologetic about being one herself—on the contrary! "Take women patients," she said. "One of the reasons I took this job was because we don't get a woman patient once in a coon's age. A man patient appreciates what is done for him. A woman just expects it and hollers for more."

"Would you be that sort of patient?" I asked, just to tease her.

"I hope not. I'm healthy, thank the Lord." She crushed out her cigarette and jumped off the bed, bouncing a little. "Got to get out of here. Scream if you want anything."

"Doris—"

"Yes?"

"You got any leave coming up?"

"I plan to take two weeks shortly. Why?"

"I was thinking. I'm going on leave—at least. I've got a shack in the Adirondacks. How about it? We could have a nice time and forget this madhouse."

She dimpled. "You know, that's mighty white of you, podnuh." She came over and kissed me full on the mouth, the first time she had done so. "And if I weren't an old married lady, with a pair of twins in the bargain, I might take you up."

"Oh."

"Sorry. But thanks for the compliment. You've made my day."

She started for the door. I called out, "Doris, wait a minute." When she stopped I added, "I didn't know. Look, why don't you take me up on it anyhow? The cabin, I mean—take your old man and the kids up there and give 'em a good time. I'll give you the combo and the transponder code."

"You mean that?"

"Of course I do."

"Well—I'll talk to you later. Thanks." She came back and kissed me again and it made me wish she had not been married, or, at least, not working at it. Then she left.

The doctor came in a bit later. While he was fiddling with the futile things doctors do, I said, "That nurse. Miss Marsden—is she married?"

"What business is it of yours?"

"I just wanted to know."

"You keep your hands off my nurses—or I'll fit you with mittens. Now stick out your tongue."

The Old Man put his head in late that afternoon. My immediate response was pleasure; the Old Man's personality is hard to shake off. Then I remembered and went cold.

"I want to talk to you," he started in.

"I don't want to talk to you. Get out."

He ignored my remarks and came in, dragging his bad leg. "Mind if I sit down?"

"You seem to be doing so."

He ignored that, too. He wrinkled his face and scowled. "You know, son, you are one of my best boys, but sometimes you are a little hasty."

"Don't let that worry you," I answered, "as soon as the doctor lets me out of here. I'm through." I had not really decided up until then, but it seemed as necessary as syrup with buckwheat cakes. I no longer trusted the Old Man; the rest was obvious.

He was not hearing anything that he did not choose to hear. "You're too hasty. You jump to conclusions. Now take this girl Mary—"

"Mary who?"

"You know who I mean; you know her as 'Mary Cavanaugh'."

"You take her."

"You jumped all over her without knowing the score. You've got her all upset. Matter of fact, you may have ruined a good agent for me."

"Hmmph! I'm in tears about it."

"Listen, you young snot, you didn't have any call to be rough on her. You don't know the facts."

I did not answer; explanations are a poor defense.

"Oh, I know that you think you do," he went on. "You think she let herself be used as bait to get you to take part in that job we did. Well, you've got it slightly wrong. She was being used as bait, but I was using her. I planned it that way."

"I know you did."

"Then why blame her?"

"Because, although you planned it, you couldn't have carried it out without her active cooperation. It's mighty big of you, you no-good, heartless bastard, to take all the blame—but you can't."

He did not hear my profanity, either. He went on, "You understand everything about it but the key point, which is—the girl didn't know."

"Hell's bells, she was there."

"So she was. Son, did you ever know me to lie to you?"

"No," I admitted, "but I don't think you would hesitate."

He looked pained but answered, "Maybe I deserve that. I'd lie to one of my own people if the country's safety depended on it. I haven't found it necessary up till now because I've been choosy about who works for me. But this time the country's welfare doesn't depend on it and I'm not lying and you'll just have to test it for yourself, any way you can figure out, and make up your mind whether or not I'm lying. That girl didn't know. She didn't know you were going to be in that room. She didn't know why you were in there. She didn't know that there was any question about who was going to sit in that chair. She didn't have the faintest suspicion that I didn't mean for her to go through with it, or that I had already decided that you were the only party who would suit me, even if I had to have you tied down and forced—which I would have done, if I hadn't had a double whammy up my sleeve to trick you into volunteering. Hell's bells yourself, son; she didn't even know you were off the sick list."

I wanted to believe it, so I did my damnedest not to believe it. If it were a lie, it would be just the shape of lie he would tell. As to whether he would bother to lie—well, getting two prime agents back into the groove might be something he would class, just now, as involving the country's safety. The Old Man had a complex mind.

"Look at me!" he added. I snapped out of my brown study and looked up. "There is something else I want you to know and I want to rub your nose in it. First off, let me say that everybody—including me—appreciates what you did, regardless of your motives. I'm putting in a letter about it and no doubt there will be a medal in due time. That stands, whether you stay with the Section or not. And if you go, I'll help you with any transfer or such you may want."

He paused for breath, then went on. "But don't go giving yourself airs as a little tin hero—"

"I won't!"

"—because that medal is going to the wrong person. Mary ought to get it.

"Now hush up; I'm not through. You had to be forced into it, like building a fire under a mule. No criticism; you had been through plenty. But Mary was a real, honest-to-God, Simon—pure volunteer. When she sat down in that chair, she didn't know what was going to happen to her. She didn't expect any last minute reprieve and she had every reason to believe that, if she got up alive, her reason would be gone, which is worse. But she did it—because she is a hero, which you miss by a couple of points."

He went on without waiting for me to reply; "Listen, son—most women are damn fools and children. But they've got more range than we've got. The brave ones are braver, the good ones are better and the vile ones are viler, for that matter. What I'm trying to tell you is: this one is more of a man than you are and you've done her a serious wrong."

I was so churned up inside that I could not judge for the life of me whether he was telling the truth, or manipulating me again. I said, "Maybe so. Maybe I lashed out at the wrong person. But if what you say is true—"

"It is."

"—it doesn't make what you did any sweeter; it makes it worse."

He took it without flinching. "Son, I'm sorry if I've lost your respect. But I'd do it again under the same circumstances. I can't be choosy about such things any more than can a commander in battle. Less, because I fight with different weapons. I've always been able to shoot my own dog. Maybe that's good; maybe that's bad— but that is what my job takes. If you are ever in my shoes, you'll have to do it, too."

"I'm not likely to be."

"Why don't you take leave, rest up, and think about it?"

"I'll take leave—terminal leave."

"Very well." He started to leave; I said,

"Wait—"

"Yes?"

"You made me one promise and I'm holding you to it. About that parasite—you said I could kill it, personally. Are you through with it?"

"Yes, I'm through with it, but—"

I started to get out of bed. "No 'buts'. Give me your gun; I'm going to kill it now."

"But you can't. It's already dead."

"What! You promised me."

"I know I did. But it died while we were trying to force you—to force it—to talk."

I sat down and started to shake with laughter. I got started and could not stop. I was not enjoying it; I could not help it.

The Old Man grasped my shoulders and shook me. "Snap out of it! You'll get yourself sick. I'm sorry about it, but there's nothing to laugh at. It could not be helped."

"Ah, but there is," I answered, still sobbing and chuckling. "It's the funniest thing that ever happened to me. All that—and all for nothing. You dirtied yourself and you loused up me and Mary—and all for no use."

"Huh? Whatever gave you that idea?"

"Eh? I know—I know everything that went on. And you didn't even get small change out of it—out of us, I should say. You didn't learn anything you didn't know before."

"The hell we didn't!"

"And the hell you did."

"It was a bigger success than you'd ever guess, son. True, we didn't squeeze anything out of it directly, before it died—but we got something out of you."

"Me?"

"Last night. We put you through it last night. You were doped, psyched, brain-waved, analyzed, wrung out, and hung out to dry. The parasite spilled things to you and they were still there for the hypno-analysts to pick up after you were free of it."

"What?"

"Where they live. We know where they come from and can fight back—Titan, sixth satellite of Saturn."

When he said it, I felt a sudden gagging constriction of my throat—and I knew that he was right.

"You certainly fought before we could get it out of you," he went on reminiscently. "We had to hold you down to keep you from hurting yourself—more."

Instead of leaving he threw his game leg over the edge of the bed and struck a cigarette. He seemed anxious to be friendly. As for me, I did not want to fight with him further; my head was spinning and I had things to get straight. Titan—that was a long way out. Mars was the farthest men had ever been, unless the Seagraves Expedition, the one that never came back, got out to the Jovian moons.

Still, we could get there, if there were a reason for it. We would burn out their nest!

Finally he got up to go. He had limped almost to the door when I stopped him again. "Dad—"

I had not called him that in years. He turned and his face held a surprised and defenseless expression. "Yes, son?"

"Why did you and mother name me 'Elihu'?"

"Eh? Why, it seemed the thing to do at the time. It was your maternal grandfather's name."

"Oh. Not enough reason. I'd say."

"Perhaps not." He turned again and again I stopped him.

"Dad—what sort of a person was my mother?"

"Your mother? I don't exactly know how to tell you. Well—she was a great deal like Mary. Yes, sir, a great deal like her." He turned and stumped out without giving me any further chance to talk.

I turned my face to the wall. After a while I steadied down.

Chapter 12

This is a personal account of my angle of view on events known to everybody. I'm not writing history. For one thing, I don't have the broad viewpoint.

Maybe I should have been sweating about the fate of the world when I was actually stewing about my own affairs. Maybe. But I never heard of a man with a blighty wound caring too much about how the battle turned out.

Anyhow, there did not seem much to worry about. I knew that the President had been saved under circumstances which would open up anybody's eyes, even a politician's, and that was, as I saw it, the last real hurdle. The slugs—the titans, that is—were dependent on secrecy; once out in the open they could not possibly hold out against the massed strength of the United States. They had no powers except those they borrowed from their slaves, as I knew better than anybody.

Now we could clean up their beachhead here; then we could go after them where they lived. But planning interplanetary expeditions was hardly my job. I knew as much about that subject as I knew about Egyptian art.

When the doctor released me I went looking for Mary. I still had nothing but the Old Man's word for it, but I had more than a suspicion that I had made a big hairy thing of myself. I did not expect her to be glad to see me, but I had to speak my piece.

You would think that a tall, handsome redhead would be as easy to find as flat ground in Kansas. She would have been had she been a member of the in staff, but she was a field agent. Field agents come and go and the resident personnel are encouraged to mind their own business. Doris had not seen her again—so she said—and was annoyed that I should want to find her.

The personnel office gave me the bland brush off. I was not inquiring officially, I did not know the agent's name, and just who did I think I was, anyway? They referred me to Operations, meaning the Old Man. That did not suit me.

I had no more luck and met with even more suspicion when I tried the door tally; I began to feel like a spy in my own section.

I went to the bio lab, could not find its chief, and talked to an assistant. He did not know anything about a girl in connection with Project Interview; the subject had been a man—he knew; he had seen the stereo. I told him to take a close look at me. He did and said, "Oh, were you that guy? Pal, you sure took a beating." He went back to scratching himself and shuffling reports.

I left without saying thank you and went to the Old Man's office. There seemed to be no choice.

There was a new face at Miss Haines's desk. I never saw Miss Haines again after the night I got taken. Nor did I ask what had become of her; I did not want to know. The new secretary passed in my I.D. code and, for a wonder, the Old Man was in and would see me.

"What do you want?" he said grumpily.

I said, "Thought you might have some work for me," which was not at all what I intended to say.

"Matter of fact, I was just fixing to send for you. You've loafed long enough." He barked something at his desk phone, stood up and said, "Come!"

I felt suddenly at peace, and followed him. "Cosmetics?" I asked.

"Your own ugly face will do. We're headed for Washington." Nevertheless we did stop in Cosmetics, but only for street clothes. I drew a gun—my own had gone where the woodbine twineth—and had my phone checked.

The door guard made us bare our backs before he would let us approach and check out. Then we tucked our shirts in and went on up, coming out in the lower levels of New Philadelphia, the first I had known as to the location of the Section's new base. "I take it this burg is clean?" I said to the Old Man.

"If you do, you are rusty in the head," he answered. "Keep your eyes peeled."

There was no opportunity for more questions. The presence of so many fully clothed humans bothered me; I found myself drawing away from people and watching for round shoulders. Getting into a crowded elevator to go up to the launching platform seemed downright reckless. When we were in our car and the controls set, I said so.

"What in the devil do the authorities in that dump think they are doing? I could swear that at least one cop we passed was wearing a hump."

"Possibly. Even probably."

"Well, for crying in church! What goes on? I thought you had this job taped and that we were fighting back on all fronts."

"We're trying to. What would you suggest we do about it?"

"Why, it's obvious—even if it were freezing cold, we ought not to see a back covered up anywhere, not until we know they are all dead."

"That's right."

"Well, then—Look, the President knows the score, doesn't he? I understand that—"

"He knows it."

"What's he waiting for? For the whole country to be taken over? He should declare martial law and get action. You told him, a long time ago."

"So I did." The Old Man stared down at the country-side. "Son, are you under the impression that the President runs the country?"

"Of course not. But he is the only man who can act."

"Mmmm—They sometimes call Premier Tsvetkov 'the Prisoner of the Kremlin'. True or not, the President is the prisoner of Congress."

"You mean Congress hasn't acted?"

"I have spent my time the past several days—ever since we stopped the attempt on the President—trying to help the President convince them. Ever been worked over by a congressional committee, son?"

I tried to figure it out. Here we sat, as stupid as dodoes walking up a gangplank to be slugged—yes, and Homo sapiens would be as extinct as the dodo if we did not move. Presently the Old Man said, "It's time you learned the political facts of life. Congresses have refused to act in the face of dangers more obvious than this one. This one isn't obvious, not until a man has had it in his lap, the way we have. The evidence is slim and hard to believe."

"But how about the Assistant Secretary of the Treasury? They can't ignore that."

"Can't they? The Assistant Secretary had one snatched off his back, right in the East Wing, and we killed two of his Secret Service guards. And now the honorable gent is in Walter Reed with a nervous breakdown and can't recall what happened. The Treasury Department gave out that an attempt to assassinate the President had been foiled—true, but not the way they meant it."

"And the President held still for that?"

"His advisers told him to wait until he can get congressional support. His majority is uncertain at best and there are stalwart statesmen in both houses who want his head on a platter. Party politics is a rough game."

"Good Lord, partisanship doesn't figure in a case like this!"

The Old Man cocked an eyebrow. "You think not, eh?"

I finally managed to ask him the question I had come into his office to ask: where was Mary?

"Odd question from you," he grunted. I let it ride; he went on, "Where she should be. Guarding the President."

We went first to a room where a joint special committee was going over evidence. It was a closed session but the Old Man had passes. When we got there they were running stereos; we slipped into seats and watched.

The films were of my anthropoid friend. Napoleon— the ape himself, shots of him with the titan on his back, then close-ups of the titan. It made me sick to see it. One parasite looks like another; but I knew which one this was and I was deeply glad it was dead.

The ape gave way to me myself. I saw myself being clamped into the chair. I hate to admit how I looked; real funk is not pretty. A voice off screen told what was going on.

I saw them lift the titan off the ape and onto my own bare back. Then I fainted in the picture—and almost fainted again. I won't describe it and it upsets me to tell about it. I saw myself writhing under the shocks given the titan—and I writhed again. At one point I tore my right hand free of the clamps, something I had not known, but which explained why my wrist was still not healed.

And I saw the thing die. That was worth sitting through the rest.

The film ended and the chairman said, "Well, gentlemen?"

"Mr. Chairman!"

"The gentleman from Indiana is recognized."

"Speaking without prejudice to the issue, I must say that I have seen better trick photography from Hollywood." They tittered and someone called out, "Hear! Hear!" I knew the ball game was gone.

The head of our bio lab testified, then I found myself called to the stand. I gave my name, address, and occupation, then perfunctorily was asked a number of questions, about my experiences under the titans. The questions were read from a sheet and the chairman obviously was not familiar with them.

The thing that got me was that they did not want to hear. Two of them were reading newspapers.

There were only two questions from the floor. One senator said to me, "Mr. Nivens—your name is Nivens?"

I agreed that it was. "Mr. Nivens," he went on, "you say that you are an investigator?"

"Yes."

"F.B.I., no doubt?"

"No, my chief reports directly to the President."

The senator smiled. "Just as I thought. Now Mr. Nivens, you say you are an investigator—but as a matter of fact you are an actor, are you not?" He seemed to be consulting notes.

I tried to tell too much truth. I wanted to say that I had once acted one season of summer stock but that I was, nevertheless, a real, live, sure—enough investigator. I got no chance. "That will do, Mr. Nivens. Thank you."

The other question was put to me by an elderly senator whose name I should have known. He wanted to know my views on using tax money to arm other countries—and he used the question to express his own views. My views on that subject are cloudy but it did not matter, as I did not get to express them. The next thing I knew the clerk was saying, "Stand down, Mr. Nivens."

I sat tight. "Look here," I said, "all of you. It's evident

that you don't believe me and think this is a put-up job. Well, for the love of heaven, bring in a lie detector! Or use the sleep test. This hearing is a joke."

The chairman banged his gavel. "Stand down, Mr. Nivens."

I stood.

The Old Man had told me that the purpose of the meeting was to report out a joint resolution declaring total emergency and vesting war powers in the President. The chairman asked if they were ready to consider the resolution. One of the newspaper readers looked up long enough to say, "Mr. Chairman, I call for clearing the committee room."

So we were ejected. I said to the Old Man, "It looks bad to this boy."

"Forget it," he said. "The President knew this gambit had failed when he heard the names of the committee."

"Where does that leave us? Do we wait for the slugs to take over Congress, too?"

"The President goes right ahead with a message to Congress and a request for full powers."

"Will he get them?"

The Old Man screwed up his face. "Frankly, I don't think he stands a chance."

The joint session was secret, of course, but we were present—direct orders of the President, probably. The Old Man and I were on that little balcony business back of the Speaker's rostrum. They opened it with full rigamarole and then went through the ceremony of appointing two members from each house to notify the President.

I suppose he was right outside for he came in at once,

escorted by the delegation. His guards were with him—
but they were all our men.

Mary was with him, too. Somebody set up a folding
chair for her, right by the President. She fiddled with a
notebook and handed papers to him, pretending to be a
secretary. But the disguise ended there; she had it
turned on full blast and looked like Cleopatra on a warm
night—and as out of place as a bed in church. I could
feel them stir; she got as much attention as the President
did.

Even the President noticed it. You could see that he
wished that he had left her at home, but it was too late to
do anything about it without greater embarrassment.

You can bet I noticed her. I caught her eye—and she
gave me a long, slow, sweet smile. I grinned like a collie
pup until the Old Man dug me in the ribs. Then I settled
back and tried to behave but I was happy.

The President made a reasoned explanation of the
situation, why we knew it to be so and what had to be done.
It was as straightforward and rational as an engineering
report, and about as moving. He simply stated facts. He
put aside his notes at the end. "This is such a strange
and terrible emergency, so totally beyond any previous
experience, that I must ask very broad powers to cope
with it. In some areas, martial law must be declared.
Grave invasions of civil guarantees will be necessary, for a
time. The right of free movement must be abridged. The
right to be secure from arbitrary search and seizure must
give way to the right of safety for everyone. Because any
citizen, no matter how respected or how loyal, may be the
unwilling servant of these secret enemies, all citizens must

face some loss of civil rights and personal dignities until this plague is killed.

"With utmost reluctance, I ask that you authorize these necessary steps." With that he sat down.

You can feel a crowd. They were made uneasy, but he did not carry them. The president of the Senate took the gavel and looked at the Senate majority leader; it had been programmed for him to propose the emergency resolution.

Something slipped. I don't know whether the floor leader shook his head or signaled, but he did not take the floor. Meanwhile the delay was getting awkward and there were cries of, "Mister President!" and "Order!"

The Senate president passed over several others and gave the flow to a member of his own party. I recognized the man—Senator Gottlieb, a wheelhorse who would vote for his own lynching if it were on his party's program. He started out by yielding to none in his respect for the Constitution, the Bill of Rights, and, probably, the Grand Canyon. He pointed modestly to his own long and faithful service and spoke well of America's place in history.

I thought he was beating the drum while the boys worked out a new shift—when I suddenly realized that his words were adding up to meaning: he was proposing to suspend the order of business and get on with the impeachment and trial of the President of the United States!

I think I tumbled to it as quickly as anyone; the senator had his proposal so decked out in ritualistic verbiage that it was a wonder that anyone noticed what he was actually saying. I looked at the Old Man.

The Old Man was looking at Mary.

She was looking back at him with an expression of extreme urgency.

The Old Man snatched a pad out of his pocket, scrawled something, wadded it up, and threw it down to Mary. She caught it, opened it, and read it—and passed it to the President.

He was sitting, relaxed and easy—as if one of his oldest friends were not at that moment tearing his name to shreds and, with it, the safety of the Republic. He put on his old-fashioned specs and read the note. He then glanced unhurriedly around at the Old Man and lifted his eyebrows. The Old Man nodded.

The President nudged the Senate president, who, at the President's gesture, bent over him. The President and he exchanged whispers.

Gottlieb was still rumbling along about his deep sorrow, but that there came times when old friendship must give way to a higher duty and therefore—The Senate president banged his gavel. "If the senator please!"

Gottlieb looked startled and said, "I do not yield."

"The senator is not asked to yield. At the request of the President of the United States, because of the importance of what you are saying, the senator is asked to come to the rostrum to speak."

Gottlieb looked puzzled but there was nothing else he could do. He walked slowly toward the front of the house.

Mary's chair blocked the little stairway up to the rostrum. Instead of getting quietly out of the way, she bumbled around, turning and picking up the chair, so that she got even more in the way. Gottlieb stopped and she brushed against him. He caught her arm, as much to steady himself as her. She spoke to him and he to her, but no one else could hear the words. Finally they got around each other and he went on to the front of the rostrum.

The Old Man was quivering like a dog in point. Mary looked up at him and nodded. The Old Man said, "Take him!"

I was over that rail in a flying leap, as if I had been wound up like a crossbow. I landed on Gottlieb's shoulders.

I heard the Old Man shout, "Gloves, son! Gloves!" I did not stop for them. I split the senator's jacket with my bare hands and I could see the slug pulsing under his shirt. I tore the shirt away and anybody could see it.

Six stereo cameras could not have recorded what happened in the next few seconds. I slugged Gottlieb back of the ear to stop his thrashing. Mary was sitting on his legs. The President was standing over me and pointing, while shouting, "There! There! Now you can all see." The Senate president was standing stupefied, waggling his gavel.

The Congress was just a mob, men yelling and women screaming. Above me the Old Man was shouting orders to the presidential guards as if he were standing on a bridge.

We had this in our favor; doors were locked and there were no armed and disciplined men present except the Old Man's own boys. Sergeants-at-arms, surely—but what are they? One elderly Congressman pulled a hogleg out of his coat that must have been a museum piece, but that was a mere incident.

Between the guns of the guards and the pounding of the gavel something like order was restored. The

President started to talk. He told them that an amazing accident had given them a chance to see the true nature of the enemy and he suggested that they file past and see for themselves one of the titans from Saturn's largest moon. Without waiting for their consent, he pointed to the front row and told them to come up.

They came.

I squatted back out of the way and wondered what was accidental about it. With the Old Man you can never tell. Had he known that Congress was infested? I rubbed a bruised knee and wondered.

Mary stayed on the platform. About twenty had filed by and a female Congressman had gotten hysterics when I saw Mary signal the Old Man again. This time I was a hair ahead of his order.

I might have had quite a fight if two of the boys had not been close by; this one was young and tough, an ex-marine. We laid him beside Gottlieb, and again the Old Man and the President and the Senate president, shouting their lungs out, restored order.

Then it was "inspection and search" whether they liked it or not. I patted the women on the back as they came by and caught one. I thought I had caught another, but it was an embarrassing mistake; she was so blubber fat that I guessed wrong.

Mary spotted two more, then there was a long stretch, three hundred or more, with no jackpots. It was soon evident that some were hanging back.

Don't let anyone tell you that Congressmen are stupid. It takes brains to get elected and it takes a practical psychologist to stay elected. Eight men with guns were not enough—eleven, counting the Old Man, Mary, and me. Most of the slugs would have gotten away if the Whip of the House had not organized help.

With their assistance, we caught thirteen, ten alive. Only one of the hosts was badly wounded.

But the Congress of the United States has not been such a shambles since Jefferson Davis announced his momentous decision. No, not even after the Bombing.

Chapter 13

So the President got the authority he needed and the Old Man was his de facto chief of staff; at last we could move fast and effectively. Oh, yes? Did you ever try to hurry a project through a bureaucracy?

"Directives" have to be "implemented"; "agencies" have to be "coordinated"—and everything has to go to the files.

The Old Man had a simple enough campaign in mind. It could not be the straightforward quarantine he had proposed when the infection was limited to the Des Moines area; before we could fight back, we had to locate them. But government agents couldn't search two hundred million people; the people had to do it themselves.

Schedule Bare Back was to be the first phase of the implementation of Operation Parasite—which makes me talk like a bureaucrat. Never mind—the idea was that everybody, everybody was to peel to the waist and stay peeled, until all titans were spotted and killed. Oh, women could have halter strings across their backs, but a parasite could not hide under a bra string.

We whipped up a visual presentation to go with the stereocast speech the President would make to the nation. Fast work had saved seven of the parasites we had flushed in the sacred halls of Congress and now they were alive on animal hosts. We could show them and we could show the less grisly parts of the film taken of me. The President himself would appear in the 'cast in shorts, and models would demonstrate what the Well Undressed Citizen Would Wear This Season, including the metal head-and-spine armor which was intended to protect a person even if a parasite got to him in his sleep.

We got it ready in one black-coffee night and the President's writers had his lines ready for him. The smash finish was to show Congress in session, discussing the emergency, and every man, woman, and page boy showing a bare back to the camera.

With twenty-eight minutes left until stereocast time the President got a call from up the street. I was present; the Old Man had been with the President all night, and had kept me around for chores. Mary was there, of course; the President was her special charge. We were all in shorts; Schedule Bare Back had already started in the White House. The only ones who looked comfortable in the get-up were Mary, who can wear anything, the colored doorman, who carried himself like a Zulu king, and the President himself, whose innate dignity could not be touched.

When the call came in the President did not bother to cut us out of his end of the conversation. "Speaking," he said. Presently he added, "You feel certain? Very well, John, what do you advise. . . . I see. No, I don't think that would work. . . . I had better come up the street. Tell them to be ready." He pushed back the phone, his face still serene, and turned to an assistant. "Tell them to hold up the broadcast." He turned to the Old Man. "Come, Andrew, we must go to the Capitol."

He sent for his valet and retired into a dressing room adjoining his office; when he came out, he was formally dressed for a state occasion. He offered no explanation, the Old Man raised an eyebrow but said nothing and I did not dare say anything. The rest of us stayed in our goose-flesh specials and so we went to the Capitol.

It was a joint session, the second in less than twenty-four hours. We trooped in, and I got that no-pants-in-church nightmare feeling, for the Congressmen and senators were dressed as usual. Then I saw that the page boys were in shorts without shirts and felt somewhat better.

I still don't understand it. It seems that some people would rather be dead than lose dignity, with senators high on the list. Congressmen, too—a Congressman is a man who wants to be a senator. They had given the President all the authority he asked for; Schedule Bare Back itself had been discussed and approved-but they did not see where it applied to them. After all, they had been searched and cleaned out; Congress was the only group in the country known to be free of titans.

Maybe some saw the holes in the argument, but not one wanted to be first in a public striptease. Face and dignity are indispensable to an office holder. They sat tight, fully dressed.

When the President took the rostrum, he simply looked at them until he got dead silence. Then slowly, calmly, he started taking off clothes.

He stopped when he was bare to the waist. He had had me worried for a moment; I think he had others worried. He then turned slowly around, lifting his arms. At last he spoke.

"I did that," he said, "so that you might see for yourself that your Chief Executive is not a prisoner of the enemy." He paused.

"But how about you?" That last word was flung at them.

The President punched a finger at the junior Whip. "Mark Cummings—how about you? Are you a loyal citizen or are you a zombie spy? Get up! Get your shirt off!"

"Mister President—" It was Charity Evans, from the State of Maine, looking like a pretty schoolteacher. She stood and I saw that, while she was fully dressed, she was in evening dress. Her gown reached to the floor, but was cut as deep as could be above. She turned like a mannequin; in back the dress ended at the base of her spine; in front it came up in two well-filled scallops. "Is this satisfactory, Mr. President?"

"Quite satisfactory, madam."

Cummings was on his feet and fumbling at his jacket; his face was scarlet. Someone stood up in the middle of the hall.

It was Senator Gottlieb. He looked as if he should have been in bed; his cheeks were gray and sunken; his lips showed cyanosis. But he held himself erect and, with incredible dignity, followed the President's example. His old-fashioned underwear was a one-piece job; he wriggled his arms out and let it dangle over his galluses. Then he, too, turned all the way around; on his back, scarlet against his fish-white flesh, was the mark of the parasite.

He spoke. "Last night I stood here and said things I would rather have been flayed alive than utter. But last night I was not my own master. Today I am. Can you not see that Rome is burning?" Suddenly he had a gun in his hand. "Up on your feet, you wardheelers, you courthouse loafers! Two minutes to get your duds off and show a bare back—then I shoot!"

Men close to him sprang up and tried to grab his arm, but he swung the gun around like a flyswatter, smashing one of them in the face. I had my own out, ready to back his play, but it was not necessary. They could see that he was as dangerous as an old bull and they backed away.

It hung in balance, then they started shucking clothes like Doukhobors. One man bolted for a door; he was tripped. No, he was not wearing a parasite.

But we did catch three. After that, the show went on the channels, ten minutes late, and Congress started the first of its "bare back" sessions.

🦅 Chapter 14 🦅

"LOCK YOUR DOORS!"
"CLOSE THE DAMPERS ON YOUR FIREPLACES!"
"NEVER ENTER A DARK PLACE!"
"BE WARY OF CROWDS!"
"A MAN WEARING A COAT IS AN ENEMY—SHOOT!"

We should have had every titan in the country spotted and killed in a week. I don't know what more we could have done. In addition to a steady barrage of propaganda the country was being quartered and sectioned from the air, searching for flying saucers on the ground. Our radar screen was on full alert for unidentified blips. Military units, from airborne troops to guided-rocket stations, were ready to smear any that landed.

Then nothing happened. There was no work for them to do. The thing fizzled like a damp firecracker.

In the uncontaminated areas people took off their shirts, willingly or reluctantly, looked around them and found no parasites. They watched their newscasts and wondered and waited for the government to tell them that the danger was over. But nothing happened and both laymen and local officials began to doubt the necessity of running around the streets in sunbathing costumes. We had shouted "Wolf!" and no wolf came.

The contaminated areas? The reports from the contaminated areas were not materially different from the reports from other areas.

Our stereocast and the follow-ups did not reach those areas. Back in the days of radio it could not have happened; the Washington station where the 'cast originated could have blanketed the country. But stereo-video rides wavelengths so short that horizon-to-horizon relay is necessary and local channels must be squirted out of local stations; it's the price we pay for plenty of channels and high resolution pictures.

In the infected areas the slugs controlled the local stations; the people never heard the warning.

But in Washington we had every reason to believe that they had heard the warning. Reports came back from— well, Iowa, for example, just like those from California. The governor of Iowa was one of the first to send a message to the President, promising full cooperation. The Iowa state police were already cruising the roads, he reported, stopping everybody and requiring them to strip to the waist. Air travel above Iowa was stopped for the duration of the emergency, just as the President had urged.

There was even a relayed stereo of the governor addressing his constituents, bare to the waist. He faced the camera and I wanted to tell him to turn around. But presently they cut to another camera and we had a close up of a bare back, while the governor's voice went cheerfully on, urging all citizens to work with the police.

If any place in the Union was a pest house of slugs, Iowa should have been it. Had they evacuated Iowa and concentrated on heavier centers of population?

We were gathered in a conference room off the President's office. The President had kept the Old Man with him, I tagged along, and Mary was still on watch. Secretary of Security Martinez was there as well as the Supreme Chief of Staff, Air Marshal Rexton. There were others from the President's "fishing cabinet", but they weren't important.

The President watched the 'cast from Iowa and turned to the Old Man. "Well, Andrew? I thought Iowa was a place we would have to fence off."

The Old Man grunted.

Marshal Rexton said, "As I figure it—mind you, I have not had much time to evaluate this situation—they have gone underground. We may have to comb every inch of every suspicious area."

The Old Man grunted again. "Combing Iowa, corn shock by corn shock, does not appeal to me."

"How else would you tackle it, sir?"

"Figure your enemy! He can't go underground. He can't live without a host."

"Very well—assuming that is true, how many parasites would you say are in Iowa?"

"Damn it, how should I know? They didn't take me into their confidence."

"Suppose we make a top estimate. If—"

The Old Man interrupted him. "You've got no basis for an estimate. Can't you folks see that the titans have won another round?"

"Eh?"

"You just heard the governor; they let us look at his back—or somebody's back. Did you notice that he didn't turn around in front of the camera?"

"But he did," someone said. "I saw him."

"I certainly had the impression that I saw him turn," said the President slowly. "You are suggesting that Governor Packer is himself possessed?"

"Correct. You saw what you were meant to see. There was a camera cut just before he was fully turned; people hardly ever notice them; they are used to them. Depend on it. Mister President, every message out of Iowa is faked."

The President looked thoughtful. Secretary Martinez shook his head emphatically and said, "Impossible. Granted that the governor's message could have been faked—a clever character actor could have faked it. Remember the inaugural address in the crisis of '96, when the President Elect was laid up with pneumonia? Granted that one such 'cast could be faked, we've had our choice of dozens of 'casts from Iowa. How about that street scene in Des Moines? Don't tell me you can fake hundreds of people dashing around stripped to their waists—or do your parasites practice mass hypnotic control?"

"They can't that I know of," conceded the Old Man. "If they can, we might as well throw in the towel and admit that the human race has been superseded. But what made you think that that 'cast came from Iowa?"

"Eh? Why, damn it, sir, it came over the Iowa channel."

"Proving what? Did you read any street signs? It looked like any typical street in a downtown retail district. Never mind what city the announcer told you it was; what city was it?"

The Secretary let his mouth hang open. I've got fairly close to the "camera eye" that detectives are supposed to have; I let that picture run through my mind—and I not only could not tell what city, I could not even place the part of the country. It could have been Memphis, Seattle, or Boston—or none of them. Allowing for special cases like Canal Street in New Orleans, or Denver's Civic Center, the downtown districts in American cities are as standardized as barber shops.

"Never mind," the Old Man went on. "I couldn't tell and I was looking for landmarks. The explanation is simple; the Des Moines station picked up a Schedule Bare Back street scene from some city not contaminated and rechanneled it under their own commentary. They chopped out anything that would localize it . . . and we swallowed it. Gentlemen, this enemy knows us, inside and out. This campaign has been planned in great detail and they are ready to outwit us in almost any move we can make."

"Aren't you being an alarmist, Andrew?" said the President. "There is another possibility, that the titans have moved somewhere else."

"They are still in Iowa," the Old Man said flatly, "but you won't prove it with that thing." He gestured at the stereo tank.

Secretary Martinez squirmed. "This is ridiculous!" he exclaimed. "You are saying that we can't get a correct report out of Iowa, as if it were occupied territory."

"That is what it is."

"But I stopped off in Des Moines two days ago, coming back from Alaska. Everything was normal. Mind you, I grant the existence of your parasites, though I haven't seen one. But let's find them where they are and root them out, instead of dreaming up fantasies."

The Old Man looked tired and I felt tired. I wondered how many ordinary people were taking it seriously, if this was what we ran into at the top.

Finally the Old Man replied, "Control the communications of a country and you control the country; that's elementary. You had better take fast steps. Mister Secretary, or you won't have any communications left."

"But I was merely—"

"You root 'em out!" the Old Man said rudely. "I've told you they are in Iowa and in New Orleans, and a dozen other spots. My job is finished. You are Secretary of Security; you root 'em out." He stood up and said, "Mister President, I've had a long pull for a man my age; when I lose sleep I lose my temper. Could I be excused?"

"Certainly, Andrew." He had not lost his temper and I think the President knew it. He doesn't lose his temper; he makes other people lose theirs.

Before the Old Man could say goodnight, Secretary Martinez interrupted. "Wait a moment! You've made some flat-footed statements. Let's check up on them." He turned to the Chief of Staff. "Rexton!"

"Uh, yes, sir."

"That new post near Des Moines, Fort something-or-other, named after what's-his-name?"

"Fort Patton."

"That's it, that's it. Well, let's not dally; get them on the command circuit—"

"With visual," put in the Old Man.

"With visual, of course, and we'll show this—I mean we'll get the true situation in Iowa."

The Air Marshal handed a by-your-leave-sir to the President, went to the stereo tank and patched in with Security General Headquarters. He asked for the officer of the watch at Fort Patton, Iowa.

Shortly thereafter the stereo tank showed the inside of a military communications center. Filling the foreground was a young officer. His rank and corps showed on his cap, but his chest was bare. Martinez turned triumphantly to the Old Man. "You see?"

"I see."

"Now to make certain. Lieutenant!"

"Yes, sir!" The young fellow looked awestruck and kept glancing from one famous face to another. Reception and bi-angle were in synch; the eyes of the image looked where they seemed to look, as if he were actually sitting in the receiver tank.

"Stand up and turn around," Martinez continued.

"Uh? Why, certainly, sir." He seemed puzzled, but he did so—and it took him almost out of scan. We could see his bare back, up to about the short ribs—no higher.

"Confound it!" shouted Martinez. "Sit down and turn around."

"Yessir!" The youth seemed flustered. He leaned over

the desk and added, "Just a moment while I widen the view angle, sir."

The picture suddenly melted and rippling rainbows chased across the tank. The young officer's voice was still coming over the audio channel. "There—is that better, sir?"

"Damn it, we can't see a thing!"

"You can't? Just a moment, sir."

We could hear him breathing heavily. Suddenly the tank came to life and I thought for a moment that we were back at Fort Patton. But it was a major on the screen this time and the place looked larger. "Supreme Headquarters," the image announced, "Communications officer of the watch. Major Donovan."

"Major," Martinez said in controlled tones, "I was hooked in with Fort Patton. What happened?"

"Yes, sir; I was monitoring it. We've had a slight technical difficulty on that channel. We'll put your call through again in a moment."

"Well, hurry!"

"Yes, sir." The tank rippled and went empty.

The Old Man stood up again. "Call me when you've cleared up that 'slight technical difficulty'. Meantime, I'm going to bed."

Chapter 15

If I have given the impression that Secretary Martinez was stupid, I am sorry. Everyone had trouble at first believing what the slugs could do. You have to see one, then you believe in the pit of your stomach.

There were no flies on Air Marshal Rexton, either. The two must have worked all night, after convincing themselves by more calls to known danger spots that "technical interruptions" do not occur so conveniently. They called the Old Man about four a.m. and he called me, using our special phones. Those flesh-embedded receptors should not be used as alarm clocks; it's too rough a way to wake a man.

They were in the same conference room, Martinez, Rexton, a couple of his high brass, and the Old Man. The President came in, wearing a bathrobe and followed by Mary, just as I arrived. Martinez started to speak but the Old Man cut in. "Let's see your back, Tom!"

The President looked surprised and Mary signaled

that everything was okay, but the Old Man chose not to see her. "I mean it," he persisted.

The President said quietly, "Perfectly correct, Andrew," and slipped his robe off his shoulders. His back was clean. "If I don't set an example, how can I expect others to cooperate?"

The Old Man started to help him back into the robe, but the President shrugged him off and hung it over a chair. "I'll just have to acquire new habits. Difficult, at my age. Well, gentlemen?"

I thought myself that bare skin would take getting used to; we made an odd group. Martinez was lean and tanned, carved smooth from mahogany. I'd judge he was part Indian. Rexton had a burned-in, high-altitude tan on his face, but from his collar line down he was as white as the President. On his chest was a black cross of hair, armpit to armpit and chin to belly, while the President and the Old Man were covered front and back with grizzled, wiry fur. The Old Man's mat was so thick that mice could have nested in it.

Mary looked like a publicity pic—low angle shot to bring out the legs and careful posing, that sort. Me—well. I'm the spiritual type.

Martinez and Rexton had been shoving push pins into a map, red for bad, green for good, and a few amber ones. Reports were still coming and Rexton's assistants kept adding new pins.

Iowa looked like measles; New Orleans and the Teche country were as bad. So was Kansas City. The upper end of the Missouri-Mississippi system, from Minneapolis and St. Paul down to St. Louis, was clearly enemy territory.

There were fewer red pins from there down to New Orleans—but there were no green ones.

There was another hot spot around El Paso and two on the East Coast.

The President looked it over calmly. "We shall need the help of Canada and Mexico," he said. "Any reports?"

"None that mean anything, sir."

"Canada and Mexico," the Old Man said seriously, "will be just a start. You are going to need the whole world with you on this job."

Rexton said, "We will, eh? How about Russia?"

Nobody had an answer to that one; nobody ever has. Too big to occupy and too big to ignore—World War III had not settled the Russian problem and no war ever would. The parasites might feel right at home behind the Curtain.

The President said, "We'll deal with that when we come to it." He drew a finger across the map. "Any trouble getting messages through to the Coast?"

"Apparently not, sir," Rexton told him. "They don't seem to interfere with straight-through relay. But all military communications I have shifted to one-link relay through the space stations." He glanced at his watch finger. "Space Station Gamma, at the moment."

"Hmmm—" said the President. "Andrew, could these things storm a space station?"

"How would I know?" the Old Man answered testily. "I don't know whether their ships are built for it or not. More probably they would do it by infiltration, through the supply rockets."

There was discussion as to whether or not the space

stations could already have been taken over; Schedule Bare Back did not apply to the stations. Although we had built them and paid for them, since they were technically United Nations territory, the President had to wait until the United Nations acted on the entire matter.

"Don't worry about it," Rexton said suddenly.

"Why not?" the President asked.

"I am probably the only one here who has done duty in a space station. Gentlemen, the costume we are now wearing is customary in a station. A man fully dressed would stand out like an overcoat on the beach. But we'll see." He gave orders to one of his assistants.

The President resumed studying the map. "So far as we know," he said, pointing to Grinnell, Iowa, "all this derives from a single landing, here."

The Old Man answered, "Yes—so far as we know."

I said, "Oh, no!"

They all looked at me and I was embarrassed. "Go ahead," said the President.

"There were at least three more landings—I know there were—before I was rescued."

The Old Man looked dumbfounded. "Are you sure, son? We thought we had wrung you dry."

"Of course I'm sure."

"Why didn't you mention it?"

"I never thought of it before." I tried to explain how it feels to be possessed, how you know what is going on, but everything seems dreamy, equally important and equally unimportant. I grew quite upset. I am not the jittery type, but being ridden by a master does something to you.

The Old Man put his hand on me and said, "Steady

down, son." The President said something soothing and gave me a reassuring smile. That stereocast personality of his is not put on; he's really got it.

Rexton said, "The important point is: where did they land? We might still capture one."

"I doubt it," the Old Man answered. "They did a cover-up on the first one in a matter of hours. If it was the first one," he added thoughtfully.

I went to the map and tried to think. Sweating, I pointed to New Orleans. "I'm pretty sure one was about here." I stared at the map. "I don't know where the others landed. But I know they did."

"How about here?" Rexton asked, pointing to the East Coast.

"I don't know. I don't know."

The Old Man pointed to the other East Coast danger spot. "We know this one is a secondary infection." He was kind enough not to say that I had been the means of infecting it.

"Can't you remember anything else?" Martinez said testily. "Think, man!"

"I just don't know. We never knew what they were up to, not really." I thought until my skull ached, then pointed to Kansas City. "I sent several messages here, but I don't know whether they were shipment orders, or not."

Rexton looked at the map; around Kansas City was almost as pin-studded as Iowa. "We'll assume a landing near Kansas City, too. The technical boys can do a problem on it. It may be subject to logistic analysis; we might derive the other landing."

"Or landings," added the Old Man.

"Eh? 'Or landings'. Certainly. But we need more reports." He turned back to the map and stared at it thoughtfully.

🖝 Chapter 16 🖜

Hindsight is confoundedly futile. At the moment the first saucer landed the menace could have been stamped out by one determined man and a bomb. At the time "The Cavanaughs"—Mary, the Old Man, and I—reconnoitered around Grinnell and in Des Moines, we three alone might have killed every slug had we been ruthless and, more important, known where they all were.

Had Schedule Bare Back been ordered during the fortnight after the first landing it alone might have turned the trick. But by the next day it was clear that Schedule Bare Back had failed as an offensive measure. As a defense it was useful; the uncontaminated areas could be kept so, as long as the slugs could not conceal themselves. It had even had mild success in offense; areas contaminated but not "secured" by the parasites were cleaned up at once . . . Washington itself, for example, and New Philadelphia. New Brooklyn, too—there I had been able to give specific advice. The entire East Coast turned from red to green.

But as the area down the middle of the country filled in on the map, it filled in red, and stayed so. The infected areas stood out in ruby light now, for the simple wall map studded with push pins had been replaced by a huge electronic military map, ten miles to the inch, covering one wall of the conference room. It was a repeater map, the master being located down in the sublevels of the New Pentagon.

The country was split in two, as if a giant had washed red pigment down the Central Valley. Two zigzag amber paths bordered the great band held by the slugs; these were overlap, the only areas of real activity, places where line-of-sight reception was possible from both stations held by the enemy and from stations still in the hands of free men. One such started near Minneapolis, swung west of Chicago and east of St. Louis, then meandered through Tennessee and Alabama to the Gulf. The other cut a wide path through the Great Plains and came out near Corpus Christi. El Paso was the center of a ruby area as yet unconnected with the main body.

I looked at the map and wondered what was going on in those border strips. I had the room to myself; the Cabinet was meeting and the President had taken the Old Man with him. Rexton and his brass had left earlier. I stayed there because I had not been told where to go and I hesitated to wander around in the White House. So I stayed and fretted and watched amber lights blink red and, much less frequently, red lights blink amber or green.

I wondered how an overnight visitor with no status managed to get breakfast? I had been up since four and my total nourishment so far had been one cup of coffee,

served by the President's valet. Even more urgently I
wanted to find a washroom. I knew where the President's
washroom was, but I did not have the nerve to use it,
feeling vaguely that to do so would be somewhere
between high treason and disorderly conduct.

There was not a guard in sight. Probably the room was
being scanned from a board somewhere; I suppose every
room in the White House has an "eye & ear" in it; but
there was no one physically in view.

At last I got desperate enough to start trying doors.
The first two were locked; the third was what I was
looking for. It was not marked "Sacred to the Chief" nor
did it appear to be booby-trapped, so I used it.

When I came back into the conference room, Mary
was there.

I looked at her stupidly for a moment. "I thought you
were with the President?"

She smiled. "I was, but I got chased out. The Old Man
took over for me."

I said, "Say, Mary, I've been wanting to talk with you
and this is the first chance I've had. I guess I—Well,
anyway, I shouldn't have, I mean, according to the Old
Man—" I stopped, my carefully rehearsed speech in ruins.
"Anyhow, I shouldn't have said what I did," I concluded
miserably.

She put a hand on my arm. "Sam. Sam, my very dear,
do not be troubled. What you said and what you did was
fair enough from what you knew. The important thing, to
me, is what you did for me. The rest does not matter—
except that I am happy again to know that you don't
despise me."

"Well, but—Damn it, don't be so noble! I can't stand it!"

She gave me a merry, lively smile, not at all like the gentle one with which she had greeted me. "Sam, I think you like your women to be a little bit bitchy. I warn you, I can be so." She went on, "You are still worried about that slap, too, I think. All right, I'll pay it back." She reached up and patted me gently on the cheek, once. "There, it's paid back and you can forget it."

Her expression suddenly changed, she swung on me—and I thought the top of my head was coming off. "And that," she said in a tense, hoarse whisper, "pays you back the one I got from your girlfriend!"

My ears were ringing and my eyes did not want to focus. If I had not seen her bare palm, I would have sworn that she had used at least a two-by-four.

She looked at me, wary and defiant, not the least apologetic—angry, rather, if dilated nostrils meant anything. I raised a hand and she tensed—but I just wanted to touch my stinging cheek. It was very sore. "She's not my girlfriend," I said lamely.

We eyed each other and simultaneously burst out laughing. She put both her hands on my shoulders and let her head collapse on my right one, still laughing. "Sam," she managed to say, "I'm so sorry. I shouldn't have done it—not to you, Sam. At least I shouldn't have slapped you so hard."

"The devil you're sorry," I growled, "but you shouldn't have put English on it. You damn near took the hide off."

"Poor Sam!" She reached up and touched it; it hurt. "She's really not your girlfriend?"

"No, worse luck. But not from lack of my trying."

"I'm sure it wasn't. Who is your girlfriend, Sam?" The words seem coquettish; she did not make them so.

"You are, you vixen!"

"Yes," she said comfortably, "I am—if you'll have me. I told you that before. And I meant it. Bought and paid for."

She was waiting to be kissed; I pushed her away. "Confound it, woman, I don't want you 'bought and paid for'."

It did not faze her. "I put it badly. Paid for—but not bought. I'm here because I want to be here. Now will you kiss me, please?"

So help me, up to that moment she had not turned on the sex, not really. When she saw that the answer was yes, she did so and it was like summer sun coming out from a cloud. That is inadequate but it will have to do.

She had kissed me once before; this time she kissed me. The French are smart; they have two words for it . . . this was the other one. I felt myself sinking into a warm golden haze and I did not ever want to come up.

Finally I had to break and gasped. "I think I'll sit down for a minute."

She said, "Thank you, Sam," and let me.

"Mary," I said presently, "Mary, my dear, there is something you possibly could do for me."

"Yes?" she said eagerly.

"Tell me how in the name of Ned a person gets anything to eat around here? I'm starved. No breakfast."

She looked startled; I suppose she had expected something else. But she answered, "Why, certainly!"

I don't know where she went nor how she did it. She

may have butted into the White House pantry and helped herself. But she returned in a few minutes with a tray of sandwiches and two bottles of beer. Corned beef and rye put the roses back in my cheeks. I was cleaning up my third when I said, "Mary, how long do you figure that meeting will last?"

"Let me see," she answered, "fourteen people, including the Old Man. I give it a minimum of two hours. Why?"

"In that case," I said, swallowing the last bite, "we have time to duck out of here, find a registry office, get married, and get back before the Old Man misses us."

She did not answer and she did not look at me. Instead she stared at the bubbles in her beer. "Well?" I insisted.

She raised her eyes. "I'll do it if you say so. I'm not welshing. But I'm not going to start out by lying to you. I would rather we didn't."

"You don't want to marry me?"

"Sam, I don't think you are ready to get married."

"Speak for yourself!"

"Don't be angry, my dear. I'm not holding out—honest. You can have me with or without a contract, anywhere, anywhen, anyway. But you don't know me yet. Get acquainted with me; you might change your mind."

"I'm not in the habit of changing my mind." She glanced up without answering, then looked away sadly. I felt my face get hot. "That was a very special circumstance," I protested. "It could not happen to us again in a hundred years. That wasn't really me talking; it was—"

She stopped me. "I know, Sam. And now you want to prove to me that it didn't really happen or at least that you are sure of your own mind now. But you don't have to prove anything. I won't run out on you and I don't mistrust you. Take me away on a weekend; better yet, move into my apartment. If you find that I wear well, there's always time to make me what great grandmother called an 'honest woman', heaven knows why."

I must have looked sullen; I felt so. She put a hand on mine and said seriously, "Take a look at the map, Sam."

I turned my head and looked. Red as ever, or more so—it seemed to me that the danger zone around El Paso had increased. She went on, "Let's get this mess cleaned up first, dear. Then, if you still want to, ask me again. In the meantime, you can have the privileges without the responsibilities."

What could be fairer than that? The only trouble was that it was not the way I wanted it. Why will a man who has been avoiding marriage like the plague suddenly decide that nothing less will suit him? I had seen it happen a hundred times and never understood it; now I was doing it myself.

Mary had to go back on duty as soon as the meeting was over. The Old Man collared me and took me for a walk. Yes, a walk, though we went only as far as the Baruch Memorial Bench. There he sat down, fiddled with his pipe, and stared into space. The day was as muggy as only Washington can get, but the park was almost deserted. People were not yet used to Schedule Bare Back.

He said, "Schedule Counter Blast starts at midnight."

I said nothing; questioning him was useless.

Presently he added, "We swoop down on every relay

station, broadcast station, newspaper office, and Western Union office in 'Zone Red'."

"Sounds good," I answered. "How many men does it take?"

He did not answer; instead he said, "I don't like it. I don't like it a little bit."

"Huh?"

"See here, bub—the President went on the channels and told everybody to peel off their shirts. We find that the message did not get through into infected territory. What's the next logical development?"

I shrugged. "Schedule Counter Blast, I suppose."

"That hasn't happened yet. Think, it has been more than twenty-four hours: what should have happened and hasn't?"

"Should I know?"

"You should, if you are ever going to amount to anything on your own. Here—" He handed me a combo key. "Scoot out to Kansas City and take a looksee. Stay away from comm stations, cops, and—shucks, you know their attack points better than I do. Stay away from them. Take a look at anything else. And don't get caught." He looked at his finger and added, "Be back here a half hour before midnight, or sooner. Get going."

"A lot of time you allow me to case a whole city," I complained. "It will take nearly three hours just to drive to Kansas City."

"More than three hours," he answered. "Don't attract attention by picking up a ticket."

"You know damn well I'm a careful driver."

"Move."

So I moved, stopping by the White House to pick up my kit. I wasted ten minutes convincing a new guard that I really had been there overnight and actually had possessions to pick up.

The combo was to the car we had come down in; I picked it up at Rock Creek Park platform. Traffic was light and I commented on it to the dispatcher as I handed in the combo. "Freight and commercial carriers are grounded," he answered. "The emergency—you got a military clearance?"

I knew I could get one by phoning the Old Man, but bothering him about minutiae does not endear one to him. I said, "Check the number."

He shrugged and slipped the combo in his machine. My hunch had been right; his eyebrows shot up and he handed it back. "How you rate!" he commented. "You must be the President's fair-haired boy."

He did not ask for my destination and I did not offer it. His machine probably broke into "Hail, Columbia!" when the Old Man's number hit it.

Once launched, I set the controls for Kansas City at legal max and tried to think. The transponder beeped as radar beams hit it each time I slid from one control block into the next, but no faces appeared on the screen. Apparently the Old Man's combo was good for the route, emergency or not.

I began to wonder what would happen when I slipped over into the red areas—and then realized what he had been driving at when he talked about "the next logical development". Would the control net pass me on through into areas we knew darn well were infested by titans?

One tends to think of communications as meaning the line-of-sight channels and nothing else. But "communications" means all traffic of every sort, even dear old Aunt Mamie, headed for California with her head stuffed with gossip. The slugs had seized the channels and the President's proclamation had not gotten through, or so we assumed—but news can't be stopped that easily; such measures merely slow it down. Behind the Soviet Curtain Aunt Sonya does not go on long trips; it ain't healthy. Ergo, if the slugs expected to retain control where they were, seizing the channels would be just their first step.

It stood to reason that they were not numerous enough to interfere with all traffic, but what would they do?

I reached only the unhelpful conclusion that they would do something and that I, being a part of "communications" by definition, had better be prepared for evasive action if I wanted to save my pretty pink skin.

In the meantime the Mississippi River and Zone Red were sliding closer by the minute. I wondered what would happen the first time my recognition signal was picked up by a station controlled by masters. I tried to think like a titan—impossible, I found, even though I had been a slave to one. The idea revolted me.

Well, then, what would a security commissar do if an unfriendly craft flew past the Curtain? Have it shot down, of course. No, that was not the answer; I was probably safe in the air.

But I had better not let them spot me landing. Elementary.

"Elementary" in the face of a traffic control net which was described proudly as the No-Sparrow-Shall-Fall plan.

They boasted that a butterfly could not make a forced landing anywhere in the United States without alerting the search & rescue system. Not quite true—but I was no butterfly.

What I wanted was to land short of the infested area and go in on the ground. On foot I will make a stab at penetrating any security screen, mechanical, electronic, manned, or mixed. But how can you use misdirection in a car making west a full degree every seven minutes? Or hang a stupid, innocent look on the nose of a duo?

If I went in on foot the Old Man would get his report come next Michaelmas; he wanted it before midnight.

Once, in a rare mellow mood, the Old Man told me that he did not bother his agents with detailed instructions—give a man a mission; let him sink or swim. I suggested that his method must use up a lot of agents.

"Some," he had admitted, "but not as many as the other way. I believe in the individual and I try to pick individuals who are survivor types."

"And how in the hell," I had asked him, "do you know when you've got a 'survivor type'."

He had grinned at me wickedly. "A survivor type is an agent who comes back. Then I know."

I had to reach a decision in the next few minutes. Elihu, I said to myself, you are about to find out which type you are—and damn his icy heart!

My course would take me in toward St. Louis, swing me in the city loop around St. Louis, and on to Kansas City. But St. Louis was in Zone Red. The military-situation map had showed Chicago as still green; as I remembered it the amber line had zigzagged west somewhere above Hannibal, Missouri—and I wanted very badly to cross the Mississippi while still in Zone Green. A car crossing that mile-wide river would make a radar blip as sharp as a desert star.

I signaled block control for permission to descend to local-traffic level, then did so without waiting, resuming manual control and cutting my speed. I headed north.

Short of the Springfield loop I headed west again, staying low. When I reached the river I crossed slowly, close to the water, with my transponder shut down. Sure, you can't shut off your radar recognition signal in the air, not in a standard rig—but the Section's cars were not standard. The Old Man was not above using gangster tricks.

I had hopes, if local traffic were being monitored while I crossed, that my blip would be mistaken for a boat on the river. I did not know certainly whether the next block station across the river was Zone Red or Zone Green, but, if my memory was correct, it should be green.

I was about to cut in the transponder again on the assumption that it would be safer, or at least less conspicuous, to get back into the traffic system when I noticed the shoreline opening up ahead of me. The map did not show a tributary there; I judged it to be an inlet, or possibly a new channel cut in the spring floods and not yet mapped. I dropped almost to water level and headed into it. The stream was narrow, meandering, and almost overhung by trees and I had no more business taking a sky car into it than a bee has of flying down a trombone—but it afforded perfect radar "shadow"; I could get lost in it.

In a few minutes I was lost, not only from any monitoring technician, but lost myself, right off the map. The channel switched and turned and cut back and I was so busy bucking the car by hand, trying to keep from crashing that I lost all track of navigation. I swore and wished that the car were a triphib so that I could land on water.

The trees suddenly broke on the left bank; I saw a stretch of level land, kicked her over and squatted her in with a deceleration that nearly cut me in two against my safety belt. But I was down and no longer trying to play catfish in a muddy stream.

I wondered what to do. There seemed to be nobody around; I judged that I was on the back end of someone's farm. No doubt there was a highway close by. I had better find it and stay on the ground.

But I knew that was silly even as I thought it. Three hours from Washington to Kansas City by air—I had completed almost all the trip and now I was how far away from Kansas City? By land, about three hours. At that rate, all I needed to make the trip complete was to park the car ten or twelve miles outside Kansas City and walk; then I would still have three hours to go.

I felt like the frog who jumped halfway to the end of the log with each hop, but never got there. I must get back into the air.

But I did not dare do so until I knew positively whether traffic here was being controlled by free men, or by slugs.

It suddenly occurred to me that I had not turned on the stereo since leaving Washington. I am not much for stereo; between the commercials and the junk they sandwich between them I sometimes wonder about "progress". But a newscast may have uses.

I could not find a newscast. I got (a) a lecture by Myrtle Doolightly, Ph.D., on Why Husbands Grow Bored, sponsored by the Uth-a-gen Hormone Company—I decided that she probably had plenty of experience in her subject; (b) a trio of girl hepsters singing 'If You Mean What I think You Mean, What are We Waiting For?;' (c) an episode in 'Lucretia Learns About Life'.

Dear Doctor Myrtle was fully dressed and could have hidden half a dozen titans around her frame. The trio were dressed about the way one would expect them to be, but they did not turn their backs to the camera. Lucretia appeared to alternate having her clothes torn off with taking them off willingly, but the camera always cut or the lights always went out just before I could check on whether or not her back was bare—of slugs, that is.

And none of it meant anything. Those programs could have been taped weeks or months before the President announced Schedule Bare Back. I was still switching channels, trying to find a newscast—or any live program— when I found myself staring into the professionally unctuous smile of an announcer. He was fully dressed.

Shortly I realized it was one of those silly give-away shows. He was saying: "—and some lucky little woman sitting by her screen right this minute is about to receive, absolutely free, a General Atomics Six-in-One Automatic Home Butler. Who will it be? You? You? Or lucky you! He turned away from scan; I could see his shoulders. They were covered by shirt and jacket and distinctly rounded, almost humped. I was inside Zone Red.

When I switched off I realized that I was being watched—by a male urchin about nine years old. He was wearing nothing but shorts, but the brown of his shoulders showed that such was his custom. I threw back the windscreen. "Hey, bub, where's the highway?"

He continued to stare before replying, "Road to Macon's up there yonder. Say, mister, that's a Cadillac Zipper, ain't it?"

"Sure thing. Where yonder?"

"Give me a ride, huh, will you?"

"Haven't got time. Where's the road?"

He sized me up before answering, "Take me along and I'll show you."

I gave in. While he climbed in and looked around, I opened my kit, got out shirt, trousers, and jackct, and put them on. I said conversationally, "Maybe I shouldn't put on this shirt. Do people around here wear shirts?"

He scowled. "I've got shirts!"

"I didn't say you didn't; I just asked if people around here wore shirts."

"Of course they do. Where do you think you are, mister; Arkansas?"

I gave up and asked again about the road. He said, "Can I punch the button when we take off, huh?"

I explained that we were going to stay on the ground. He was frankly annoyed but condescended to point out a direction. I drove cautiously as the car was heavy for unpaved countryside. Presently he told me to turn. Quite a bit later I stopped the car and said, "Are you going to show me where that road is, or am I going to wallop your backsides?"

He opened the door and slid out. "Hey!" I yelled.

He looked back. "Over that way," he admitted. I turned

the car, not really expecting to find a highway, but finding one, nevertheless, only fifty yards away. The brat had caused me to drive around three sides of a large square.

If you could call it a highway—there was not an ounce of rubber in the paving. Still, it was a road; I followed it to the west. All in all, I had wasted more than an hour.

Macon, Missouri seemed normal—much too normal to be reassuring, as Schedule Bare Back obviously had not been heard of here. There were a number of bare backs, but it was a hot day. There were more backs that were covered and any of them might have concealed a slug. I gave serious thought to checking this town, rather than Kansas City, then beating back the way I had come, while I could. Pushing further into country which I knew to be controlled by the masters made me as nervous as a preacher at a stag party; I wanted to run.

But the Old Man had said "Kansas City"; he would take a dim view of a substitute. Finally I drove the belt around Macon and pulled into a landing flat on the far side. There I queued up for local traffic launching and headed for Kansas City in a mess of farmers' copters and suchlike local craft. I would have to hold local speeds all across the state, but that was safer than getting into the hot pattern with my transponder identifying my car to every block control station.

The field was automatically serviced, no attendants, not even at the fuelling line. It seemed probable that I had managed to enter the Missouri traffic pattern without arousing suspicion. True, there was a block control station back in Illinois which might be wondering where I had gone, but that did not matter.

☞ Chapter 17 ☜

Kansas City is an old-fashioned city; it was not hurt in the bombings; except on the East Side where Independence used to be. Consequently, it was never rebuilt. From the southeast you can drive almost downtown, as far as Swope Park, without having to choose between parking or paying toll to enter the city proper.

One can fly in and make another choice: land in the landing flats north of the Missouri River and take the tunnels into the city, or land on the downtown platforms south of Memorial Hill.

I decided against both of these; I wanted the car near me but I did not want to have to pick it up through a checking system. If it came to a pinch, I could not shoot my way out while offering my combo to a parking attendant. I did not like tunnels in a pinch, either—nor launching platform elevators. A man can be trapped in such.

Frankly I did not want to go into the city at all.

I roaded the car on Route 40 and drove into the

Meyer Boulevard toll gate. The line waiting to pay toll for the doubtful privilege of driving on a city street was quite long; I began to feel hemmed in as soon as another car filled in behind me and wished mightily that I had decided to park and go in by the public passenger ways. But the gatekeeper took my toll without glancing at me. I glanced at him, all right, but could not tell whether or not he was being ridden.

I drove through the gate with a sigh of relief—only to be stopped just beyond the gate. A barrier dropped in front of me and I just managed to stop the car, whereupon a cop stuck his head in the side I had open. "Safety check," he said. "Climb out."

I protested that my car had just been inspected. "No doubt," he agreed, "but the city is having a safety drive. Here's your car check. Pick it up just beyond the barrier. Now get out and go in that door." He pointed to a low building a few steps from the curb.

"What for?"

"Eyesight and reflexes," he explained. "Come on. You're holding up the line."

In my mind's eye, I saw the map, with Kansas City glowing red. That the city was "secured" I was sure; therefore this mild-mannered policeman was almost surely hag-ridden. I did not need to look at his shoulders.

But, short of shooting him and making an emergency take-off from that spot, there was nothing I could do but comply. With a normal, everyday cop I would have tried the bribe direct, slipping him money as he handed me my car check. But titans don't use money.

Or do they?

I got out, grumbling, and walked slowly toward the building. The door near me was marked "IN"; there was one at the far end marked "OUT"; a man came out from it as I approached. I wanted very badly to ask him what he had found.

It was a temporary building with an old-style unpowered door. I pushed it open with a toe and glanced both sides and up before I entered. It seemed safe. Inside was an empty anteroom with open door beyond.

Someone inside called out, "Come in." Still as cautious as the setup permitted, I went in.

There were two men, both in white coats, one with a doctor's speculum strapped to his head. He looked up and said briskly, "This won't take a minute. Step over here." He closed the door I had entered; I heard the latch click.

It was a sweeter setup than we had worked out for the Constitution Club; had I had time I would have admired it. Spread out on a long table were transit cells for masters, already opened and warmed. The second man had one ready—for me, I knew—and was holding it tilted toward him, so that I could not see the slug inside. The transit cells would not arouse alarm in the minds of victims; medical men always have things at hand which are odd to the layman.

As for the rest, I was being invited to place my eyes against the goggles of a quite ordinary visual acuity tester. The "doctor" would keep me there, blindfolded without knowing it and reading test figures, while his "assistant" fitted me with a master. No violence, no slips, no protests.

It was not even necessary, as I had learned during my own "service", to bare the victim's back. Just touch the master to the bare neck, then let the new recruit himself adjust his clothing to cover his master before he left.

"Right over here," the "doctor" repeated. "Place your eyes against the eyepieces."

Moving very quickly I went to the bench on which was mounted the acuity tester and started to comply. Then I turned suddenly around.

The assistant had moved in closer: the cell was ready in his hands. As I turned he tilted it away from me. "Doctor," I said, "I wear contact lenses. Should I take them off?"

"No, no," he snapped. "Let's not waste time."

"But, Doctor," I protested, "I want you to see how they fit. Now I've had a little trouble with this left one—" I lifted both hands and pulled back the upper and lower lids of my left eye. "See?"

He said angrily, "This is not a clinic. Now, if you please—" They were both within reach; lowering my arms in a mighty bear hug I got them both—and grabbed with clutched fingers at the spot between each set of shoulder blades. With each hand I struck something soft and mushy under the coats and felt revulsion shake me at the touch.

Once I saw a cat struck by a ground car; the poor thing leapt straight up about four feet with its back arched the wrong way and all limbs flying. These two unlucky men did the same sort of thing; they contorted in every muscle in a grand spasm as if every motor cell in each body had been stimulated at once.

Which is perhaps just what happened when I clutched and crushed their masters.

I could not hold them; they jerked out of my arms and

flopped to the floor. But there was no need to hold them; after that first boneshaking convulsion they went limp, unconscious, possibly dead.

Someone was knocking at the door. I called out, "Just a moment. The doctor is busy." The knocking stopped. I made sure that the door was fastened, then went back, bent over the "doctor" and pulled up his coat to see what I had done to his master.

The thing was a ruptured, slimy mess, already beginning to stink. So was the one on the other man—which facts pleased me heartily as I was determined to burn the slugs if they were not already dead and I was not sure that I could do so without killing the hosts as well. I left the men, to live or die—or be seized again by titans, as might be. I had no way to help them.

The masters waiting in their cells were another matter. With a fan beam and a max charge I burned them all in seconds only. There were two large crates against the wall. I did not know that they contained masters but I had no reason to believe otherwise; I beamed them through and through until the wood charred.

The knocking at the door resumed. I looked around hastily for somewhere to hide the two men. There was nowhere at all, so I decided to execute the classic military maneuver. As I was about to go out the exit, I felt that something was missing. I hesitated and looked around again.

The room was almost bare; there seemed to be nothing suited to my purpose. I could use clothing from the "doctor" or his helper, but I did not want to touch them. Then I noticed the dust cover for the acuity tester lying on the bench. I loosened my shirt, snatched up the dust cover, wadded it up, and stuffed it under my shirt between my shoulder blades. With my shirt collar fastened and my jacket zipped tightly it made a bulge of the proper size.

Then I went out, "—a stranger and afraid, into a world I never made."

As a matter of fact I was feeling pretty cocky.

Another cop took my car check. He glanced sharply at me, then motioned me to climb in. I did so and he said, "Go to police headquarters, under the City Hall."

" 'Police headquarters, the City Hall'," I repeated and gunned her ahead. I started in that direction and turned onto Nichols Freeway. I came to a stretch where traffic thinned out and punched the button to shift license plates, hoping that no one would notice. It seemed possible that there was already a call out for the plates I had been showing at the toll gate. I wished that I had been able to change the car's colors and body lines as well.

Before the freeway reached Magee Traffic Way, I turned into a down ramp and stuck thereafter to residential side streets. It was eighteen hundred, zone six time, and I was due in Washington in four and one-half hours.

✒ Chapter 18 ✒

The city did not look right. I tried to discount my own keyed-up state and to see what was actually there—not what I expected to see nor what I was expected to see. Superficially there was nothing wrong, but it did not have the right flavor, as if it were a clumsily directed play. I kept trying to put my finger on it; it kept slipping away.

Kansas City has many wide neighborhoods made up of family units a century old or more. Time seems to have passed them by; kids roll on lawns and householders sit in the cool of the evening on their front porches, just as their great-grandparents did. If there are bomb shelters around, they do not show. The queer, old, bulky houses, fitted together piece by piece by guildsmen long since dead, have homely charm. Seeing them, one wonders how Kansas City got its gamy reputation; those old neighborhoods feel like an enclave of security, impregnable, untouchable.

I cruised through, dodging dogs and rubber balls and

toddlers who chased after each, and tried to get the feel of the place. It was the slack of the day, time for the first drink, for watering lawns, and for neighborly chatting.

And so it seemed. Ahead of me I saw a woman bending over a flower bed. She was wearing a sun suit and her back was bare as mine—more so, for I had that wad of cloth stuffed under my jacket. But clearly she was not wearing a master, nor were the two young kids with her. So what could be wrong?

It was a hot day, hotter even than Washington had been; I began to look for bare shoulders, sun-suited women and men in shorts and sandals. Kansas City, despite its reputation, is in the Bible Belt and feels its puritanical influence. People there do not strip to the weather with the cheerful unanimity of Laguna Beach or Coral Gables. An adult fully covered up is never conspicuous, even on the hottest day.

So I found people dressed both ways—but the proportions were wrong. Sure, there were plenty of kids dressed for the weather, but in several miles of driving I saw the bare backs of only five adult women and two adult men.

I should have seen more like five hundred. It was a hot day.

Cipher it out. While some jackets undoubtedly did not cover masters, by simple proportion well over ninety percent of the population must be possessed.

This city was not "secured" the way we had secured New Brooklyn; this city was saturated. The masters did not simply hold key points and key officials; the masters were the city.

I felt a panicky urge to blast off right from the street

and streak out of Zone Red at emergency maximum. They knew that I had escaped the toll gate trap; they would be looking for me. I might be the only free man driving a car in the entire city—and they were all around me!

I fought it down. An agent who gets the wind up is no use to himself or his boss and is not likely to get out of a tight spot. But I had not fully recovered from what it had done to me to be possessed; it was hard to be calm.

I counted ten, delayed my reactions, and tried to figure the situation. It seemed that I must be wrong; there could not possibly be enough masters available to permit them to saturate a city with a million population. I remembered my own experiences hardly two weeks earlier; I recalled how we picked our recruits and made each new host count. Of course that had been a secondary invasion in which we had depended on shipments, whereas Kansas City almost certainly had had a flying saucer land nearby.

Still it did not make sense; it would have taken, I felt sure, not one saucer but a dozen or more, to carry enough masters to saturate Kansas City. If there had been that many surely the space stations would have spotted them, radar-tracked their landing orbits.

Or could it be that they had no trajectories to track? That they simply appeared instead of swooping down like a rocket? Maybe they used that hypothetical old favorite, the "space-time warp"? I did not know what a space-time warp was and I doubted if anyone knew, but it would do to tag a type of landing which could not be spotted by radar. We did not know what the masters were capable of in the way of engineering and it was not safe to judge their limitations by our own.

But the data I had led to a conclusion which contradicted common logic; therefore I must check before I reported back. One thing seemed sure: if I assumed that the masters had in fact almost saturated this city, then it was evident that they were still keeping up the masquerade. For the time being they were permitting the city to look like a city of free human beings. Perhaps I was not as conspicuous as I feared.

While I was thinking I had moseyed along another mile or so, going nowhere. Once I found myself heading into the retail district around the Plaza; I swung away; where there are crowds, there are cops. But I skimmed the edge of the district and in so doing passed a public swimming pool. I observed it and filed what I had seen. My mind works by delays and priorities; an item having a low priority is held until the circuits are cleared and ready for it.

To put it bluntly, I am subject to doubletakes.

I was several blocks away before I reviewed the swimming pool datum; it had not been much: the gates were locked and it carried a sign—"CLOSED FOR THE SEASON".

A swimming pool closed down during the hottest part of the summer? What did it mean? Nothing at all; swimming pools have gone out of business before and will again. On the other hand it was contrary to the logic of economics to close such an enterprise during the season of greatest profit except through utter necessity. The odds against it were long.

But a swimming pool was the one place where the masquerade could not possibly be maintained. From the viewpoint of humans a closed pool was less conspicuous than a pool unpatronized in hot weather. And I knew that the masters noted and followed the human point of view in their maneuvers—shucks, I had been there!

Item: a trap at the city's toll gates; item: too few sun suits; item: a closed swimming pool.

Conclusion: the slugs were incredibly more numerous than had been dreamed by anyone—including myself who had been possessed by them.

Corollary: Schedule Counter Blast was based on a mistaken estimate of the enemy and would work as well as hunting rhinoceri with a slingshot.

Counter argument: what I thought I saw was physically impossible. I could hear Secretary Martinez's restrained sarcasm tearing my report to shreds. My guesses referred only to Kansas City and were insufficiently grounded even there. Thank you kindly for your interest but what you need is a long rest and freedom from nervous strain. Now, gentlemen—

Pfui!

I had to have something strong enough for the Old Man to convince the President over the reasonable objections of his official advisers—and I had to have it right away. Even with a total disregard of traffic laws I could not clip much off two and a half hours running time back to Washington.

What could I dig up that would be convincing? Go farther downtown, mingle with crowds, and then tell Martinez that I was sure that almost every man I passed was possessed? How could I prove it? For that matter, how could I myself be certain; I did not have Mary's special talent. As long as the titans kept up the farce of "business as usual" the tell-tales would be subtle, a superabundance of round shoulders, a paucity of bare ones.

True, there was the toll gate trap. I had some notion now of how the city had been saturated, granting a large enough supply of slugs. I felt sure that I would encounter another such trap on the way out and that there would be others like it on launching platforms and at every other entrance and exit to the city proper. Every person leaving would be a new agent for the masters; every person entering would be a new slave.

This I felt sure of without being inclined to test it by visiting a launching platform. I had once set up such a trap in the Constitution Club; no one who entered it had escaped.

I had noticed a vendo-printer for the Kansas City Star on the last corner I had passed. Now I swung around the block and came back to it, pulled up, and got out. I shoved a dime in the slot and waited for my paper to be printed. It seemed to take unusually long, but that was my own nervousness, I felt that every passer-by was staring at me.

The Star's format had its usual dull respectability—no excitement, no mention of an emergency, no reference to Schedule Bare Back. The lead news story was headed PHONE SERVICE DISRUPTED BY SUNSPOT STORM, with a subhead City Semi-Isolated by Solar Static. There was a 3-col, semi-stereo, trukolor of the sun, its face disfigured by cosmic acne. The pic carried a Palomar date line, as did one of the substories.

The picture was a good fake—or perhaps they pulled a real one out of the paper's library. It added up to a convincing and unexciting explanation of why Mamie Schultz, herself free of parasites, could not get her call through to Grandma in Pittsburgh.

The rest of the paper looked normal. I tucked it under my arm to study later and turned back to my car . . . just as a police car glided silently up and cramped in across the nose of it. A cop got out.

A police car seems to condense a crowd out of air. A moment before the comer was deserted—else I would never have stopped. Now there were people all around and the cop was coming toward me. My hand crept closer to my gun; I would have dropped him had I not been sure that most, if not all, of those around me were equally dangerous.

He stopped in front of me. "Let me see your license," he said pleasantly.

"Certainly, officer," I agreed. "It's clipped to the instrument board of my car." I stepped past him, letting it be assumed that he would follow me. I could feel him hesitate, then take the bait. I led him around to the far side, between my car and his. This let me see that he did not have a mate in his car, a most welcome variation from human practice. More important, it placed my car between me and the too—innocent bystanders.

"Right there," I said, pointing inside, "it's fastened down." Again he hesitated, then looked—just long enough for me to use the new technique I had developed through necessity. My left hand slapped down on his shoulders and I clutched with all my strength.

It was the "struck cat" all over again. His body seemed to explode so violent was the spasm. I was in the car and gunning it almost before he hit the pavement.

And none too soon. The masquerade broke as suddenly as it had in Barnes's outer office; the crowd closed in. One young woman clung by her nails to the smooth outside of the car for fifty feet or more before she fell off. By then I was making speed and still accelerating. I cut in and out of oncoming traffic, ready to take to the air but lacking space.

A cross street showed up on the left; I slammed into it. It was a mistake; trees arched over it and I could not take off. The next turn was even worse; I cursed the city planners who had made Kansas City so parklike.

Of necessity I slowed down. Now I was cruising at a conservative city speed, still watching for a street which would carry me to some boulevard wide enough for an illegal take-off. My thoughts began to catch up with me and I realized that there was no sign of pursuit. My own too-intimate knowledge of the masters came to my aid. Except for "direct conference" a titan lives in and through his host; he sees what the host sees; receives and passes on information through whatever organs and by whatever means are available to the host.

I knew that. So I knew that it was unlikely that any of the slugs at the corner had been looking for that particular car other than the one inhabiting the body of a policeman—and I had settled with it!

Now, of course, the other parasites present would be on the lookout for me, too—but they had only the bodily abilities and facilities of their hosts. I decided that I need treat them with no more respect, or only a little more respect, than I would give to any casual crowd of witnesses, i.e., ignore them; change neighborhoods and forget it.

For I had nearly thirty minutes of grace left and I had decided what it was I needed as proof; a prisoner, a man who had been possessed and could tell what had happened to the city. I had to rescue a host.

I had to capture a man who was possessed, capture him without hurting him, kill or remove his rider, and kidnap him back to Washington. I had not time to pick a victim, to make plans; I must act now. Even as I decided, I saw a man walking in the block ahead. He was carrying a briefcase and stepping along like a man who sees home and supper ahead. I pulled alongside him and said, "Hey!"

He stopped. "Eh?"

I said, "I've just come from City Hall. No time to explain—slide in here and we'll have a direct conference."

He answered, "City Hall? What are you talking about?"

I said, "Change in plans. Don't waste time. Get in!"

He backed away. I jumped out of the car and grabbed at his hunched shoulders.

Nothing happened—nothing, save that my hand struck bony human flesh, and the man began to yell.

I jumped back into the car and got out of there fast. When I was blocks away I slowed and thought it over. Could it be that I was wrong, that my nerves were so overwrought that I saw signs of titans where there were none?

No! For the moment I had the Old Man's indomitable will to face facts, to see them as they were. The toll gate, the sun suits, the swimming pool, the cop at the vendo-printer . . . those facts I knew—and this last fact simply meant that I had hit the double-zero, rolled boxcars, picked the one man in ten, or whatever the odds were, who was not yet recruited. I speeded up, looking for a new victim.

He was a middle-aged man watering his lawn, a figure so bucolic and out-of-this-century that I was half a mind to pass him by. But I had no time left—and he wore a heavy sweater which bulged suspiciously. Had I seen his wife on the veranda I would have gone past, for she was dressed in bra and skirt and so could not have been possessed.

He looked up inquiringly as I stopped. "I've just come from City Hall," I repeated. "You and I need a direct conference right away. Get in."

He said quietly, "Come in the house for it. That car is too public."

I wanted to refuse but he had already turned and was heading for the house. As I came up by him he whispered, "Careful. The woman is not of us."

"Your wife?"

"Yes."

We stopped on the porch and he said, "My dear, this is Mr. O'Keefe. We have some business to discuss. We'll be in the study."

She smiled and answered, "Certainly, my love. Good evening, Mr. O'Keefe. Sultry, isn't it?"

I agreed that it was and she went back to her knitting. We went on inside and the man ushered me into his study. Since we were both keeping the masquerade I went in first, as befitted a visitor being escorted. I did not like turning my back on him.

For that reason I was half expecting it. He hit me near the base of the neck. But I rolled with it and went down almost unhurt. I continued to roll and fetched up on my back.

In training school they used to slap us with sandbags for trying to get up, once down. I recall my savate instructor saying in a flat Belgian accent, "Brave men get up again— and die. Be a coward—fight from the floor."

So I was on my back and threatening him with my heels as soon as I hit. He danced back out of range. Apparently he did not have a gun and I could get at mine. But there was an open fireplace in the room, a real one, complete with poker, shovel, and tongs. He circled toward it.

There was a small table just out of my reach. I half rolled, half lunged, grabbed a leg and threw it. It caught him in the face as he was grabbing the poker. Then I was on him.

His master was dying in my fingers and he himself was convulsing under its last, terrible command when I became aware of nerve-shattering screams. His wife was standing in the doorway. I bounced up and let her have one, right about her double chin. She went down in mid scream and I returned to her husband.

A limp man is amazingly hard to lift; it took me longer to get him up and across my shoulders than it had to silence him. He was heavy. Fortunately I am a big husky, all hands and feet; I managed a lumbering dog trot toward the car. I doubt if the noise of our fight disturbed anyone but my victim's wife, but her screams must have aroused half that end of town. There were people popping out of doors on both sides of the street. So far, none of them was near, but I was glad to see that I had left the car door open. I hurried toward it.

Then I was sorry; a brat who looked like the twin of the one who had given me trouble earlier was inside fiddling with the controls. Cursing, I dumped my prisoner in the lounge circle and grabbed at the kid. The boy shrank back and struggled, but I tore him loose and threw him out—straight into the arms of the first of my pursuers.

That saved me. He was still untangling himself as I slammed into the driver's seat and shot forward without bothering with door or safety belt. As I took the first corner the door swung shut and I almost went out of my seat; I then held a straight course long enough to fasten the belt. I cut sharp on another corner, nearly ran down a ground car coming out, and went on.

I found the wide boulevard I needed—the Paseo, I think—and jabbed the take-off key. Possibly I caused several wrecks; I had no time to worry about it. Without waiting to reach altitude I wrestled her to course east and continued to climb as I made easting. I kept her on manual across Missouri and expended every launching unit in her racks to give her more speed. That reckless and illegal action may have saved my neck; somewhere over Columbia, just as I fired the last one, I felt the car shake to concussion. Someone had launched an interceptor, a devil-chaser would be my guess—and the pesky thing had fused where I had just been.

There were no more shots, which was good, as I would have been a duck on water from then on. My star-board impeller began to run hot immediately thereafter, possibly from the near miss or perhaps simply from abuse. I let it heat, praying that it would not fly apart, for another ten minutes. Then, with the Mississippi behind me and the indicator way up into "danger" I cut it out and let the car limp along on the port unit. Three hundred was the best she would do—but I was out of Zone Red and back among free men.

Up until then I had not had time to give my passenger more than a glance. He lay where I had slung him, sprawled on the floor pads, unconscious or dead. Now that I was back among men and no longer had the power for illegal speeds there was no reason not to go automatic. I flipped on the transponder, signaled a request for block assignment, and put the controls on automatic without waiting for permission. A block control technician might curse me out and even note my signal for a citation, but they would fit me into the system somehow. I swung around into the lounge and looked my man over.

He was breathing but still out. There was a welt on his face where I had clipped him with the table, but no bones seemed broken and I doubted that he would be unconscious from that cause. I slapped his face and dug my thumbnails into his ear lobes but I could not rouse him.

The dead slug was beginning to stink but I had no way to dispose of it. I let him be and went back to the control seat.

The chronometer read twenty-one thirty-seven Washington time—and I still had better than six hundred miles to go. At my best speed on one power plant, allowing nothing for landing, for tearing over to the White House and finding the Old Man, I would reach Washington a few minutes after midnight. So I had already failed to carry out the letter of my orders and the Old Man was sure as the devil going to make me stay in after school for it.

I took a chance and tried to start the starboard impeller. No dice—it was probably frozen solid and needing a major overhaul. Perhaps just as well, as anything that goes that fast can be explosively dangerous if it gets out of balance—so I desisted and tried to raise the Old Man by phone.

The phone would not work. Perhaps I had jiggered it in one of the spots of exercise I had been forced to take that day but I had never had one fail me before. Printed circuits, transistors, and the whole works being embedded in plastic made those units almost as shock resistant as a proximity fuse. I put it back in my pocket, feeling that this was one of those days when it was just not worthwhile to get out of bed. I turned to the car's communicator and punched the emergency tab.

"Control," I called out. "Control! This is an emergency!"

The screen lighted up and I was looking at a young man. He was, I saw with relief, bare-skinned so far as he appeared in the screen. "Control answering—Block Fox Eleven. What are you doing in the air? I've been trying to raise you ever since you entered my block."

"Never mind!" I snapped. "Patch me into the nearest military circuit. This is crash priority!"

He looked uncertain, but the screen flickered and went blank. Shortly another picture built up showing a military message center—and that did my heart good, as every person in sight was stripped to the waist. The foreground was occupied by a young watch officer; I could have kissed him. Instead I said, "Military emergency—patch me through to the Pentagon and there to the White House."

"Who are you?"

"No time, no time! I'm a civil agent and you wouldn't recognize my I.D. if you saw it. Hurry!"

I might have talked him into it but he was shouldered out of scan by an older man, a wing commander by his cap insignia. "Land at once!" was all that he said.

"Look, skipper," I said. "This is a military emergency; you've got to put me through. I—"

"This is a military emergency," he interrupted, "and all civil craft have been grounded for the past three hours. Land at once."

"But I've got to—"

"Land or be shot down. We are tracking you; I am about to launch an interceptor to burst a half mile ahead of you. Hold your course, or make any maneuver but landing, and the next one will burst on."

"Will you listen, please? I'll land, but I've got to get—" He switched off, leaving me with my jaw pumping air.

The first burst seemed considerably short of a half mile ahead of me; I landed.

I cracked up in doing it, but without hurting myself or my passenger. I did not have long to wait. They had me flare-lighted and were swooping down on me before I had satisfied myself that the boat wouldn't move. They took me in and I met the wing commander personally. He even put my message through after his psych squad got through giving me the antidote for the sleep test. By then it was one-thirteen, zone five—and Schedule Counter Blast had been underway for exactly that hour and thirteen minutes.

The Old Man listened to a summary, grunted, then told me to shut up and see him in the morning.

𝍱 Chapter 19 𝍱

If the Old Man and I had gone to the National Zoological Gardens instead of sitting around in the park, it would not have been necessary for me to go to Kansas City. The ten titans we had captured at the joint session of Congress, plus two the next day, had been entrusted to the director of the zoo to be placed on the shoulders of unlucky anthropoids—chimps and orangutans, mostly. No gorillas.

The director had had the apes locked up in the zoo's veterinary hospital. Two chimpanzees, Abelard and Heloise, were caged together; they had always been mates and there seemed to be no reason to separate them. Maybe that sums up our psychological difficulty in dealing with the titans; even the men who transplanted the slugs to the apes still thought of the result as apes, rather than as titans.

The treatment cage next to that of the two chimps was occupied by a family of tuberculous gibbons. They were not used as hosts, since they were sick, and there was no communication between cages. They were shut one from another by sliding, gasketed panels and each cage had its own air-conditioning. I've been in worse hospitals; I remember one in the Ukraine—

Anyhow, the next morning the panel had been slid back and the gibbons and the chimps were all in together. Abelard, or possibly Heloise, had found some way to pick the lock. The lock was supposed to be monkey proof, but it was not ape-cum-titan proof. Don't blame the designer of the lock.

Two chimps plus two titans plus five gibbons—the next morning there were seven apes ridden by seven titans.

This was discovered two hours before I left for Kansas City, but the Old Man had not been notified. Had he been, he would have known that Kansas City was saturated. I might have figured it out for myself. Had the Old Man known about the gibbons, Schedule Counter Blast would not have taken place.

Schedule Counter Blast was the worst wet firecracker in military history. The evolution was beautifully worked out and the drops were made simultaneously just at midnight, zone five, on over ninety-six hundred communication points—newspaper offices, block controls, relay stations, and so forth. The raiding squad were the cream of our sky-borne forces, mostly veteran non-coms, and with them, technicians to put each communication point back into service.

Whereupon the President's speech and the visual display would go out from each local station; Schedule Bare Back would take effect all through the infected territory; and the war would be over, save for minor mopping up.

Ever see a bird hurt itself by flying into a glass window? The bird is not stupid; he simply did not have all the data.

By twenty-five minutes after midnight reports started coming in that such-and-such points were secured. A little later there were calls for help from other points. By one in the morning most of the reserves had been committed but the operation was clearly going well—so well, indeed, that unit commanders were landing and were reporting from the ground.

That was the last anybody ever heard of them.

Zone Red swallowed up the task force as if it had never existed—over eleven thousand military craft, more than a hundred and sixty thousand fighting men and technicians, seventy-one group commanders and—why go on? The United States had received its worst military setback since Black Sunday. Not in numbers, for there was not a city bombed, but in selected quality.

Let me make it clear that I am not criticizing Martinez, Rexton, the General Staff, or those poor devils who made the drop. The program was properly planned, it was based on what appeared to be a true picture, and the situation called for fast action with the best we had. If Rexton had sent any but his best boys he would have earned a court martial; the Republic was at stake and he had the sense to realize it.

But he did not know about the seven apes.

It was nearly daylight, so I understand, before Martinez and Rexton got it through their heads that the messages they had gotten back about successes were actually faked, fakes sent by their own men—our own men—but hag-ridden, possessed, and brought into the masquerade. After my report, more than an hour too late to stop the raids, the Old Man had tried to get them not to send in any more men, but they were flushed with success and anxious to make a clean sweep.

The Old Man asked the President to insist on visual checks of what was happening, but the operation was being controlled by relay through Space Station Alpha and there just aren't enough channels to parallel audio with video through a space station. Rexton had said, "They know what they are up against; quit worrying. As fast as we get local stations back in our hands, our boys will patch back into the ground relay net and you will have all the visual evidence you want."

The Old Man had pointed out that by then it would be too late. Rexton had burst out, "Confound it, man! —I can't stop soldiers in action to have them take pictures of bare backs. Do you want a thousand men to let themselves be killed just to quiet your jitters?"

The President had backed him up.

By early morning they had their visual evidence. Stereo stations in the Central Valley were giving out with the same old pap; Rise and Shine with Mary Sunshine, Breakfast with the Browns, and such junk. There was not a station with the President's stereocast, not one that even conceded that anything had happened. The military dispatches tapered off and stopped around four o'clock and Rexton's frantic calls were not answered. Task Force Redemption of Schedule Counter Blast ceased to exist— spurlos versenkt.

I got this not from the Old Man but from Mary. Being

the President's little shadow who went in and out with him, she had a box seat. I did not get to see the Old Man until nearly eleven the next morning. He let me report without comment, and without bawling me out, which was worse.

He was about to dismiss me when I put in, "How about my prisoner? Didn't he confirm my conclusions?"

"Oh, him? Still unconscious, by the last report. They don't expect him to live. The psychotechnicians can't get anything out of him."

"I'd like to see him."

"You stick to things you understand."

"Well—have you got something for me to do?"

"Not at the moment. I think you had better—No, do this: trot down to the National Zoo. You'll see some things that may put a different light on what you picked up in Kansas City."

"Huh?"

"Look up Doctor Horace, he's the Assistant Director. Tell him I sent you."

So I went down to see the animals. I tried to find Mary, but she was tied up.

Horace was a nice little guy who looked like one of his own baboons; he turned me over to a Doctor Vargas who was a specialist in exotic biologies—the same Vargas who was on the Second Venus Expedition. He told me what had happened and I looked at the gibbons, meantime rearranging my prejudices.

"I saw the President's broadcast," he said conversationally, "weren't you the man who—I mean, weren't you the—"

"Yes, I was 'the man who'," I agreed shortly.

"Then you can tell us a great deal about these phenomena. Your opportunities have been unique."

"Perhaps I should be able to," I admitted slowly, "but I can't."

"Do you mean that no cases of fission reproduction took place while you were, uh, their prisoner?"

"That's right." I thought about it and went on, "At least, I think that's right."

"Don't you know? I was given to understand that, uh, victims have full memory of their experiences?"

"Well, they do and they don't." I tried to explain the odd detached frame of mind of a servant of the masters.

"I suppose it could happen while you sleep."

"Maybe. Besides sleep, there is another time, or rather times, which are difficult to remember. During conference."

"Conference?"

So I explained. His eyes lit up, "Oh, you mean 'conjugation'."

"No, I mean 'conference'."

"We mean the same thing. Don't you see? Conjugation and fission—they reproduce at will, whenever the food supply, that is to say the supply of hosts, permits. Probably one contact for each fission; then, when the opportunity exists, fission—two fully adult daughter parasites in a matter of hours. . . or less, possibly."

I thought it over. If that were true—and looking at the gibbons, I could not doubt it—then why had we depended on shipments at the Constitution Club? Or had we? In fact I did not know; I did what my master wanted done and saw only what came under my eyes. But why had we not saturated New Brooklyn as Kansas City had been saturated. Lack of time?

It was clear how Kansas City had been saturated. With plenty of "livestock" at hand and a space ship loaded with transit cells to draw from the titans had reproduced to match the human population.

I am no biologist, exotic or otherwise, but I can do simple arithmetic. Assume a thousand slugs in that space ship, the one we believed to have landed near Kansas City; suppose that they could reproduce when given the opportunity every twenty-four hours.

First day, one thousand slugs.

Second day, two thousand.

Third day, four thousand.

At the end of the first week, the eighth day, that is—a hundred and twenty-eight thousand slugs.

After two weeks, more than sixteen million slugs.

But we did not know that they were limited to spawning once a day; on the contrary the gibbons proved they weren't. Nor did we know that a flying saucer could lift only a thousand transit cells; it might be ten thousand—or more—or less. Assume ten thousand as breeding stock with fission every twelve hours. In two weeks the answer comes out—

MORE THAN TWO AND A HALF TRILLION!!!!

The figure did not mean anything; it was cosmic. There aren't anything like that many people on the whole globe, not even if you counted in apes.

We were going to be knee deep in slugs—and that before long. I felt worse than I had in Kansas City.

Dr. Vargas introduced me to a Doctor McIlvaine of the Smithsonian Institution; McIlvaine was a comparative psychologist, the author, so Vargas told me, of 'Mars, Venus, and Earth: A Study in Motivating Purposes'. Vargas seemed to expect me to be impressed but I was not as I had not read it. Anyhow, how can anyone study the motives of Martians when they were all dead before we swung down out of trees?

They started swapping trade talk not intelligible to an outsider; I continued to watch the gibbons. Presently McIlvaine asked me, "Mr. Nivens, how long does a conference last?"

"Conjugation," Vargas corrected him.

"Conference," McIlvaine repeated. "Keep your mind on the more important aspect."

"But, Doctor," Vargas insisted, "there are parallels in terrestrial biology. In primitive reproduction, conjugation is the means of gene exchange whereby mutation is spread through the body of the—"

"You are being anthropocentric, Doctor. You do not know that this life form has genes."

Vargas turned red. "I presume you will allow me gene equivalents?" he said stiffly.

"Why should I? I repeat, sir, that you are reasoning by analogy where there is no reason to judge that analogy exists. There is one and only one characteristic common to all life forms and that is the drive to survive."

"And to reproduce," insisted Vargas.

"Suppose the organism is immortal and has no need to reproduce?"

"But—" Vargas shrugged. "Your question is not

germane; we know that they reproduce." He gestured at the apes.

"And I am suggesting," McIlvaine came back, "that this is not reproduction, but a single organism availing itself of more space, as a man might add a wing to his house. No, really. Doctor, I do not wish to be offensive, but it is possible to get so immersed in the idea of the zygote-gamete cycle that one forgets that there may be other patterns."

Vargas started out, "But throughout the entire system—"

McIlvaine cut him short. "Anthropocentric, terrocentric, solocentric—it is still a provincial approach. These creatures may be from outside the solar system entirely."

I said, "Oh, no!" I had had a sudden flash picture of the planet Titan and with it a choking sensation.

Neither one paid any attention to me. McIlvaine continued, "If you must have analogy, take the amoeba—an earlier, more basic, and much more successful life form than ours. The motivational psychology of the amoeba—"

I switched off my ears; I suppose free speech gives a man the right to talk about the 'psychology' of an amoeba, but I don't have to listen. They never did get back to asking me how long a conference takes, not that I could have told them. A conference is, well—timeless.

They did do some direct experimentation which raised my opinion of them a little. Vargas ordered brought in a baboon who was wearing a slug and had him introduced into the cage with the gibbons and the chimps. Up to then the gibbons had been acting like gibbons, grooming each other and such, except that they seemed rather quiet—and kept a sharp eye on our movements. As soon as the newcomer was dumped in they gathered in a ring facing outwards and went into direct conference, slug to slug. McIlvaine jabbed his finger excitedly at them. "You see? You see? Conference is not for reproduction, but for exchange of memory. The organism, temporarily divided, has now re-identified itself."

I could have told him the same thing without the double talk; a master who has been out of touch always gets into direct conference as soon as possible.

"Hypothesis!" Vargas snorted. "Pure hypothesis—they have no opportunity to reproduce just now. George!" He ordered the boss of the handling crew to bring in another ape.

"Little Abe?" asked the crew boss.

"No, I want one which is not supporting a parasite. Let me see—make it Old Red."

The crew boss glanced at the gibbons, looked away at once, and said, "Gripes, Doc, I'd rather you didn't pick on Old Red."

"This won't hurt him."

"Why can't I bring in Satan? He's a mean bastard anyway."

"All right, all right! But hurry it up; you are keeping Dr. McIlvaine waiting."

So they brought in Satan, a coal black chimp. He may have been aggressive elsewhere; he was not so here. They dumped him inside, he took one look around, shrank back against the door, and began to whine. It was like watching an execution; I could not stand to look but I couldn't look away. I had had my nerves under control—a man can get used to anything; there are people who make their livings by pumping out cesspools—but the ape's hysteria was contagious. I wanted to run.

At first the hag-ridden apes did nothing; they simply stared at him like a jury. It went on that way for a long while. Satan's whines changed to low, sobbing moans and he covered his face with his hands. Presently Vargas said, "Doctor! Look!"

"Where?"

"Lucy—the old female. There." He pointed.

It was the matriarch of the family of consumptive gibbons. Her back was toward us; I could see that the slug thereon had humped itself together. An iridescent line ran down the center of it.

It began to split as an egg splits. In a few minutes only, the division was complete. One new slug centered itself over her spine; the other flowed down her back. She was squatting, buttocks almost to the floor; it slithered off and plopped gently on the concrete.

It crept slowly toward Satan. The ape must have peeked through his fingers, for he screamed hoarsely— and swarmed up into the top of the cage.

So help me, they sent a squad to arrest him. Four of the biggest: two gibbons, a chimp, and a baboon. They tore him loose and hauled him down and held him face down on the floor.

The slug slithered closer.

It was a good two feet away when it grew a pseudopod— slowly, at first—a slimy stalk that weaved around like a cobra. Then it lashed out and struck the ape on the foot. The others promptly let go of him but Satan did not move.

The titan seemed to pull itself in by the extension it had formed and attached itself to Satan's foot. From there it crawled up; when it reached the base of his spine the ape stirred. Before it was settled at the top of his back Satan sat up. He shook himself and joined the others, stopping only to look us over.

Vargas and McIlvaine started talking excitedly, apparently quite unmoved otherwise. I wanted to smash something—for me, for Satan, for the whole simian race.

Vargas was insisting that nothing had been proved, while McIlvaine maintained that we were seeing something new to our concepts; an intelligent creature which was, by the fashion in which it was organized, immortal and continuous in its personal identity—or its group identity; the argument grew confused. In any case McIlvaine was theorizing that such a creature would have continuous memory of all its experiences, not just from the moment of fission, but back to its racial beginning. He described the slug as a four dimensional worm in space-time, intertwined with itself as a single organism, and the talk grew so esoteric as to be silly.

As for me, I did not know and did not care. All very interesting, no doubt, but the only way I cared about slugs was to kill them. I wanted to kill them, early and often and as many as possible.

About that uninterrupted "racial memory" idea: wouldn't it be rather cumbersome to be able to recall exactly what you did the second Wednesday in March a million years ago?

☞ **Chapter 20** ☜

For a wonder, when I got back the Old Man was available and wanted to talk. The President had left to address a secret session of the United Nations and the Old Man had not been included in the party. I wondered if he had fallen out of official favor, but I did not say so.

He had me report fully on what I had seen at the zoo and questioned me closely; he had not been down there himself. I added my opinion of Vargas and McIlvaine. "A couple of boy scouts," I complained, "comparing stamp collections. They don't realize it's serious."

The Old Man took time out before answering. "Don't sell those boys short, son," he advised me. "They are more likely to come up with the answer than are you and I."

"Humph!" I said, or something stronger. "They are more likely to let those slugs escape. Remember Graves?"

"I do remember Graves. You don't understand scientific detachment."

"I hope I never do!"

"You won't. But it's the ignition system of the world; without it, we're sunk. Matter of fact, they did let one escape."

"Huh?"

"Didn't they tell you about the elephant?"

"What elephant? They damn near didn't tell me anything; they got interested in each other and ignored me."

"Sure that's not what's biting you? About the elephant: an ape with a rider got out, somehow. Its body was found trampled to death in the elephant house. And one of the elephants was gone."

"You mean there is an elephant loose with a slug on him!" I had a horrid vision of what that could mean—something like a tank with a cybernetic brain.

"Her," the Old Man corrected me, "it was a cow elephant. I didn't say so, anyhow. They found her over in Maryland, quietly pulling up cabbages. No parasite."

"Where did the slug get to?" Involuntarily I glanced around. The Old Man chuckled.

"Don't worry; I don't have it in here. But a duo was stolen in the adjoining village. I'd say the slug is somewhere west of the Mississippi by now."

"Anybody missing?"

He shrugged again. "How can you tell, in a free country? At least, the titan can't hide on a human host anywhere short of Zone Red."

That seemed true; Schedule Bare Back appeared to be operating one hundred percent. That made me think of something else, something I had seen at the zoo and had not reasoned through. Whatever it was, it eluded me. The Old Man went on, "It's taken drastic action to make the bare-shoulders order stick, though. The President has had a flood of protests on moral grounds, not to mention the National Association of Men's Haberdashers."

"Huh?"

"You would think we were trying to sell their daughters down to Rio, the way some of them carry on. There was a delegation in, called themselves The Mothers of the Republic, or some such nonsense."

"The President's time is being wasted like that, at a time like this?"

"McDonough handled them. But he roped me in on it, damn his eyes." The Old Man looked pained. "We told them that they could not see the President unless they stripped absolutely naked. That stopped 'em."

The thought that had been bothering me came to the surface. "Say, boss, you might have to."

"Have to what?"

"Make people strip naked."

He chewed his lip and looked worried. "What are you driving at?"

"Do we know, as a certainty, that a slug can attach itself to its host only near the base of the brain?"

"You should know, better than I do."

"I thought I did, but now I'm not sure. That's the way we always did it, when I was, uh, with them." I recounted again, in more detail, what I had seen when Vargas had had poor old Satan exposed to a slug. "That ape moved as soon as the thing reached the base of his spine, clear down at his tail bone. Maybe they prefer to ride up near the brain—I'm sure they do. But maybe they don't have to. Maybe they could ride down inside a man's pants and just put out an extension to the end of his spinal cord."

"Hmm . . . you'll remember, son, that the first time I had a crowd searched for one I made everybody peel clear down to the buff. That was not accidental; I wanted to be sure."

"I think you were justified. See here; they might be able to conceal themselves anywhere on the body, if they have to. Inside a pair of shorts, for example. Of course you couldn't hide anything under some shorts—" I was thinking of the skin-tight things that Mary wore. "—but take those droopy drawers you've got on. One could hide in them and it would just make you look a bit satchel fannied—a bit more, I should say."

"Want me to take 'em off?"

"I can do better than that; I'll give you the Kansas City Clutch." My words were joking but I was not; I grabbed at the bunchiness of his pants and made sure he was clean. If he had not been, he would have contorted and gone unconscious had I clutched a parasite. He submitted to it with good grace, then gave me the same treatment.

"But we can't," he complained as he sat down, "go around slapping women on the rump. It won't do."

"You may have to," I pointed out, "or make everybody strip."

"We'll run some experiments."

"How?" I asked.

"You know that head-and-spine armor deal? It's not worth much, except to give a feeling of security to any-body who bothers to wear one. I'll tell Doctor Horace to take an ape, fit an armor to him so that a slug can't reach anything but his legs, say—and see what happens. Or use some other method to limit the area of attack, and vary the areas, too. We'll find out."

"Uh, yes. But don't have him use an ape, boss."

"Why not?"

"Well—they're too human."

"Damn it, bub, you can't make an omelet—"

"—without breaking eggs. Okay, okay, but I don't have to like it. Anyhow, we'll find out."

I could see that he did not like what he was thinking. "I hope it turns out that you are wrong. Yes, sir, I surely do. It has been hard enough to get their shirts off; I'd hate like the very deuce to try to get 'em to take off their drawers as well." He looked worried.

"Well, maybe it won't be necessary."

"I hope not."

"By the way, we're moving back to the old nest."

"How about the New Philadelphia hide-out?" I asked.

"We'll keep both. This war may go on a long time."

"Speaking of such, what have you got for me now?"

"Well, now, as I said, this is likely to prove a long war. Why don't you take some leave? Indefinite—I'll call you back when I need you."

"You always have," I pointed out. "Is Mary going on leave?"

"What's that got to do with it?"

"I asked you a straight question, Boss."

"Mary is on duty, with the President."

"Why? She's done her job, and nobly. You aren't depending on her being able to smell out a slug, not if I know you. You don't need her as a guard; she's too good an agent to waste on such work."

"See here—when did you get so big that you are telling me how to use other agents? Answer that and make it good."

"Oh, skip it, skip it," I told him, my temper very much out of hand. "Let it lay that if Mary isn't taking leave, I don't want leave—and none of your business why."

"That's a nice girl."

"Did I say she wasn't? Keep your nose out of my affairs. In the meantime, give me a job to do."

"I say you need to take leave."

"So you can make damn sure that I don't have any free time when Mary has? What is this? A YWCA?

"I say you need leave because you are worn out."

"Hunh!"

"You are a fair-to-good agent when you are in shape. Right now you aren't; you've been through too much. No, shut up and listen: I send you out on a simple assignment. Penetrate an occupied city, look it over and see everything there is to see and report back by a certain time. What do you do? You are so jittery that you hang around in the suburbs and are afraid to go downtown. You don't keep your eyes open and you damn near get caught three times. Then when you do head back, you get so nervy that you burn out your ship and fail to get back in time to be of any use. Your nerve is shot and your judgment with it. Take leave—sick leave, in fact."

I stood there with my ears burning. He did not directly blame me for the failure of Schedule Counter Blast but he might as well have. I felt that it was unfair—and yet I knew that there was truth in it. My nerves used to be like rock, and now my hands trembled when I tried to strike a cigarette.

Nevertheless he let me have an assignment—the first and only time I have ever won an argument with him.

A hell of an assignment—I spent the next several days lecturing to brass, answering fool questions about what titans eat for lunch, explaining how to tackle a man who was possessed. I was billed as an "expert" but half the time my pupils seemed sure that they knew more about slugs than I did.

Why do people cherish their preconceptions? Riddle me that.

✍ Chapter 21 ✍

Operation Parasite seemed to come to a dead stop during this period. The titans continued to hold Zone Red, but they could not break out without being spotted. And we did not try to break in for the good reason that every slug held one of our own people as hostage. It was a situation which might go on for a long time.

The United Nations were no help. The President wanted a simple act of cooperation—Schedule Bare Back on a global scale. They hemmed and hawed and sent the matter to committee for investigation. The plain truth was they did not believe us; that was always the enemy's great advantage—only the burned believed in the fire.

Some nations were safe from the slugs through their own customs. A Finn who did not strip down and climb into a steam bath, in company, every day or so would have been conspicuous. The Japanese, too, were casual about undressing. The South Seas were relatively safe, as were large parts of Africa. France had gone enthusiastically

nudist, on weekends at least, right after World War III—
a slug would have a tough time hiding in France.

But in countries where the body-modesty taboo
meant something a slug could stay hidden until his host
began to stink. The United States itself, Canada—
England, most particularly England. "Aren't you getting
excited over nothing, old chap? Take off my weskit? Now,
really!"

They flew three slugs (with apes) to London; I understand that the King wanted to set an example as the
President had, but the Prime Minister, egged on by the
Archbishop of Canterbury, would not let him. The
Archbishop had not even bothered to look; moral behavior
was more important than mundane peril. Nothing about
this appeared in the news and the story may not be true,
but English skin was not exposed to the cold stares of
neighbors.

The Cominform propaganda system began to blast us
as soon as they had worked out a new line. The whole
thing was an "American Imperialist fantasy" intended to
"enslave the workers"; the "mad dogs of capitalism" were
at it again.

I wondered why the titans had not attacked Russia
first; Stalinism seemed tailor-made for them. On second
thought, I wondered if they had. On third thought I
wondered what difference it would make; the people
behind the Curtain had had their minds enslaved and
parasites riding them for three generations. There might
not be two kopeks difference between a commissar with a
slug and a commissar without a slug.

There would be one change: their intermittent purges

would take a different form; a "deviationist" would be "liquidated" by plastering a titan on his neck. It wouldn't be necessary to send him to the gas chamber.

Except when the Old Man picked me to work with him I was not close to the center of things; I saw the war with the titans as a man sees hurricanes—his small piece only. I did not see the Old Man soon and I got my assignments from Oldfield, his deputy. Consequently I did not know of it when Mary was relieved from special duty with the President. I ran into her in the lounge of the Section offices. "Mary!" I yelped and fell over my feet getting to her.

She gave me that long, slow, sweet smile and moved over to make room for me. "Hello, darling!" she whispered. She did not ask me what I had been doing, nor scold me that I had not been in touch with her, nor even comment on how long it had been. Mary always let the water over the dam take care of itself.

Not me—I babbled. "This is wonderful! I thought you were still tucking the President into his beddy-bye. How long have you been here? Do you have to go back right away? Say, can I dial you a drink—no, you've got one." I started to dial for an old-fashioned and discovered that Mary had already done so; it popped out almost into my hand. "Huh? How'd this get here?"

"I ordered it when you came in the door."

"You did? Mary, did I tell you that you are wonderful?"

"No."

"Very well, then, I will: You're wonderful."

"Thank you."

I went on, "This calls for a celebration! How long are

you free? Say, couldn't you possibly get some leave? They can't expect you to be on duty twenty-four hours a day, week after week, with no time off. I think I'll go right straight to the Old Man and tell him just what—"

"I'm on leave, Sam."

"—just what I think of that sort of—Huh?"

"I'm on leave now."

"You are? For how long?"

"Subject to call. All leaves read that way now."

"But—How long have you been on leave?"

"Since yesterday. I've been sitting here, waiting for you to show up."

"Yesterday!" And I had spent yesterday giving more kindergarten lectures to brass hats who did not want them. "Oh, for the love of—" I stood up. "Stay right where you are. Don't move. I'll be right back."

I rushed over to the operations office. I got in to see the chief deputy by insisting that I had a very urgent matter that he had to attend to. Oldfield looked up when I came in and said in a surly tone, "What do you want?"

"Look, chief, that series of bedtime stories I'm scheduled to tell: better cancel them."

"Why?"

"I'm a sick man; I've been due for sick leave for a long time. Now I've just got to take it."

"You're sick in the head, if you ask me."

"That's right; I'm sick in the head. Sometimes I hear voices. People have been following me around. I keep dreaming I'm back with the titans." That last point was regrettably true.

"But since when has this being crazy been any

handicap in this section?" He leaned back and waited for me to argue the point.

"Look—do I get leave or don't I?"

He fumbled through papers on his desk, found one and tore it up. "Okay. Keep your phone handy; you're subject to recall. Get out."

I got. Mary looked up when I came in and gave me the soft warm treatment again. I said, "Grab your things; we're leaving."

She did not ask where; she simply stood up. I snatched my drink, gulped half of it and spilled the rest. We went up and were out on the pedestrian level of the city before either one of us said anything. Then I asked, "Now—where do you want to get married?"

"Sam, we discussed that before."

"Sure we did and now we are going to do it. Where?"

"Sam, Sam my very dear—I will do what you say. But I am bound to tell you that I am still opposed to it."

"Why?"

"Sam, let's go straight to my apartment. I'd like to cook dinner for you."

"Okay, you can cook dinner—but not in your apartment. And we get married first."

"Please, Sam!"

I heard somebody say, "Keep pitching, kid. She's weakening." I looked around and found that we were playing to a good-sized gallery.

I swept an arm wide, almost clipping the youngster who had given me the advice and shouted irritably, "Haven't you people got anything else to do? Go get drunk!"

Somebody else said, "I'd say he ought to take her offer; he won't get a better one."

I grabbed Mary by the arm and hurried her away from there. I did not say another word until I had gotten her into a cab and closed off the driver's compartment from the lounge. "All right," I said gruffly, "why not get married? Let's have your reasons."

"Why get married, Sam? I'm yours; you don't need a contract."

"Why? Because I love you; that's one reason, damn it!"

She did not answer for quite a while; I thought I had offended her. When she did I could hardly hear her. "You hadn't mentioned that before, Sam."

"Hadn't I? Oh, I must have. I'm sure I have."

"No, I'm sure, quite sure, that you haven't. Why didn't you?"

"Unh, I don't know. Just an oversight, I guess. I'm not right sure what the word 'love' means."

"Neither am I," she said softly, "but I love to hear you say it. Say it again, please."

"Huh? Okay. I love you. I love you, Mary."

"Oh, Sam!"

She snuggled in against my shoulder and began to tremble. I shook her a little. "How about you?"

"Me? Oh, I love you, Sam. I do love you. I've loved you ever since—"

"Ever since when?"

I thought she was going to say that she had loved me ever since I took her place in Project Interview; what she said was, "I've loved you ever since you slapped me."

Is that logic?

The driver was cruising slowly east along the Connecticut coast; I had told him just to drive around. I had to wake him up before I could get him to land us in Westport. We went straight to the City Hall.

I stepped up to a counter in the Bureau of Sanctions and Licenses and said to a clerk there, "Is this where we get married?"

"That's up to you," he answered. "Hunting licenses on the left, dog licenses on the right, this desk is the happy medium—I hope." He leered at me.

I don't like smart boys and the gag was ancient. "Very well," I said stiffly, "will you oblige by issuing us a license?"

"Sure thing. Everybody ought to get married at least once; that's what I keep telling my old lady." He got out a large printed form. "Let's have your serial numbers."

We gave them to him. He slid the form into a typer and recorded them. "Now—are either of you married in any other state?" We said that we weren't; he went on, "You're sure, now? If you are and don't tell me, so I can put a rider on this showing the other contracts, this contract ain't valid."

We told him again that we weren't married anywhere. He shrugged and went on, "Term, renewable, or lifetime? If it's over ten years, the fee is the same as for lifetime; if it's under six months, you don't need this; you get the short form from that vendo machine over there by the wall."

I looked at Mary; she said in a very small voice, "Lifetime."

The clerk looked surprised. "Lady, are you sure you know what you're doing? The renewable contract, with the automatic option clause, is just as permanent and you don't have to go through the courts if you change your mind."

I said, "You heard the lady! Put it down."

"Okay, okay—either party, mutual consent, or binding?"

"Binding," I answered and Mary nodded.

"Binding it is," he agreed, stroking the typer. "Now we come to the meat of the matter: who pays and how much? And is it salary or endowment?"

I said, "Salary"; I didn't own enough to set up a fund.

At the same time and in a firm voice Mary said, "Neither."

The clerk said, "Huh?"

"Neither one," Mary repeated. "This is not a financial contract."

The clerk stopped completely, looked at me, and then looked at Mary. "Now, look, lady," he said reasonably, "don't be foolish. You heard the gentleman say that he was willing to do the right thing."

"No."

"Hadn't you better talk it over with your lawyer before you go ahead with this? There's a public communicator out in the hall."

"No!"

"Well—I'm darned if I see what you need a license for."

"Neither do I," Mary told him.

"You mean you don't want this?"

"No! Put it down the way I told you to. 'No salary'."

The clerk looked helpless but bent over the typer

again. "I guess that's all we need," he said finally. "You've kept it simple, I'll say that for you. 'Do—you both—solemnly—swear—that—the—above—facts—are—true—to—the—best—of—your—knowledge—and—belief—that—you—aren't—entering—into—this—agreement—uninfluenced—by—drugs—or—other—illegal—inducements—and—that—there—exists—no—other—covenants—nor—other—legal—impediments—to—the—execution—and—registration—of—the—above—contract?' "

We both said that we did and we were and it was and there weren't. He pulled the form out of the typer. "Let's have your thumb prints . . . okay; that'll be ten dollars, including the federal tax." I paid him and he shoved the form into the copier and threw the switch. "Copies will be mailed to each of you," he announced, "at your serial-number addresses. Now—what type of ceremony are you looking for? Maybe I can be of help."

"We don't want a religious ceremony," Mary told him and I agreed.

He nodded. "Then I've got just what you're looking for. Old Doctor Chamleigh. He's completely non-sectarian, best stereo accompaniment in town, all four walls and full orchestra. He gives you the whole works, fertility rites and everything, but dignified. And he tops it off with a fatherly straight-from-the-shoulder word of advice. Makes you feel married."

"No." This time I said it.

"Oh, come, now!" the clerk said to me. "Think of the little lady. If she sticks by what she just swore to—and I'm not saying she won't—she'll never have another chance.

Every girl is entitled to a formal wedding. Honest—I don't get much of a commission out of it."

I said, "See here, you can marry us, can't you? Go ahead. Get it over with!"

He looked surprised and said, "Didn't you know? In this state you marry yourself. You've been married, ever since you thumb-printed the license."

I said, "Oh—" Mary didn't say anything. We left.

I hired a duo at the landing flat north of town; the heap was ten years old and smelled of it but it had full-automatic and that was all that really mattered. I looped around the city, cut across Manhattan Crater, and set the controls. We didn't talk much; there didn't seem to be much to say just yet. I was happy but terribly nervous—and then Mary put her arms around me and after a bit I wasn't nervous any longer but happier than ever. After a long time that seemed short I heard the BEEEEP! beep-beep BEEEEP! of the beacon at my shack in the mountains, whereupon I unwound myself, took over manual, and landed. Mary said sleepily, "Where are we?"

"At my cabin in the mountains," I told her.

"I didn't know you had a cabin in the mountains. I thought you were headed for my apartment."

"What, and risk those bear traps? Anyhow, it's not mine; it's ours."

She kissed me again and I loused up the landing. She slid out ahead of me while I was securing the board, then I followed and found her staring at my shack. "Sweetheart, it's beautiful!"

"You can't beat the Adirondacks," I agreed. There was

a slight haze with the sun low in the west, giving that wonderful, depth upon depth, stereo look that you never get anywhere else. "I picked this place for the view."

She glanced at it and said, "Yes, yes—but I didn't mean that. I meant your—our cabin. Let's go inside, right now."

"Suits," I agreed, "but it's really just a simple shack." Which it was—not even an indoor pool. I had kept it that way on purpose; when I came up here I didn't want to feel that I had brought the city with me. The shell was conventional steel-and-fiberglass construction but I had had it veneered in duroslabs which could not be told from real logs unless you took a knife to them. The inside was just as simple—a big living room with a real, wood-burning fireplace, deep plain-colored rugs, and plenty of low chairs. The services were all in a Kompacto special, the shell of which was buried under the foundation—air-conditioner, power pack, cleansing system, sound equipment, plumbing, radiation alarm, servos—everything but the deep-freeze and the other kitchen equipment, out of sight and out of mind. Even the stereo screens were covered up and would not be noticed unless in use. It was about as near as a man could get to a real log cabin and still have inside plumbing.

"I think it's just lovely," Mary said seriously. "I wouldn't want to have an ostentatious place."

"You and me both." I worked the combo and the front door dilated; Mary was inside at once. "Hey! Come back here!" I yelled.

She did so. "What's the matter, Sam? Did I do something wrong?"

"You sure did." I dragged her back to me, then swung her up in my arms and carried her across the threshold. I kissed her as I put her down. "There. Now you are in your own house, properly."

The lights had come on as we entered the house. She looked around her, then turned and threw her arms around my neck. "Oh, darling, darling! I can't see—my eyes are all blurry."

Mine were blurry, too, so we took time out for mutual treatment. Then she started wandering around, touching things. "Sam, if I had planned it all myself, it would have been just this way."

"It hasn't but one bathroom," I apologized. "We'll have to rough it a bit."

"I don't mind. In fact I'm glad; now I know you didn't bring any of those women of yours up here."

"What women?"

"You know darn well what women. If you had been planning this as a nest, you would have included a woman's bathroom."

"You know too much."

She did not answer but wandered on out into the kitchen. I heard her squeal. "What's the matter?" I asked, following her out.

"I never expected to find a real kitchen in a bachelor's lodge."

"I'm not a bad cook myself. I wanted a kitchen so I bought one."

"I'm so glad. Now I will cook you dinner."

"It's your kitchen; suit yourself. But don't you want to wash up? You can have first crack at the shower if you want it. And tomorrow we'll get a catalog and you can pick out a bathroom of your own. We'll have it flown in."

"No hurry," she said. "You take the first shower. I want to start dinner."

So I did. I guess she did not have any trouble figuring out the controls and filing system in the kitchen, for about fifteen minutes later while I was whistling away in the shower, letting the hot water soak in, I heard a tap on the shower door. I looked through the translucent panel and saw Mary silhouetted there.

"May I come in?" she called out.

"Sure, sure!" I said, "Plenty of room." I opened the door and looked at her. She looked good. For a moment she stood there, letting me look but with a sweet shyness on her face that I had never seen before.

I put on an expression of utter surprise and said, "Honey! What's the matter? Are you sick?"

She looked startled out of her wits and said, "Me? What do you mean?"

"There's not a gun on you anywhere."

She giggled and came at me. "Idiot!" she squealed and started to tickle me. I got her left arm in a bonebreaker but she countered with one of the nastiest judo tricks that ever came out of Japan. Fortunately I knew the answer to it and then we were both on the bottom of the shower and she was yelling, "Let me up! You're getting my hair all wet."

"Does it matter?" I asked, not moving. I liked it there.

"I guess not," she answered softly and kissed me. So I let her up and we rubbed each other's bruises and giggled. It was quite the nicest shower I have ever had.

Mary and I slipped into domesticity as if we had been married for twenty years. Oh, not that our honeymoon was humdrum, far from it, nor that there weren't a thousand things we still had to learn about each other—the point was that we already seemed to know the necessary things about each other that made us married. Especially Mary.

I don't remember those days too clearly, yet I remember every second of them. I went around feeling gay and a bit confused. My Uncle Egbert used to achieve much the same effect with a jug of corn liquor, but we did not even take tempus pills, not then. I was happy; I had forgotten what it was like to be happy, had not known that I was not happy. Interested, I used to be—yes. Diverted, entertained, amused—but not happy.

We did not turn on a stereo, we did not read a book—except that Mary read aloud some Oz books that I had. Priceless items, they were, left to me by my great-grandfather; she had never seen any. But that did not take us back into the world; it took us farther out.

The second day we did go down to the village; I wanted to show Mary off. Down there they think I am a writer and I encourage the notion, so I stopped to buy a couple of tubes and a condenser for my typer and a roll of copy tape, though I certainly had no intention of doing any writing, not this trip. I got to talking with the storekeeper about the slugs and Schedule Bare Back—sticking to my public persona of course. There had been a local false alarm and a native in the next town had been shot by a trigger-happy constable for absent-mindedly showing up in public in a shirt. The storekeeper was indignant. I suggested that it was his own fault; these were war conditions.

He shook his head. "The way I see it we would have had no trouble at all if we had tended to our own business. The Lord never intended men to go out into space. We should junk the space stations and stay home; then we would be all right."

I pointed out that the slugs came here in their own ships; we did not go after them—and got a warning signal from Mary not to talk too much.

The storekeeper placed both hands on the counter and leaned toward me. "We had no trouble before space travel; you'll grant that?"

I conceded the point. "Well?" he said triumphantly.

I shut up. How can you argue?

We did not go into town after that and saw no one and spoke to no one. On the way home (we were on foot) we passed close to the shack of John the Goat, our local hermit. Some say that John used to keep goats; I know he smelled like one. He did what little caretaking I required and we respected each other, that is, we saw each other only when strictly necessary and then as briefly as possible. But, seeing him, I waved.

He waved back. He was dressed as usual, stocking cap, an old army blouse, shorts, and sandals. I thought of warning him that a man had been shot nearby for not complying with the bare-to-the-waist order, but decided against it. John was the perfect anarchist; advice would have made him only more stubborn. Instead I cupped my hands and shouted, "Send up the Pirate!" He waved again and we went on without coming within two hundred feet of him, which was about right unless he was downwind.

"Who's the Pirate, darling?" Mary asked.

"You'll see."

Which she did; as soon as we got back the Pirate came in, for I had his little door keyed to his own meow so that he could let himself in and out—the Pirate being a large and rakish torn cat, half red Persian and half travelling salesman. He came in strutting, told me what he thought of people who stayed away so long, then headbumped my ankle in forgiveness. I reached down and roughed him up, then he inspected Mary.

I was watching Mary. She had dropped to her knees and was making the sounds used by people who understand cat protocol, but the Pirate was looking her over suspiciously. Suddenly he jumped into her arms and commenced to buzz like a faulty fuel meter, while bumping her under the chin.

I sighed loudly. "That's a relief," I announced. "For a moment I didn't think I was going to be allowed to keep you."

Mary looked up and smiled. "You need not have worried; I get along with cats. I'm two-thirds cat myself."

"What's the other third?"

She made a face at me. "You'll find out." She was scratching the Pirate under the chin; he was stretching his neck and accepting it, with an expression of indecent and lascivious pleasure. I noticed that her hair just matched his fur.

"Old John takes care of him while I'm away," I explained, "but the Pirate belongs to me—or vice versa."

"I figured that out," Mary answered, "and now I belong to the Pirate, too; don't I, Pirate?"

The cat did not answer but continued his shameless lallygagging—but it was clear that she was right. Truthfully

I was relieved; aelurophobes cannot understand why cats matter to aelurophiles, but if Mary had turned out not to be one of the lodge it would have fretted me.

From then on the cat was with us—or with Mary—almost all the time, except when I shut him out of our bedroom. That I would not stand for, though both Mary and the Pirate thought it small of me. We even took him with us when we went down the canyon for target practice. I suggested to Mary that it was safer to leave him behind but she said, "See to it that you don't shoot him. I won't."

I shut up, somewhat stung. I am a good shot and remain so by unrelenting practice at every opportunity—even on my honeymoon. No, that's not quite straight; I would have skipped practice on that occasion had it not turned out that Mary really liked to shoot. Mary is not just a good trained shot; she is the real thing, an Annie Oakley. She tried to teach me, but it can't be taught, not that sort of shooting.

I asked why she carried more than one gun. "You might need more than one," she told me. "Here—take my gun away from me."

I went through the motions of a standing, face-to-face disarm, bare hands against gun. She avoided it easily and said sharply, "What are you doing? Disarming me, or asking me to dance? Make it good."

So I made it good. I'll never be a match—medal shot but I stood at the top of my class in barroom. If she had not given in to it, I would have broken her wrist.

I had her gun. Then I realized that a second gun was pressing against my belly button. It was a lady's social gun, but perfectly capable of making two dozen widows without recharging. I looked down, saw that the safety was off, and knew that my beautiful bride had only to tense one muscle to burn a hole through me. Not a wide one, but sufficient.

"Where in the deuce did you find that?" I asked—and well I might, for neither one of us had bothered to dress when we came out. The area was very deserted and often it did not seem worthwhile to take the trouble; it was my land.

So I was much surprised as I would have sworn that the only gun Mary had with her was the one she had carried in her sweet little hand.

"It was high up on my neck, under my hair," she said demurely. "See?" I looked. I knew a phone could be hidden there but I had not thought of it for a gun—though of course I don't use a lady-size weapon and I don't wear my hair in long flame-colored curls.

Then I looked again, for she had a third gun shoved against my ribs. "Where did that one come from?" I asked.

She giggled. "Sheer misdirection; it's been in plain sight all the time." She would not tell me anything further and I never did figure it out. She should have clanked when she walked—but she did not. Oh my, no!

I found I could teach her a few things about hand-to-hand, which salved my pride. Bare hands are more useful than guns anyhow; they will save your life oftener. Not that Mary was not good at it herself; she packed sudden death in each hand and eternal sleep in her feet. However, she had the habit, whenever she lost a fall, of going limp and kissing me. Once, instead of kissing her back, I shook her and told her she was not taking it seriously. Instead of cutting out the nonsense, she continued to remain limp, let her voice go an octave lower, and said, "Don't you realize, my darling, that these are not my weapons?"

I knew that she did not mean that guns were her weapons; she meant something older and more primitive. True, she could fight like a bad-tempered Kodiak bear and I respected her for it, but she was no Amazon. An Amazon doesn't look that way with her head on a pillow. Mary's true strength lay in her other talents.

Which reminds me; from her I learned how it was that I was rescued from the slugs. Mary herself had prowled the city for days, not finding me, but reporting accurately the progress with which the city was being "secured". Had she not been able to spot a possessed man, we might have lost many agents fruitlessly—and I might never have gotten free from my master. As a result of the data she brought in, the Old Man drew back and concentrated on the entrances and exits to the city. And I was rescued, though they weren't waiting for me in particular . . . at least I don't suppose they were.

Or maybe they were. Something Mary said led me to think that the Old Man and she had worked watch on and watch off, heel-and-toe, covering the city's main launching platform, once it was evident that there was a focal point active in the city. But that could not have been correct— the Old Man would not have neglected his job to search for one agent. I must have misunderstood her.

I never got a chance to pursue the subject; Mary did not like digging into the past. I asked her once why the Old Man had relieved her as a presidential guard. She said, "I stopped being useful at it," and would not elaborate. She knew that I eventually would learn the reason: that the slugs had found out about sex, thus rendering her no longer useful as a touchstone for possessed males. But I did not know it then; she found the subject repulsive and refused to talk about it. Mary spent less time borrowing trouble than anyone I ever knew.

So little that I almost forgot, during that holiday from the world, what it was we were up against.

Although she would not talk about herself, she let me talk about myself. As I grew still more relaxed and still happier I tried to explain what had been eating me all my life. I told her about resigning from the service and the knocking around I had done before I swallowed my pride and went to work for the Old Man. "I'm a peaceable guy," I told her, "but what's the matter with me? The Old Man is the only one I've ever been able to subordinate myself to—and I still fight with him. Why, Mary? Is there something wrong with me?"

I had my head in her lap; she picked it up and kissed me. "Heavens, boy, don't you know? There's nothing really wrong with you; it's what has been done to you."

"But I've always been that way—until now."

"I know, ever since you were a child. No mother and an arrogantly brilliant father—you've been slapped around so much that you have no confidence in yourself."

Her answer surprised me so much that I reared up. Me? No confidence in myself? "Huh?" I said. "How can you say that? I'm the cockiest rooster in the yard."

"Yes. Or you used to be. Things will be better now." And there's where it stood for she took advantage of my change in position to stand up and say, "Let's go look at the sunset."

"Sunset?" I answered. "Can't be—we just finished breakfast." But she was right and I was wrong, a common occurrence.

The mix-up about the time of day jerked me back to reality. "Mary, how long have we been up here? What's the date?"

"Does it matter?"

"You're damn right it matters. It's been more than a week. I'm sure. One of these days our phones will start screaming and then it's back to the treadmill."

"In the meantime what difference does it make?"

She was right but I still wanted to know what day it was. I could have found out by switching on a stereo screen, but I would probably have bumped into a newscast—and I did not want that; I was still pretending that Mary and I were away in a different world, a safe world, where titans did not exist. "Mary," I said fretfully, "how many tempus pills have you?"

"None."

"Well—I've got enough for both of us. Let's stretch it out, make it last a long time. Suppose we have just twenty-four more hours; we could fine it down into a month, subjective time."

"No."

"Why not? Let's carpe that old diem before it gets away from us."

She put a hand on my arm and looked up into my eyes. "No, darling, it's not for me. I must live each moment as it comes and not let it be spoiled by worrying about the moment ahead." I suppose I looked stubborn for she went on, "If you want to take them, I won't mind, but please don't ask me to."

"Confound it. I'm not going on a joy ride alone." She did not answer, which is the damnedest way of winning an argument I know of.

Not that we argued. If I tried to start one—which I did, more than once—Mary would give in and somehow it would work out that I was mistaken. I did try several times to find out more about her; it seemed to me that I ought to know something about the woman I was married to. To one question she looked thoughtful and answered presently, "I sometimes wonder whether I ever did have a childhood—or was it something I dreamed last night?"

I asked her point blank what her name was. "Mary," she said tranquilly.

"Mary really is your name, then?" I had long since told her my right name, but we had agreed to go on using "Sam".

"Certainly it's my name, dear. I've been 'Mary' since you first called me that."

"Oh. All right, your name is Mary. You are my beloved Mary. But what was your name before?"

Her eyes held an odd, hurt look, but she answered steadily, "I was once known as 'Allucquere'."

"'Allucquere'," I repeated, savoring it. "Allucquere. What a strange and beautiful name. Allucquere. It has a rolling majesty about it. My darling Allucquere."

"My name is Mary, now." And that was that. Somewhere, somewhen, I was becoming convinced, Mary had been hurt, badly hurt. But it seemed unlikely that I was ever going to know about it. She had been married before, I was fairly certain; perhaps that was it.

Presently I ceased to worry about it. She was what she was, now and forever, and I was content to bask in the warm light of her presence. "Age cannot wither her nor custom stale her infinite variety."

I went on calling her "Mary" since she obviously preferred it and that was how I thought of her anyhow, but the name that she had once had kept running through my mind. Allucquere . . . Allucquere . . . I rolled it around my tongue and wondered how it was spelled.

Then suddenly I knew how it was spelled. My pesky packrat memory had turned up the right tab and now was pawing away at the shelves in the back of my mind where I keep the useless junk that I don't think about for years on end and am helpless to get rid of. There had been a community, a colony that used an artificial language, even to given names—

The Whitmanites, that was it—the anarchist-pacifist cult that got kicked out of Canada, then failed to make a go of it in Little America. There was a book, written by their prophet. The Entropy of Joy—I had not read it but I had skimmed it once; it was full of pseudomathematical formulas for achieving happiness.

Everybody is for "happiness", just as they are against "sin", but the cult's practices kept getting them in hot water. They had a curious and yet very ancient solution to their sexual problems, a solution which appeared to suit them but which produced explosive results when the Whitmanite culture touched any other pattern of behavior. Even Little America had not been far enough away for them; I had heard somewhere that the remnants had emigrated to Venus—in which case they must all be dead by now.

I put it out of my mind. If Mary were a Whitmanite, or had been reared that way, that was her business. I certainly was not going to let the cult's philosophy cause us a crisis now or ever; marriage is not ownership and wives are not property.

If that were all there was to what Mary did not want me to know about her, then I simply would not know it. I had not been looking for virginity wrapped in a sealed package; I had been looking for Mary.

🪶 **Chapter 22** 🪶

The next time I mentioned tempus pills, she did not argue but suggested that we hold it down to a minimum dose. It was a fair compromise—and we could always take more.

I prepared it as injections so that it would take hold faster. Ordinarily I watch a clock after I've taken tempus; when the second hand stops I know that I'm loaded. But my shack has no clocks and neither of us was wearing ring-watches. It was just sunrise and we had been awake all night, cuddled upon a big low half-moon couch in front of the fireplace.

We continued to lie there for a long time, feeling good and dreamy, and I was half considering the idea that the drug had not worked. Then I realized that the sun had stopped rising. I watched a bird fluttering past the view window. If I stared at him long enough, I could see his wings move.

I looked back from it to my wife, admired the long sweep of her limbs and the sudden, rising curves. The

Pirate was curled up on her stomach, a cubical cat, with his paws tucked in as a muff. Both of them seemed asleep. "How about some breakfast?" I said, "I'm starved."

"You fix it," she answered. "If I move, I'll disturb Pirate."

"You promised to love, honor, and fix me breakfast," I replied and tickled the soles of her feet. She gasped and drew up her legs; the cat squawked and landed on the floor.

"Oh dear!" she said, sitting up. "You made me move too fast and now I've offended him."

"Never mind the cat, woman; you're married to me." But I knew that I had made a mistake. In the presence of others, people not under the drug, one should move with great care. I simply hadn't thought about the cat; no doubt he thought we were behaving like drunken jumping jacks. I intentionally slowed down and tried to woo him.

No use—he was streaking toward his door. I could have stopped him, for to me his movement was a molasses crawl, but had I done so I would simply have frightened him more. I let him go and went to the kitchen.

Do you know, Mary was right; tempus fugit drug is no good for honeymoons. The ecstatic happiness that I had felt before was masked by the euphoria of the drug, though I did not feel the loss at the time because the drug's euphoria is compelling. But the loss was real; I had substituted for the true magic a chemical fake.

And there are some precious things which cannot or should not be hurried. Mary was right, as usual. Nevertheless it was a good day—or month, however you care to look at it. But I wished that I had stuck to the real thing.

Late that evening we came out of it. I felt the slight irritability which marks the loosening hold of the drug, found my ringwatch and timed my reflexes. When they were back to normal I timed Mary's, whereupon she informed me that she had been out of it for twenty minutes or so—pretty accurate matching of dosage to have been based on body weights alone.

"Do you want to go under again?" she asked me.

I pulled her to me and kissed her. "No; frankly, I'm glad to be back."

"I'm so glad."

I had the usual ravenous appetite that one has afterward no matter how many times one eats while under; I mentioned it. "In a minute," she said. "I want to call Pirate. He has not been in all day."

I had not missed him during the day—or "month"—just past; the euphoria is like that. "Don't worry about it," I told her. "He often stays out all day."

"He has not before."

"He has with me," I answered.

"I think I offended him—I know I did."

"Then he is probably down at Old John's. That is his usual way of punishing me when he does not like the service. He'll be all right."

"But it's late at night—I'm afraid a coyote might get him."

"Don't be silly; there are no coyotes this far east."

"A fox, then—or something. Do you mind, darling? I'll just step out and call him." She headed for the door.

"Put on something, then," I ordered. "It will be nippy out there."

She hesitated, then went back to the bedroom and got a negligee I had bought for her the day we had gone down to the village. She went out; I put more wood on the fire and went into the kitchen.

She must have left the door dilated for, while I was trying to make up my mind between convenience of a "Soup-to-Nuts" and the pleasure of planning a meal from separate units, I heard her saying, "Bad, bad cat! You worried mama," in that cooing voice suitable for babies and felines.

I called out, "Fetch him in and close the door—and mind the penguins!" She did not answer and I did not hear the door relax, so I went back into the living room.

She was just coming in and did not have the cat with her. I started to speak and then caught sight of her eyes. They were staring, filled with unspeakable horror. I said, "Mary!" and started toward her.

She seemed to see me and turned back toward the door; her movements were jerky, spasmodic. As she turned I saw her shoulders.

Under the negligee was a hump.

I don't know how long I stood there. Probably a split second but it is burned into me as endless. I jumped toward her and grabbed her by the arms. She looked at me and her eyes were no longer wells of horror but merely dead.

She gave me the knee.

I squeezed and managed to avoid the worst of it. Look—I know you don't tackle a dangerous opponent by grabbing his upper arms, but this was my wife. I couldn't come at Mary with a feint-shift-and-kill.

But the slug had no compunctions about me. Mary—or it—was giving me everything she had and I had all I could do to keep from killing her. I had to keep her from killing me—and I had to kill the slug—and I had to keep the slug from getting at me or I would not be able to save her.

I let go with one hand and jabbed at her chin. The blow should have knocked her out but it did not even slow her down. I grabbed again, with both arms and legs, trying to encase her in a bear hug to immobilize her without injuring her. We went down together, Mary on top. I shoved the top of my head into her face to stop her biting me.

I held her so, curbing her strong body by sheer bulk of muscle. Then I tried to paralyze her with nerve pressure, but she knew what I was up to, knew the key spots as well as I did—and I was lucky that I was not myself paralyzed.

There was one thing left that I could do: clutch the slug itself-but I knew the shattering effect that had on the host. It might not kill her; again it might. It was sure to hurt her horribly. I wanted to make her unconscious, then remove the slug gently before I killed it . . . drive it off with heat or force it to turn loose with mild shocks.

Drive it off with heat—

But I was given no time to develop the idea; she got her teeth in my ear. I shifted my right arm and grabbed at the slug. Nothing happened. Instead of sinking my fingers into a slimy mess I found that this slug had a horny, leathery covering; it was as if I had clutched a football. Mary jerked when I touched it and took away part of my ear, but there was no bone-crushing spasm; the slug was still alive and in control of her.

I tried to get my fingers under it, to pry it loose; it clung like a suction cup. My fingers would not go under.

In the meantime I was suffering damages in other places. I rolled over and got to my knees, still hugging her. I had to let her legs free and that was bad, but I bent her across a knee and then struggled to my feet. I dragged and carried her to the fireplace.

She knew what I was doing and almost got away from me; it was like trying to wrestle a mountain lion. But I got her there, grabbed her by her mop of hair and slowly forced her shoulders over the fire.

I meant—I swear that I meant only to singe it, force it to drop off to escape that heat. But she struggled so hard that I slipped, banging my own head against the arch of the opening and dropping her shoulders against the coals.

She screamed and bounded out of the fire, carrying me with her. I struggled to my feet, still dazed by the wallop I had taken in the head, and saw her collapsed on the floor. Her hair, her beautiful hair, was burning.

So was her negligee. I slapped at them both with my hands. The slug was no longer on her. Still crushing the flames with my hands I glanced around and saw it lying on the floor in front of the fireplace—and the Pirate was sniffing at it.

"Get away from there!" I yelled. "Pirate! Stop that!" The cat looked up inquiringly, as if this were some new and interesting game. I went on doing what I had to do, making absolutely certain that the fire was out, both hair and clothing. When I was sure, I left her; there was not even time to make certain that she was still alive. There was something more urgent to do.

What I wanted was the fireplace shovel; I did not dare risk touching the thing with my hands. I turned to get the shovel.

But the slug was no longer on the floor; it had gotten Pirate. The cat was standing rigid, feet wide apart, and the slug was settling into place.

Perhaps it would have been better had I been a few seconds later; perhaps the slug, mounted on the cat, would have escaped outdoors. I would not have pursued it into the dark. I don't think I would have. But I dived at Pirate and got him by his hind legs just as he made his first controlled movement.

Handling a frenzied, full-grown cat with bare hands is reckless at best; controlling one which is already controlled by a titan is impossible. Hands and arms being slashed by claws and teeth at every step, I hurried again to the fireplace.

This time I made sure. Despite Pirate's wails and struggles I forced the slug against the coals and held it there, cat fur and my hands alike burning, until the slug dropped off directly into the flames. Then I took Pirate out and laid him on the floor. He was no longer struggling. I did for him what I had done for Mary, made sure that he was no longer burning anywhere and went back to Mary.

She was still unconscious. I squatted down beside her and sobbed.

An hour later I had done what I could for Mary. Her hair was almost gone from the left side of her head and there were burns on her shoulders and neck. But her pulse was strong, her respiration steady though fast and light, and I did not judge that she would lose much body fluid. I dressed her burns—I keep a rather full stock out there in the country—and gave her an injection to make her sleep. Then I had time for Pirate.

He was still on the floor where I had left him and he did not look good. He had gotten it much worse than Mary and probably flame in his lungs as well. I thought he was dead, but he lifted his head when I touched him. "I'm sorry, old fellow," I whispered. I think I heard him mew.

I did for him what I had done for Mary, except that I was afraid to give him a soporific. After that I went into the bathroom and looked myself over.

The ear had stopped bleeding and I decided to ignore it, for the time being. Someday, when I had time, it would need to be rebuilt. My hands were what bothered me. I stuck them under hot water and yelped, then dried them in the air blast and that hurt, too. I could not figure out how I could dress them, and, besides, I needed to use them.

Finally I dumped about an ounce of the jelly for burns into each of a pair of plastic gloves and put them on. The stuff included a local anesthetic; I could get by. Then I went to the stereophone and called the village medical man. I explained to him carefully and correctly what had happened and what I had done about it and asked him to come at once.

"At night?" he said. "You must be joking."

I said that I decidedly was not joking.

He answered, "Don't ask the impossible, man. Yours makes the fourth alarm in this county; nobody goes out at night. You've done everything that can be done tonight; I'll stop in and see your wife first thing in the morning."

I told him to go straight to the devil first thing in the morning and switched off.

Pirate died a little after midnight. I buried him at once so that Mary would not see him. Digging hurt my hands but he did not take a very big hole. I said goodbye to him and came back in. Mary was resting quietly; I brought a chair to the bed and watched over her. Probably I dozed from time to time; I can't be sure.

Chapter 23

About dawn Mary began to struggle and moan. I stepped to the bed and put a hand on her. "There, baby, there— It's all right. Sam's here."

Her eyes opened and for a moment held the same horror they had held when she was first possessed. Then she saw me and relaxed. "Sam! Oh, darling, I've had the most terrible dream."

"It's all right," I repeated.

"Why are you wearing gloves?" She became aware of her own dressings; she looked dismayed and said, "It wasn't a dream!"

"No, dearest, it wasn't a dream. But it's all right; I killed it."

"You killed it? You're sure it's dead?"

"Quite sure." The house still reeked with the stench of its dying.

"Oh. Come here, Sam. Hold me tight."

"I'll hurt your shoulders."

"Hold me!" So I did, while trying to be careful of her

burns, although she seemed indifferent to them. Presently her trembling slowed down and stopped almost completely. "Forgive me, darling—I'm being weak and womanish."

"You should have seen the shape I was in when they got me back."

"I did see. Now tell me what happened; I must know. The last I remember you were trying to force me into the fireplace."

"Look. Mary, I couldn't help it; I had to—I couldn't get it off!"

She shook my shoulders and now it was she comforting me. "I know, darling, I know—and thank you for doing it! Thank you from the bottom of my heart. Again I owe you everything."

We both cried a bit and presently I blew my nose and went on, "You did not answer when I called you, so I went into the living room and there you were."

"I remember—oh darling, I tried so hard!"

I stared at her. "I know you did—you tried to leave. But how did you? Once a slug gets you, that's it. There's no way to fight it."

"Well, I lost—but I tried." There was no answer to the mystery. Somehow, Mary had forced her will against that of a parasite—and that can't be done. I know. True, she had succumbed, but I knew then that I was married to a human who was tougher and stronger than I was, despite her lovely curves and her complete femininity.

I had a sneaking hunch that had Mary not been able to resist the slug by some amount, however slight, I would have lost the struggle, handicapped as I was by what I could not do.

"I should have used a light, Sam," she went on, "but it never occurred to me to be afraid here." I nodded; this was the safe place, like crawling into bed or into sheltering arms. "Pirate came to me at once. I didn't see the thing until I had reached down and touched him. Then it was too late." She sat up, supporting herself on one arm. "Where is he, Sam? Is he all right? Call him in."

So I had to tell her about Pirate. She listened without expression, nodded and never referred to him again. I changed the subject by saying, "Now that you are awake I had better fix you some breakfast."

"Don't go!" I stopped. "Don't go out of my sight at all," she went on, "Not for any reason. I'll get up in a moment and get breakfast."

"The hell you will. You'll stay right in that bed, like a good little girl."

"Come here and take off those gloves. I want to see your hands." I did not take them off—could not bear to think about it; the anesthesia had worn off. She nodded and said grimly, "Just as I thought. You were burned worse than I was."

So she got breakfast. Furthermore she ate—I wanted nothing but a pot of coffee. I did insist that she drink a lot, too; large area burns are no joke. Presently she pushed aside her plate, looked at me and said, "Darling, I'm not sorry it happened. Now I know. Now we've both been there." I nodded humbly, knowing what she meant. Sharing happiness is not enough. She stood up and said, "Now we must go."

"Yes," I agreed, "now we must go. I want to get you to a doctor as soon as possible."

"I did not mean that."

"I know you didn't." There was no need to discuss it further; we both knew that the music had stopped and that now was time to go back to work. The heap we had arrived in was still sitting on my landing flat, piling up rental charges. It took about three minutes to burn the dishes, switch off everything but the permanent circuits, and get ready. I could not find my shoes but Mary remembered where I had left them.

Mary drove, because of my hands. Once in the air she turned to me and said, "Let's go straight to the Section offices. We'll get treatment there and find out what has been going on—or are your hands hurting too badly?"

"Suits," I agreed. My hands were hurting but they would not be any worse for another hour of waiting. I wanted to learn the situation as soon as possible—and I wanted to get back to work. I asked Mary to switch on the squawk screen; I was as anxious to catch a newscast now as I had been anxious to avoid them before. But the car's communication equipment was as junky as the rest of it; we could not even pick up audio. Fortunately the remote-control circuits were still okay, or Mary would have had to buck it through traffic by hand.

A thought had been fretting me for some time; I mentioned it to Mary. "A slug would not mount a cat just for the hell of it, would it?"

"I suppose not."

"But why? It doesn't make sense. But it has to make sense; everything they do makes sense, grisly sense, from their viewpoint."

"But it did make sense. They caught a human that way."

"Yes, I know. But how could they plan it? Surely there aren't enough of them that they can afford to place themselves on cats on the off chance that the cat might catch a human. Or are there enough?" I remembered the speed with which a slug on an ape's back had turned itself into two, I remembered Kansas City, saturated, and shivered.

"Why ask me, darling? I don't have an analytical brain." Which was true, in a way; there is nothing wrong with Mary's brain but she jumps logic and arrives at her answers by instinct. Me, I have to worry it out by logic.

"Drop the modest little girl act and try this on for size: the first question is, 'Where did the slug come from?' It didn't walk; it had to get to the Pirate on the back of another host. What host? I'd say it was Old John—John the Goat. I doubt if Pirate would have let any other human get close to him."

"Old John?" Mary closed her eyes, then opened them. "I can't get any feeling about it. I was never close to him."

"It does not matter; by elimination I think it must be true. Old John wore a coat when everyone else was complying with the Bare Back order . . . getting away with it because he shuns people. Ergo, he was hag-ridden before Schedule Bare Back. But that does not get me any further. Why would a slug single out a hermit way up in the mountains?"

"To capture you."

"Me?"

"To recapture you."

It made some sense. Possibly any host that ever escaped them was a marked man; in that case the dozen-odd

Congressmen and any others we had rescued—including Mary—were in special danger. I'd mark that down to report for analysis. No, not Mary—the only slug that knew she had been possessed was dead.

On the other hand they might want me in particular. What was special about me? I was a secret agent. More important, the slug that had ridden me must have known what I knew about the Old Man and known that I had access to him. That would be reason enough to try to get me back. I held an emotional certainty that the Old Man was their principal antagonist; the slug must have known that I thought so; he had full use of my mind.

That slug had even met the Old Man, talked with him. Wait a minute, that slug was dead. And my theory came tumbling down.

And built up again at once. "Mary," I asked, "have you used your apartment since the morning you and I had breakfast there?"

"No. Why?"

"Don't. Don't go back there for any purpose. I recall thinking, while I was with them, that I would have to booby-trap it."

"Well, you didn't, did you? Or did you?"

"No, I did not. But it may have been booby-trapped since then. There may be the equivalent of Old John waiting, spider fashion, for you—or me—to return there." I explained to her McIlvaine's theory about the slugs, the "group memory" idea. "I thought at the time he was spinning the dream stuff scientists are so fond of. But now I don't know; it's the only hypothesis I can think of that covers everything . . . unless we assume that the titans are so stupid that they would as soon try to catch fish in a bathtub as in a brook. Which they aren't."

"Just a moment, dear—by Dr. McIlvaine's theory each slug is really every other slug; is that it? In other words that thing that caught me last night was just as much the one that rode you when you were with them as was the one that actually did ride you—Oh, dear, I'm getting confused. I mean—"

"That's the general idea. Apart, they are individuals; in direct conference they merge their memories and Tweedledum becomes exactly like Tweedledee. Then, if that is true, this one last night remembers everything it learned from me provided it had direct conference with the slug that rode me, or any other slug that had had, or a slug that had been linked through any number of slugs by direct conference to the slug that had ridden me, after the time it did—which you can bet it did, from what I know of their habits. It would have—the first one, I mean . . . wait a minute; this is getting involved. Take three slugs; Joe, Moe, and uh, Herbert. Herbert is the one last night; Moe is the one which—"

"Why give them names if they are not individuals?" Mary wanted to know.

"Just to keep them—No reason; let it lie that if McIlvaine is right there are hundreds of thousands, maybe millions, of slugs who know exactly who you and I are, by name and by sight and everything, know where your apartment is, where my apartment is, and where our cabin is. They've got us on a list."

"But—" She frowned. "That's a horrid thought, Sam. How would they know when to find us at the cabin? You didn't tell anybody we were going and I did not even know. Would they simply stake it out and wait? Yes, I suppose they would."

"They must have. We don't know that waiting matters to a slug; time may mean something entirely different to them."

"Like Venerians," she suggested. I nodded; a Venerian is likely as not to "marry" his own great-great-granddaughter—and be younger than his descendants. It depends on how they estivate, of course.

"In any case," I went on, "I've got to report this, including our guesses as to what is behind it, for the boys in the analytical group to play with."

I was about to go on to say that, if we were right, the Old Man would have to be especially careful, as it was he and not Mary and myself that they were after. But my phone sounded for the first time since my leave had started. I answered and the Old Man's voice cut in ahead of the talker's: "Report in person."

"We're on our way," I acknowledged. "About thirty minutes."

"Make it sooner. You use Kay Five; tell Mary to come in by Ell One. Move." He switched off before I could ask him how he had known that Mary was with me.

"Did you get it?" I asked Mary.

"Yes, I was in the circuit."

"Sounds as if the party was about to start."

It was not until we had landed that I began to realize how drastically the situation had changed. We were complying with Schedule Bare Back; we had not heard of

Schedule Sun Tan. Two cops stopped us as we got out. "Stay where you are!" one of them ordered. "Don't make any sudden moves."

You would not have known they were cops, except for the manner and the drawn guns. They were dressed in gun belts, shoes, and skimpy breech clouts—little more than straps. A second glance showed their shields clipped to their belts. "Now," the same one went on, "Off with those pants, buddy."

I did not move quickly enough to suit him. He barked, "Make it snappy! There have been two shot trying to escape already today; you may be the third."

"Do it, Sam," Mary said quietly. I did it. My shorts were a one-piece garment, with the underwear part built in; without them, I stood dressed in my shoes and a pair of gloves, feeling like a fool—but I had managed to keep both my phone and my gun covered up as I took off my shorts.

The cop made me turn around. His mate said, "He's clean. Now the other one." I started to put my shorts back on and the first cop stopped me.

"Hey! You looking for trouble? Leave 'em off."

I said reasonably, "You've searched me. I don't want to get picked up for indecent exposure."

He looked surprised, then guffawed and turned to his mate. "You hear that. Ski? He's afraid he'll be arrested for indecent exposure."

The second one said patiently, "Listen, yokel, you got to cooperate, see? You know the rules. You can wear a fur coat for all of me—but you won't get picked up for indecent exposure; you'll get picked up DOA. The

Vigilantes are a lot quicker to shoot than we are." He turned to Mary. "Now, lady, if you please."

Without argument Mary started to remove her shorts. The second cop said kindly, "That isn't necessary lady, not the way those things are built. Just turn around slowly."

"Thank you," Mary said and complied. The policeman's point was well taken; Mary's briefies appeared to have been sprayed on, and her halter also quite evidently contained nothing but Mary.

"How about those bandages?" the first one commented. "Her clothes sure can't cover anything." I thought, brother, how wrong you are; I'll bet she's packing at least two guns this minute, besides the one in her purse—and I'll bet one of them is ready to heat up quicker than yours! But what I said was,

"She's been badly burned. Can't you see that?" He looked doubtfully at the sloppy job I had done on the dressings; I had worked on the principle that, if a little is good, more is better, and the dressing across her shoulders where she had been burned the worst undoubtedly could have concealed a slug, if that had been the purpose. "Mmmm . . ." he said, "If she was burned."

"Of course she was burned!" I felt my judgment slipping away; I was the perfect heavy husband, unreasonable where my wife was concerned. I knew it—and I liked it that way. "Damn it, look at her hair! Would she ruin a head of hair like that just to fool you?"

The first cop said darkly, "One of them would."

The more patient one said, "Carl is right. I'm sorry, lady; we'll have to disturb those bandages."

I said excitedly, "You can't do that! We're on our way to a doctor. You'll just—"

Mary said, "Help me, Sam. I can't take them off myself."

I shut up and started to peel up one corner of the big dressing, my hands trembling with rage. Presently the older, more kindly one whistled and said, "I'm satisfied. How about you, Carl?"

"Me, too. Ski. Gripes, girlie, it looks like somebody tried to barbecue you. What happened?"

"Tell them, Sam."

So I did. The older cop finally commented, "I'd say you got off easy—no offense, madam. So it's cats, now, eh? Dogs I knew about. Horses, yes. But cats—you wouldn't think the ordinary cats could carry one." His face clouded. "We got a cat and now we'll have to get rid of it. My kids won't like that."

"I'm sorry," Mary told him and sounded as if she meant it.

"It's a bad time for everybody. Okay, folks, you can go—"

"Wait a minute," the first one said. "Ski, if she goes through the streets with that thing on her back somebody is likely to burn her."

The older one scratched his chin. "That's true," he said to Mary. "I'd say you couldn't stand to have that dressing off. We'll just have to dig up a prowl car for you."

Which they did—one was just landing and they hailed it. I had to pay the charges on the rented wreck, then I went along, as far as Mary's entrance. It was in a hotel, through a private elevator; I got in with her to avoid explanations, then went back up after she had gotten out at a level lower than the obvious controls of the car provided for. I was tempted to go on in with her, but the Old Man had ordered me to come in by Kay Five, so Kay Five it was.

I was tempted, too, to put my shorts back on. In the prowl car and during a quick march through a side door of the hotel, with police around us to keep Mary from being shot, I had not minded so much—but it took nerve to step out of the elevator and face the world without pants.

I need not have worried. The short distance I had to go was enough to show me that a fundamental custom had gone with last year's frost. Most men were wearing straps—codpieces, really—as the cops had been, but I was not the only man in New Brooklyn stark naked to his shoes. One in particular I remember; he was leaning against a street roof stanchion and searching with cold eyes every passer-by. He was wearing nothing but slippers and a brassard lettered with "VIG"—and he was carrying an Owens mob gun under his arm.

I saw three more like him before I reached Kay Five; I was glad that I was carrying my shorts.

Some women were naked, some were not—but those who were not might as well have been—string brassieres, translucent plastic trunks, nothing that could possibly hide a slug.

Most of the women, I decided, would have looked better in clothes, preferably togas. If this was what the preachers had been worrying about all these years, then they had been barking up the wrong tree; it was nothing to arouse the happy old beast in men. The total effect was depressing. That was my first impression—but before I got to my destination even that had worn off. Ugly bodies weren't any more noticeable than ugly taxicabs; the eye discounted them automatically. And so it appeared to be with everybody else, too; those on the streets seemed to have acquired utter indifference. Maybe Schedule Bare Back got them ready for it.

One thing I did not notice consciously until much later: after the first block I was unaware of my own nakedness. I noticed other people long after I had forgotten my own bare skin. Somehow, some way, the American community had been all wrong about the modesty taboo and had been wrong for centuries.

When tackled firmly, it was as empty as the ghost that turns out to be a flapping window drape. It did not mean a thing, either pro or con, moral or immoral. Skin was skin and what of it?

I was let in to see the Old Man at once. He looked up and growled, "You're late."

I answered, "Where's Mary?"

"In the infirmary, getting treated and dictating her report. Let's see your hands."

"I'll show them to the doctor, thanks," I replied, making no move to take off the gloves. "What's up?"

"If you would ever bother to listen to a newscast," he grumbled, "you would know what was up."

Chapter 24

I'm glad I had not looked at a newscast; our honeymoon would never have gotten to first base. While Mary and I had each been telling the other how wonderful the other one was the war had almost been lost—and I was not sure about that "almost". My suspicion that the slugs could, if necessary, hide themselves on any part of the body and still control hosts had proved to be right—but I had guessed that from my own experience on the streets. It had been proved by experiments at the National Zoo before Mary and I had holed up on the mountain, although I had not seen the report. I suppose the Old Man knew it; certainly the President knew it and the other top VIPs.

So Schedule Sun Tan replaced Schedule Bare Back and everybody skinned down to the buff.

Like hell they did! The matter was still "Top Secret" and the subject of cabinet debates at the time of the Scranton Riot. Don't ask me why it was top secret, or even restricted; our government has gotten the habit of classifying anything as secret which the all-wise statesmen and bureaucrats decide we are not big enough boys and girls to know, a Mother-Knows-Best-Dear policy. I've read that there used to be a time when a taxpayer could demand the facts on anything and get them. I don't know; it sounds Utopian.

The Scranton Riot should have convinced anybody that the slugs were loose in Zone Green despite Schedule Bare Back, but even that did not bring on Schedule Sun Tan. The fake air-raid alarm on the east coast took place, as I figure it, the third day of our honeymoon; there had not been any special excitement in the village when we visited it the day before that and certainly no vigilante activity. After the false air-raid alarm it took a while to figure out what had happened, even though it was obvious that lighting could not fail by accident in so many different shelters.

It gives me the leaping horrors to think about it even now—all those people crouching in the darkness, waiting for the all-clear, while zombies moved among them, slapping slugs on them. Apparently in some air raid bunkers the recruitment was one hundred percent. They did not have a chance.

So there were more riots the next day and we were well into the Terror, though we did not know it. Technically, the start of vigilantism came the first time a desperate citizen pulled a gun on a cop—Maurice T. Kaufman of Albany and the cop was Sergeant Malcolm MacDonald. Kaufman was dead a half second later and MacDonald followed him in a few minutes, torn to pieces by the mob, along with his titan master. But the Vigilantes did not really get going until the air-raid wardens put organization into the movement.

The wardens, being mostly aboveground at the time the coup in the bunkers took place, largely escaped— but they felt responsible. Not that all Vigilantes were wardens, nor all wardens Vigilantes—but a stark naked, armed man on the street was as likely to be wearing a warden's armband as the "VIG" brassard. Either way, you could count on him shooting at any unexplained excrescence on a human body—shoot and investigate afterward.

While my hands were being treated and dressed I was brought up to date concerning the period (it turned out to be two weeks) that Mary and I had spent at the cabin. By the Old Man's orders the doctor gave me a short shot of tempus before he worked on me and I spent the time— subjective, about three days; objective, less than an hour—studying stereo tapes through an over-speed scanner. This gadget has never been released to the public, though I have heard that it is bootlegged at some of the colleges around examination week. You adjust the speed to match your subjective time rate, or a little faster, and use an audio frequency step-down to let you hear what is being said. It is hard on the eyes and usually results in a splitting headache—but it is a big help in my profession.

It was hard to believe that so much could have happened in so short a time. Take dogs. A Vigilante would kill a dog on sight, even though it was not wearing a slug— because it was even money that it would be wearing one before next sunrise, that it would attack a man and that the titan would change riders in the dark.

A hell of a world where you could not trust dogs!

Apparently cats were hardly ever used because of their smaller size. Poor old Pirate was an exceptional case.

In Zone Green dogs were almost never seen now, at least by day. They filtered out of Zone Red at night, traveled in the dark and hid out in the daytime. They kept showing up, even on the coasts. It made one think of the werewolf legends. I made a mental note to apologize to the village doctor who had refused to come to see Mary at night— after I pasted him one.

I scanned dozens of tapes which had been monitored from Zone Red; they fell into three time groups: the masquerade period, when the slugs had been continuing the "normal" broadcasts; a short period of counter-propaganda during which the slugs had tried to convince citizens in Zone Green that the government had gone crazy—it had not worked as we had not relayed their casts, just as they had not relayed the President's proclamation—and, finally, the current period in which pretense had been dropped, the masquerade abandoned.

According to Dr. McIlvaine the titans have no true culture of their own; they are parasitic even in that and merely adapt the culture they find to their own needs. Maybe he assumes too much, but that is what they did in Zone Red. The slugs would have to maintain the basic economic activity of their victims since the slugs themselves would starve if the hosts starved. To be sure, they continued that economy with variations that we would not use—that business of processing damaged and excess people in fertilizer plants, for example—but in general farmers stayed farmers, mechanics went on being mechanics, and bankers were still bankers. That last seems silly, but the experts claim that any "division-of-labor" economy requires an accounting system, a "money" system.

I know myself that they use money behind the Curtain, so he may be right—but I never heard of "bankers" or "money" among ants or termites. However, there may be lots of things I've never heard of.

It is not so obvious why they continued human recreations. Is the desire to be amused a universal need? Or did they learn it from us? The "experts" on each side of the argument are equally emphatic—and I don't know. What they picked from human ideas of fun to keep and "improve on" does not speak well for the human race although some of their variations may have merit—that stunt that they pulled in Mexico, for example, of giving the bull an even break with the matador.

But most of it just makes one sick at the stomach and I won't elaborate. I am one of the few who saw even transcriptions on such things, except for foolhardy folk who still held out in Zone Amber; I saw them professionally. The government monitored all stereocasts from Zone Red but the transcriptions were suppressed under the old Comstock "Indecency" Law—another example of "Mother-Knows-Best", though perhaps Mother did know best in this case. I hope that Mary, in her briefing, did not have to look at such things, but Mary would never say so if she had.

Or perhaps "Mother" did not "Know Best"; if anything more could have added to the determination of men still free to destroy this foul thing it would have been the "entertainment" stereocast from stations inside Zone Red. I recall a boxing match cast from the Will Rogers Memorial Auditorium at Fort Worth—or perhaps you would call it a wrestling match. In any case there was a ring and a referee and two contestants pitted against each other. There were even fouls, i.e., doing anything which might damage the opponent's manager—I mean "master", the opponent's slug.

Nothing else was a foul—nothing! It was a man versus a woman, both of them big and husky. She gouged out one of his eyes in the first clinch, but he broke her left wrist which kept the match on even enough terms to continue. It ended only when one of them had been so weakened by loss of blood that the puppet master could no longer make the slave dance. The woman lost—and died, I am sure, for her left breast was almost torn away and she had bled so much that only immediate surgery and massive transfusions could have saved her. Which she did not get; the slugs were transferred to new hosts at the end of the match and the inert contenders were dragged out.

But the male slave had remained active a little longer than the female, slashed and damaged though he was, and he finished the match with a final act of triumph over her which I soon learned was customary. It seemed to be a signal to turn it into an "audience participation show", an orgy which would make a witches' Sabbat seem like a sewing circle.

Oh, the slugs had discovered sex, all right!

There was one more thing which I saw in this and other tapes, a thing so outrageous, so damnably disgusting that I hesitate even to mention it, though I feel I must—there were men and women here and there among the slaves, humans (if you could call them that) without slugs . . . trusties . . . renegades—

I hate slugs but I would turn from killing a slug to kill one such. Our ancestors believed that there were men who would willingly sign compacts with the Devil; our ancestors were partly right: there are men who would, given the chance.

Some people refuse to believe that any human being turned renegade; those who disbelieve did not see the suppressed transcriptions. There was no chance for mistake; as everyone knows, once the masquerade was no longer useful to the slugs, the wearing of clothes was dropped in Zone Red even more thoroughly than it was under Schedule Sun Tan in Zone Green; one could see. In the Fort Worth horror which I have faintly sketched above the referee was a renegade; he was much in the camera and I was able to be absolutely sure. I knew him by sight, a well-known amateur sportsman, a "gentleman" referee. I shan't mention his name, not to protect him but to protect myself; later on I killed him.

We were losing ground everywhere; that I knew before they finished treating my hands. Ours was a holding action only; our methods were effective only in stopping the spread of the infection and not fully effective in that. To fight them directly we would have to fight our own people, bomb our own cities, with no certainty of killing the humps. What we needed was a selective weapon, one that would kill slugs but not men, or something that would disable humans or render unconscious without killing and thereby permit us to rescue our compatriots. No such weapon was available, though the scientists were all busy on the problem, from the comedy team of McIlvaine & Vargas down to the lowliest bottle-washer in the Bureau of Standards. A "sleep" gas would have been perfect, but it is lucky that no such gas was known before the invasion, or the slugs could have used it against us; it would have cut both ways. It must be remembered that the slugs then had as much, or more, of the military potential of the United States at their disposal as had the free men.

Stalemate—with time on the side of the enemy. There were the fools who wanted to H-bomb the cities of the Mississippi Valley right out of existence, like curing a lip cancer by cutting off the head, but they were offset by their twins who had not seen slugs, did not believe in slugs, and felt that the whole matter was a violation of states' rights and Schedule Sun Tan a tyrannical Washington plot. These second sort were fewer each day, not because they changed their minds but because the Vigilantes were awfully eager.

Then there was the tertium quid, the flexible mind, the "reasonable" man who hardly had a mind to change— he favored negotiation; he thought we could "do business" with the titans. One such committee, a delegation from the caucus of the opposition party in Congress, actually attempted negotiation. Bypassing the State Department they got in touch via a linkage rigged across Zone Amber with the Governor of Missouri, and were assured of safe conduct and diplomatic immunity—"guarantees" from a titan, but they accepted them; they went to St. Louis— and never came back. They sent messages back; I saw one such, a good rousing speech adding up to, "Come on in; the water is fine!"

Do steers sign treaties with meat packers?

North America was still the only known center of infection. The only action by the United Nations, other than placing the space stations at our disposal, was to remove temporarily to Geneva. No aggression by any other nation was involved and it was even argued that the slugs—if they existed—were technically an epidemic disease rather than a potential source of war and therefore of no interest to the Security Council. It was voted, with twenty-three nations abstaining, to define it as "civil disorder" and to urge each member nation to give such aid as it saw fit to the legitimate governments of the United States, Mexico, and Canada.

What each might have "seen fit" was academic; we did not know what to ask for.

It remained a creeping war, a silent war, with battles lost before we knew they were joined. After the debacle of Schedule Counter Blast, conventional weapons were hardly used, except in police action in Zone Amber— which was now a double no-man's-land on each side of Zone Red, from the trackless Canadian forests to the Mexican deserts. It was almost deserted in the daytime of any life larger than birds and mice, save for our own patrols. At night our scouts drew back and the dogs came through—and other things, perhaps.

At the time Mary and I arrived back only one atom bomb had been used in the entire war and that against a flying saucer that landed near San Francisco just south of Burlingame. Its destruction was according to doctrine, but the doctrine was now under criticism; the saucer should have been captured for study, so it was argued, if we were to learn enough about our foe to fight successfully. I found my sympathies with those who wanted to shoot first and study later.

By the time the dose of tempus was beginning to wear off I had a picture of the United States in a shape that I had not imagined even when I was in saturated Kansas City—a country undergoing a Terror. Friend might shoot friend, or wife denounce husband. Rumor of a titan could drum up a mob on any street, with Old Judge Lynch baying in their van. To rap on a door at night was to invite a blast through the door rather than a friendly response. Honest folk stayed home; at night the dogs were out— and others.

The fact that most of the rumored discoveries of slugs were baseless made the rumors no less dangerous. It was not exhibitionism which caused many people to prefer outright nudity to the tight and scanty clothing permitted under Schedule Sun Tan; even the skimpiest clothing invited a doubtful second look, a suspicion that might be decided too abruptly. The head-and-spine armor was never worn now; the slugs had faked it and used it almost at once. And there had been the case of a girl in Seattle; she had been dressed in sandals and a big purse, nothing else—but a Vigilante who apparently had developed a nose for the enemy followed her and noticed that she never, under any circumstances, moved the purse from her right hand, even when she opened it to make change.

She lived, for he burned her arm off at the wrist, and I suppose that she had a new one grafted on; the supply of such spare parts was almost a glut. The slug was alive, too, when the Vigilante opened the purse—but not for long.

When I came across this in the briefing I realized with a shudder that I had not been too safe even in carrying my shorts through the streets; any slug-sized burden was open to suspicion.

The drug had worn off by the time I scanned this incident and I was back in contact with my surroundings. I mentioned the matter to the nurse. "Mustn't worry," she told me. "It does no good. Now flex the fingers of your right hand, please."

I flexed them, while she helped the doctor spray on surrogate skin. I noticed that she was taking no chances; she wore no bra at all and her so-to-speak shorts were actually more of a G-string. The doctor was dressed about the same. "Wear gloves for rough work," the doctor cautioned, "and come back next week."

I thanked them and went to the operations office. I looked for Mary first, but found that she was busy in Cosmetics.

☞ **Chapter 25** ☜

Hands all right?" the Old Man asked when they let me in.

"They'll do. False skin for a week. They do a graft job on my ear tomorrow."

He looked vexed. "I forgot your ear. There's no time for a graft to heal; Cosmetics will have to fake one for you."

"The ear doesn't matter," I told him, "but why bother to fake it? Impersonation job?"

"Not exactly. Now that you've been briefed, what do you think of the situation?"

I wondered what answer he was fishing for. "Not good," I conceded. "Everybody watching everybody else. Might as well be behind the Curtain. Shucks," I admitted, going overboard, "this is worse. You can usually bribe a communist, but what bribe can you offer a slug?"

"Hmm—" he commented. "That's an interesting thought. What would constitute a bribe inducement to a titan?"

"Look, that was a rhetorical question. I—"

"And my restatement of it was not rhetorical; we'll farm it out for theoretical investigation."

"Grabbing at straws these days, aren't you?"

"Precisely. Now about the rest of your comment; would you say that it was easier to penetrate and maintain surveillance in the Soviet Union or in Zone Red. Which would you rather tackle?"

I eyed him suspiciously. "There's a catch in this. You don't let a man pick his assignment."

"I asked you for a professional opinion."

"Mmmm . . . I don't have enough data. Tell me; are there slugs behind the Curtain?"

"That," he answered, "is just what I would like to find out."

I realized suddenly that Mary had been right; agents should not marry. If this job were ever finished, I wanted to hire out to count sheep for a rich insomniac or, something equally soft. "This time of year," I said, "I think I'd want to enter through Canton. Unless you were figuring on a drop?"

"What makes you think I want you to go into the USSR?" he asked. "We might find out what we want to know quicker and easier in Zone Red."

"Huh?"

"Certainly. If there is infection anywhere but in this continent, the titans in Zone Red must know about it. Why go half around the globe to find out?"

I put aside the plans I had been forming to be a Hindu merchant, travelling with his wife, and thought about what he was saying. Could be . . . could be. "How in the devil can Zone Red be penetrated now?" I asked. "Do I wear a plastic imitation slug on my shoulder blades? They'd catch me the first time I was called on for direct conference. Or before."

"Don't be a defeatist. Four agents have gone in already."

"And come back?"

"Well, no, not exactly. That's the rub."

"And you want me to be the fifth? Have you decided that I've cluttered up the payroll long enough?"

"I think the others used the wrong tactics—"

"Obviously!"

"The trick is to convince them that you are a renegade. Got any ideas?"

The idea was overwhelming, so much so that I did not answer at once. Finally I burst out, "Why not start me easy? Can't I impersonate a Panama pimp for a while? Or practice being an ax murderer? I have to get into the mood for this."

"Easy," he said. "It may not be practical—"

"Hmmph!"

"But you might bring it off. You've had more experience with their ways than any agent I've got. You must be rested up, aside from that little singe you got on your fingers. Or maybe we should drop you near Moscow and let you take a direct look. Think it over. Don't get into a fret about it for maybe another day."

"Thanks. Thank you too much." I changed the subject. "What have you got planned for Mary?"

"Why don't you stick to your own business?"

"I'm married to her."

"Yes."

"Well, for the love of Pete! Is that all you've got to say? Don't you even want to wish me luck?"

"It strikes me," he said slowly, "that you have had all the luck one man could ask for. You have my blessing, for whatever it's worth."

"Oh. Well, thanks." I am slow in some ways, but I plead the excuse that I had had much on my mind—up to that moment it had not occurred to me that the Old Man might have had something directly to do with Mary's leave and mine falling together so conveniently. I said, "Look here. Dad—"

"Huh?" It was the second time I had called him that in a month; it seemed to put him on the defensive.

"You meant for Mary and me to marry all along. You planned it that way."

"Eh? Don't be ridiculous. I believe in free will, son— and free choices."

"Provided the choice suits you."

"See here, we discussed this once before—"

"I know we did. Never mind; I'm hardly in a position to be angry about it. It's just that I feel like a prize stallion being led into the pen. Why did you do it? It wasn't sentiment about 'young love' and such twaddle; I know you better than that."

"I did not do anything, I tell you. As for approving of it—well, the race must go on, so they tell me. If it doesn't, everything else we do is pointless—even this war."

"Like that, eh? You would send two agents on leave in the middle of a battle—to catch yourself a grandson?" I did a rapid summing up and added, "I'll bet you used a slide rule."

He colored. "I don't know what you are talking about. You both were entitled to leave; the rest was accidental."

"Hmm! Accidents don't happen; not around you. Never mind; I'm a willing victim. Now about the job; give me a bit longer to size up the possibilities, if you really mean to let me pick my own method. Meantime, I'll see Cosmetics about a rubber ear."

I did not see a man about an ear, not then, for, as I was heading into Cosmetics, I met Mary coming out. I had not intended to let myself be surprised into endearments around the Section, but I was caught off guard. "Darling! They fixed you!"

She turned slowly around and let me look. "Good job, isn't it?"

It was a good job. I could not tell that her hair had ever been burned. Besides that, they had done a make-up job on her shoulders over the temporary skin that was quite convincing, but I had expected that. It was the hair that fooled me. I touched it gently and examined the hair line on the left side. "They must have taken it all off and started fresh."

"No, they simply matched it."

"Now you've got your favorite gun cache back."

"Like this?" she said, dimpling. She adjusted her curls with her left hand—then suddenly she had a gun in each hand. And again I did not know where the second one had come from.

"That's papa's good girl! If you ever have to, you can make a living as a night-club magician. But seriously, don't let a Vigilante catch you doing that trick; he might get jumpy."

"One won't catch me," she assured me solemnly. I wondered about the verb. We went to the staff lounge and found a quiet place to talk. We did not order drinks; we did not seem to need such. We talked over the situation and found that each had been briefed. I did not tell Mary about my proposed assignment, and, if she had one, she did not mention it; we were back with the Section and indoctrinated habits are hard to break.

"Mary," I said suddenly, "are you pregnant?"

"It's too early to tell, dear," she answered, searching my eyes. "Do you want me to be?"

"Yes."

"Then I'll try very hard to be."

❦ **Chapter 26** ❦

We finally decided to attempt to penetrate the Curtain rather than Zone Red. The evaluation group had advised that there was no chance of impersonating a renegade; their advice would not have stopped the Old Man, but it agreed with his opinion and mine. The question hinged on, "How does a man get to be a renegade? Why do the titans trust him?"

The question answers itself; a slug knows its host's mind. Verbal guarantees would mean nothing to a titan—but if the titan, through once possessing a man's mind, knows that he is a natural renegade, a man who can be had, then it may suit the slug's purposes to let him be renegade rather than host. But first the slug had to plumb the vileness in the man's mind and be sure of its quality.

We did not know this as fact but as logical necessity. Human logic—but it had to be slug logic, too, since it fitted what the slugs could and could not do. As for me, it was not possible even under deep hypnotic instruction to pass myself off to a slug in possession of my mind as a candidate for renegade. So the psycho lads decided—and to which I said "Amen!"; it saved me from telling the Old Man that I would not volunteer to let myself be caught by a slug and it saved him from rigging some damned logical necessity which would force me into "volunteering".

It may seem illogical that titans would "free" a host even though they knew that the host was the sort who could be owned. But the advantages to them show up through analogy: the commissars will not willingly let any of their slave-citizens escape; nevertheless they send out thousands of fifth columnists into the territory of free men. Once outside, these agents can choose freedom and many do, but most of them don't—as we all know too well. They prefer slavery.

In the renegades the slugs had a supply of "trustworthy" fifth columnists—"trustworthy" is not the right word but the English language has no word for this form of vileness. That Zone Green was being penetrated by renegades was certain—but it is hard to tell a fifth columnist from a custard head; it always has been. The ratio of damn fools to villains is high.

So I got ready to go. I took under light hypnosis a refresher in the languages I would need with emphasis on shibboleth phrases of the latest meanderings of the Party Line. I was provided with a personality and coached in a trade which would permit me to travel, repairman for irrigating pumps—and given much money. If it suited me, my trade would let me hint that a pump had been sabotaged. Coercion, intimidation, blackmail, and bribery are especially useful behind the Curtain; the people have lived under a terror so long that they have no defenses; their puppet strings are always at hand.

I was to be dropped, rather than let to crawl under the Curtain. If I failed to report back, other agents would follow. Probably other agents would anyhow—or already had gone. I was not told; what an agent does not know he cannot divulge, even under drugs.

The reporting equipment was a new model and a joy to have. Ultramicrowave stuff with the directional cavity no bigger than a teacup and the rest, power pack and all, hardly larger than a loaf of bread, with the whole thing so well shielded that it would not make a Geiger counter even nervous. Strictly horizon range—I was to aim it at whatever space station was above the horizon. It had to be aimed closely, which required me to seal into my mind the orbital tables of all three space stations and a navigational grid of the territory I was to operate in. The handicap was really its prime advantage; the highly directional quality of the sender meant that it would not be detected save by wild accident.

I had to drop through their screen but it would be under a blanket of anti-radar "window" to give their search technicians fits. They would know that something was being dropped, but they would not know what, nor where, nor when, for mine would not be the only blanket, nor the only night of such tactics.

Once I had made up my mind whether the USSR was or was not slug infested I was to dictate a report to whatever space station was in sight, the line-of-sight, that is; I can't pick out a space station by eye and I doubt those who say they can. Report made, I was free to walk, ride, crawl, sneak and/or bribe my way out if I could.

The only trouble was that I never had a chance to use these preparations; the Pass Christian saucer landed.

The Pass Christian saucer was only the third to be seen after landing. Of the first two, the Grinnell saucer had been concealed by the slugs—or perhaps it took off again—and the Burlingame saucer was a radioactive memory. But the Pass Christian saucer was tracked and was seen on the ground almost at once.

It was tracked by Space Station Alpha—and recorded as an extremely large meteorite believed to have landed in or near the Gulf of Mexico. Which fact was not connected with the Pass Christian saucer until later but which, when it was, told us why we had failed to spot other landings by radar screen . . . the saucers came in too fast.

The saucers could be "seen" by radar—the primitive radar of sixty-odd years ago had picked them up many times, especially when cruising at atmospheric speeds while scouting this planet. But our modern radar had been "improved" to the point where saucers could not be seen; our instruments were too specialized. Electronic instruments follow an almost organic growth toward greater and greater selectivity. All our radar involves discriminator circuits and like gimmicks to enable each type to "see" what it is supposed to see and not bother with what it should ignore. Traffic block control sees atmospheric traffic only; the defense screen and fire control radars see what they are supposed to see—the fine screen "sees" a range from atmospheric speeds up to orbiting missiles at five miles a second; the coarse screen overlaps the fine screen, starting down at the lowest wingless-missile speed and carrying on up into the highest spaceship speeds relative to Earth and somewhat higher—about ten miles per second.

There are other selectivities—weather radar, harbor radar, and so forth. The point is none of them sees objects at speeds over ten miles per second . . . with the single exception of meteor-count radars in the space stations, which are not military but a research concession granted by the U.N. to the Association for the Advancement of Science.

Consequently the "giant meteor" was recorded as such and was not associated with flying saucers until later.

But the Pass Christian saucer was seen to land. The submersible cruiser U.N.S. Robert Fulton on routine patrol of Zone Red out of Mobile was ten miles off Gulfport with only her receptors showing when the saucer decelerated and landed. The spaceship popped up on the screens of the cruiser as it dropped from outer-space speed (around fifty-three miles per second by the space station record) to a speed the cruiser's radars would accept.

It came out of nothing, slowed to zero, and disappeared from the screen—but the operator had a fix on the last blip, less than twenty miles away on the Mississippi coast. The cruiser's skipper was puzzled. The radar track surely could not be a ship, since ships don't decelerate at fifty gravities. It did not occur to him that g's might not matter to a slug. He swung his ship over and took a look.

His first dispatch read: SPACESHIP LANDED BEACH WEST OF PASS CHRISTIAN MISSISSIPPI. His second was: LANDING FORCE BEACHING TO CAPTURE.

If I had not been in the Section offices I suppose I would have been left out of the party. As it was my phone shrilled so, that I bumped my head on the study machine I was using and swore. The Old Man said, "Come at once. Move!"

It was the same party we had started with so many weeks—or was it years?—before, the Old Man, Mary, and myself. We were in the air and heading south at emergency maximum, paying no attention to block controls and with our transponder sending out the police warning, before the Old Man told us why.

When he did tell us, I said, "Why the family group? You need a full-scale air task force."

"It will be there," he answered grimly. Then he grinned, his old wicked grin, an expression I had not seen since it started. "What do you care?" he jibed. "The 'Cavanaughs' are riding again. Eh, Mary?"

I snorted. "If you want that sister-and-brother routine, you had better get another boy."

"Just the part where you protect her from dogs and strange men," he answered soberly. "And I do mean dogs and I do mean strange men, very strange men. This may be the payoff, son."

I started to ask him more but he went into the operator's compartment, closed the panel, and got busy at the communicator. I turned to Mary. She snuggled up with a little sigh and said, "Howdy, Bud."

I grabbed her. "Don't give me that 'Bud' stuff or somebody's going to get a paddling."

✥ **Chapter 27** ✥

We were almost shot down by our own boys, then we picked up an escort of two Black Angels who throttled back and managed to stay with us. They turned us over to the command ship from which Air Marshal Rexton was watching the action. The command ship matched speeds with us and took us inboard with an anchor loop—I had never had that done before; it's disconcerting.

Rexton wanted to spank us and send us home, since we were technically civilians—but spanking the Old Man is a chore. They finally unloaded us and I squatted our car down on the sea-wall roadway which borders the Gulf along there—scared out of my wits, I should add, for we were buffeted by A.A. on the way down. There was fighting going on above and all around us, but there was a curious calm near the saucer itself.

The outlander ship loomed up almost over us, not fifty yards away. It was as convincing and as ominous as the plastic-board fake in Iowa had been phony. It was a discus in shape and of great size; it was tilted slightly toward us, for it had grounded partly on one of the magnificent high-stilted old mansions which line that coast. The house had collapsed but the saucer was partly supported by the wreckage and by the six-foot-thick trunk of a tree that had shaded the house.

The ship's canted attitude let us see that the upper surface and what was surely its airlock—a metal hemisphere, a dozen feet across, at the main axis of the ship, where the hub would have been had it been a wheel. This hemisphere was lifted straight out or up from the body of the ship some six or eight feet. I could not see what held it out from the hull but I assumed that there must be a central shaft or piston; it came out like a poppet valve.

It was easy to see why the masters of the saucer had not closed up again and taken off from there; the airlock was fouled, held open by a "mud turtle", one of those little amphibious tanks which are at home on the bottom of a harbor or crawling up onto a beach—part of the landing force of the Fulton.

Let me set down now what I learned later; the tank was commanded by Ensign Gilbert Calhoun of Knoxville; with him was Powerman 2/c Florence Berzowski and a gunner named Booker T. W. Johnson. They were all dead, of course, before we got there.

The car, as soon as I roaded it, was surrounded by a landing force squad commanded by a pink-cheeked lad who seemed anxious to shoot somebody or anybody. He was less anxious when he got a look at Mary but he still refused to let us approach the saucer until he had checked with his tactical commander—who in turn consulted the skipper of the Fulton. We got an answer back in a short time, considering that the demand must have been referred to Rexton and probably clear back to Washington.

While waiting I watched the battle and, from what I saw, was well pleased to have no part of it. Somebody was going to get hurt—a good many had already. There was a male body, stark naked, just behind the car—a boy not more than fourteen. He was still clutching a rocket launcher and across his shoulders was the mark of the beast, though the slug was nowhere around. I wondered whether the slug had crawled away and was dying, or whether, perhaps, it had managed to transfer to the person who had bayoneted the boy.

Mary had walked west on the highway with the downy young naval officer while I was examining the corpse. The notion of a slug, possibly still alive, being around caused me to hurry to her. "Get back into the car," I said.

She continued to look west along the road. "I thought I might get in a shot or two," she answered, her eyes bright.

"She's safe here," the youngster assured me. "We're holding them, well down the road."

I ignored him. "Listen, you bloodthirsty little hellion," I snapped, "get back in that car before I break every bone in your body!"

"Yes, Sam." She turned and did so.

I looked back at the young salt. "What are you staring at?" I demanded, feeling edgy and needing someone to take it out on. The place smelled of slugs and the wait was making me nervous.

"Nothing much," he said, looking me over. "In my part of the country we don't speak to ladies that way."

"Then why in the hell don't you go back where you come from?" I answered and stalked away. The Old Man was missing, too; I did not like it.

An ambulance, coming back from the west, ground to a halt beside me. "Has the road to Pascagoula been opened?" the driver called out.

The Pascagoula River, thirty miles or so east of where the saucer had landed, was roughly "Zone Amber" for that area; the town of that name was east of the river's mouth and, nominally at least, in Zone Green—while sixty or seventy miles west of us on the same road was New Orleans, the heaviest concentration of titans south of St. Louis. Our opposition came from New Orleans while our nearest base was in Mobile.

"I haven't heard," I told the driver.

He chewed a knuckle. "Well . . . I made it through once; maybe I'll make it back all right." His turbines whined and he was away. I continued to look for the Old Man.

Although the ground fighting had moved away from the site, the air fighting was all around and above us. I was watching the vapor trails and trying to figure out who was what and how they could tell, when a big transport streaked into the area, put on the brakes with a burst of rato units, and spilled a platoon of sky boys. Again I wondered; it was too far away to tell whether they wore slugs or not. At least it came in from the east, but that did not necessarily prove anything.

I spotted the Old Man, talking with the commander of the landing force. I went up and interrupted. "We ought to get out of here, boss. This place is due to be atom-bombed about ten minutes ago."

The commander answered me. "Relax," he said blandly, "the concentration does not merit A-bombing, not even a pony bomb."

I was just about to ask him sharply how he knew that the slugs would figure it that way, when the Old Man interrupted. "He's right, son." He took me by the arm and walked me back toward the car. "He's perfectly right, but for the wrong reasons."

"Huh?"

"Why haven't we bombed the cities they hold? They won't bomb this area, not while that ship is intact. They don't want to damage it; they want it back. Now go on back to Mary. Dogs and strange men—remember?"

I shut up, unconvinced. I expected us all to be clicks in a Geiger counter any second. Slugs, fighting as individuals, fought with gamecock recklessness—perhaps because they were really not individuals. Why should they be any more cautious about one of their own ships? They might be more anxious to keep it out of our hands than to save it.

We had just reached the car and spoken to Mary when the still-damp little snottie came trotting up. He halted, caught his breath, and saluted the Old Man. "The commander says that you are to have anything you want, sir—anything at all!"

From his manner I gathered that the answering dispatch had probably been spelled out in asterisks, accompanied by ruffles and flourishes. "Thank you, sir," the Old Man said mildly. "We merely want to inspect the captured ship."

"Yes, sir. Come with me, sir." He came with us instead,

having difficulty making up his mind whether to escort the Old Man or Mary. Mary won. I came along behind, keeping my mind on watching out and ignoring the presence of the youngster. The country on that coast, unless gardened constantly, is practically jungle; the saucer lapped over into a brake of that sort and the Old Man took a shortcut through it. The kid said to him. "Watch out, sir. Mind where you step."

I said, "Slugs?"

He shook his head. "Coral snakes."

At that point a poisonous snake would have seemed as pleasant as a honey bee, but I must have been paying some attention to his warning for I was looking down when the next thing happened.

I first heard a shout. Then so help me, a Bengal tiger was charging us.

Probably Mary got in the first shot. I know that mine was not behind that of the young officer; it might even have been ahead. I'm sure it was—fairly sure, anyhow. It was the Old Man who shot last.

Among the four of us we cut that beast so many ways that it would never be worth anything as a rug. And yet the slug on it was untouched; I fried it with my second bolt. The young fellow looked at it without surprise. "Well," he said, "I thought we had cleaned up that load."

"Huh? What do you mean?"

"One of the first transport tanks they sent out. Regular Noah's Ark. We were shooting everything from gorillas to polar bears. Say, did you ever have a water buffalo come at you?"

"No and I don't want to."

"Not near as bad as the dogs, really. If you ask me, those things don't have much sense." He looked at the slug, quite unmoved, while I was ready as usual to throw up.

We got up out of there fast and onto the titan ship—which did not make me less nervous, but more. Not that there was anything frightening in the ship itself, not in its appearance.

But its appearance wasn't right. While it was obviously artificial, one knew without being told that it was not made by men. Why? I don't know. The surface of it was dull mirror, not a mark on it—not any sort of a mark; there was no way to tell how it had been put together. It was as smooth as a Jo block.

I could not tell of what it was made. Metal? Of course, it had to be metal. But was it? You would expect it to be either bitterly cold—or possibly intensely hot from its landing. I touched it and it was not anything at all, neither cold nor hot. Don't tell me it just happened to be exactly ninety-eight and six-tenths. I noticed another thing presently; a ship that size, landing at high speed, should have blasted a couple of acres. There was no blast area at all; the brake around it was green and rank.

We went up to the parasol business, the air lock, if that is what it was. The edge was jammed down tight on the little mud turtle; the armor of the tank was crushed in, as one might crush a pasteboard box with the hand. Those mud turtles are built to launch five hundred feet deep in water; they are strong.

Well, I suppose this one was strong. The parasol arrangement had damaged it, but the air lock had not closed. On the other hand the metal, or whatever the spaceship's door was made of, was unmarked by the exchange.

The Old Man turned to me. "Wait here with Mary."

"You're not going in there by yourself?"

"Yes. There may be very little time."

The kid spoke up. "I'm to stay with you, sir. That's what the commander said."

"Very well, sir," the Old Man agreed. "Come along." He peered over the edge, then knelt and lowered himself by his hands. The kid followed him. I felt burned up—but had no desire to argue the arrangements.

They disappeared into the hole. Mary turned to me and said, "Sam—I don't like this. I'm afraid."

She startled me. I was afraid myself—but I had not expected her to be. "I'll take care of you."

"Do we have to stay? He did not say so, quite."

I considered it. "If you want to go back to the car I'll take you back."

"Well . . . no, Sam, I guess we have to stay. Come closer to me." She was trembling.

I don't know how long it was before they stuck their heads over the rim. The youngster climbed out and the Old Man told him to stand guard. "Come on," he said to us, "it's safe—I think."

"The hell it is," I told him, but I went because Mary was already starting. The Old Man helped her down.

"Mind your head," he said. "Low bridge all the way."

It is a platitude that unhuman races produce unhuman works, but very few humans have ever been inside a Venerian labyrinth and still fewer have seen the Martian ruins—and I was not one of the few. I don't know what I expected. Superficially the inside of the saucer was not, I suppose, too startling, but it was strange. It had been thought out by unhuman brains, ones which did not depend on human ideas in fabricating, brains which had never heard of the right angle and the straight line or which regarded them as unnecessary or undesirable. We found ourselves in a very small oblate chamber and from there we crawled through a tube about four feet thick, a tube which seemed to wind down into the ship and which glowed from all its surface with a reddish light.

The tube held an odd and somewhat distressing odor, as if of marsh gas, and mixed with it faintly was the reek of dead slugs. That and the reddish glow and the total lack of heat response from the wall of the tube as my palms pressed against it gave me the unpleasant fancy that I was crawling through the gut of some unearthly behemoth rather than exploring a strange machine.

The tube branched like an artery and there we came across our first Titanian androgyne. He—let me call it "he"—was sprawled on his back, like a child sleeping, his head pillowed on his slug. There was a suggestion of a smile on the little rosebud mouth; at first I did not realize that he was dead.

At first sight the similarities between the Titanian people and ourselves are more noticeable than the differences; we impress what we expect to see on what we do see, as a wind-sculptured rock may look like a human head or a dancing bear. Take the pretty little "mouth" for example; how was I to know that it was an organ for breathing solely?

Conceded that they are not human and that, despite the casual similarities of four limbs and a head-like protuberance, we are less like them than is a bullfrog like a bullpup; nevertheless the general effect is pleasing, not frightening, and faintly human. "Elfin" I should say—the elves of Saturn's moons. Had we met them before the slugs we call titans possessed them I think we could have gotten along with them. Judged by their ability to build the saucers they were our equals—if they did build them. (Certainly the slugs did not build them; slugs are not builders but thieves, cosmic cuckoos.)

But I am letting my own later thoughts get in the way. When I saw the little fellow I managed to draw my gun. The Old Man, anticipating my reaction, turned and said, "Take it easy. It's dead—they are all dead, smothered in oxygen when the tank ruined their air seal."

I still had my gun out. "I want to burn the slug," I insisted. "It may still be alive." It was not covered by the horny shell we had lately come to expect but was naked, moist and ugly.

He shrugged. "Suit yourself. It can't possibly hurt you."

"Why not?"

"Wrong chemistry. That slug can't live on an oxygen breather." He crawled across the little body, giving me no chance to shoot had I decided to. Mary, always so quick with a gun, had not drawn but had shrunk against my side and was breathing in sharp little sobbing gasps. The Old Man stopped and said patiently, "Coming, Mary?"

She choked and then gasped, "Let's go back! Let's get out of here!"

I said, "She's right. This is no job for three people; this is something for a research team and proper equipment."

He paid no attention to me. "It has to be done, Mary. You know that. And you have to be the one to do it."

"Why does she have to do it?" I demanded angrily.

Again he ignored me. "Well, Mary?"

From somewhere inside herself she called on reserves. Her breathing became normal, her features relaxed, and she crawled across the slug-ridden elfin body with the serenity of a queen going to the gallows. I lumbered after them, still hampered by my gun and trying not to touch the body.

We came at last to a large chamber. It may have been the control room, for there were many of the dead little elfin creatures in it, though I saw nothing resembling (to my eye) instruments or machinery. Its inner surface was cavitated and picked out with lights much brighter than the reddish illumination and the chamber space was festooned with processes as meaningless to me as the convolutions of a brain. I was troubled again with the thought—completely wrong, I know now—that the ship itself was a living organism.

The Old Man paid no attention but crawled on through and into another ruddy-glowing tube. We followed its contortions to a place where it widened out to ten feet or more with a "ceiling" overhead almost tall enough to let us stand erect. But that was not what caught our eyes; the walls were no longer opaque.

On each side of us, beyond transparent membranes, were thousands on thousands of slugs, swimming, floating, writhing in some fluid which sustained them.

Each tank had an inner diffuse light of its own and I could see back into the palpitating mass—and I wanted to scream.

I still had my gun out. The Old Man reached back and placed his hand over the bell of it. "Don't yield to temptation," he warned me. "You don't want to let that loose in here. Those are for us."

Mary looked at them with a face too calm. Thinking back, I doubt that she was fully conscious in the ordinary sense. I looked at her, glanced back at the walls of that ghoulish aquarium, and said urgently, "Let's get out of here if we can—then just bomb it out of existence."

"No," he said quietly, "there is more. Come." The tube narrowed in again, then enlarged and we were again in a somewhat smaller chamber like that of the slugs. Again there were transparent walls and again there were things floating beyond them.

I had to look twice before I could fully make out and believe what I saw.

Floating just beyond the wall, face down, was the body of a man—a human. Earth-born man—about forty to fifty years old. He was grizzled and almost bald. His arms were curved across his chest and his knees were drawn up, as if he were sleeping safe in bed—or in the womb.

I watched him, thinking terrible thoughts. He was not alone; there were more beyond him, male and female, young and old—but he was the only one I could see properly and he got my attention. I was sure that he was dead; it did not occur to me to think otherwise—then I saw his mouth working—and then I wished he were dead.

Mary was wandering around in that chamber as if she were drunk—no, not drunk but preoccupied and dazed. She went from one transparent wall to the other, peering intently into the crowded, half-seen depths. The Old Man looked only at her. "Well, Mary?" he said softly.

"I can't find them!" she said piteously in a voice like a little girl's. She ran back to the other side.

The Old Man grasped her arm and stopped her. "You're not looking for them in the right place," he said firmly. "Go back where they are. Remember?"

She stopped and her voice was a wail. "I can't remember!"

"You must remember . . . now. This is what you can do for them. You must return to where they are and look for them."

Her eyes closed and tears started leaking from them. She gasped and choked. I pushed myself between them and said, "Stop this! What are you doing to her?"

He grabbed me with his free hand and pushed me away. "No, son," he whispered fiercely. "Keep out of this—you must keep out."

"But—"

"No!" He let go of Mary and led me away to the entrance. "Stay there. And, as you love your wife, as you hate the titans, do not interfere. I shan't hurt her—that's a promise."

"What are you going to do?" But he had turned away. I stayed, unwilling to let it go on, afraid to tamper with what I did not understand.

Mary had sunk down to the floor and now squatted on it like a child, her face covered with her hands. The Old

Man went back to her, knelt down and touched her arm. "Go back," I heard him say. "Go back to where it started."

I could barely hear her answer, "No . . . no."

"How old were you? You seemed to be about seven or eight when you were found. It was before that?"

"Yes—yes, it was before that." She sobbed and collapsed completely to the floor. "Mama! Mama!"

"What is your mama saying?" he asked gently.

"She doesn't say anything. She's looking at me so queerly. There's something on her back. I'm afraid, I'm afraid!"

I got up and hurried toward them, crouching to keep from hitting the low ceiling. Without taking his eyes off Mary the Old Man motioned me back. I stopped, hesitated. "Go back," he ordered. "Way back."

The words were directed at me and I obeyed them— but so did Mary. "There was a ship," she muttered, "a big shiny ship—" He said something to her; if she answered I could not hear it. I stayed back this time and made no attempt to interfere. I could see that he was doing her no physical hurt and, despite my vastly disturbed emotions, I realized that something important was going on, something big enough to absorb the Old Man's full attention in the very teeth of the enemy.

He continued to talk to her, soothingly but insistently. Mary quieted down, seemed to sink almost into a lethargy, but I could hear that she answered him. After a while she was talking in the monotonous logorrhea of emotional release. Only occasionally did the Old Man prompt her.

I heard something crawling along the passage behind me. I turned and drew my gun, with a wild feeling that we were trapped. I almost shot him before I realized that it was the ubiquitous young officer we had left outside. "Come on out!" he said urgently. He pushed on past me out into the chamber and repeated the demand to the Old Man.

The Old Man looked exasperated beyond endurance. "Shut up and don't bother me," he said.

"You've got to, sir," the youngster insisted. "The commander says that you must come out at once. We're falling back; the commander says he may have to use demolition at any moment. If we are still inside—blooie! That's it."

"Very well," the Old Man agreed in unhurried tones. "We're coming. You go out and tell your commander that he must hold off until we get out; I have vitally important information. Son, help me with Mary."

"Aye, aye, sir!" the youngster acknowledged. "But hurry!" He scrambled away. I picked up Mary and carried her to where the chamber narrowed into a tube; she seemed almost unconscious. I put her down.

"We'll have to drag her," the Old Man said. "She may not come out of this soon. Here—let me get her up on your back, you can crawl with her."

I paid no attention but shook her. "Mary," I shouted, "Mary! Can you hear me?"

Her eyes opened. "Yes, Sam?"

"Darling—we've got to get out of here, fast! Can you crawl?"

"Yes, Sam." She closed her eyes again. I shook her again. "Mary!"

"Yes, darling? What is it? I'm so tired."

"Listen, Mary—you've got to crawl out of here. If you don't the slugs will get us—do you understand?"

"All right, darling." Her eyes stayed open this time but were vacant. I got her headed up the tube and came along after her. Whenever she faltered or slowed I slapped at her. I lifted and dragged her through the chamber of the slugs and again through the control room, if that is what it was. When we came to the place where the tube was partly blocked by the dead elfin creature she stopped; I wormed my way past her and moved it, stuffing it into the branching tube. There was no doubt, this time, that its slug was dead; I gagged at the job. Again I had to slap her into cooperation.

After an endless nightmare of leaden-limbed striving we reached the outer door and the young officer was there to help us lift her out, him pulling and the Old Man and me lifting and pushing. I gave the Old Man a leg up, jumped out myself, and took her away from the youngster. It was quite dark.

We went back the long way past the crushed house, avoiding the jungle-like brake, and thence down to the beach road. Our car was no longer there; it did not matter for we found ourselves hurried into a "mud turtle" tank—none too soon, for the fighting was almost on top of us. The tank commander buttoned up and the craft lumbered off the stepped-back seawall and into the water. Fifteen minutes later we were inside the Fulton.

And an hour later we disembarked at the Mobile base. The Old Man and I had bad coffee and sandwiches in the wardroom of the Fulton, some of the Wave officers had taken Mary and cared for her in the women's quarters.

She joined us as we left and seemed entirely normal. I said, "Mary, are you all right?"

She smiled at me. "Of course, darling. Why shouldn't I be?"

A small command ship and an escort took us out of there. I had supposed that we were headed back to the Section offices, or more likely to Washington. I had not asked; the Old Man was in no mood to talk and I was satisfied simply to hold Mary's hand and feel relieved.

The pilot put us into a mountainside hangar in one of those egg-on-a-plate maneuvers that no civilian craft can accomplish—in the sky at high speed, then in a cave and stationary. Like that. "Where are we?" I asked.

The Old Man did not answer but got out; Mary and I followed. The hangar was small, just parking space for about a dozen craft, an arresting platform, and a single launching rack; it contained only two other ships besides ours. Guards met us and directed us on back to a door set in the living rock; we went through and found ourselves in an anteroom. An unseen metallic voice told us to strip off what little we wore. I did not mind being naked but I hated to part with my gun and phone.

We went on inside and were met by a young fellow whose total clothing was an armband showing three chevrons and crossed retorts. He turned us over to a girl who was wearing even less, as her armband had only two chevrons. Both of them noticed Mary, each with typical gender response. I think the corporal was glad to pass us on to the captain who received us.

"We got your message," the captain said. "Dr. Steelton is waiting."

"Thank you, ma'am," the Old Man answered. "The sooner, the better. Where?"

"Just a moment," she said, went to Mary and felt through her hair. "We have to be sure, you know," she said apologetically. If she was aware of the falseness of much of Mary's hair, she did not mention it and Mary did not flinch. "All right," she decided, "let's go." Her own hair was cut mannishly short, in crisp gray waves.

"Right," agreed the Old Man. "No, son, this is as far as you go."

"Why?" I asked.

"Because you damn near loused up the first try," he explained briefly. "Now pipe down."

The captain said, "The officers' mess is straight down the first passageway to the left. Why don't you wait there?"

So I did. On the way I passed a door decorated primly in large red skull-and-crossbones and stenciled with: WARNING—LIVE PARASITES BEYOND THIS DOOR; in smaller letters it added Qualified Personnel Only—Use Procedure "A".

I gave the door a wide berth.

The officers' mess was the usual clubroom and there were three or four men and two women lounging in it. No one seemed interested in my presence, so I found an unoccupied chair, sat down, and wondered just who you had to be to get a drink around this joint. After a time I was joined by a large male extrovert wearing a colonel's insignia on a chain around his neck; with it was a Saint Christopher's medal and an I.D. dog tag. "Newcomer?" he asked.

I admitted it. "Civilian expert?" he went on.

"I don't know about 'expert'," I replied. "I'm a field operative."

"Name? Sorry to be officious," he apologized, "but I'm alleged to be the security officer around here. My name's Kelly."

I told him mine. He nodded. "Matter of fact I saw your party coming in. Mine was the voice of conscience, coming out of the wall. Now, Mr. Nivens, how about a drink? From the brief we had on you, you could use one."

I stood up. "Whom do I have to kill to get it?"

"—though as far as I can see," Kelly went on sometime later, "this place needs a security officer the way a horse needs roller skates. We should publish our results as fast as we get them. This isn't like fighting a human enemy."

I commented that he did not sound like the ordinary brass hat. He laughed and did not take offense. "Believe me, son, not all brass hats are as they are pictured—they just seem to be."

I remarked that Air Marshal Rexton struck me as a pretty sharp citizen.

"You know him?" the colonel asked.

"I don't know him exactly, but my work on this job has thrown me in his company a good bit—I last saw him earlier today."

"Hmm—" said the colonel. "I've never met the gentleman. You move in more rarefied strata than I do, sir."

I explained that it was mere happenstance, but from then on he showed me more respect. Presently he was telling me about the work the laboratory did. "By now we know more about those foul creatures than does Old Nick himself. But do we know how to kill them without killing their hosts? We do not.

"Of course," he went on, "if we could lure them one at a time into a small room and douse them with anesthetics, we could save the hosts—but that is like the old saw about how to catch a bird: naturally it's no trouble if you can sneak up close enough to put salt on its tail. I'm not a scientist myself—just the son of a cop and a cop myself under a different tag—but I've talked to the scientists here and I know what we need. This is a biological war and it will be won by biological warfare. What we need is a bug, one that will bite the slug and not the host. Doesn't sound too hard, does it? It is. We know a hundred things that will kill the slug—smallpox, typhus, syphilis, encephalitis lethargica, Obermeyer's virus, plague, yellow fever, and so on. But they kill the host, too."

"Couldn't they use something that everyone is immune to?" I asked. "Take typhoid—everybody has typhoid shots. And almost everybody is vaccinated for smallpox."

"No good—if the host is immune, the parasite doesn't get exposed to it. Now that the slugs have developed this outer cuticle the parasite's environment is the host. No, we need something the host will catch and that will kill the slug, but won't give the host more than a mild fever or a splitting headache."

I started to answer with some no-doubt brilliant thought when I saw the Old Man standing in the doorway. I excused myself and went to him. "What was Kelly grilling you about?" he asked.

"He wasn't grilling me," I answered.

"That's what you think. Don't you know what Kelly that is?"

"Should I?"

"You should. Or perhaps you shouldn't; he never lets his picture be taken. That's B. J. Kelly, the greatest scientific criminologist of our generation."

"That Kelly! But he's not in the army."

"Reserve, probably. But you can guess how important this laboratory is. Come on."

"Where's Mary?"

"You can't see her now. She's recuperating."

"Is she—hurt?"

"I promised you she would not be hurt. Steelton is the best in his line. But we had to go down deep, against a great deal of resistance. That's always rough on the subject."

I thought about it. "Did you get what you were after?"

"Yes and no. We got a great deal, but we aren't through."

"What were you after?"

We had been walking along one of the endless underground passageways of which the place was made. Now he turned us into a small, empty office and we sat down. The Old Man touched the communicator on the desk and said, "Private conference."

"Yes, sir," a voice answered. "We will not record." A green light came on in the ceiling.

"Not that I believe them," the Old Man complained, "but it may keep anyone but Kelly from playing it back. Now, son, about what you want to know; I'm not sure you are entitled to it. You are married to the girl, but that does not mean that you own her soul—and this stuff comes from down so deep that she did not know she had it herself."

I said nothing; there was nothing to say. He went on presently in worried tones, "Still—it might be better to tell you enough so that you will understand. Otherwise you would be bothering her to find out. That I don't want to happen, I don't ever want that to happen. You might throw her into a bad wingding. I doubt if she'll remember anything herself—Steelton is a very gentle operator—but you could stir up things."

I took a deep breath. "You'll have to judge. I can't."

"Yes, I suppose so. Well, I'll tell you a bit and answer your questions—some of them—in exchange for a solemn promise never to bother your wife with it. You don't have the skill."

"Very well, sir. I promise."

"Well—there was a group of people, a cult you might call them, that got into disrepute."

"I know—the Whitmanites."

"Eh? How did you know? From Mary? No, she couldn't have; she didn't know herself."

"No, not from Mary. I just figured it out."

He looked at me with odd respect. "Maybe I've been underestimating you, son. As you say, the Whitmanites. Mary was one of them, as a kid in Antarctica."

"Wait a minute!" I said. "They left Antarctica in—" The wheels buzzed in my mind and the number came up. "—in 1974."

"Surely. What about it?"

"But that would make Mary around forty years old. She can't be."

"Do you care?"

"Huh? Why, no—but she can't be."

"She is and she isn't. Just listen. Chronologically her age is about forty. Biologically she is in her middle twenties. Subjectively she is even younger, because she doesn't remember anything, not to know it, earlier than about 1990."

"What do you mean? That she doesn't remember I can understand—she never wants to remember. But what do you mean by the rest?"

"Just what I said. She is no older than she is because— you know that room where she started to remember? She spent ten years and probably more floating in suspended animation in just such a tank as that."

Chapter 28

Time was when I was immune to emotional shocks. But as I get older, I don't get tougher; I get softer. Being in love has a lot to do with it, too. The thought of Mary, my beloved Mary, swimming in that artificial womb, neither dead nor alive but preserved like a pickled grasshopper, was too much for me.

I heard the Old Man saying, "Take it easy, son. She's all right."

I said, "Go ahead."

Mary's overt history was simple, although mystifying. She had been found in the swamps near Kaiserville at the North Pole of Venus—a little girl who could give no account of herself and who knew only her name—Allucquere. Nobody spotted the significance of the name and a child of her (apparent) age could not be associated with the Whitmanites debacle in any case; the 1980 supply ship had not been able to find any survivor of their "New Zion" colony. Its plantations had returned to the swamp; the dwellings were ruptured shells, hidden in rank growth. More than ten years of time and more than two hundred miles of jungle separated the little waif of Kaiserville from the God-struck colonists of New Zion.

At that time, an unaccounted-for Earth child on Venus was little short of incredible. Like finding the cat locked in the icebox, it called for explanation. But there was no one around with the intellectual curiosity to push the matter. Kaiserville still does not have a sweet reputation; in those days it was made up of miners, doxies, company representatives of the Two Planets Corporation—and nothing else. I don't suppose that shoveling radioactive mud in the swamps leaves much energy for wonder.

Apparently she grew up using poker chips for toys and calling every woman in crib row "mother" or "auntie". In turn they shortened her name to "Lucky". The Old Man did not go into detail about who paid her way back to Earth and why, and he avoided my questions. The real question was where she had been from the time New Zion was eaten up by the Venerian jungle and just what had happened to the colony.

The only record of those things was buried in Mary's mind, locked tight with terror and despair.

Sometime before 1980—about the same time as the flying saucer reports from Russo-Siberia, or a year or so earlier—the titans had discovered the New Zion colony. If you place it one Saturn year earlier than the invasion of Earth, the times fit fairly well. It does not seem likely that the titans were looking for Earthmen on Venus; more probably they were scouting Venus as they had long scouted Earth. Or they may have known just where to look; we know that they kidnapped Earthmen at intervals over the course of two or more centuries; they may have captured someone on Earth whose brain could tell them where to find the New Zion colony. Mary's dark memories could contain no clue to that.

Mary saw the colony captured, saw her parents turned into zombies who no longer cared for her. Apparently she herself was not possessed, or she may have been possessed and turned loose, the titans finding a weak and ignorant young girl an unsuitable slave. In any case, for what was to her baby mind an endlessly long time, she hung around the slave colony, unwanted, uncared for, but unmolested, scavenging like a mouse for her living. On Venus the slugs were moving in to stay; their principal slaves were Venerians and the New Zion colonists were only incidental. It is sure that Mary saw her parents being placed in suspended animation—for later use in the invasion of Earth? Probable, but not certain.

In due course she herself was grabbed and placed in the tanks. Inside a titan ship? At a titan base on Venus itself? More probably the latter, as when she awoke, she was still on Venus. There are many such gaps. Were the slugs that rode the Venerians identical with the slugs which rode the colonists? Possible—since both Earth and Venus have oxy-carbon economy. The slugs seem to be endlessly protean but they surely have to adapt themselves to the biochemistry of their hosts. Had Venus an oxy-silicon economy like Mars, or a fluorine economy, the same parasite type could not possibly have fed on both.

But the gist of the matter lay in the situation as it was when Mary was removed from the artificial incubator. The titan invasion of Venus had failed, or was failing. Almost certainly she was possessed as soon as they removed her from the tank—but Mary had outlived the slug that possessed her.

Why had the slugs died? Why had the invasion of Venus failed? It was for clues to these that the Old Man and Dr. Steelton had gone fishing in Mary's brain.

I said, "Is that all?"

He answered, "Isn't that enough?"

"It raises as many questions as it answers," I complained.

"Of course there is more," he told me, "a great deal more. But you aren't a Venerian expert of any sort, nor a psychologist, so you won't be called on to evaluate it. I've told you what I have so that you will know why we have to work on Mary and so that you won't question her about it. Be good to her, boy; she's had more than her share of grief."

I ignored the advice; I can get along or not get along with my own wife without help, thank you. "What I can't figure out," I answered, "is why you ever had Mary linked up with flying saucers in the first place? I can see now that you took her along on that first trip to Iowa on purpose. You were right, granted—but why? And don't give me any malarkey."

The Old Man himself looked puzzled. "Son, do you ever have hunches?"

"Lord, yes!"

"What is a 'hunch'?"

"Eh? It's a belief that something is so, or isn't so, without evidence. Or a premonition that something is going to happen—or a compulsion to do something."

"Sloppy definitions. I'd call a hunch the result of automatic reasoning below the conscious level on data you did not know you possessed."

"Sounds like the black cat in the coal cellar at midnight. You didn't have any data, not then. Don't tell me that your unconscious mind works on data you are going to get, next week. I won't believe it."

"Ah, but I did have data."

"Huh?"

"What's the last thing that happens to a candidate before he is certified as an agent in our section?"

"The personal interview with you."

"No, no!"

"Oh—the trance analysis." I had forgotten hypno-analysis for the simple reason that the subject never remembers it; he's off somewhere else, wherever it is you go when you're asleep. "You mean you had this data on Mary then. It wasn't a hunch at all."

"No again. I had some, a very little of it—Mary's defenses are strong. And I had forgotten what little I knew, in my conscious memory. But I knew that Mary was the agent for this job. Later on I played back her hypno interview; then I knew that there must be more. We tried for it—and did not get it. But I knew that there had to be more."

I thought it over. "You must have been pretty cocky certain that it was worth digging out; you sure put her over the bumps to get it."

"I had to. I'm sorry."

"Okay, okay." I waited a moment, then said, "Look—what was there in my hypno record?"

"That's not a proper question."

"Nuts."

"And I couldn't tell you if I would. I have never listened to your analysis, son."

"Huh?"

"I had my deputy play it, then asked him if there were anything in it which I should know. He said there wasn't so I never played it."

"So? Well—thanks."

He merely grunted, but I felt warmer toward him than I had in a long time. Dad and I have always managed to embarrass each other.

☞ Chapter 29 ☜

The slugs had died from something they contracted on Venus. That much we knew, or thought we knew. We weren't likely to get another chance in a hurry to collect direct information as a dispatch came in while the Old Man and I were still talking, telling us that Rexton had finally ordered the Pass Christian saucer bombed to keep it from falling back in the hands of the titans. I think that the Old Man had hoped to get at those human beings whom we knew to be inanimate prisoners in that ship, find some way to breathe life into them, and question them.

Well, that chance was gone—what they could dig out of Mary had better be the answer. Assuming that some infection peculiar to Venus was fatal to slugs but not fatal to humans—at least Mary had lived through it—then the thing to do was to test them all and determine which one. Just dandy! —it was like examining every grain of sand on a wide beach to locate the one with square edges!

The problem was somewhat simplified by there

being no need to check the Venus diseases known to be fatal to Earthmen. Perhaps it had been one of such, but, if so, no matter; we could as well use smallpox. But the list of diseases native to Venus which kill Earthmen is surprisingly short and the list of those which are not fatal but merely nastily annoying is very long—from the standpoint of a Venerian bug we must be too strange a diet to suit his taste. If a Venerian bug has a viewpoint, which I doubt, McIlvaine's silly ideas notwithstanding.

The problem was made harder by the fact that the types of diseases native to Venus which were represented by living cultures on Earth were strictly limited in number, i.e., the grain of sand we sought might not be on this beach. To be sure, such an omission could be repaired— in a century or so of exploration and research on a strange planet.

In the meantime there was beginning to be a breath of frost in the air; Schedule Sun Tan could not go on forever.

They had to go back where they hoped the answer was—into Mary's brain. I did not like it, but I could not stop it. She did not appear to know why she was being asked to submit, over and over again, to hypnotics—or perhaps she would not tell. She seemed serene, but the strain showed—circles under her eyes, things like that. Finally I went to the Old Man and told him that it had to stop. "You know better than that, son," he said mildly.

"The hell I do! If you haven't gotten what you want from her by now, you'll never get it."

"Have you any idea of how long it takes to search all the memories in a person's mind, even if you limit yourself to a particular period? It takes exactly as long as the period itself. What we need—if it's there at all—may be subtle."

"'If it's there at all,'" I repeated. "You don't know that it is. See here—if Mary miscarries as a result of this, I'll break your neck personally."

"And if we don't succeed," he answered gently, "you will wish to heaven that she had. Or do you want to raise up kids to be hosts to titans?"

I chewed my lip. "Why didn't you send me to the USSR as you planned to, instead of keeping me around?"

"Oh, that—In the first place I want you here, with Mary, keeping her morale up—instead of acting like a spoiled brat! In the second place, it isn't necessary, or I would have sent you."

"Huh? What happened? Did some other agent report in?"

He stood up and started to leave. "If you would ever learn to show a grown-up interest in the news of the world, you would know."

I said, "Huh?" again, but he did not answer; he left.

I hurried out of there and brought myself up to date. My one-track mind has never been able to interest itself in the daily news; for my taste this dinning into the ears and eyes of trivia somewhere over the horizon is the bane of so-called civilization and the death of serious thinking. But I do miss things.

This time I had managed to miss the first news of the Asiatic plague. I had had my back turned on the biggest—no, the second biggest—news story of the century, the only continent-wide epidemic of the Black Death since the seventeenth century.

I could not understand it. Communists are crazy, granted—but I had been behind the Curtain enough to know that their public health measures were as good as ours and even better in some ways, for they were carried out "by the numbers" and no nonsense tolerated. And a country has to be, quite literally, lousy to permit the spread of plagues—rats, lice, and fleas, the historical vectors. In such respects the commissars had even managed to clean up China to the point, at least, that bubonic plague and typhus were sporadically endemic rather than epidemic.

Now both plagues were spreading like gossip across the whole Sino-Russo-Siberian axis, to the point where the soviet government system had broken down and pleas were being sent via the space stations for U.N. help. What had happened?

Out of my own mind I put the pieces together; I looked up the Old Man again. "Boss—there were slugs behind the Curtain."

"Yes."

"You knew? Well, for cripes sake—we'd better do something fast, or the whole Mississippi Valley will be in the shape that Asia is in. Just one rat, one little rat—" I was thinking back to my own time among the slugs, something I avoided doing when possible. The titans did not bother about human sanitation. My own master had not caused me to bathe, not once. I doubted if there had been a bath taken between the Canadian border and New Orleans since the slugs dropped the masquerade as unnecessary. Lice—Fleas—

The Old Man sighed. "Maybe that's the best solution. Maybe it's the only one."

"You might as well bomb them, if that's the best we have to offer. It would be a cleaner way to die."

"So it would. But you know that we won't. As long as there is a chance of cleaning out the vermin without burning down the barn, we'll keep on trying."

I mulled it over at great length. We were in still another race against time. Fundamentally the slugs must be too stupid to keep slaves; perhaps that was why they moved from planet to planet—they spoiled what they touched. After a while their hosts would die out and then they needed new hosts.

Theory, just theory—I brushed it aside. One thing was sure: what had happened behind the Curtain would happen in Zone Red unless we found a way to kill off the slugs, and that mighty soon! Thinking about it, I made up my mind to do something I had considered before—force myself into the mind-searching sessions being conducted on Mary. If there were something in her hidden memories which could be used to kill slugs, possibly I might see it where others had failed. In any case I was going in, whether Steelton and the Old Man liked it or not. I was tired of being treated like a cross between a prince con-sort and an unwelcome child.

🦇✷ **Chapter 30** ✷🦇

Since our arrival Mary and I had been living in a cubicle about the size of a bass drum. It had been intended for one junior officer; the laboratory had not been planned for married couples. We were as crowded as a plate of smorgasbord but we did not care.

I woke up first the next morning and made my usual quick check to be sure that a slug had not gotten to her. While I was doing so, she opened her eyes and smiled drowsily. "Go back to sleep," I said. "You've got another thirty minutes."

But she did not go back to sleep. After a while I said, "Mary, do you know the incubation period for bubonic plague?"

She answered, "Should I know? One of your eyes is slightly darker than the other."

I shook her. "Pay attention, wench. I was in the lab library last night, doing some rough figuring. As I get it, the slugs must have moved in on our commie pals at least three months before they invaded us."

"Yes, of course."

"You knew? Why didn't you say so?"

"Nobody asked me. Besides, it's obvious."

"Oh, for heaven's sake! Let's get up; we'll be late for breakfast."

Before we left the cubicle I said, "Parlor games at the usual time this morning?"

"Yes."

"Mary, you never talk about what they ask you."

She looked surprised. "But I never know."

"That's what I gathered. Deep trance with a 'forgetter' order, eh?"

"I suppose so."

"Hmm . . . well, there will be some changes made. Today I am going in with you."

All she said was, "Yes, dear."

They were gathered as usual in Dr. Steelton's office, the Old Man, Steelton himself, a Colonel Gibsy who was chief of staff, a lieutenant colonel whom I knew only by sight, and an odd lot of sergeant-technicians, j.o.'s, and flunkies. In the army it seems to take an eight-man working party to help a brass hat blow his nose; that is one reason why I left the service.

The Old Man's eyebrows shot up when he saw me but he said nothing. A sergeant who seemed to be doorman tried to stop me. "Good morning, Mrs. Nivens," he said to Mary; then to me he added, "I don't seem to have you on the list."

"I'm putting myself on the list," I announced to the entire room and pushed on past him.

Colonel Gibsy glared at me and turned to the Old

Man with one of those "Hrrumph-hrrumph-what's-all-this?" noises. The Old Man did not answer but his eyebrows went still higher. The rest looked frozen faced and tried to pretend they weren't there—except one WAC sergeant who could not keep from grinning.

The Old Man got up, said to Gibsy, "Just a moment. Colonel." and limped over to me. In a voice that reached me alone, he said, "Son, you promised me."

"And I withdraw it. You had no business exacting a promise from a man about his wife. You were talking out of turn."

"You've no business here, son. You are not skilled in these matters. For Mary's sake, get out."

Up to that moment it had not occurred to me to question the Old Man's right to stay—but I found myself announcing my decision as I made it. "You are the one with no business here—you are not an analyst. So get out."

The Old Man glanced at Mary and so did I. Nothing showed in her face; she might have been waiting for me to make change. The Old Man said slowly, "You been eating raw meat, son?"

I answered, "It's my wife who is being experimented on; from here on I make the rules—or there won't be any experiments."

Colonel Gibsy butted in with, "Young man, are you out of your mind?"

I said, "What's your status here?" I glanced at his hands and added, "That's a V.M.I, ring, isn't it? Have you any other qualifications? Are you an M.D.? Or a psychologist?"

He drew himself up and tried to look dignified—pretty

difficult dressed in your skin, unless your dignity is built in, the way Mary's is. "You seem to forget that this is a military reservation."

"And you seem to forget that my wife and I aren't military personnel!" I added, "Come on, Mary. We're leaving."

"Yes, Sam."

I added to the Old Man, "I'll tell the offices where to send our mail." I started for the door with Mary following me.

The Old Man said, "Just a moment, as a favor to me." I stopped and he went on to Gibsy, "Colonel, will you step outside with me? I'd like a word in private."

Colonel Gibsy gave me a general-court-martial look but he went. We all waited. Mary sat down but I did not. The juniors continued to be poker-faced, the lieutenant colonel looked perturbed, and the little sergeant seemed about to burst. Steelton was the only one who appeared unconcerned. He took papers out of his "incoming" basket and commenced quietly to work on them.

It was ten or fifteen minutes later that a sergeant came in. "Dr. Steelton, the Commanding Officer says to go ahead."

"Very well. Sergeant," he acknowledged, then looked at me, and said, "Let's go into the operating room."

I said, "Not so fast. Who are the rest of these super-numeraries? How about them?" I indicated the lieutenant colonel.

"Eh? He's Dr. Hazelhurst—two years on Venus."

"Okay, he stays." I caught the eye of the sergeant with the grin and said, "What's your job here, sister?"

"Me? Oh, I'm sort of a chaperone."

"I'm taking over the chaperone business. Now, Doctor, suppose you sort out the spare wheels from the people you actually need for your work."

"Certainly, sir." It turned out that he wanted no one but Colonel Hazelhurst. I gathered an impression that he was glad to get rid of the gallery. We went on inside—Mary, myself, and the two specialists.

The operating room contained a psychiatrist's couch surrounded by a semi-circle of chairs. The double snout of a tri-dim camera poked unobtrusively out of the overhead; I suppose the mike was hidden in the couch. Mary went to the couch and sat down; Dr. Steelton got out an injector. "We'll try to pick up where we left off, Mrs. Nivens."

I said, "Just a moment. You have records of the earlier attempts?"

"Of course."

"Let's play them over first. I want to come up to date."

He hesitated, then answered, "If you wish. Mrs. Nivens, I suggest that you wait in my office. No, it will take quite a long time; suppose I send for you later?"

It was probably just the contrary mood that I was in; bucking the Old Man had gotten me hiked up with adrenaline. "Let's find out first if she wants to leave."

Steelton looked surprised. "You don't know what you are suggesting. These records would be emotionally disturbing to your wife, even harmful."

Hazelhurst put in, "Very questionable therapy, young man."

I said, "This isn't therapy and you know it. If therapy

had been your object you would have used eidetic recall technique instead of drugs."

Steelton looked worried. "There was not time for that. We had to use rough methods for quick results. I'm not sure that I can authorize the subject to see the records."

Hazelhurst put in, "I agree with you. Doctor."

I exploded. "Damn it, nobody asked you to authorize anything and you haven't got any authority in the matter. Those records were snitched right out of my wife's head and they belong to her. I'm sick of you people trying to play God. I don't like it in a slug and I don't like it any better in a human being. She'll make up her own mind whether or not she wants to see them and whether or not I or anybody else will see them. Now ask her!"

Steelton said, "Mrs. Nivens, do you wish to see your records?"

Mary answered, "Yes, Doctor, I'd like very much to see them."

He seemed surprised. "Uh, to be sure. Do you wish to see them by yourself?" He glanced at me.

"My husband and I will see them. You and Dr. Hazelhurst are welcome to remain, if you wish."

Which they did. Presently a whole stack of tape spools were brought in, each labeled with attributed dates and ages. It would have taken us hours to go through them all, so I discarded those which concerned Mary's life after about 1991. I could not see how they could affect the problem and Mary could see them later if she wished.

We started out with her very early life. Each record started with the subject—Mary, that is—choking and groaning and struggling the way people always do when they are being forced back on a memory track which they would rather not follow, then would come the reconstruction, both in Mary's voice and in other voices. What surprised me most was Mary's face—in the tank, I mean. We had the magnification stepped up so that the stereo image of her face was practically in our laps and one could follow every change of expression.

First her face became that of a little girl—oh, her features were the same grown-up features but I knew that I was seeing my darling as she must have been when she was very small. It made me hope that we would have a little girl ourselves.

Then her expression would change to match when other actors out of her memory took over. It was like watching an incredibly able monologist playing many parts.

Mary took it with apparent serenity but her hand stole into mine. When we came to the terrible part when her parents changed, became not her parents but slaves of slugs, she clamped down on my fingers so hard that it would have crushed a hand less hamlike than my own. But she controlled herself.

I skipped over the spools marked "period of suspended animation". I was surprised to find that there were a great many of them; I would have thought that there was nothing to dig out of the memory of a person in such a condition. Be that as it may, I could not see how she could have learned anything during that period which would tell us how the slugs had died, so I left them out and proceeded to the group concerned with the time from her resuscitation to the group concerned with her rescue from the swamps.

One thing was certain from her expressions in the imaged record: she had been possessed by a slug as soon as she was revived. The dead quality of her face was that of a slug not bothering to keep up a masquerade; the stereocasts from Zone Red were full of that expression. The barren qualities of her memories from that period confirmed it.

Then, rather suddenly, she was no longer hag-ridden but was again a little girl, a very sick and frightened little girl. There was a delirious quality to her remembered thoughts, but, at the last, a new voice came out loud and clear; "Well, skin me alive come Sunday! Look, Pete—it's a little girl!"

Another voice answered, "Alive?" and the first voice answered, "I don't know."

The rest of that tape carried on into Kaiserville, her recovery, and many new voices and memories; presently it ended.

"I suggest," Dr. Steelton said as he took the tape out of the projector, "that we play another one of the same period. They are all slightly different and this period is the key to the whole matter."

"Why, Doctor?" Mary wanted to know.

"Eh? Of course you need not see them if you don't want to—but this period is the one which we are actually investigating. From your memories we must build up a picture of what happened to the parasites on Venus, why they died. In particular, if we could tell just what killed the titan which, uh, possessed you before you were found— what killed it and left you alive—we might well have the weapon we need."

"But don't you know?" Mary asked wonderingly.

"Eh? Not yet, not yet—but we'll get it. The human memory is an amazingly complete record, even though unhandy to use."

"But I can tell you now—I thought you knew. It was 'nine-day fever'."

"What?" Hazelhurst was out of his chair as if prodded.

"But of course. Couldn't you tell from my face? It was utterly characteristic—the mask, I mean. I saw it several times; I used to nurse it back ho—back in Kaiserville, because I had had it once and was immune to it."

Steelton said, "How about it Doctor? Have you ever seen a case of it?"

"Seen a case? No, I can't say that I have; by the time of the second expedition they had the vaccine for it. I'm thoroughly acquainted with its clinical characteristics, of course."

"But can't you tell from this record?"

"Well," Hazelhurst answered carefully, "I would say that what we have seen is consistent with it—but not conclusive, not conclusive."

"What's not conclusive?" Mary said sharply. "I told you it was 'nine-day fever'."

"We must be sure," Steelton said apologetically.

"How sure can you get? There is no question about it. I was told that I had had nine-day fever, that I had been sick with it when Pete and Frisco found me. I nursed other cases later and I never caught it again. I remember what their faces looked like when they were ready to die—just like my own face in the record. Anyone who has ever seen a case never forgets it and could not possibly mistake it for anything else. What more do you want? Fiery letters in the sky?" I have never seen Mary so close to losing her temper—except once. I said to myself: look out, gentlemen, better duck!

Steelton said, "I think you have proved your point, dear lady—but tell me: you were believed to have no memory of this period and my own experience with you leads me to think so. Now you speak as if you had direct, conscious memory—yes?"

Mary looked puzzled. "I remember it now—I remember it quite clearly. I haven't thought about it in many years."

"I think I understand." He turned to Hazelhurst. "Well, Doctor? Do we have a culture of it in the laboratory? Have your boys done any work on it?"

Hazelhurst seemed stunned. "Work on it? Of course not! It's utterly out of the question—nine-day fever! We might as well use polio—or typhus. I'd rather treat a hangnail with an ax!"

I touched Mary's arm and said, "Let's go, darling. I think we have done all the damage we can." As we left I saw that she was trembling and that her eyes were full of tears. I took her into the messroom for systemic treatment—distilled.

Later on I bedded Mary down for a nap and sat with her until I was sure she was asleep. Then I looked up my father; he was in the office they had assigned to him. The green privacy light was already on. "Howdy," I said.

He looked at me speculatively. "Well, Elihu, I hear that you hit the jackpot."

"I prefer to be called 'Sam'," I answered.

"Very well, Sam. Success is its own excuse; nevertheless the jackpot appears to be disappointingly small. The situation seems to be almost as hopeless as before. Nine-day fever, no wonder the colony died out and the slugs as well. I don't see how we can use it. We can't expect everyone to have Mary's indomitable will to live."

I understood him; the fever carried a 98-percent plus death rate among unprotected Earthmen. With those who had taken the shots the rate was an effective zero—but that did not figure. We needed a bug that would just make a man sick—but would kill his slug. "I can't see that it makes much difference," I pointed out. "It's odds-on that you will have typhus—or plague—or both—throughout the Mississippi Valley in the next six weeks."

"Or the slugs may have learned a lesson from the setback they took in Asia and will start taking drastic sanitary measures," he answered. I had not thought of that; the idea startled me so that I almost missed the next thing he said, which was: "No, Sam, you'll have to devise a better plan than that."

"I'll have to? I just work here."

"You did once—but now you've taken charge. I don't mind; I was ready to retire anyhow."

"Huh? What the devil are you talking about? I'm not in charge of anything—and don't want to be. You are head of the Section."

He shook his head. "A boss is the man who does the bossing. Titles and insignia usually come after the fact, not before. Tell me—do you think Oldfield could take over my job?"

I considered it and shook my head; Dad's chief deputy

was the executive officer type, a "carry-outer", not a "think-upper". "I've known that you would take over, some day," he went on. "Now you've done it—by bucking my judgment on an important matter, forcing your own on me, and by being justified in the outcome."

"Oh, rats! I got bull-headed and forced one issue. It never occurred to you big brains that you were failing to consult the one real Venus expert you had on tap—Mary, I mean. But I didn't expect to find out anything; I had a lucky break."

He shook his head. "I don't believe in luck, Sam. Luck is a tag given by the mediocre to account for the accomplishments of genius."

I placed my hands on the desk and leaned toward him. "Okay, so I'm a genius—just the same you are not going to get me to hold the sack. When this is over Mary and I are going up in the mountains and raise kittens and kids. We don't intend to spend our time bossing screwball agents."

He smiled gently as though he could see farther into the future than I could. I went on, "I don't want your job—understand me?"

"That is what the Devil said to the Deity after he displaced him—but he found he could not help himself. Don't take it so hard, Sam. I'll keep the title for the present and give you all the help I can. In the meantime, what are your orders, sir?"

Chapter 31

The worst of it was, he meant it. I tried to correct matters by going limp on him, but it did not work. A top-level conference was called late that afternoon; I was notified but I stayed away. Shortly a very polite little WAC came to tell me that the commanding officer was waiting and would I please come at once?

So I went—and tried to stay out of the discussion. But my father has a way of conducting any meeting he is in, even if he is not in the chair, by looking expectantly at the one he wants to hear from. It's a subtle trick, as the group does not know that it is being led.

But I knew. With every eye in the room on you, it is easier to voice an opinion than to keep quiet. Particularly as I found that I had opinions.

The meeting was largely given over to moaning and groaning about the utter impossibility of using nine-day fever against the slugs. Admitted that it would kill slugs—it would even kill Venerians who can be chopped in two and still survive. But it was sure death to any human—or almost any human; I was married to one who had survived—death to the enormous majority. Seven to ten days after exposure, then curtains.

"Yes, Mr. Nivens?" It was the commanding general, addressing me. I hadn't said anything but Dad's eyes were on me, waiting.

"I think there has been a lot of despair voiced at this session," I said, "and a lot of opinions given that were based on assumptions. The assumptions may not be correct."

"Yes?"

I did not have an instance in mind; I had been shooting from the hip. I continued to do so. "Well . . . for example—I hear constant reference to nine-day fever as if the 'nine-day' part were an absolute fact. It's not."

The boss brass shrugged impatiently. "It's a convenient tag—it averages nine days."

"Yes—but how do you know it lasts nine days—for a slug?"

By the murmur with which it was received I knew that I had hit the jackpot again.

A few minutes later I was being invited to explain why I thought the fever might run a different time in slugs and, if so, why it mattered. I began to feel like the after-dinner speaker who wishes he had not gotten up in the first place. But I bulled on ahead. "As to the first point," I said, "according to the record I saw this morning in the only case we know about the slug did die in less than nine days—quite a lot less. Those of you who have seen the records on my wife—and I gather that entirely too many of you have—are aware that her parasite left her, presumably dropped off and died, long before the eighth-day crisis. One datum does not fair a curve, but if it is true and experiments show it to be, then the problem is very different. A man infected with the fever might be rid of his slug in—oh, call it four days. That gives you five days to catch him and cure him."

The general whistled. "That's a pretty heroic solution, Mr. Nivens. How do you propose to cure him? For that matter, how do you propose to catch him? I mean to say, suppose we do plant an epidemic of nine-day fever in Zone Red, it would take some incredibly fast footwork— in the face of stubborn resistance, remember—to locate and treat more than fifty million people before they died of the fever."

It was a hot potato, so I slung it right back. I wondered as I did so how many "experts" made their names by passing the buck. "As to the second question, that is a logistical and tactical problem—your problem, not mine. As to the first, there is your expert." I pointed to Dr. Hazelhurst. "Ask him."

Hazelhurst huffed and puffed and I knew how he felt. Insufficient former art . . . more research needed . . . experiments would be required . . . he seemed to recall that some work had been done toward an antitoxin treatment but the vaccine for immunizing had proven so successful that he was not sure the antitoxin had ever been perfected. Anyway, everyone who went to Venus nowadays was immunized before leaving. He concluded lamely by saying that the study of the exotic diseases of Venus was necessarily still in its infancy.

The general interrupted him as he was finishing.

"This antitoxin business—how soon can you find out about it?"

Hazelhurst said he would get after it at once, there was a man at the Sorbonne he wanted to phone.

"Do so," his commanding officer said. "You are excused."

Hazelhurst came buzzing at our door before breakfast the next morning. I was annoyed but tried not to show it when I stepped out into the passage to see him. "Sorry to wake you," he said, "but you were right about that antitoxin matter."

"Huh?"

"They are sending me some from Paris; it should arrive any minute now. I do hope it's still potent."

"And if it isn't?"

"Well, we have the means to make it. We'll have to make it, of course, if this wild scheme is used—millions of units of it."

"Thanks for telling me," I said. "I know the general will be pleased." I started to turn away; he stopped me.

"Uh, Mr. Nivens—"

"Yes?"

"About the matter of vectors—"

"Vectors?" At the moment all the word meant to me was little arrows pointing in various directions.

"Disease vectors. We can't use rats or mice or anything like that. Do you happen to know how the fever is transmitted on Venus? By a little flying rotifer, the Venerian equivalent of an insect—but we don't have such here and that is the only way it can be carried."

"Do you mean to say you couldn't give it to me if you tried? Even with a jugful of live culture?"

"Oh, yes—I could inject you with it. But I can't picture a million paratroopers dropping into Zone Red and asking the parasite-ridden population to hold still while they gave them injections." He spread his hands helplessly.

Something started turning slowly over in my brain . . . a million men, in a single drop. "Why ask me?" I said. "It seems to be a medical problem."

"Uh, yes, it is of course. I just thought—Well, you seemed to have a ready grasp—" He paused.

"Thanks." My mind was struggling with two problems at once and beginning to have traffic problems. How many people were there in Zone Red? "Let me get this straight: suppose you had the fever and I didn't; I could not catch it from you?" The drop could not be medical men; there weren't that many.

"Not very easily. If I took a live smear from my throat and placed it in your throat, you might contract it. If I opened a vein of mine and made a trace transfusion to your veins, you would be sure to be infected with it."

"Direct contact, eh?" How many people could one paratrooper service? Ten? Twenty? Thirty? Or more? "If that is what it takes, you don't have any problem."

"Eh?"

"What's the first thing one slug does when he runs across another slug he hasn't seen lately?"

"Conjugation!"

" 'Direct conference', I've always called it—but then I use the sloppy old slug language for it. Do you think that would pass on the disease?"

"Think so? I'm sure of it! We have demonstrated, right here in this laboratory, that there is actual exchange of living protein during conjugation. They could not possibly escape direct transmission; we can infect the whole colony as if it were one body. Now why didn't I think of that?"

His words roused out a horrid memory, something about, "Would that my subjects had but one neck—" But I refrained from quoting it. "Don't go off half cocked," I said. "Better try it first. But I suspect that it will work."

"It will, it will!" He started to go, then stopped. "Oh, Mr. Nivens, would you mind very much—I know it's a great deal to ask—"

"What is? Speak up; I'm getting hungry." Actually I was anxious to work out the rest of the other problem.

"Well, would you consider permitting me to announce this method of vectoring in my report this morning? I'll give you full credit, but the general expects so much and this is just what I need to make my report complete." He looked so anxious that I almost laughed.

"Not at all," I said. "It's your department."

"That's decent of you. I'll try to return the favor." He turned away feeling happy and I turned back feeling the same way. I was beginning to like being a "genius".

I waited before reopening the door to our cubicle until I had straightened out in my mind all the main features of the big drop. Then I went in. Mary opened her eyes when I came in and gave me that long heavenly smile. I reached down and smoothed her hair. "Howdy, flame top, did you know that your husband is a genius?"

"Yes."

"You did? You never said so."

"You never asked me."

❀   ❀   ❀

Hazelhurst gave credit all right; he referred to it as the "Nivens vector". I suppose it was natural that I should be asked to comment, though Dad looked my way first.

"I agree with Dr. Hazelhurst," I started out, "subject to experimental confirmation as outlined. However, he has properly left open for discussion certain aspects which are tactical rather than medical. While it is true that the entire body of titans might be infected from one contact, important considerations of timing—crucial, I should say—" I had worked out my whole opening speech, even to the hesitations, while eating breakfast. Mary does not chatter at breakfast, thank goodness!

"—require vectoring from many focal points. If we are to save a nominal hundred percent of the population of Zone Red, it is necessary that all the parasites be infected at as nearly the same time as possible in order that rescue squads may enter Zone Red after the slugs are no longer dangerous and before any host has passed the point where antitoxin can save him. The problem is susceptible to mathematical analysis—" Sam boy, I said to myself, you old phony, you could not solve it with an electronic integrator and twenty years of sweat. "—and should be turned over to your analytical section. However, let me sketch out the factors. Call the number of vector origins 'X'; call the number of rescue workers who must be dropped 'Y'. There will be an indefinitely large number of simultaneous solutions, with the optimum solution depending on logistic factors. Speaking in advance of rigorous mathematical treatment—" I had done my very damnedest with a slipstick, but I did not mention that. "—and basing my opinions on my own unfortunately-too-intimate knowledge of their habits, I would estimate that—"

They let me go right ahead. You could have heard a pin drop, if anybody in that bare-skinned crew had had a pin. The general interrupted me once when I placed a rather low estimate on "X"; "Mr. Nivens. I think we can assure you of any number of volunteers for vectoring."

I shook my head. "You can't accept volunteers, General."

"I think I see your objection. The disease would have to be given time to establish itself in the volunteer and the timing might be dangerously close for his safety. But I think we could get around that—a gelatin capsule with the antitoxin embedded in tissue, or something of the sort. I'm sure the staff could work it out."

I thought they could, too, but I did not say that my real objection was a deep-rooted aversion to any additional human soul having to be possessed by a slug. "You must not use human volunteers, sir. The slug will know everything that his host knows—and he simply will not go into direct conference; he'll warn the others by word of mouth instead." I did not know that I was right but it sounded plausible. "No, sir, we will use animals—apes, dogs, anything large enough to carry a slug but incapable of human speech, and in sufficient quantities to infect the whole group before any slug knows that it is sick."

I went on to give a fast sketch of the final drop, Schedule Mercy, as I visualized it. "We can assume that the first drop—Schedule Fever—can start as soon as we are sure that we will have enough units of antitoxin for the second drop. In less than a week thereafter there should be no slug left alive on this continent."

They did not applaud, but it felt that way. The general adjourned the meeting and hurried away to call Air Marshal Rexton, then sent his aide back to invite me to lunch. I sent word that I would be pleased provided the invitation included my wife, otherwise I would be unable to accept.

Dad waited for me outside the conference room. "Well, how did I do?" I asked him, more anxiously than I tried to sound.

He shook his head. "Sam, you wowed 'em. You have the makings of a politician. No, I think I'll sign you up for twenty-six weeks of stereo instead."

I tried not to show how much I was pleased. I had gotten through the whole performance without once stammering; I felt like a new man.

✎ Chapter 32 ✎

That ape Satan which had wrung my heart so back at the National Zoo turned out to be as mean as he was billed, once he was free of his slug. Dad had volunteered to be the test case for the Nivens-Hazelhurst theories, but I put my foot down and Satan drew the short straw.

Dad made an issue out of it; he had some silly idea that it was up to him to be possessed by a slug, at least once. I told him that we had no time to waste on his sinful pride. He grew huffy but I made it stick.

It was neither filial affection nor its neo-Freudian antithesis that caused me to balk him; I was afraid of the combination of Dad-cum-slug. I did not want him on their side even temporarily and under laboratory conditions. Not with his shifty, tricky mind! I did not know how he would manage to escape nor what he would do to wreck our plans, but I was morally certain he would, once possessed.

People who have never experienced possession, even

those who have seen it, cannot appreciate that the host is utterly against us—with all his abilities intact. We could not risk having Dad against us—and I swung enough weight to overrule him.

So we used anthropoid apes for the experiments. We had on hand not only apes from the National Zoological Gardens but simian citizens from half a dozen zoos and a couple of circuses. I did not select Satan for the job; I would have let the poor beast be. The look of patient suffering on his face made one forget the slug on his back.

Satan was injected with nine-day fever on Wednesday the 13th. By Friday the fever had established; another chimp-cum-slug was introduced into his cage; the two slugs immediately went into direct conference, after which the second ape was removed.

On Sunday the 17th Satan's master shriveled up and fell off—dead. Satan was immediately injected with the antitoxin. Late Monday the other slug died and its host was dosed.

By Wednesday Satan was well though a bit thin and the second ape, Lord Fauntleroy, was on the road to recovery. I gave Satan a banana to celebrate and he took off the first joint of my left index finger and me with no time for a repair job. It was no accident either; that ape was nasty.

But a minor injury could not depress my spirits. After I had it dressed I looked for Mary, as I wanted to crow; I failed to find her and ended up in the messroom, wanting someone with whom to share a toast.

The place was empty; everyone in the labs—except me—was working harder than ever, mounting Schedule

Fever and Schedule Mercy. By order of the President all possible preparations were taking place in this one lab in the Smoky Mountains. The apes for vectoring, some two hundred of them, were here, and both the culture and the antitoxin were being "cooked" here; the horses needed for serum were stalled in what had been an underground handball court.

The million-plus men necessary for the Schedule Mercy drop could not be here, but they would know nothing about it until alerted a few hours before the drop, at which time each would be issued a hand gun and two bandoleers of individual dose antitoxin injectors. Those who had never parachuted before would not be given a chance to practice; they would each be pushed, if necessary, by some sergeant with a large foot. Everything possible was being done to keep the secret close; the only way I could see that we could lose (now that we knew that our theories worked) would be for the titans to find out our plans, through a renegade or by whatever means. Too many good plans have failed because some fool told his wife about it in bed.

If we failed to keep this secret, our ape disease vectors would never get into direct conference; they would be shot on sight wherever they appeared in the titan nation. But I relaxed over my first drink, happy and reasonably sure that the secret could not leak. Traffic with the laboratory was "incoming only" until after Drop Day and Colonel Kelly censored or monitored all communication outward— Kelly was no fool.

As for a leak from outside, the chances were slight. The general, Dad, Colonel Gibsy, and myself had gone to the White House the week before, there to see the President and Marshal Rexton. I had already convinced Dad that the way to keep this secret was not to share it with anybody; he put on a histrionic exhibition of belligerence and exasperation that got him what we wanted; in the end even Secretary Martinez was bypassed. If the President and Rexton could keep from talking in their sleep for another week, I did not see how we could miss.

A week would be none too soon; Zone Red was spreading. The counterattack they had launched at Pass Christian had not stopped there. The slugs had pushed on and now held the Gulf coast past Pensacola and there were signs that more was to come. Perhaps the slugs were growing tired of our resistance and might decide to waste human raw material by A-bombing the cities we still held. If so, we would find it hard to stop; a radar screen can alert your defenses, but it won't stop a determined attack.

But I refused to worry about that. One more week—

Colonel Kelly came in, looked around the otherwise empty room, came over and sat down beside me. "How about a drink?" I suggested. "I feel like celebrating."

He examined the hairy paunch bulging out in front of him and said, "I suppose one more beer wouldn't put me in any worse shape."

"Have two beers. Have four—a dozen." I dialed for him, and told him about the success of the experiments with the apes.

He nodded. "Yes, I had heard. Sounds good."

" 'Good', the man says! Colonel, we are on the one yard line and goal to go. A week from now the game will be won."

"So?"

"Oh, come now!" I answered, irritated by his manner. "In a short time you'll be able to put your clothes back on and lead a normal life. Or don't you think our plans will work?"

"Yes, I think they will work."

"Then why the crepe-hanging?"

Instead of answering directly he said, "Mr. Nivens, you don't think that a man with my pot belly enjoys running around without his clothes, do you?"

"I suppose not. As for myself, I'm beginning to find it pleasant. I may hate to have to give it up—saves time and it's comfortable."

"You need not worry about having to give it up. This is a permanent change."

"Huh? I don't get you. You said our plans would work and now you talk as if Schedule Sun Tan would go on forever."

"In a modified way, it will."

I said, "Pardon me? I'm stupid today."

He dialed for another beer. "Mr. Nivens, I never expected to live to see a military reservation turned into a ruddy nudist camp. Having seen it happen, I never expect to see us change back—because we can't. Pandora's box has a one-way lid. All the king's horses and all the king's men—"

"Conceded," I answered. "Things never go back quite to what they were before. Just the same, you are exaggerating. The day after the President rescinds Schedule Sun Tan the suspended blue laws will go into effect and a man without pants will be liable to arrest."

"I hope not."

"Huh? Make up your mind."

"It's made up for me. Mr. Nivens, as long as there exists a possibility that a slug is alive the polite man must be willing to bare his entire body on request—or risk getting shot. Not just this week and next week but twenty years from now, or a hundred. No, no!" he said, seeing that I was about to interrupt, "I am not disparaging your fine plans—but pardon me if I say that you have been too busy with their details to notice that they are strictly local and temporary. For example—have you made any plans for combing the Amazonian jungles, tree by tree?"

He went on apologetically, "Just a rhetorical inquiry. This globe has nearly sixty million square miles of dry land; we can't begin to search it and clean out the slugs. Shucks, man, we haven't made a dent in the rats and we've been at that a long time. Titans are trickier and more prolific than rats."

"Are you trying to tell me it's hopeless?" I demanded.

"Hopeless? Not at all. Have another drink. I'm trying to say that we are going to have to learn to live with this horror, the way we had to learn to live with the atom bomb."

I went away feeling dashed and not at all cocky. I wanted to find Mary. Some days, it occurred to me, the "genius" business wasn't worth the trouble.

Chapter 33

We were gathered in the same conference room in the White House; it put me in mind of the night after the President's message many weeks before. Dad was there; so were Mary and Rexton and Martinez. None of the "fishing cabinet" was present but their places were filled by our own lab general, by Dr. Hazelhurst, and by Colonel Gibsy. Martinez was busy trying to restore his face after having been told that he had been shunted out of the biggest show of his own department.

Nobody paid him any attention. Our eyes were on the big map still mounted across one wall; it had been four and a half days since the vector drop of Schedule Fever but the Mississippi Valley still glowed in ruby lights.

I was getting jittery, although the drop had been an apparent success and we had lost only three craft. According to the equations every slug within reach of direct conference should have been infected three days ago, with an estimated twenty-three percent overlap. The operation had been computed to contact about eighty percent of the slugs in the first twelve hours alone, mostly in the large cities.

Soon, slugs should start dying a damn sight faster than flies ever did—if we were right.

I forced myself to sit still and wondered whether those ruby lights covered a few million very sick slugs—or merely two hundred dead apes. Had somebody skipped a decimal point? Or blabbed? Or had there been an error in our reasoning so colossal that we could not see it?

Suddenly a light blinked green, right in the middle of the board; everybody sat up. Right on top of it a voice began to come out of the stereo gear though no picture built up. "This is Station Dixie, Little Rock," a very tired southern voice said. "We need help very badly. Anyone who is listening, please be good enough to pass on this message: Little Rock, Arkansas, is in the grip of a terrible epidemic. Notify the Red Cross. We have been in the hands of—" The voice trailed off, whether from weakness or transmission failure I could not be sure.

I remembered to breathe. Mary patted my hand and I sat back, relaxing consciously. It was joy too great to be pleasure. I saw now that the green light had not been Little Rock, but farther west in Oklahoma. Two more lights blinked green, one in Nebraska and one north of the Canadian line. Another voice came over, a twangy New England voice; I wondered how he had gotten into Zone Red.

"A little like election night, eh, chief?" Martinez said heartily.

"A little," the President agreed, "but we do not usually

get returns from Old Mexico." He pointed to the board; a pair of green lights were showing in Chihuahua.

"By George, you're right. Well, I guess 'State' will have some international incidents to straighten out when this is over, eh?"

The President did not answer and he shut up, to my relief. The President seemed to be talking to himself; he noticed me watching him, smiled, and spoke out loud:

"' 'Tis said that fleas have little fleas,

Upon their backs to bite 'em,

And little fleas have lesser fleas,

And so, ad infinitum.'"

I smiled to be polite though I thought the notion was gruesome, under the circumstances. The President looked away and said, "Would anyone like supper? I find that I am hungry, for the first time in days."

By late the next afternoon the board was more green than red. Rexton had caused to be set up two annunciators keyed into the command center in the New Pentagon; one showed percentage of completion of the complicated score deemed necessary before the big drop; the other showed the projected time of drop. The figures on it changed from time to time, sometimes up, sometimes down. For the past two hours they had been holding fairly steady around 17.43, East Coast time.

Finally Rexton stood up. "I'm going to freeze it at seventeen forty-five," he announced. "Mr. President, if you will excuse me?"

"Certainly, sir."

Rexton turned to Dad and myself. "If you two Don Quixotes are still determined to go, now is the time."

I stood up. "Mary, you wait for me."

She asked, "Where?" It had already been settled— and not peacefully! —that she was not to go.

The President interrupted. "I suggest that Mrs. Nivens stay here. After all, she is a member of the family."

With the invitation he gave us his best smile and I said, "Thank you, sir." Colonel Gibsy got a very odd look.

Two hours later we were coming in on our target and the jump door was open. Dad and I were last in line, after the kids who would do the real work. My hands were sweaty and I stunk with the old curtain going-up stink. I was scared as hell—I never like to jump.

🦅 Chapter 34 🦅

Gun in my left hand, antitoxin injector ready in my right, I went from door to door in my assigned block. It was an older section of Jefferson City, slums almost; it consisted of apartment houses built fifty years ago. I had given two dozen injections and had three dozen to go before it would be time for me to rendezvous at the State House. I was getting sick of it.

I knew why I had come— it was not just curiosity; I wanted to see them die! I wanted to watch them die, see them dead, with a weary hate that passed all other needs. But now I had seen them dead and I wanted no more of it; I wanted to go home, take a bath, and forget it.

It was not hard work, just monotonous and nauseating. So far I had not seen one live slug, though I had seen many dead ones. I had burned one skulking dog that appeared to have a hump; I was not sure as the light had been bad. We had hit shortly before sundown and now it was almost full dark.

The worst of it was the smells. Whoever compared the odor of unwashed, lousy, diseased humans with that of sheep was no friend to decent sheep.

I finished checking the rooms of the apartment building I was in, shouted to make sure, and went out into the street. It was almost deserted; with the whole population sick with the fever we found few on the streets. The lone exception was a man who came weaving toward me, eyes vacant. I yelled, "Hey!"

He stopped. I said, "You are sick, but I've got what you need to get well. Hold out your arm."

He struck at me feebly. I hit him carefully with my gun and he went face down. Across his back was the red rash of the slug; I avoided that area, picked a reasonably clean and healthy patch over his kidney and stuck in the injector, bending it to break the point after it was in. The units were gas-loaded; nothing more was needed. I did not even withdraw it, but left him.

The first floor of the next house held seven people, most of them so far gone that I did not bother to speak but simply gave them their shots and hurried on. I had no trouble. The second floor was like the first.

The top floor had three empty apartments, at one of which I had to bum out the lock to enter. The fourth flat was occupied, in a manner of speaking. There was a dead woman on the floor of the kitchen, her head bashed in. Her slug was still on her shoulders, but merely resting there, for it was dead, too, and beginning to reek. I left them quickly and looked around.

In the bathroom, sitting in an old-fashioned bathtub, was a middle-aged man. His head slumped on his chest and his wrist veins were open. I thought he was dead but he looked up as I bent over him. "You're too late," he said dully. "I killed my wife."

Or too soon, I thought. From the appearance of the bottom of the tub and by his gray face, five minutes later would have been better. I looked at him, wondering whether or not to waste an injection. He spoke again. "My little girl—"

"You have a daughter?" I said loudly. "Where is she?"

His eyes flickered but he did not speak. His head slumped forward again. I shouted at him, then felt his jaw line and dug my thumb into his neck, but could find no pulse. As a favor to him I burned him carefully through the base of the brain before I left.

The child was in bed in one of the rooms, a girl of eight or so who would have been pretty had she been well. She roused and cried and called me Daddy. "Yes, yes," I said soothingly, "Daddy's going to take care of you." I gave her the injection in her leg; I don't think she noticed it.

I turned to go but she called out again. "I'm thirsty. Want a drink of water." So I had to go back into that bathroom again.

As I was giving it to her my phone shrilled and I spilled some of it. "Son! Can you hear me?"

I reached for my belt and switched on my phone. "Yes. What's up?"

"I'm in that little park just north of you. Can you come? I'm in trouble."

"Coming!" I put down the glass and started to leave— then caught by indecision, I turned back. I could not leave my new friend to wake up in that charnel house, a parent dead in each room. I gathered her up in my arms and stumbled down to the second floor. There I entered the first door I came to and laid her on a sofa. There were people in the flat, probably too sick to bother with her, but it was all I could do.

"Hurry, son!"

"On my way!" I dashed out of there and wasted no more breath talking to him, but made speed. Dad's assignment was directly north of mine, paralleling it and fronting on one of those pint-sized downtown parks. When I got around the block I did not see him at first and ran on past him.

"Here, son, over here—at the car!" This time I could hear him both through the phone and my bare ear. I swung around and spotted the car, a big Cadillac duo much like the Section often used. There was someone inside but it was too dark for me to see whether or not it was the Old Man. I approached cautiously until I heard him say, "Thank God! I thought you would never come," and knew that it was he.

I had to duck to get in through the door. It was then that he clipped me.

I came to, to find my hands tied and my ankles as well. I was in the second driver's seat of the car and the Old Man was in the other, at the controls. The wheel on my side was latched up out of the way. The sudden realization that the car was in the air brought me fully awake.

He turned and said cheerfully, "Feeling better?" I could see his slug, riding high on his shoulders.

"Some better," I admitted.

"Sorry I had to hit you," he went on, "but there was no other way."

"I suppose not."

"I'll have to leave you tied up for the present; you know that. Later on we can make better arrangements." He grinned, his old wicked grin. Most amazingly his own personality came through with every word the slug said.

I did not ask what "better arrangements" were possible; I did not need nor want to know. I concentrated on checking my bonds; I need not have bothered—the Old Man had given them his personal attention.

"Where are we going?" I asked.

"South." He fiddled with the controls. "'Way south. Just give me a moment to lay this heap in the groove and I will explain what's in store for us." He was busy for a few seconds, then said, "There—that will hold her until she levels off at thirty thousand."

The mention of that much altitude caused me to take a quick look at the control board. The duo did not merely look like one of the Section's cars; it actually was one of our souped-up jobs. "Where did you get this car?" I asked.

"The Section had it cached in Jefferson City. I looked, and, sure enough, nobody had found it. Fortunate, wasn't it?"

There could be a second opinion on that point, I thought, but I did not argue. I was still checking the possibilities—and finding them somewhere between slim and hopeless. My own gun was gone, as I could tell by the pressure. He was probably carrying his on the side away from me; it was not in sight.

"But that was not the best of it," he went on; "I had

the good luck to be captured by what was almost certainly the only healthy master in the whole of Jefferson City—
not that I believe in luck. So we win after all." He chuckled.
"It's like playing both sides of a very difficult chess game."

"You did not tell me where we are going?" I persisted.
I did not know that it would help, but I was getting
nowhere fast and talking was the only action open to me.

He considered. "Out of the United States, certainly.
My master may be the only one free of nine-day fever in
the whole continent and I don't dare take a chance. I think
the Yucatan peninsula would suit us—that's where I've got
her pointed. We can hole up there and increase our
numbers and work on south. When we do come back—
and we will! —we won't make the same mistakes."

I said, "Dad, can't you take these ties off me? I'm losing
circulation. You know you can trust me."

"Presently, presently—all in good time. Wait until we
go full automatic." The car was still climbing; souped up
or not, thirty thousand was a long pull for a car that had
started out as a family model.

I said, "You seem to forget that I was with the masters
a long time. I know the score—and I give you my word of
honor."

He grinned. "Don't teach grandma how to steal sheep.
If I let you loose now, you'll kill me or I'll have to kill you.
And I want you alive. We're going places, son—you and
me. We're fast and we're smart and we are just what the
doctor ordered."

I did not have an answer. He went on, "Just the
same—about you knowing the score: why didn't you tell
me the score, son? Why did you hold out on me?"

"Huh?"

"You didn't tell me how it felt. Son, I had no idea that a man could feel such a sense of peace and contentment and well-being. This is the happiest I've been in years, the happiest since—" he suddenly looked puzzled, and then went on, "since your mother died. But never mind that; this is better. You should have told me."

Disgust suddenly poured over me and I forgot the cautious game I was playing. "Maybe I didn't see it that way. And neither would you, you crazy old fool, if you didn't have a filthy slug riding you, talking through your mouth, thinking with your brain!"

"Take it easy, son," he said gently—and so help me, his voice did soothe me. "You'll know better in a little while. Believe me, this is what we were intended for, this is our destiny. Mankind has been divided, warring with himself. The masters will make him whole again."

I thought to myself that there were probably custard heads just screwy enough to fall for such a line—surrender their souls willingly for a promise of security and peace. But I did not say so; I was clamping my jaws to keep from throwing up.

"But you need not wait much longer," he said suddenly, glancing at the board. "I'll nail her down in the groove." He adjusted his dead-reckoner bug, checked his board, and set his controls. "That's a relief. Next stop: Yucatan. Now to work." He got out of his chair and knelt beside me in the crowded space. "Got to be safe," he said, as he strapped the safety belt across my middle.

I brought my knees up in his face.

He reared up and looked at me without anger.

"Naughty, naughty. I could resent that—but the masters don't go in for resentment. Now be good." He went ahead, checking my wrists and feet. His nose was bleeding but he did not bother to wipe it. "You'll do," he said. "Now be patient; it won't be long."

He went back to the other control seat, sat down and leaned forward, elbows on knees. It brought his master directly into my view.

Nothing happened for some minutes, nor could I think of anything to do other than strain at my bonds. By his appearance, the Old Man was asleep, but I placed no trust in that.

A line formed straight down the middle of the horny brown covering of the slug.

As I watched it, it widened. Presently I could see the clotted opalescent horror underneath. The space between the two halves of the shell widened—and I realized that the slug was fissioning, sucking life and matter out of the body of my father to make two of itself.

I realized, too, with rigid terror, that I had no more than five minutes of individual life left to me. My new master was being born and soon would be ready to mount me.

Had it been humanly possible for flesh and bone to break the ties on me I would have broken them. I did not succeed. The Old Man paid no attention to my struggles. I doubt if he were conscious; the slugs must surely give up some measure of control while they are occupied with splitting. It must be that they simply immobilize the slave. As may be—the Old Man did not move.

By the time I had given up, worn out and sure that I could not break loose, I could see the ciliated silvery line down the center of the slug proper which means that fission is about to be complete. It was that which changed my line of reasoning, if there were reason left in my churning skull.

My hands were tied behind me, my ankles were tied, and I was belted tight across the middle to the chair. But my legs, even though fastened together, were free from my waist down; the seat had no knee belts.

I slumped down in the chair to get even more reach and swung my legs up high. I brought them down smashingly across the board—and set off every launching unit in her racks at once.

That adds up to a lot of g's—how many, I don't know, for I don't know how full her racks were. But there were plenty. We were both slammed back against the seats. Dad much harder than I was, since I was strapped down. He was thrown against the back of his seat, with his slug, open and helpless, crushed between the two masses.

It splashed.

And Dad himself was caught in that terrible, total reflex, that spasm of every muscle that I had seen three times before. He bounced forward against the wheel, face contorted, fingers writhing.

The car dived.

I sat there and watched it dive, if you call it sitting when you are held in place only by the belt. If Dad's body had not hopelessly fouled the controls I might have been able to do something about it—gotten her headed up again perhaps—with my bound feet. As it was, I tried but with no success at all. The controls were probably jammed as well as fouled.

The altimeter was clicking away busily. We had dropped to eleven thousand feet before I found time to glance at it. Then it was nine . . . seven . . . six—and we entered our last mile.

At fifteen hundred the radar interlock with the altimeter cut in and the nose units fired one at a time. The belt buffeted me across the stomach each time and I finally did throw up. I was thinking that I was saved, that now the ship would level off—though I should have known better. Dad being jammed up against the wheel as he was.

I was still thinking so as we crashed.

I came to by becoming slowly aware of a gently rocking motion. I was annoyed by it, I wanted it to stop; even a slight motion seemed to cause me more pain than I could bear. I managed to get one eye open—the other would not open at all—and looked dully around for the source of my annoyance.

Above me was the floor of the car, but I stared at it for a long time before I placed it as such. By the time I figured out what it was I was somewhat aware of where I was and what had happened. I remembered the dive and the crash—and realized that we must have crashed not into the ground but into some body of water—the Gulf of Mexico—but I did not really care.

With a sudden burst of grief I mourned my father.

The broken belt of my seat was flapping uselessly just above me. My hands were still tied and so were my ankles, and one arm at least seemed to be broken. One eye was stuck shut and it hurt me to breathe; I quit taking stock of my injuries. Dad was no longer plastered against the wheel and that puzzled me. With painful effort I rolled my head over to see the rest of the car with my one good eye. He was lying not far from me, three feet or so, from my head to his. He was bloody and cold and I was sure that he was dead. I think it took me about a half hour to cross that three feet.

I lay face to face with him, almost cheek to cheek. So far as I could tell there was no trace of life, nor, from the odd and twisted way in which he lay, did it seem possible.

"Dad," I said hoarsely. Then I screamed it. "Dad!"

His eyes flickered but did not open. "Hello, son," he whispered. "Thanks, boy, thanks—" His voice died out.

I wanted to shake him but all I could do was shout. "Dad! Wake up—are you all right?"

He spoke again, as if every word were a painful task. "Your mother—said to tell you . . . she was—proud of you." His voice died out again and his breathing was labored in that ominous dry-stick sound.

"Dad," I sobbed, "don't die—I can't get along without you."

His eyes opened wide. "Yes, you can, son." He paused and labored, then added, "I'm hurt, boy." His eyes closed again.

I could not get any more out of him, though I shouted and screamed. Presently I lay my face against his and let my tears mix with the dirt and blood.

☞ **Chapter 35** ☜

And now to clean up Titan!

Each of us who are going is writing one of these reports, for we know that we may not come back. If not, this is our legacy to free human beings—all that we learned and all that we know of how the titan parasites operate and what must be guarded against. For Kelly was right; there is no getting Humpty-Dumpty back together. In spite of the almost complete success of Schedule Mercy there is no way to be sure that the slugs are all gone. No longer ago than last week it was reported that a bear was shot, up Yukon way, wearing a hump.

The race will have to be always on guard; most especially it will have to be on guard about twenty-five years from now if we don't come back—but the flying saucers do. We don't know why the titan monsters follow the twenty-nine year cycle of Saturn's "year", but they do. The human race has many cycles which match the Earth year; the reasons may be equally simple for the titans. We hope that they are active only at one period of their "year"; if they are. Operation Vengeance may have easy pickings. Not that we are counting on it. I am going out, heaven help us, as an "applied psychologist (exotic)", but I am also a combat trooper, as is every one of us, from chaplain to cook. This is for keeps and we intend to show those slugs that they made the mistake of tangling with the toughest, meanest, deadliest, most unrelenting—and ablest—form of life in this section of space, a critter that can be killed but can't be tamed.

(I have a private hope that we will find some way to save the little elf creatures, the androgynes. We weren't able to save any of those in the saucer we found near Kansas City when the fighting was over, but that doesn't prove anything. I think we could get along with the elves. They are probably the real natives of Titan, anyhow; certainly they aren't related to the slugs.)

Whether we make it, or not, the human race has got to keep up its well-earned reputation for ferocity. If the slugs taught us anything, it was that the price of freedom is the willingness to do sudden battle, anywhere, any time, and with utter recklessness. If we did not learn that, well— "Dinosaurs, move over! We are ready to become extinct."

For who knows what dirty tricks may be lurking around this universe? The slugs may be simple and open and friendly compared with, let us say, the natives of the planets of Sirius. If this is just the opener, we had better learn from it for the main event. We thought space was empty and that we were automatically the lords of creation—even after we "conquered" space we thought so; Mars was already dead and Venus had not really gotten started. Well, if Man wants to be top dog—or even a respected neighbor—he'll have to fight for it. Beat the plowshares back into swords; the other was a maiden aunt's fancy.

Every one of us who is going has been possessed at least once. Only those who have been hag-ridden can know how tricky the slugs are, how constantly one must be on guard—or how deeply one must hate. The trip, they tell me, will take about twelve years, which will give Mary and me time to finish our honeymoon. Oh, yes, Mary is going; most of us are married couples and the single men are balanced by an equal number of single women. Twelve years isn't a trip; it's a way of living.

When I told Mary that we were going to Saturn her single comment was, "Yes, dear."

We'll have time for two or three kids, too. As Dad says, "The race must go on, even if it doesn't know where."

This report is loose-jointed in spots, and I can see that some must be cut and some must be censored before it is transcribed. But I have put everything into it, as I saw it and as I felt it, for war with another race is psychological war, not war of gadgets, and what I thought and what I felt may be more important than what I did.

I am finishing this report in Space Station Beta, from which we will transship to our vessel U.N.S. Avenger. I will not have time to make corrections; this will have to go as is, for the historians to have fun with. We said good-by to Dad last night at Pikes Peak Port and left our little girl with him. She did not understand and that was hard. But it was better so—and Mary and I will look into the matter of having another, at once.

When I said good-by Dad corrected me. "So long, you mean. You'll be back and I intend to hang on, getting crankier and meaner every year, until you do." I said I hoped so. He nodded. "You'll make it. You're too tough and mean to die. I've got a lot of confidence in you and the likes of you, son."

We are about to transship. I feel exhilarated. Puppet masters—the free men are coming to kill you!

Death and Destruction!

☞ Afterword ☜
by
Sarah A. Hoyt

When I first read *The Puppet Masters* I was very young. I don't remember my age exactly, but I remember it was the beginning of summer vacation and that the book was carefully taken from my brother's room after he left for college classes.

You see, he was sure science fiction books would be bad for me because sometimes they had sex scenes. I was, of course, determined to read these books. Not because of the sex. I'd already managed to read most of Masters and Johnson's—it did wonders for my English—while standing by my brother's desk, ready to drop it and run if I heard his step on the stairs.

Mostly, I wanted to read science fiction because the books were "grownup stuff" that my brother didn't want me reading. And most of the stuff I read was desperately bad. And most of it has been—mercifully—forgotten.

The Puppet Masters—most of Heinlein—was different. Looking back, it is hard to imagine—objectively—why I took to both the book or Heinlein; why I returned to the book again and again, and why Heinlein moved right up on my list of authors to look for—and later buy, when I had the money and went to school in the city.

I've been giving this some thought because a week after I was asked to write this, it was brought to my attention there are people—granted most of them very young, one way or another—who think Heinlein is irrelevant because no one in his stories uses cell phones, personal computers, the internet, gaming systems, because there is no web of communications girding the planet and because he failed to anticipate myriad advancements, large and small. At the same time, of course, we lack flying cars and moon colonies.

To an extent this baffles me. It seems to view science fiction as—somehow—a side field to futurism, or perhaps to psychic endeavors. If this were true, then all the writers of science fiction would be experts in the field they write about. And what they write would be more extrapolation of where science is going and less story.

The fact is that a good science fiction writer—and Heinlein was a very good one—is not a soothsayer, or a prophet, blinking into the sparkling crystal ball of future technology and making sense of the penumbras of knowledge yet to be. No. A good science fiction writer is more like a cartographer mapping territory that by its very nature cannot and will not be known, sitting at the known edge of the present—the farthest we've gotten on the land of time—in a tower that looks a little way over the oceans of the future. From his glimmers of this ocean—mostly obtained by reading the scientists—he gathers rumors and hopes, fears and warnings. These then he distillates into a map.

Oh, the map will almost for sure be distorted. He will make small islands into continents, and some continents will be missed all together. But if this cartographer knows human nature—and Heinlein did—he will retain enough of those rumors, those shadows, those ideas, to make a map that warns of where there are likely to be dragons and also indicate clear sailing and good prospects ahead.

Is this what science fiction is supposed to do?

I believe so. I believe science fiction is a way for humanity to cope with the ever accelerating rate of change. True or false, well-foreseen or not, science fiction books show us pathways that the future *might* take, ways that things might go. And—the best ones show us how humans react to certain types of situations, and thus prepare us for situations that might be very different than those they are actually depicting but that, yet, follow the same general pattern. And the best of all show us the path to retaining our humanity and morality in a future we can't even clearly dream.

At this as at so many other things, Heinlein was a master of the craft.

Unlike a certain generation of writers which would come later and who viewed it as their sworn goal in life to always and forever sound the warning about technology, till it became a merged tolling of "repent, repent" and "unclean, unclean", Heinlein never lost his faith in technology and in the ultimate triumph of what I would, for lack of better words, call the American ideal.

I know whence I speak of when it comes to that "American ideal" because I came at it as a foreigner. I was born to Portuguese parents in Portugal, in a village at the edge of a great city. In that country, crushed under the weight of a history so ponderous that anything less than a hundred years old is considered merely old news and needing substantial yellowing of the newspapers on which it was first printed before it acquires the dignity and patina of a historical lesson.

My first encounters with Heinlein shocked me terribly. Take the way that his characters complained about taxes. Didn't the people around me complain about taxes? Oh, yes, occasionally. But not in the same way. The people around me might complain that taxes on them in particular were too high. That this class or that was being favored. But they never, not for a moment, doubted the government's right—almost divine right—to levy taxes and to levy them in any way they wished.

Heinlein's idea that the individual was the source of the authority—and the money—of the government and that he had the right to complain about anything or everything that took his fancy shocked me. And then, because I'm not put together right, it brought me back to read more. And eventually it convinced me of the validity of this American idea that right and might reposes in the individual.

Life, liberty, the pursuit of happiness, every man born equal—I wonder if people who grew up with it from birth realize how crazy, how revolutionary, how outrageous these ideas are. How historically "unsound". And how they are woven into every sentence, every character, every situation in Heinlein's books.

Which brings us right around to my two favorites among all of Heinlein's work—*The Moon is a Harsh Mistress* and *The Puppet Masters*. One of which details the promise of representative democracy and the other its limitations when faced with something that impairs the functioning of the individual or collective channels of information.

Because I was lucky enough to be asked to write the afterword to *The Puppet Masters* we will concentrate on it.

On the face of it, *The Puppet Masters* is an invasion from space book. It seems almost a cliché now, after the continuous barrage of aliens and invaders and predators and possibly predators on invading aliens that keep my children attached to the TV screen.

And yet, for my money, *The Puppet Masters* remains both the most accurate in how crisis and resolution proceed in a democracy—save for the "easy" solution of the Nine Days Fever, but the man had, after all, a deadline and a word count to respect—and the scariest.

First, let's establish that whatever details of future technology he got wrong, the parasites are at least perfectly plausible. Recent research indicates, for instance, that Toxoplasma gondii can alter the behavior of infected rats in ways that makes them more likely to be eaten by cats, the host of choice for Toxoplasma. So it is plausible that aliens could take over humans and change their behavior and, perhaps, make use of the human's own intelligence—throughout *The Puppet Masters* we're never absolutely sure that the creatures are of themselves intelligent and not dependent on the host's mental resources, as they are on the host's oxygen.

However, because this is a Heinlein book, the mind parasites are not just mind parasites. I was going to write about how it is a perfect metaphor—and to an extent a roadmap—to the type of war we find ourselves involved in currently. Then it occurred to me that, just like I found books that had been printed thirty or forty years before I read them, these words might be found after this war is won, and seem irrelevant to a new generation.

It is not that my words might be irrelevant which disturbs me. It is the fact that I think Heinlein's book— which clearly could not have been written with the current war in mind—applies to every war fought between a representative, democratic government and a dictatorship or an ideological group organized on dictatorial principles.

I read somewhere that he viewed *The Puppet Masters* as his metaphor for the Cold War. And perhaps he did. It could also have been about the Second World War or, if my recently acquired collection of bound periodicals of World War One is correct, about that one too.

What do I mean exactly? I can see people scratching their heads and saying that if this book on space parasites is a good metaphor for all that, then "See Spot Run" must be a wonderful metaphor for the human existence.

This is where I have to clarify that though I have a degree in literature, I never considered myself one of *them*, so if I say this is a metaphor for something, it is such a plain metaphor that blind men can see it blinking at them with neon brightness through the deepest midnight gloom.

Surely I can't mean that when we are at war with a totalitarian state or ideology they send soup-plate sized aliens to attach to our nervous system? Well . . . not literally. Not yet.

Heinlein's life coincided with the period of ascendancy, monopoly and concentration of what became known as mass media. I am informed enough to be aware that newspapers and pamphlets, broadsheets and plays had an influence on public opinion long before Heinlein's life time. In Richelieu's time pamphlets were important tools of propaganda. And it could be argued that Shakespeare was the Tudors' greatest publicist.

But Heinlein's lifetime saw the rise of a media that was both image-based—and therefore not dependent on the literacy of the public—and by its very nature concentrated upon a very few outlets.

That he was aware of the danger of this is clear when he notes in *The Puppet Masters* "Control the communications of the country, and you control the country; that's elementary." And indeed it is and it was long before he wrote this book. What wasn't obvious, and I know still isn't—is how relatively easy it is to lie with mass media and images. Particularly if you are a totalitarian regime—a Puppet Master.

I remember in the Seventies walking to the train station in downtown Porto and walking past a stand of magazines, the front of which was ornamented with copy after shining copy of *Soviet Life*. Glamour and glitz, recipes and fashions, and not a hint of poverty anywhere, not a glimmer of doubt, not a hint that everything was not as it should be in the worker's paradise. The same stand sold *Times magazine* and *Newsweek*, showing worried expressions and people wondering when the stagflation was going to end.

Did I believe the Soviet Union was better? No. But I am one of the few people whom too-glossy an image puts off, one of the few people who thinks too perfect an image of necessity hides something underneath.

A totalitarian regime, something controlled by a few puppet masters, is always at an advantage in controlling the flow of communication. A democracy is always more fractured, more full of doubt, more worried about whether the enemy is really an enemy or whether our own side is wrong. And if you think that is a feature of the current war only, you haven't read nearly enough about the Cold War or World War Two. (For that matter, there are people walking around among us who in those wars were the equivalent of the collaborationists in *The Puppet Masters*, the ones who didn't need to be ridden and who would do the bidding of the enemy willingly. They too have yet to admit they did anything wrong.)

Part of the genius of Heinlein in this book is that he shows us the enormity—the impossibility—of the threat in the characters' minds from the beginning. A UFO? Come on. Sam makes an impassioned plea that these were all proven to be fake. From the beginning. Every right thinking person knew it. Why, their society had proved that UFOs were part of the madness of the crazy years. Digby's evaluating integral for second and higher order data gave a certainty that 93.7 percent of the flying saucer appearances were hallucination. (Death camps? In Germany? You must be kidding. Germany is a civilized nation.)

The characters are forced to accept the threat, the enormity of it little by little, with incontrovertible facts and *their own personal research*. And though the main characters are both operatives, they are not told to research anything. Their boss orders them to go on vacation. But they research. They inform themselves. They find out the truth.

Even then, note that as the main characters—and their boss—have a pretty good picture of what humanity is facing, the government won't move on it. The president as good as tells their boss, who is a good friend, an invaluable aide and a trusted operative, that he's crazy or having a breakdown. And once they convince the president, they have to convince Congress. All in the face of an enormous and ruthless threat.

And meanwhile, all through it, the broadcasts from the occupied zones maintain the masquerade. The people in the occupied zones claim that they are the sane ones, they are the normal ones. They are upholding the laws of the land, while the rest of the country seems to have gone chasing, willy-nilly, down some blind alley of madness that they have escaped. And though in the free zone, the majority of the population remains unaffected, many of them also believe that there are no aliens and that government has gone mad. After all, it is far more rational than thinking about space aliens taking over. Far less scary too. If people admitted there were such a thing as space aliens, they would have to fight. As long as they don't admit it, they can pretend the situation is normal.

It's much easier to believe the worst of our own citizens—of the other party, the other race, the other class, those goofballs in DC, anything—than to believe that something or someone ruthless and utterly unprincipled wants to kill us. (Why, we're pretty nice people. How can they hate us? They don't even know us.) It is easier to believe that it is our own president, our own Congress, those people up the street, who have gone crazy, who are paranoid, racist, evil, than to believe that our deaths are the path to some stranger's idea of world domination and paradise on Earth.

You see, we know our neighbors, our president, our Congress. We know those people down the street. We can call them evil all we want to, but deep inside, we know they're safe to attack. The very fact that we're here, in the United States, means we can say whatever we want to, doesn't it? No one is going to hurt us. (As for publishing the Danish cartoons of Mohammed, why, we're not doing it because we're being sensitive! Sensitive, I tell you. It has nothing to do with being afraid for our heads and their precarious attachment to our necks.)

While re-reading *The Puppet Masters* last week I couldn't help snorting when Sam—still somewhat naive— tells his boss he can't believe this would involve partisan politics. The mechanisms along which collective resolutions must be made, in *Puppet Masters* is almost painfully familiar. Every order, every attempt to contravene enemy action must go through our democratic institutions which are, of necessity, filled with partisan interests. Whatever else they are—and it could be said they're mechanisms for ensuring a degree of individual freedom—they are also a way of forming a hierarchy and of fighting for personal power. This dual nature infuses everything. And in *The Puppet Masters* each attempt to defend humanity from the aliens must go through this narrow sieve. As must our attempts to defend democracy and freedom.

All right, so no one is asking us to undress—yet—though I've often suspected that it will inevitably come to that while flying. (I also noted, with a grin, his comparison of the very half-hearted security measures before they meet the president with the far more effective ones behind the curtain. Another price of individual freedom.) But there are other taboos, other restrictions and characteristics which are just as important—perhaps more important—to us nowadays as the nudity taboo was when Heinlein wrote this. I have a great deal of trouble imagining that any men would put up much of a fight these days if they were told to strip to the waist. Women might put up a bit more of a fight, but if they could wear halters or bikini tops, it would probably not be a huge taboo to break.

However, try violating other taboos, principles, even, on which the country was founded. Try listening in on a private conversation—even one that happens between foreign nationals, but whose transmission passes through national phone companies—try putting a bug in a religious establishment. These taboos exist still, and anyone who thinks doing such things is needed to defend us from the enemy will fight for the right to break every single one of them.

Am I saying that taboos and principles of individual privacy are bad things? Am I saying it is a bad thing that approval for actions against the enemy must undergo the slow approval of democratic institutions? No. As a country founded on neither race nor creed, but only on principle, we do have to hold on to those founding principles tightly. And they are not a crippling disadvantage. Not so long as our information organs work, not so long as an informed and free citizenry eventually becomes aware of the danger and decides to defend itself.

Why is it not a bad thing? After all, in the book, Mr. Nivens, Sam's boss—and father—knows what to do right from the beginning. After all, Sam says that if they had taken control earlier, quarantined Iowa, gone in and killed all the Titans, they could easily have saved lives and strife. The same is true of every war. I keep hearing how if the—eventual—Allies had intervened earlier in World War II it would have saved countless lives.

But that type of action, single-handedly, almost always requires an individual to take it. A single person who takes command, who sees the trouble and the danger and who is willing to risk it all and take actions that might seem reckless to others.

This is easy in a dictatorship, not so easy under a representative government, particularly not one that prides itself on checks and balances which—at least theoretically—are supposed to keep government power in check.

And the truth is, if the people we elect as presidents were saints—if each and every one of them were exceptionally pure of heart and mind and soul—then perhaps we could do without our safeties, our protections, our doubts and our finger pointing. Perhaps.

But the people we elect for chief executive—and the ones we elect for the Congress, as well—are all too human, with the same feet of clay as the rest of us. The limitations on their power keeps them, if not honest, at least from doing too much damage out of misguided good intentions—or misguided evil intentions, some of them.

Does this mean we are forever hampered in fighting against evil? Does this mean that America's representative republic is—as well as revolutionary and amazing—doomed? What an ill-behaved alien calls it in *Glory Road* "The noble experiment"?

Perhaps. There are days when I get up in the morning and I take a look around and I think we have lost our civilizational confidence; that the West as the West goes is ripe for the taking. Part of it is that of course democracies are more likely to self-criticize. And part of it is the misguided—and poisonous—twin notions that culture is genetic and that therefore all cultures are equally valid. (i.e., to condemn any culture is to be guilty of racism, since culture is inborn.)

(If you don't believe me on this, look at any school curriculum. Culture and ancestry are used interchangeably, as they are in almost every conversation. I'm more acutely aware of this than most, since every stranger finds it incumbent upon him or herself to tell me that I must teach Portuguese to my American-born American-raised sons, or deprive them of their "culture." I would accept the idea that it would be good for them to know the language spoken by half of their ancestors, but Portuguese is not now and has never been their "culture.")

On the heels of these misguided notions follows the even more poisonous notion of ancestral guilt. That because our ancestors were "imperialists" or oppressed people in other parts of the world, we owe anyone who was ever oppressed—a fate that is bizarrely assumed never to have befallen any Caucasian population— the courtesy of rolling over and dying on command.

This notion is more prevalent in Europe than here, but it has made inroads here as well, because in our hyper connected world no bad notion is so self-evidently foolish as to be universally ridiculed.

The restrictions on government action—in fact, the whole notion of a representative government grounded on individual liberty—are only good for the organization of free individuals. That is, the only work if at some point men and women are willing to think rationally and realize that for this time being, for this little while, we must drop the overcoat and unbutton the pants.

Of course, in such cases we must remember the ideals and checks and balances on state power as the way of living we should return to—in some form—when the crisis is gone. And before we give them up, we must make sure the Titans are real. Sometimes I think we have lost that; that we fear our own system more than any other; that we think our own culture is uniquely evil.

But then, here and there, slowly, there are glimmers of hope, flashes of sanity. There are people who go to the remote corners of the world to see how things are for themselves. They are willing to talk. You can read their reports and judge of their veracity .

In the end—as Heinlein was at pains to show—once free men finally realize they are under attack, they are far more capable, more cunning, more inventive than those who are enslaved.

Time and time again in previous wars, after long hesitations and when everything looked lost, free men, aware of the danger, have moved to stop it.

I am Heinleinian enough to believe this will happen

again. For one, I share his belief that America is the best thing ever to happen to humanity—that it is, to quote *Farnham's Freehold*—the last best hope of mankind.

I believe too in the goodness of America—and being foreign born I do not hesitate to say that America *is* good. Given our military might it would be easy for us to take by force most of the riches in the world. We don't. We pay for them. We talk. We negotiate. We appease. We do not use force unless we believe we must. Or, to quote my friend Dave Freer, "Americans are very bad Imperialists. All they want to do is go back home." The goodness of America is derived from the goodness of the individuals in our country. I believe that the individual, allowed to be free, is ultimately the best master of his own passions and his own well-being. I believe, as Heinlein did, that most people are good. Ignorant, misguided, often annoying, but good. With very few exceptions, they would not knowingly side with evil.

The "knowingly" is the problem.

We do not have brain parasites riding our shoulders— yet. Who knows what time travel and the future will bring?—We do not have parasites controlling our bodies, speaking through our mouths.

And yet there is more than one form of mind control. In a democracy, where all voices are equally free, it is easy for individuals to become confused. There is some indication we instinctively believe the most consistent narrative— and always the least scary one to our own beliefs and to ourselves. Not necessarily the true one.

So, what would you believe? Aliens from space? Or that the president, Congress, and those vigilantes with guns and armbands on the corner have gone insane? Which one scares you more?

Living in a Western democracy—and living in the States, above all—confers on us many benefits. We need not fear famine. The occasional excess of power will be corrected. Our lives will be longer, more comfortable and cleaner than the dreams of royalty in the past.

What does it demand of us in return?

It demands that we, as the characters in Heinlein's *The Puppet Masters*, inform ourselves. That we do not believe the reports that might or might not be coming out of the occupied zone. That we do not believe the reports that might or might not be coming out of a crazy Congress, an unstable White House, a zany State Department.

If you're reading this and our problems with Islamists are still not solved, and you haven't read the Koran or informed yourself—from more than one source—about the life and times of Mohammed, you are a person in an overcoat, fully buttoned down because it's cold out and you don't believe there is any danger. If you read this at any time and you don't regularly take the time to inform yourself and to read something more than your local paper, or do more than watch your TV news; if you implicitly buy the coherent—coordinated?—story pouring out of these means of mass communication, you are Senator Martinez shouting that of course there were no parasites in Iowa. Look at all the transmissions coming through and showing people following the bareback schedule.

Informing yourself is neither easy nor painless. It is easier now than it has been for most of humanity's lifespan, of course, and easier even than in Heinlein's alternate future world. Unlike Sam and Mary you do not have to go to the library, occupy a reading room and wait for the information to arrive. You can type search terms into an internet engine and be more information rich than you can handle.

There is perhaps too much information. As a news junkie myself, I can easily spend two-three hours I don't really have, every day, reading on the day's events and trying to hear from all the perspectives. And then I think about it.

It is neither immediate nor effortless. Not ultimately. It is never effortless when the conclusions one must arrive at are scary. It is not easy to think about what to do next and how to go forward when all the options seem equally bad.

Somehow when faced with a tyranny that wants to obliterate us, our freedoms or our nation, our options are never an obvious multiple choice: a) a lot of deaths, b) endless strife, c) a big heaping bowl of chocolate ice cream. Those who pretend that there is a cost free and in fact pleasurable solution to any difficult problem are usually selling you snake oil. And the price will always be more than you want to pay.

In the same way, the solution is rarely to just sit still within our borders. When Sam confronts the irate storekeeper, the storekeeper says none of this would have happened if only we hadn't messed around in space. How many times have we heard this? The US tried the isolationist route, too, in World Wars One and Two. Worked great didn't it? Can you imagine if we had stuck to it in World War Two? Jawohl?

The problem with dictatorships—as I read somewhere recently—and with poisonous ideologies, too, is that they are like sharks. They must keep moving forward or die. What caused their aggression is not what you did. It's who they are.

I am not telling you what to believe. Heinlein would not tell you what to believe. His third objective in writing his books—right after feeding his family and telling an entertaining story—was his hope of making people think. That is my hope for you too. Go back, re-read *The Puppet Masters*. Then whatever happens to be facing this country at the time, go and think about it. Read the news—read the news from more than one source. Remember if they all echo each other too precisely, it's probably arranged— and think about it. And always distrust totalitarian regimes. Particularly those that promise you paradise whether religious or secular.

Yes, they are often more "efficient" than democracies. They put out a better story. And all they want in return for it is the hearts and souls and minds of everyone who lives under them and those foolish enough to believe them.

You are a free man (even if—or perhaps particularly if—you happen to be a woman). The price of that freedom is constant vigilance. Not vigilance by governments, or even by "rough men" ready to "do violence" on your behalf. Those are needed too, but remember the genius and the wonder of America—what made me fall in love not just with one of its citizens but with the country itself—is that the government rules with the consent and by the right of the governed.

What this awesome power requires of you is that you

remain informed; that you make sure that whoever controls your mind is not a parasite bent only on using you for his purpose. You owe it to yourself not to be afraid of the truth no matter how dark or how unpleasant it is when you find it. And you owe it to yourself to fight to keep your freedom.

Not all of us are fit or able to serve our country with our bodies. There are few of us who are unfit to serve her with our minds, our words and our work.

In the end, I believe that freedom and free men will win. I believed this through all those dark days in the Seventies, when even my eleventh grade history book hailed communism as the end of history and the perfect and future nirvana that waited us all. In the end I believe when danger is perceived, we will unbutton our overcoats and shed our pants, too, if needed. Metaphorically, of course—which is far more difficult than merely removing clothing.

I'd like to believe we'll do it early enough that things can go back to how they were. But perhaps that is already a forlorn dream. Perhaps we too must always watch for the stray tiger come out of some forgotten jungle, carrying a hump on its back. In a world grown very, very small one parasite might be enough to contaminate an entire region.

And while the Nine Day Fever might seem like a contrived solution, fit to end the book when it must be ended, and perhaps as a nod to H.G. Wells, it too is a symbol—something extracted from Mary's memory, something she is afraid of facing, but must face if she wants to continue living as a free woman. The innermost fear has to be conquered and the innermost peace sacrificed.

In the real world we did defeat fascism and the Soviet Union is no more. Oh, communism, fascism and their close cousins will rise again, possibly under other names. They will rise again—doubtless—full of threat and wrapped in promise. Humans being humans will continue to crave Nirvana. But humans, being humans, will also continue to reject that most false of all promises—the idea that perfection and happiness for all passes through the obliteration of the individual.

For all our faults, for the seeming precipices of horror and danger that each new technology appears to open at our feet, the future in general—and excepting some short and exceptionally disgusting episodes—has been better than the past.

I hope we can say, with Sam, at the end of *The Puppet Masters*, in response to the Titan's offer of Nirvana and world wide peace, that humanity has always rejected that offer and this time it will be no different.

Being free was never easy. Our oldest account of freed slaves tells us of their sitting by their fires in the desert and lamenting the lost fleshpots of Egypt, when they had eaten well in captivity and oppression. And while I've never seen this with my own eyes, it is said that the freed lion will still pace within the limits of its no-longer-present cage as though bars still confined him.

As Heinlein says in *The Puppet Masters*, to remain free we must remain alert. We must remain aware. We must be able to detect the parasites impinging on our electronic senses, on our perceptions of the world. It is our responsibility as free individuals.

And then in the end—past the dark spots and the

places in the map where there be dragons—we will survive and win. And in space or at the end of time, we'll meet the next enemy or the next challenge.

When things are at their darkest, I remember Heinlein's words which I know are addressed to all the enemies of the free human mind, to any parasites that would prey on humanity:

I feel exhilarated. Puppet masters—the free men are coming to kill you!